Old Enough to Love…

By: Kristi Pelton

Dedication

Wow... I clearly need to thank my family who tolerated pizza rolls and chicken sticks when I was too engrossed in my writing to stop. I would like to thank my parents who introduced me to Oregon and its beauty when I was a kid; and now creating new memories with my boys.

Olivia...what can I say? You've read it a hundred times with a smile and you always continued to push me. We did it together! To the Barnes and Noble writers group: Alice, Karen, Mark, Phil, Dennis and George...and those now in Heaven: Bill, Eleanor, Karleen. It's because of all of you that I continued.

Lisa Loewen...bless you! Thanks for your help in editing and non-tabbing!

Creating this work of fiction has been a blast...thank you to Journey, Kid Rock, Eminem, Gasoline Heart, and T-Swift for keeping the vibes going when I got lost.

Go Ducks...Go Jayhawks...Go Cubs

Mom, Dad, Kevin, Ben and Zach...I love you.

Prologue

My body felt weak. I felt weak, pathetic. He'd experienced the world and I'd experienced nothing. He moved toward me—felt sorry for me. I was the girl who could barely breathe on her own.

"Don't touch me," I warned and he took another step. "Get out of my house."

He retreated. He was leaving. That was for the best. He stopped at my desk and snatched up my inhaler then turned toward me shaking it.

"NO!" I hit his chest with my fist but he didn't flinch. "I hate you," I said coldly and tried to shove him.

"No. You don't. You hate what I did. Now use the inhaler." The softness in his tone hurt my heart even more.

My teeth clenched together and I refused. I was being stupid. I knew I needed the albuterol. My breaths were short and coming quicker.

"Come on Em. Take it."

Being stubborn was one thing, being this stupid was another. I'm not sure I was done making my point, but my chest was done. I knew this because the lack of oxygen had left my arms limp and light-headedness crept into me.

His arm wrapped around my waist and moved me to the bed. My head rested on his shoulder for its final time; as he slid the inhaler between my already parted lips, I wondered if he saw the irony in what was happening. As he compressed the tube and the mist entered my mouth providing my lungs with relief, he was essentially giving me life. But it was a life that I knew I would live without him now. The irony of this situation was that he was saving me yet emotionally killing me all within a few moments.

ONE

Emma

"Come on, Reesy," I shouted to our ten-year-old weimaraner. Her tail snapped back and forth as she whipped past me and up the hill. Summer vacation was finally over and this was our last day at the beach. Usually, this was my favorite place in the world but this summer completely sucked. As I ran toward our house, sand oozed over my freshly painted toe nails and nestled between my toes ready to stowaway.

A familiar whistle resonated over the roar of the waves. Saying goodbye to Austin was the worst part of my summer. He stood on the third floor deck of the most photographed home on the beach and shot me deuces, our greeting and farewell every summer. I flicked a peace sign in return and forced a smile. I'd had a crush on him forever. Our four year age difference wasn't much to me, but I was like a little sister to him. I realized now, that would never change. It had always been a tossup, who I was going to marry or, at the very least, offer up my virginity to…Austin Falsone or Grant Meiers. Austin lived here in Cannon Beach. Grant would return to Ashland with us. They were as different as Lil' Wayne and Michael Buble. With Grant, I pictured living on a beach, our blonde hair, blue-eyed kids wearing wet suits and catching the surf. With Austin, our brown-eyed, brown-haired kids were dressed in khaki shorts and polos, tossing frisbees. I knew for years that one of those scenarios would play out, but every summer my hopes of finding love dwindled. I was fifteen and outside of a few truth or dare games with my brother's friends, love…romance had eluded me. Austin turned away and I watched him disappear between the French doors to his bedroom.

Reesy waited for me, alongside a fresh pile of steaming dog crap. "Nice, Reesy. Thanks." A great end to an already crappy summer.

Mom forced us to carry plastic bags to keep the beaches clean. I didn't really care that there was plastic between me and the crap; it was still freaking disgusting. And even though I wasn't touching it, the warmth through the bag made me shudder; plus, I could still smell it. Holding my breath, I pulled it into the bag, tied the end and sidestepped the beach grass. Ryan was at the back door laughing. Older brothers were a pain, but at times, my overprotective one was a bigger pain than most. Reesy perched herself right in front of him waiting for attention.

"Great news. You're riding with mom," he said and his lip pulled into a bigger grin just before he crunched into an apple.

"NO!"

He shrugged. "She wants to talk to you."

"What about?" I demanded.

Reesy almost purred as he rubbed her ears. "The punk."

"He's not a punk!"

"Let's go, Reesy." Ryan patted his thigh. "You're wrong Emma. He is a punk. A punk who better keep his hands off you."

The only thing I prayed for all summer was to feel 'his' touch once more and Ryan was the one person who would keep that from happening. Before I could control it, the bag and its warm contents left my hands and nailed Ryan in the back. He glanced over his shoulder at the plastic covered crap on the ground. I ran past and pounded his arm as hard as I could.

"You're the punk! Come on, Reesy."

Ryan continued rubbing her floppy ears so she stayed put. Nice! Even betrayed by the dog.

TWO

Mom was driving; I stubbornly kept my eyes locked on the edge of Highway 1. The view of the Pacific was freakishly awesome but no matter how often we drove it, it stressed me out. Scared of breaking through a guard rail and ending up in the blue water, I covered my ears with my Beats and closed my eyes.

Over the past couple of years, my brother and I had fought about who got to ride with Dad (the non-talker)—today, I lost, which sucked. My feet stuck out the open window and I tried to fake sleep. We'd barely past Tillamook before I felt the predictable tap on my arm. I opened my eyes, paused Adele and removed an earpiece.

"What?"

"You ready to talk?"

"About what?" Of course I knew what it was about. I looked at her out the corner of my eye. A lazy smile touched the sides of her mouth. She was pretty with her light brown hair pulled into a baseball cap. Outside of her inquisitive nature into every aspect of my life, she was beautiful and eloquent and funny. People migrated to her and an unspoken thrill shot through me when they would say that I was a miniature, Katie Hendricks or Kate, as she preferred. I didn't see it though.

She hit the brakes with a sudden jolt, which made my stomach lurch. I peeked and saw the brake lights of my dad's Land Rover as he slowed for an RV making the twists ahead. Passing was not an option on this road and unless the RV pulled off at one of the many lookout points or lighthouses, we were in for a long ride. *Ugh!* Seeing Reesy look out the back window of the Rover at us, made me smile. She liked me best.

Mom and I were in her silver Honda S2000 convertible with the top down. There were only a few months out of the year in Oregon that the top could be down and August was one of them. Ashland was still three hours away.

"Emma. Really?"

"Really what, Mom? It's not worth talking about."

"Sweetheart," she said with a pitiful inflection. "I know this summer was hard for you. Given what happened, right before we left. This is the first year I've reconsidered our texting and cell phone rule."

"Such a stupid rule," I muttered softly unsure if she heard. No texting allowed on the summer getaway. What a load of crap! Our house on Cannon Beach was awesome but staying for two months was brutal. No phone calls, no texts…strictly 'family time' is what she called it. I called it my father's lame attempt at fighting technology and controlling my life. Ryan called it bullshit; one summer he actually bought a cheap phone and paid for minutes. I was too scared to outright break the rules but snuck a couple of calls on his.

Summers in Cannon were easier on Ryan. First off, he was a dude—a dude's dude. As long as he had Grant, a football and some chicks, he was golden. The Meiers vacationed from Ashland to the beach just like us. Seth Meiers was a freshman at the U of O. And Grant, well, he and Ryan were both turning 18…SENIORS! Their summer consisted of football, girls, more football and more girls. Cannon Beach was ideal for them—a tourist spot that brought in a new crop of girls, weekly.

The boys had it right, the girls were completely predictable. Cannon was never what people expected. Upon arrival, they would find a cold beach and even more frigid water. Sure enough, these teenage girls would arrive *beach equipped* with their swimsuits— voila, senior guys to the rescue—always prepared with an extra sweatshirt or jacket. Conversation started and a week-long relationship begun. Obviously starry eyed and pathetic in their simple thinking, most girls were had from the beginning with my brother and his best bud. Watching them exchange addresses as the girls bit their cheeks and fought back tears—VOMIT!

I swore to myself years ago I would never reduce myself to such lies and tactics, but the guys never really seemed interested in me.

"Emma, after that night, you asked us for space. We've given it to you. But we need to address it now." She took a sip of her Diet Coke.

Fortunately, the wind had shifted my hair to the left side of my head and created a curtain between us. "Mom. It doesn't matter. An entire summer has gone by. He probably forgot about me, anyway." The thought made my stomach twist.

"I seriously doubt that. You are a beautiful girl."

The word *girl* made me cringe, and I turned toward the ocean taking in a slow breath of air.

"I know you think you probably know everything when it comes to sex and relationships, but honey, I want to make sure if you have any questions that you come to me."

The wind blew my hair back and I offered her a smile. "I don't have any questions." I had *SO* many questions, I didn't know where to start. I knew how to get pregnant and how not to get pregnant. But the rest was a little fuzzy. Oral sex really scared me and sex itself, I could only imagine. Watching *Fast Times at Ridgemont High* with Ryan and his buddies was somewhat educational. I remembered in the movie that Brad jacked off in the bathroom thinking about Linda; then she busted him and got grossed out. Stacy got pregnant by Mike in an act that didn't look like much fun. So, it wasn't as if I was dying to do the deed, but I wanted to know the drill.

"Not yet. But, Emma." She paused and I didn't like her tone. "Guys your brother's age have a mindset that is…"

"Perverted?"

She smiled. "I was going to say, sexual. And if you and Zach start dating, do we need to discuss abstinence and/or protection?"

My face flushed; I was thankful the sun was out hoping the reddening in my cheeks would not be as noticeable. "Mom!" I had only started my period five months ago. Mom says she was a late bloomer too. She also said it came with the territory of being a preemie. That was the story of my life.

"Honey, in June, when your father and I got home from Santa Monica and found the two of you together…" She alluded to it as if I'd forgotten. I was certain I would never forget that night. God! That had only been the greatest night of my pathetic life.

THREE

Exactly 71 days ago

The door bell rang as I finished drying my legs. I hurriedly tossed my towel on the hook and slammed the shower door, wincing as the glass rattled. I threw on my ratty PAC-12 T-shirt, sweat shorts and flew down the stairs. The shadow outside on the porch turned to leave.

"Hold up!" I shouted throwing open the door as he swiveled around. Water dripped on my shoulders from my wet strands of hair and I stood staring at him. His hair held the rain that had fallen from his car to the door. Attitude crept into me when he lowered his chin to look down at me, surprised to see a five-foot dwarf before him. (I was four feet, ten inches to be exact.)

"Hi," he greeted with an exaggerated animation, as if I was in a Girl Scout outfit selling Thin Mints and had just rung *his* door bell.

I felt my lip snarl. "Hey," I said coolly, trying not to stare, but his deep chocolate eyes immediately caught my attention.

"Is Ryan here?" he asked still speaking as if I were a child.

"Nope," I snipped.

One side of his mouth pulled upward. "Oookaaay. When will he be?"

I let out an inflated breath and glanced at the clock behind me, then shrugged. My brother and his big punk-ass friends were annoying. I didn't know this one.

He chuckled and the hair on my neck stood on end. He knew he was hot! He waited, silently. Was he expecting *me* to say something? My eyes widened and brows reached their peak on my forehead. "What?" I nearly shouted.

A gust of wind caused rain to sweep under the porch and spray his face. "May I wait, inside?"

My head instantly began shaking from side to side. "Neg-a-tive. You are a stranger and I am just a little girl." Sarcasm dripped from my words.

This freakishly hot guy dragged his hands down his face and for the first time I noticed his smile. He leaned toward me, invading my space, and I drew myself away, suddenly feeling jittery inside. With the doorknob in his hand, he closed the door between us. I stood confused until I heard the chime a second time. Without me touching the door, it opened. He smiled a smile I could only describe as breathtaking and extended his hand. My eyes moved from his mouth to his extended hand then finally, landed on his eyes.

"Hi. My name is Zach Owens. I'm a friend of Ryan's. I understand he is not at home, but do you mind if I wait?"

His face was tan and his teeth were white which led me to swipe my tongue over mine.

"What's your name?" he asked.

What was my name? "Um, Emma." I stepped back so he could come in, suddenly paranoid I wasn't wearing a bra. Not that it mattered; I had no boobs.

"Umemma? That's one I've never heard before." He winked.

Between my stomach doing a back flip and blood rushing to my face, I forced a laugh; I also recognized what he was doing. Ryan had warned me about the guys who had one thing on their mind. "Well, it's just Emma. And FYI, your little smile may work for most, but I'm not your typical girl."

His smile broadened. "Ryan's supposed to have some football camp information for me."

Football. Of course. I shrugged glancing around the room for any papers lying around.

"Hmmm. I give." If there was one thing I was good at, it was hostility toward my brother's buddies. His little posse of friends served as my protectors much longer than appreciated and it didn't appear they were giving it up anytime soon. This guy was at least six feet, maybe taller, and though he wasn't grotesquely muscular like Ryan, he was well built.

My T-shirt was wet from my dripping hair. "I'm gonna go dry my hair."

"Go for it," he said with indifference.

I rolled my eyes, making sure he saw.

Once I reached the top of the stairs, I burst into the bathroom, brushed my teeth, slathered on deodorant, dabbed on some make up, fastened my bra and took the stairs two at a time.

"Ryan still not here?" I asked, winded as I entered the living room.

His expression was one of confusion and my annoyance resurrected.

"What?" I inquired.

"Your hair. Thought you were gonna dry it."

I reached up and fingered the wet strands as his white teeth became visible again. *Oh my God!* I think maybe he even laughed out loud. "Yeah. Well, I was wondering if you wanted me to text Ryan and let him know you're here. That way you can get what you need and *leave.*"

He fought hard unable to hide his full-blown smile. "I can wait a few," he said raking his fingers through his wet brown hair.

"Whatever, suit yourself."

I returned—with dry hair. "So, you're new?" He followed me into the kitchen and sat at a barstool.

"I am. Been here a couple of months. I haven't seen you around either."

I'd have remembered if I'd seen him before, but I refused to tell him I was a freshman. "Hmm. Well, obviously—I'm Ryan's little sister."

"I figured that much. You are in fact little. How old are you?"

This guy seemed insistent on pissing me off. "Where you from?" I asked ignoring the question.

His fingers intertwined on the granite countertop. "Wow, must be the hair," he muttered under his breath.

I tried my best to give him my evil glare. "Do you not think, I've not heard them all before, Tomato head, Carrot top, Rose top, Ginger, Fireball, Pippi, Peppermint Patty—whatever. Please, please, enlighten me with a new one. "

There was no mistaking his laugh now. "A. That was a double negative. B. This has nothing to do with your hair. C. For such a tiny lil thing, you're pretty feisty. And D." The proximity between us closed as he scooted his chair closer. Was he looking at my nose?

"What's D?" I barely squeaked out.

"D," he said with his breath blowing across my face. "You're strawberry blonde and Peppermint Patty had way more freckles." His finger playfully tapped the end of my nose. "Now, how old are you?"

My heart was literally going to beat up and out of my throat if that was possible. "Tell me where you're from first."

His eyes narrowed, sadly. I'd hit a nerve. Something was wrong. "San Francisco."

He wasn't happy there. I could tell. Change the subject. "So…what do you think of our city?"

He snickered. "City?"

Wow! I hated that response more.

"This isn't a city. San Francisco! That's a city."

OK. I was way off the mark. I couldn't read him yet and I was exceptional at reading guys. He liked *his* city?

"Have you ever been?" This time, his brows raised and I noticed his long, silky lashes.

"No."

His eyes suddenly widened. "Emma. It's awe-some."

I smiled at his level of enthusiasm, or maybe it was the way my name sounded coming out of his mouth, or maybe it was the way he made awesome sound like it was two words.

"Tell me."

And he did. He talked for nearly twenty minutes about his life there. His school. His friends. His laughter was infectious. Then once again, his tone turned sad. I think I understood. He didn't want to come here. He hated it here…*my* city. His mood had shifted. What made him so unhappy?

"Can you hear that?" I asked, pointing to the ceiling where the music softly played? My dad loved music and our entire house echoed his love.

"The music?"

I nodded.

"Yes."

I had an idea. "Stay here," I instructed with a pointing finger.

He glanced at me suspiciously. "OK," he agreed.

I hurried to the stereo and flipped through our CD's till I found Journey's greatest hits. I hoped he knew the song. Of course he knew the song. If he loved San Francisco that much, he knew the song. Number 7. Play. I ran back. As I stepped into the kitchen, the song started. His dark eyes fixed on mine. *Hmm. Still serious.* He either didn't know the song or it brought back a bad memory. I swallowed hard questioning my strategy to play *Lights*. Had I made him miss his city more? Remorse swarmed within me as he got to his feet. He was leaving. I didn't want him to go. I wanted to know Zach Owens more than I'd wanted to know anyone.

When the lights go down in the city.....

"I'm sorry," I said chewing on my thumbnail.

A softness touched his face. What was he thinking? He closed the distance between us and blood raced through my veins. "Thank you," he whispered.

My upper teeth pressed into my bottom lip. Had he liked it? My neck ached from looking up at him. I wanted him to kiss me but I knew that wouldn't happen. Especially if he knew my brother.

"Have I kept you from something?"

Nothing came to mind. "No." My voice was barely audible.

"No, really? What were you going to do tonight before I showed up?" He was still close and I could smell his breath.

"I'd uh, rented a movie."

"See there. I did interrupt." His smile was gentle.

He wanted out of here. I looked down at the carpet.

"We can start it, I mean, while I wait for Ryan."

Embarrassingly, no nice words came to mind. I didn't know how to communicate with a guy outside of talking about how the Ducks played in the game against the Trojans. How many rushing versus passing yards. I could do angry so much better than this...this unknown feeling. Why would he want to watch a movie with me? I forced myself to think of what Ryan would say. One reason...Sex! I managed a nod then said, "Don't think something's goin' down between us."

Both his hands shot up, palms forward like he was in a standoff but surrendering. "I will be on my best behavior." The sexy grin crept across his face again and deep down, I was scared I was toast.

I still, two months later, couldn't remember what brought on the kiss. *Oh, the kiss.* I remember laughing at the movie until a small snort came from my throat.

"You snorted?" he asked laughing.

I shook my head adamantly. "No. I didn't," I said, blushing ten shades of red.

Then his fingers dug into my sides and I laughed hysterically, my obnoxious laugh irritating even me. Suddenly, he stopped and our eyes locked, all humor gone from his.

"May I kiss you?" he whispered.

Once again, I was unable to answer verbally so I nodded weakly.

He moved slowly toward me tilting his head to the right so I tilted mine. My heart found a disjointed rhythm as his tongue peeked out moistening his lips. I did the same. Then, our lips met. I was certain he didn't inhale but my breath was taken from me as we kissed. His tongue touched my upper lip softly then moved back into his mouth. The kiss lasted at least ten seconds maybe longer. And when I opened my eyes, he was looking at me. I hadn't kissed a lot of guys and worried if I'd failed epically. His thumb moved down my jaw.

"How old are you, Emma?"

I contemplated lying. The one word on the tip of my tongue felt like it would burn a hole. "Fifteen," I said honestly, wondering if this is where he drew the line.

He didn't seem to flinch at the word I hated but he did pull away slightly. "I'm distracting you from your movie." He smiled such a perfect smile. "What are the suitcases for?" He pointed to the corner of the hallway.

I told him about Cannon Beach and our annual getaway but couldn't stop thinking about the kiss. It was perfect. Soft. Warm. Wet, but not sloppy gross wet like I'd seen on TV—just right. I wanted to try again. But, instead, we finished the movie, or at least I did. He fell asleep next to me and I nodded off only to be awakened by my father hovering over us like a nostril-flared steaming bull. *That* was the last time I'd seen Zach Owens. I only wish I knew what he remembered about that night.

Four

Zach~exactly 71 days ago

The house was nicer than I expected for this small pissant town but Ryan's country- boy-hick truck wasn't in the driveway. Maybe he left the paperwork. That would be better anyway, so I didn't have to see his arrogant ass. I popped open the door to the Jeep and the never ending rain sprayed over my face. It was hard not to notice the awesome view from his porch. The Siskiyou Mountains spreading as far as my eyes could see. Yet, I refused to like this place. This 'town' as people called it. Town, a noun, defined as an urban area that has a name, defined boundaries, and local government, and that is larger than a village and generally smaller than a city. Hmmm, smaller than a city? Really??? San Francisco's population is sitting at nearly 820,000 while this town sits at 21,000. Keep trying Ashland. You only have eight hundred thousand more to go.

I stood in the rain, staring at the houses below, seeing only roofs. I'd never seen houses stacked into the side of a mountain quite like they were here. It was admittedly beautiful. But, in San Francisco, this mountainside would crumble with a minor quake.

I finally rang the bell. After the second ring, I started to leave then heard someone shout. A girl. My brows instinctively rose at the high pitch of the voice and I hoped for a California dime. The door flew open and a girl half my height stood there in a PAC-12 T-shirt with dripping wet hair. Not what I expected.

"Hi," I said. Always wanted to be friendly to wee ones.

"Hey."

I figured she was intimidated by my size. Be nicer, I thought to myself. "Is Ryan here?" My juvenile tone sickened me.

She shifted her weight to her other hip almost as if I was the one annoying her- almost. "Nooope."

This time it was *my* mouth that pulled into a half smile. The feminine smell of her soap or shampoo or something wafted through the air and hit me. Easy Slick, she's way too young.

"Oookaay. When will he be?" I really didn't want to tolerate this little thing but then she let out a sigh as if I was putting her out, are you kidding me?

When she swiveled at the waist, her calves flexed and it suddenly hit me that maybe she wasn't as young as I originally thought. Just little.

She shrugged and it irritated the crap out of me that she didn't act like most girls. If she was indeed around my age, why didn't her eyes blink faster or why didn't she flirt like a normal chick. Surely, she was attracted to me. I couldn't help but stare at her pacific blue eyes as I tried to figure her out. No makeup. Small boobs. Great legs. Terrific teeth—though no real smile yet. This intrigued me. Females were nothing, if not predictable. Jackson, Will, Travon and I all agreed on that, and though I had unwillingly moved away, our competition was still alive and well. This girl may be a perfect score.

"What?' she nearly shouted and brought me out of my daze as a gust of wind blew the rain under the porch and across my face. Hopefully, wiping my face would motivate her to issue an invitation inside, but no go. Evidence built rapidly that this was not a normal girl.

"May I wait inside?" I asked wondering if she was dense. She shook her head. She said negative as if it were three words and mentioned something about me being a stranger. This kid was good and obviously the sister of the punk I didn't like. Didn't that just up the ante? Charm—do your thing I instructed, making mental notes as the hits just kept on coming. So I smiled and bared my fresh braces-free teeth to her—a smile most girls fall victim to.

Within a moment of the smile, I invaded her space with my much larger body. Her smell consumed me and there was no question what I wanted now, all five feet of her, if that. Yet, it was shocking how quickly that feeling faded when I spotted a hint of fear in her eyes as I grabbed the door and closed it between us. It only took a short second to register that she wasn't tough at all, that my presence unsettled her. I could not bully this girl—ever. My guess was that living with her brother was torture enough. Instinct told me that she wanted to be loved, taken care of, and I was the one to do that, albeit temporarily. I rang the bell and opened the door once again. This time, her eyes held no fear, only confusion. As I extended my hand to shake hers, her pouty little lips fell open. Finally, she was speechless. Baby steps. I was in the door and soon enough I'd be in her pants. Wow, her hand was tiny and I released it quickly.

"What's your name?" I asked.

She seemed confused by the question. "Um, Emma."

Now flustered. There was no doubt I would bang this chic.

"Umemma? That's one I've never heard before." I added a wink and as her eyes darted away, I knew she was toast.

"Well, it's just Emma," she said then placed both her hands on her tiny little hips. "And FYI, your little smile may work for most but I'm not your typical girl."

What the…? Damn. I smiled to hide my frustration. "Ryan's supposed to have some football camp information for me."

Her tiny shoulders jetted up then down as her eyes scanned the room. "Hmmm. I give. I'm gonna go dry my hair."

I couldn't read this girl for anything. Most girls were putty in my hands at this point, prime for molding. This fiery little thing didn't want anywhere near me. Yet she trusted me enough to leave me standing here.

"Go for it," I said like I didn't give a shit and when her eyes rolled, I wanted to laugh out loud. Did I truly annoy her or was that just for show?

Once she disappeared, I cracked my neck trying to relieve the increasing tension. I hadn't worked this hard for a chick in a while and still wasn't sure if this girl was worth it. But given her size and demeanor, she had to be a virgin. In fact, I'd put money on it. Though she was pretty stinking decent at telling me off, she was hiding something. Every girl has a weakness; I would expose hers and use it to my benefit.

In the living room, one wall was lined with family pictures. Most were on a beach—certainly not a California one. Every frame was filled with Emma and a group of guys. Some I knew. Some I didn't. Her brother stood over her in nearly every photo, obviously serving as protector. An even bigger challenge had certainly presented itself than just nailing her.

"Ryan still not here?" she asked as she strode quietly into the room with her hair still wet.

"What?" she asked.

"Your hair. Thought you were gonna dry it."

Her rounded eyes led me to believe that she had forgotten what she went upstairs for to begin with and if I could have patted my own back, I would have. Zach had done his job, now it was just a matter of breaking down these walls that I'm sure her douche bag brother helped create.

"Yeah, well, I was wondering if you wanted me to text Ryan and let him know you're here. That way you can get what you need and leave."

I think she put extra emphasis on the word leave, and I couldn't hide my smile from her any longer. Was she trying to come across mean? She had the scare factor of a declawed kitten.

"I can wait a few."

"Whatever, suit yourself," she spat out and held up an index finger though I got the feeling she wanted it to be her middle finger. I wanted to assure her that I was going nowhere but she didn't give me the time. Yet, because of the makeup on her face that wasn't there before and the small dab of perfume that she now wore, I knew she'd let me spend time with her.

The blow dryer blared away, a floor above me and I moved to another wall that held much older pictures. She was little and wore wire rimmed glasses. Tiny didn't cover her size in some of them and an unexpected smile crept over my face. In every picture, someone hovered over this girl like a guardian angel. My cheeks relaxed as the smile vanished when I came to the last photo of her and her brother on a hospital bed. The paleness of her face was like nothing I'd ever seen and the oxygen tubes coming from her nose were miniscule in size. Was she sick?

"So, you're new?"

Her voice startled me and I followed her into the kitchen. "I am. Been here a couple of months. I haven't seen you around either."

"Hmm. Well, obviously, I'm Ryan's little sister."

Duh. "I figured that much. You are in fact little. How old are you?"

The flare in her nostrils was not a good sign. "Where you from?" she countered.

A feeling in the pit of my stomach told me that this little thing had never been challenged much. Given her history on the wall she had been catered to. I figured it was time for a challenge.

"Must be the hair," I whispered loud enough for her to hear. Waiting…

Her eyes narrowed. I wondered if this was her angry face. "Do you not think, I've not heard them all before, Tomato head, Carrot top, Rose top, Ginger, Fireball, Pippi, Peppermint Patty— whatever. Please, please, enlighten me with a new one. "

Holy shit! Tears stung my eyes from the uncontained laughter. She misconstrued everything I said. Typical girl. But speaking of challenges, I'd never had anyone challenge me quite like this. "A. That was a double negative. B. This has nothing to do with your hair. C. For such a tiny lil' thing, you're pretty feisty. And D." I positioned my chair closer to hers and I imagined her heart picked up a beat or two.

"What's D?" she asked sounding like a mouse.

"D. You are a strawberry blonde AND Peppermint Patty had way more freckles." When my index finger tapped the end of her nose, I noticed she barely had any. "Now, how old are you?"

"Tell me where you're from first."

As stubborn as this girl was, my heart fell just saying the words. "San Francisco."

"So what do you think of our little city?" She seemed so proud.

"City??" My voice rose unintentionally and for a moment I hated that because her reaction was nearly to cower.

But really, what a freaking joke. Incomparable. Distaste filled my mouth. "This isn't a city. San Francisco, that's a city."

She only nodded and I think I'd hurt her feelings. It wasn't her fault that this crappy little town was her world. If I planned to bone her just like the other girls over the past 12 months, I was going to have to focus.

"Have you ever been there?" I asked.

"No."

"Emma, it's awe-some." As the words came out, her eyes flickered and the ocean that I loved came alive inside of them. I forced myself to look away.

"Tell me," she asked eagerly.

So, I did. Told her about my old high school, about my friends, about the food, and the things to do, but it simply reinforced why I hated it here.

"Can you hear that?" She pointed to the ceiling.

I listened. Nickelback? "Yes."

Her hand waved. "Stay here."

"OK." I pulled a piece of gum from my pocket and tossed it in my mouth. The granite was smooth as I ran my hands over the clean stone. This whole kitchen was spotless. A brown dog suddenly shot into the kitchen and introduced itself to my legs sniffing every inch.

"Hey buddy." I nudged her ears and her tail whacked the island with a thud, thud, thud.

The music echoed over the speakers and an unexpected solace inched through me. *When the lights go down in the city....* Journey sang and she waited in the archway of the kitchen measuring my response. I wouldn't tell her that Otis Redding's *Sitting on the Dock of the Bay* was my favorite but this was a close second. The unfamiliar feeling inside my chest made me anxious, creasing my brow, which, by reading her expression, caused her anxiety in return. She had reached out to me through song. She had reached out to someone that she shouldn't trust. I got to my feet and moved toward her.

"I'm sorry," she quickly whispered and started to make a meal of her thumb nail. A nervous habit obviously that I noted. I towered over her and she seemed intimidated. Terrifying her was

NOT my objective, but it was sort of cute to see her neck at a ninety degree angle as she looked up at me.

"Thank you," I said softly.

When her upper teeth pressed into her bottom lip my thoughts bordered on inappropriate and I backed away. The next thing I knew we were heading back into the living room to watch some movie she'd rented, and as much as I wanted to distance myself, I found it utterly impossible.

She giggled a lot during the movie, which made me smile, but when a full blown snort came from her little body, I lost it.

"You snorted!" I laughed.

She shook her head and the smell of her shampoo wafted through the air and blasted me. Refocus.

"No I didn't." Blood invaded her cheeks making her more vulnerable to me than before. Thoughts raced through my head like a barrage of bullets whizzing past. I could bag this chick right now, walk away and only be shy a few points of an official win or explore this feeling that she sparked in me. The difficulty of the latter was ten-fold.

I glanced at her. She was still attempting to contain her laughter but failing miserably. Keeping it playful, I began tickling her and before I knew it, laughter filled the silence between us. But in the end, silence was victorious after our eyes locked in a way confirming she wanted me. Locked in a way that mine had many times with the female species, usually with the girl wanting me more than me wanting her, but I wasn't sure in this case. I was on my knees after the tickle fest and she was lying on her side in a defenseless position.

"May I kiss you?" I asked her. The throbbing of my heart scared me. It hadn't beat so hard in months, maybe a full year, and I anticipated her response. Her head nodded, or did it? I wanted it to, but it wasn't until I tilted my head and she reacted accordingly, moistening her lips, I did it. I moved in, brushing her lips with mine. Touching her lip with my tongue, savoring the taste of her and realizing that this could possibly be her first kiss. I wasn't sure, but I wanted to know. What could she have possibly seen in me to bestow such trust? I was not trustworthy and I would prove that. My hand touched her hip. *God, she was tiny.* I stopped the kiss and looked at her. Her eyes were still closed and I wondered if she was breathing. Deep down, I knew I could have her.

FIVE

Emma

I glared at my mom in the car. "I don't know why you don't believe me. Daddy acted like a psycho that night. I'm sure that Zach doesn't even want to see me."

"Your father was, as was I, shocked to see you and him sleeping on our sofa."

"You treated him terrible. Like we were naked or something." I rubbed my temples as the red returned to my cheeks. I was glad to be gone all summer. Though the thought of seeing him again thrilled me to the bone, it also mortified me.

When I woke up that night and saw my dad standing over me with rage burning in his eyes, I was confused until I realized Zach was still there. Then I realized what my dad must be thinking. There was no way I could allow him to voice those thoughts. Little did my father know that this sweet guy wanted nothing more to do with me. After what must have been a torturous and inexperienced kiss, he chose sleep!!

"Daddy. Stop," I begged.

"Stop? I have only just gotten started."

Zach rose to meet my father's eyes. "Sir. I am so sorry. I was waiting for Ryan and…"

The tightness in my father's jaw and protrusion of his chest was pretty indicative of hostility and it was obvious I wouldn't walk away from this a winner.

"My name is Zach Owens, Sir," Zach continued.

"My name is Matt Hendricks, and this is my fifteen year old daughter you were sleeping with."

My father was determined and unwavering in his stance and though I didn't remember Zach leaving, I remember feeling like Iraq after some shock and awe mission- completely paralyzed from the attack and unable to recover. Even two months later, it seemed raw.

"Emma, we both feel bad about what happened. But we were taken back by it. You were in eighth grade. HEL-LO!" Her eyes were wide. She always said hello…like she was trying to get my attention…or like I was too stupid to grasp what she was saying.

"I'm a freshman, Mom."

"You're right. With so much experience under your belt."

I grunted and hated myself for resorting to such an immature sound. Ryan was up with Dad probably chatting about the girls he'd conquered this summer, bumping fists with my father and discussing football plays.

"Why can Ryan do anything he wants with a girl and I fall asleep with a guy fully clothed and I'm a 'ho. It's so totally not fair."

My mom's eyes shot daggers.

Whew. I could tell she was pissed and done with me for a while. An unavoidable smile touched my lips.

Not that I was expecting to see Zach staked out at the city limits with a huge banner as I came back into town. After all, our uneventful arrival into Ashland was later than expected, but my eyes scanned every car as we drove including scouring the Burger King parking right off the 5.

Once home, I bolted from the car, tore through the house and grabbed my cell phone scrolling quickly through the texts looking for an unfamiliar number. I never had the chance to give him my number. Then again, he never asked.

My pounding heart took my breath away.

"Hey Runt. Go grab some crap." Ryan hit me with his duffle bag.

"Give me a sec." I kept scrolling as Reesy darted around the kitchen smelling for any unfamiliar scent.

"Did Zachy-poo text?"

"Shut up, you 'tard." I turned away from him.

"He's too old for you and you're not dating him. Where's my phone?" he asked and dropped his heavy bag on my foot.

Ouch! "Ryan!" I didn't have time for his games. I tried to shove him but his freakishly large body didn't budge.

Ryan and I were siblings, but there was nothing about us that remotely resembled each other. For some unfair reason I'd gotten my grandmother's reddish blonde hair while Ryan's was a beautiful beach blonde, at least during the summer. I barely came up to his rib cage and he was easily six foot something and weighed over two hundred. If he wasn't my brother, I'm sure I'd think he was hot because all the girls did.

My heart sunk as he scrolled through the names on his phone. Outside of Ali and Lauren texting in the past few days there were none on mine.

The night before school, I didn't sleep well. It was too quiet. The roar of the crashing waves in my ear for the past two months seemed a constant now. I missed it.

The forecast was sunny and a warm eighty-five which, compared to the sixty-five on the beach, was a heat wave. I wore my plaid mini skirt and two tanks—dressier than normal but I had a guy to impress. I snarfed down a banana as I ran out the door.

Ryan pulled into the back of the lot, where all the seniors parked, which meant I had to tolerate seeing his dumb jock friends. Once we parked, they rushed his truck, which was typical, following our summer hiatus. Brett worked the shocks of the truck, rocking it up and down with his foot.

"What's up?" Ryan shouted slamming his door.

"Testosterone," I whispered under my breath and grabbed my backpack.

"Hey Runt! I think you've grown." Connor lifted me up and over his head. I dropped my backpack and opted to hold my skirt down. This is what I'd always been to them—a little rag doll— picked up and dragged around. Maybe fun when I was little but now, annoying.

"Connor, please." I glared at Ryan.

"Put her down, dude," Ryan said.

Connor immediately slid me off his shoulder, and on the way down, I spotted him—Zach Owens across the parking lot talking to Estelle Kramer. *ESTELLE? Crap.* I hid behind the older boys for a moment and spied between them. Zach's posture was relaxed, too relaxed and his hands rested in his khaki pockets. Estelle was laughing, all 5 foot 8 inches with her glorious mane of black hair flowing half way down her back. I swallowed as I felt the banana rise in the back of my throat. Zach was tanner from the summer sun, his light brown hair touched with golden highlights. Dark sunglasses hid his eyes and when he laughed, my heart fluttered.

Ryan, Connor, Brett and Grant started walking toward the main building, which meant I had to move. Thankfully, I was positioned in the middle as we made our entrance inside.

"So, Runt..."

I cringed. "Stop calling me that. All of you, please stop!" I begged and it wasn't the first time.

Grant tickled the back of my neck. "She's no runt. Believe me boys; I saw Runt every day this summer at the beach. Our Runt is growing up. Mmmm!"

At that very moment, every one of them looked at me as if I was just being introduced to them for the first time. A mask of confusion clouded their faces and blood crept up mine. My eyes widened then closed. Grant Meiers just said *mmmm* in relation to me? WTF? I bit my lip. By the end of summer, Grant's blonde hair touched his shoulders and his loose curls drove girls crazy. He was last year's homecoming king for crying out loud. Stop the madness!

I opened my eyes in time to watch my brother grip Grant in a headlock.

"Stop checkin' out my sister, you freak!" Ryan shouted and shoved him playfully. Grant grinned and threw his arm around my neck.

"Hey, Emma."

I heard the voice and spun around trying unsuccessfully to maneuver out from under Grant's arm. Zach was approaching my brother from behind. I darted out from under Grant's possession.

Ryan glanced at me and my mile-wide smile then rotated his mammoth body stopping Zach in his path. Zach's eyes abandoned mine and settled on Ryan's. I swallowed dryly.

"EMMA!" the voices were shrill. Ali and Lauren were rushing to me. "How was the beach? When did you get home?" The warning bell suddenly sounded.

My index finger would hold them off only for a sec, so I spun back to Zach who back stepped away from Ryan's intense glare, but not without a fierce glower of his own. With the hint of a smile, he veered down the senior's hall without another look my way. *Thanks, Ryan.* My shoulders slumped knowing my chances of seeing him again today were slim; BUT…he remembered me!

SIX

I found my first and second hours without a problem but my third period, Advanced Algebra, was clear across the school. After snatching the book from my locker, I hoofed it past the cafeteria, up to the second floor and through the hall. The bell rang just as I stepped in. I hated advanced placement classes.

"Hey Runt," Grant whispered.

I smiled. Great, this would make Ryan happy—me being in the same class as his buddies. Seriously, Grant in Advanced Alegbra? I didn't figure him smart enough. Front row was all that was available, naturally, and I took the closest seat, in front of Grant. Mr. Bowman had written what looked like a homework assignment on the board and I jotted it down in my notebook.

"Please open your books to page 14."

Math concepts. This was going to be fun.

"I believe I recognize most of you. Some of you because you failed this class before and are attempting it again." Bowman smiled deviously. "And some of you I just know. First row, first seat, introduce yourself."

Oh God! That's me. "Um…Emma." My face felt hot. "Emma Hendricks."

"Any relation to our quarterback?"

"Yes. He's my brother." Ryan's little sister, Runt. That's who I was. The quarterback's little sis. Ryan Hendricks, star football player and his kid sister.

"Mr. Owens. Mr. Meiers. Did you have something to add?"

Owens? My eyes widened and I stared down at my notebook. There was only one Owens in this school and that was Zach. Was he in this class? What had he and Grant said? I fought the urge to turn and look, hiding behind my drape of strawberry blonde hair. My chest tightened.

Grant's pencil eraser jabbed me in the back. "What?" I whispered.

"You're singing, where's your inhaler," he said quietly.

I concentrated on his words for a moment then heard myself. A soft wheeze accompanied each breath. I reached for my purse, but Grant had already retrieved my albuterol inhaler from the top and was shaking it dutifully. I lowered my head and did one quick puff, shoving it back in my bag.

"Thanks," I whispered over my shoulder.

The hour seemed to drag past. When the bell rang, I gathered my books and casually glanced back—the room was half empty and no Zach. But, Estelle swayed gracefully between the desks. *Even worse!*

"Hey, Emma," she greeted. "How's Ryan?"

She was so pretty. "Fine, I guess. Haven't you talked to him?" I hated when girls asked me about my brother. He was a player and everyone knew it. And here stood Estelle, with her ebony hair and perfect body—asking me about him. Wait, maybe this was a good thing. Maybe she'd stay away from Zach.

"He hasn't really talked to me since prom," she complained.

"Hmm, well, we were gone most of the summer." I moved to the door hoping for an easy escape.

"Tell him hi for me." She beat me out the door. "Hi Zach," she chimed.

I heard her greeting before my eyes found him. Suddenly my throat went dry—again.

"Are you going my way?" Estelle asked with a mild southern drawl—she was from Seattle.

I tried not to roll my eyes. Mainly, because they were too busy searching for him.

"Hey 'Stelle. I'm not sure. Hey, Emma. Where you headed?" His eyes met mine.

This time it was my eyes that danced from him to her and back to him. As hard as I fought—a smile touched the corners of my mouth. My arms felt weak and I tightened my grip on my Algebra book. Estelle's eyes narrowed back at me, apparently not feeling the camaraderie we had just shared.

She stepped closer to Zach touching his bicep with her hand. "Emma is Ryan's sister *and* a freshman."

My mind was racing. Estelle said 'Ryan's sister' like it was a crime and the word 'freshman' hissed off her tongue. I, of course, said nothing. But she was right; Ryan had run off every guy I'd ever liked. Not that there were many, but even his friends knew I was off limits.

"Hey, Runt." Connor whacked me with a book from behind.

"Hey, Con." I couldn't pull my eyes away to look at Connor and was getting more annoyed each time I was referred to as Runt.

I watched Zach, eager for his response. My eyes were wide and Estelle's smoky lashes fluttered.

"We were all freshman once." He smiled and strolled in my direction.

Estelle flipped around stomping away.

No words came from my mouth as much as I wanted them to.

His eyes bore into mine. "So. Where you headed?" he asked. He was walking me to class?

"Um…I…gym…P.E. I have P.E." I had three words to get out and couldn't do that clearly. My thumb acting on its own accord pointed toward the gym.

"Well, we don't have much time. You're gonna be late." He whirled me in the opposite direction. It must have been obvious I was unable to do it on my own. His hand rested at the small of my back, as he directed me through the hallway toward the gym. A jolt of electricity shot through my body as his hand shifted up and down. We moved fast and didn't talk. As we neared the gym, he glanced at his watch.

"About 20 seconds to spare."

"Now, *you're* gonna be late." I smiled guiltily but I didn't really feel bad.

"I have Spanish. Ms. Padilla won't care. Do you want me to put your Algebra book in my locker?" he offered.

"That's OK. Thanks though. I should go." God, I did not want to leave. His beautiful brown eyes seemed amused. Had I said something?

"OK. I'll see you after." He smiled then jogged down the hall.

I wished I'd let him take my book. Then I would have had to get it after school because of the homework assignment. What did he mean 'I'll see you after'—after what? After class? After school?

Gym passed more slowly than Algebra and when the bell rang, I left by the same door I came in so there would be no confusion. Zach was waiting, his big brown eyes staring at me. I fought a smile and didn't win. I couldn't believe this was happening.

"Hungry?" he asked.

"Kind of."

"You staying on campus?"

I shrugged. I hadn't given it much thought and had never had a choice. Ali and Lauren would be looking for me.

"Do you want to walk across the street?" he asked.

"Sure."

We swung by his locker, and I threw my stuff in after all, then headed down the stairs and out the front. The sky was overcast and smelled of smoke from the California fires.

"How was your summer?" he asked.

"It was OK. Kinda boring." We walked close. I wondered if he could hear my heart. "Yours?"

"Stuck here most of it. Went back to the City for a week. Anyway. I wanted to talk to you."

"Kay." I felt sick.

He shook his head. "This summer. Before you left. That night."

My head was going to explode with embarrassment. "It's OK. It doesn't matter. It's fine."

His head snapped sideways, his eyes confused. "What do you mean?"

He didn't want me. A nervous laugh answered his question. "It's cool. No worries."

"But your dad, he was pretty upset."

I looked at him, confused by his words. Now, *I* didn't understand.

"Your dad was upset," he attempted to explain.

I blushed. "I'm sorry about that." God, was I sorry. So this was a guilt thing. Apologize to the little girl who got in trouble.

"No, don't be. It wasn't your fault. He had a right to be upset. I should never have fallen asleep."

"Oh, absolutely. Sleep is off limits in our house." I laughed nervously again. *Sleep is off limits in our house???*

He lowered his brow and though he smiled, his eyes were serious. I found my cheek with my teeth.

"It was a nice night," I said and couldn't believe those words just came out either. I stared at the grass.

He stopped before we went in the cafe and brushed my cheek with his thumb but said nothing.

The place was loud and we stood in line to order.

"Hey, Runt."

I tensed and whirled around to see Grant.

"Grant, stop calling me that," I said forcefully.

Zach leaned in and grasped my hand. My heart fluttered and I glanced up at him. Grant frowned as he noticed our hands and with his elbow, he nudged the guy behind him. Ryan turned slowly around, eyeing us. Self conscious, I loosened my hold on Zach's hand. Ryan scooted out of the booth. *Oh, God.*

"You are an idiot." Ryan scowled at me.

Tears swelled in my eyes. *Don't cry. Don't cry.*

"Hey!" Zach cautioned Ryan and reached for my hand again.

Shocked, my eyes searched Zach's angry face. No one stood up to Ryan. I watched Ryan's lips purse and his eyes roll at Grant; then Ryan spun me in the opposite direction before Zach got my hand and shoved me out the door.

"Freshman-can't-leave-campus. You-have-a-closed-lunch, dumbass." His words were slow and well articulated.

I fought off the urge to cry. "I didn't know."

Zach stepped up. "It's my fault. I'm the one who asked her. And she's not a dumbass." Zach shot Ryan a look daring him to a challenge. This time, Zach's hand slid perfectly into mine. "Let's get you back," he said.

"You're gonna have a detention and I already told you…he's too freaking old for you," Ryan shouted behind us. "You better leave her alone, Owens."

I was mortified. I was ecstatic. The first guy who'd ever stood up to my brother and at this moment I didn't even have the courage to look at him. I stole my hand from his and folded my arms across my chest, barely catching a glimpse of him; and his mouth turned down at the corners. Was he upset or scared or disgusted? Maybe Ryan frightened him. But he didn't look frightened.

"I'm sorry, I ruined your lunch." Those were the only words I could offer. I was sure things couldn't get worse.

"I'm the one who should be sorry. I didn't know the rule." He quickened his pace as we entered the school and I struggled to keep up, but wondered if he was trying to get away from me. "God, things are so different here. I'll try to get you out of the detention. Maybe they'll give it to me." He smiled apologetically.

"It's OK." My voice was weak. I was weak.

"What's the deal with you and Meiers?"

Meiers? "Grant?"

"Emma! Over here," Ali shouted.

Zach automatically steered us in that direction. They were closing down the lunch line and I could read the thought on his face. I smiled. "It's OK. I'm not that hungry." I was starving.

"Miss Hendricks. This week you get a free pass for being late. Are you aware of the closed lunch for freshman?" Mr. Ming, our principal, asked confronting me.

I nodded. "I am now." I looked around and Zach was gone. Good thing he didn't have to witness my admonishment.

"Hey. Where have you been?" Lauren asked.

I told them what had happened and they were awestruck with the Zach thing. Who was I kidding...*I* was awestruck.

"He's a senior," Ali said as if I wasn't aware of that fact.

"Zach Owens likes you?" Lauren questioned like it was an inconceivable thought.

"Thank you," I said sarcastically. I hadn't told my two best friends about the out of this world kiss we shared two months ago. I knew they'd enjoy it almost as much as I had so I told the story.

"So anyway. It was perfect. He smelled so good...and God...the way he wrapped his arms around me...it's like I fit perfectly. His hands were so big and his kiss—oh—my—God." I closed my eyes as the words came out and remembered just like I had all summer. "I so want to kiss him again." There was a thud on the table; I opened my eyes. A package of individually wrapped peanut butter and crackers lay on the table in front of me. Across the table, Ali and Lauren's eyes focused above my head. Ali's mouth hung open and Lauren looked away. My heart dropped into my stomach and I felt sick. I tilted my head back till it bumped his chest and he tilted his head down until we stared at each other. He held my head in his palms, grinned then leaned in to my ear and whispered. "Eat."

I buried my head in my hands. This was the best and worst day ever. The best because of Zach. The worst because I was a freshman, a runt, and a dumbass.

SEVEN

Zach

The first flights of stairs were easy at the speed I took them. When I finally reached the top, an ache ripped through my calves and I zipped into the bathroom. Empty. Thank God, though the rank urine stench was company enough.

I paced trying to breathe with my fingers laced behind my head, but the tension held its ground, stubbornly fighting me. I searched for something worthy of my fist but adding destruction of property to my juvenile record wouldn't help. Settling, my foot made contact with a four inch metal pipe. The jolt brought me out of the emotional pit I'd fallen into, if only for a minute.

I caught sight of myself in the mirror. Leaving California was supposed to be a new start. I disgusted myself. Why was I so angry? Was it because I'd left everything I loved in the city? Was it about her douche bag brother who thought he could call the shots? Or maybe the rage of her father that night? The first girl who had really caught my attention and everyone around her hated me.

I replayed the events of the night her parents walked in, like I had all summer. Just what I needed, a family already questioning my intentions when I did nothing but kiss the fifteen year old girl. Her father was completely unwavering in his stance. It wasn't fair and clearly obvious which parent Ryan took after.

The pain in my foot was diminishing and replaced with a pain in my chest. The inviting thought of her tongue tracing over my lip flooded back. I shook the thought from my mind. 'I'm fifteen' I heard over and over again in my head like a mantra. Not that fifteen was bad. I'd banged a fifteen year old before. But she was different. There was something about her that got me. Something about her that needed me. I adjusted my crotch and chuckled thinking about what she needed. Her kiss held innocence. I could only imagine the extent of her innocence.

I remembered sitting in my Jeep that night staring up at the house, not wanting to leave her there alone to fight our battle. *OUR battle*? The curtains in the front window pulled apart in the middle then closed. I wondered if it was her then figured it was probably her father.

"Shit!" I hissed as I pounded the steering wheel.

As I reversed down the drive, I watched the curtain, nothing. I rolled down the window and spit. As I licked the residue from my bottom lip, I tasted who I knew I was going to fight hard to forget.

Now, in the bathroom of this pathetic high school, in this shithole excuse of a town, I decided exactly what I wanted and what I was going to get.

EIGHT

Emma

Cross Country meeting and first run today. I qualified for the state run last year but as an eighth grader, I wasn't allowed to go. The expectations for me this year made me nervous. I'd run on the beach every day this summer and felt more than ready.

It was our second year with cross country and Ali and I were excited. We changed in the locker room and met Coach Jones on the track.

"All right, kids. There's a storm movin' in so we're stayin' on the track today. I want three miles. Twelve laps. I need your physicals in this basket before you run and take these forms home to your parents. Be sure you stretch. Our first meet is September 7th."

Wow. No introductions or anything. Ali and I raised our brows simultaneously, giggled then started hamstring stretches.

"So, tell me about the beach."

I shrugged. "Nothing to tell."

"Yeah, but you were with your brother and Grant Meiers. It doesn't get any better than that."

Once upon a time, I would have agreed with her but not today. "Ali...Grant's like my brother."

"Yes. But he's gorgeous and so is Ryan. Plus you've been in love with Grant since birth."

I rolled my eyes. Had she seen Zach? "Come on. Let's go."

We made our way around the track as the football team burst onto the field. Could this be more perfect? My heart accelerated from the one lap around the track and skipped a beat or two when I spotted Zach, #18. I hadn't seen him since lunch. I realized I would live every day for third period—who would have thought I'd be this excited about Advanced Algebra.

"Em?"

"What?"

"What's it like?

"What?" My breathing had reached a sustainable level.

"A good kiss…I mean a really good kiss?"

I chuckled. "You ask like I'm all experienced. We kissed one time. And besides, you kissed Jacob after the spring dance." I had no doubt my kiss beat hers.

"Oh, please. He pecked me like a chicken."

I laughed out loud. "I don't know, Al. It was great. Like I said at lunch before I got busted. How freaking embarrassing was that?"

Creepy dark clouds moved overhead and a light mist began to fall. As I rounded the corner, Zach, Ryan and Coach Saia stood together. Zach's hands rested on his hip and he eyeballed Ryan, whose arms were flailing while he seemed to be berating the coach. I blinked hard to clear the rain accumulated on my lashes. Coach poked his finger in Ryan's chest, said something and left them both. Zach began to step away and Ryan grabbed his arm. My stomach knotted as Ryan's mouth began to move. Then, as if I'd called their names, they both looked at me. First Zach, then Ryan. My eyes dropped to the track.

"Did you use your tongue?"

"What?"

"Your tongue? When you kissed him?"

"ALI!" Oh my God. As distracted as I was, just the thought of it made my insides tingle.

"What? We've always told each other everything. Besides, I know you did or you would have said no."

I bumped her pushing her sideways on the track but she fell back in rhythm. "A little. But it wasn't like you shove the whole thing in; like in the movies…it's softer…we just kind of touched them. I so can not believe I'm saying this."

"Doesn't Zach have a friend you could set me up with?"

Ali was so pretty with her thick blond hair and she'd blossomed sooner than me. At 5'5'', she stood over me by five inches. Her bra size was probably a C and I was still an A, at best. Her complexion was her only downfall but she had a special soap and cream. Even Ryan thought she was hot—but he wouldn't be caught dead dating a freshman.

"We're not *dating*."

We were on lap eight—only four to go and rain was coming down. Only on the corners could I get a glimpse of him. They were running two sets of offense. Ryan and Zach both quarterbacking. *Uh-oh.*

By lap twelve, my clothes were nearly dragging the ground and Ali and I headed back to the locker room.

Ryan's truck was a good jaunt so we didn't bother to change into dry clothes, grabbed our book bags and darted to the parking lot. The truck was, of course, locked. Football must have been over because the guys were no longer on the field. I dropped the tailgate and we waited in the downpour.

"So, how was Austin this summer?" she asked bumping my shoulder with hers.

"As gorgeous and rich as ever. We held hands, twice, but in that I-love-you-like-a-sister-way."

Ali shook her head. "Wow, you must really like Zach, because Grant Meiers said you looked good this morning and you and Austin held hands and those are the two boys you've been in love with for as long as I've known you."

I grinned from ear to ear and shrugged.

"Isn't Austin in college now?" she asked.

"Yep. Freshman."

"Would Katie and Matt let you date a college guy?"

"Well, Austin's different. I've known him for…forever. Doesn't matter, Ryan wouldn't let me date him or anybody."

"What about Zach?"

"Hey, you two." Ryan said. "Grab the blanket out of the carrier so you don't ruin my leather." He seemed annoyed.

Ali and I jumped out of the bed, grabbed the blanket, threw it in the cab and slid in finding relief from the pelting rain. A light tap at the window startled me. Zach stood at the passenger side window in the rain. Ryan rolled the window down from his side. I stared at Zach.

"What?" Ryan barked.

Zach's eyes narrowed protecting them from the water. "I have your sister's book."

He passed the book to me through the window. "Sorry, it's a little wet."

I'd forgotten about my Algebra book. Why was he addressing my brother instead of me? "Thanks," I whispered. His eyes met mine for a second then flickered away.

"Yup," he said flatly.

The window went up and I watched him jog down the sidewalk. As I folded my arms across my chest, a frustrated sigh slid through my teeth.

Ali didn't live far from the school and once she'd gotten out, I unleashed.

"Can you please tell me what *that* was about?" my voice was harsh.

"What?" he looked surprised at my anger.

"Zach! You weren't even nice to him. Then today, at lunch, did you have to call me a dumbass?"

"You're acting stupid, Em." He turned up the knob on the radio, blaring the obnoxious hip-hop.

"Ryan. I'm not stupid. I like Zach and you were mean. I'm telling Mom and Dad what you said to me in front of everyone. I didn't know I couldn't leave and Zach didn't either."

He shrugged. "Maybe you're both stupid."

"What is your problem?" I flipped the radio to a different station. "He's nice and I think he likes me. Besides he's on your team. Coach won't let you be mean."

He pulled the truck into our driveway and thrust it into park. "Team has nothing to do with it when he wants my position." Ryan jerked his backpack from behind the seat and slammed the door.

The truck was quiet. So. That's what this was about. Football. Zach wanted to be the quarterback? I shivered at the thought of Zach and Ryan going head to head. Football was Ryan's life. He'd already gotten a letter of interest from U of O and UCLA. No one from Ashland had been recruited D-1 before. I couldn't imagine Coach Saia taking that from him. I had a hunch this wasn't going to turn out well—no matter what.

I started dinner, as expected, and went with the easiest thing I could find. Spaghetti. By the time I'd browned the beef, Dad had gotten home. He always beat Mom but realtor hours were weird. My dad was a CPA and partner in a firm downtown and except for the first four months of the year, his hours were flexible.

"Hey, big freshman girl. How was the first day?"

"Fine," I lied, sliding the uncooked pasta into the boiling water.

"How are your classes?"

"Good." There was some truth.

"Where's your brother?"

"Upstairs, holed up in his room, pouting like a little girl."

My father's raised brows wanted further explanation.

"Some guy wants his position in football. He is freakin' out about it."

"I'll go talk to him." He kissed my head and grabbed a bite of the cooked beef. I smacked his hand with the spatula.

Ryan had been on the phone when Dad went upstairs and now dinner was the time for sorting this out.

"Your sister said someone else is wanting to quarterback?"

Ryan shoved a wad of spaghetti in his mouth and eyeballed me.

"Sounds like someone is going to have to do a little better." Dad continued.

"Matt. He works hard as it is." Mom defended her son.

"Katie. He's never had competition before. He's never had to work. He's a few months away from signing with the Ducks."

Ryan shot his chair back and stood. "Never had to work? I work my ass off, Dad. Here. At the beach. It doesn't matter. I'm in shape and ready. The reason, *ZACH*..." his name was emphasized in my direction. "wants my position is because I missed the first week of conditioning due to the damn mandatory family getaway. So, he filled in and evidently did a great job. So coach wants to try us both there."

"Honey, sit down, please." Mom tried to calm Ryan, her voice always soothing.

Dad faced me. I knew this was going to happen. "Is this your Zach...the 'we just fell asleep' Zach?"

Ryan bellied up to the table again and grinned at me. "I don't think Zach slept much this summer. Rumor has it he and Estelle became pretty good friends."

"Shut up, Ryan." *Estelle?* I wasn't sure the noodles were going to go down my throat.

"Well, you need to know. This guy's a jackass."

I swallowed some water to help the noodles along then scooted my chair back from the table and tossed my breadstick onto my plate. What was he talking about? Zach didn't like Estelle. I started thinking about the look in her eyes today when he chose me. The daggers she shot across the hall in my direction. Was she jealous...of me? I was no longer hungry.

"Ryan and Emma, sit down," Dad demanded. "We will not allow someone...anyone to come between us. Do you understand me? This behavior and these attacks and your language..." he pointed at Ryan. "...will not be tolerated."

"He's too old for her," Ryan spouted off.

"That will be our decision. Not yours. Am I clear?"

Ryan shook his head and wouldn't look at me. His jaw was tight. I wanted to punch him.

I hid out in my room for the rest of the night. About 9:30 my phone buzzed with a text The area code was different than ours—415. Ours was 541. How weird is that!

May I call?

I bit my lip.

I Googled the area code. SAN FRAN!

I jumped up and down typing in yes so fast that I spelled it wrong twice.

Within an extremely long minute, my phone rang.

"Hey," I said.

"Hey."

"Hey," I said a second time. "How's it goin?" I wondered if he heard the smile in my voice.

"Um, it's ok, I guess."

"You guess?"

"Look, I'm sorry about after school. Your brother is kind of upset with me and I was... I don't know." He got quiet.

I sat quietly twisting my hair desperately wanting to say something but unsure what to say. It was never a good thing when conversation was left up to me. I wanted to ask him about Estelle.

"What are you doing Friday?" he asked.

"I'm not sure. Why?" Butterflies soared through my stomach.

"There are a few of us heading to Crescent City to hang out at the beach, build a fire—you know the drill."

There lay the problem. I didn't know the drill. This was all new to me.

"Apparently, it's a good hour and half drive but this is one of the few weekends we won't have a football game. Plus the weather is supposed to be awesome."

"That sounds fun. When are you leaving?"

"We'll probably head out after school. I can pick you up at your house."

Problem number two. I wasn't sure how this would fly with my folks. "Can I let you know?"

"Sure. We can talk tomorrow."

"OK."

"I'll talk to you then," he said.

"Bye," I whispered.

I plowed my fingers through my hair. How was this going to work? My brother hated the guy I was falling for and my dad didn't care for him much more than my brother. I had to somehow sway my mom to let this happen and that wasn't a guarantee. I pulled the covers up over my head without getting undressed and said a prayer.

NINE

The ride to school the next morning was quiet. The roar of the truck seemed louder. How could silence be so noticeable? Ryan and I had never been like this before and I wasn't sure who was angrier or more stubborn. Did he think I was betraying him by liking Zach? I was dying to know the gossip about Estelle and decided to ask him what he'd heard. I turned the radio down.

"Ryan?"

"What?" His tone was sharp.

"I know how you feel about Zach. But what did he say about Estelle?"

"You know what, Em. Ask him. He's your prince."

I looked out my window. "Why are you being such a jerk? I just want to know."

"You want to know what it's like to date a senior guy? Well, this is it." He parked in his spot, got out and met up with Connor, Grant and Brett. Zach and Josh were walking up ahead of them and Estelle and Claire toddled behind. I stayed in the truck, waited and watched not wanting to be late on the second day of school but not finding the courage to move without my entourage. Grant turned once and looked back at me, slowing in his step just a bit. Finally, I spotted Lauren, alone. I hurried out of the truck and hustled toward her. "Hey," I said, winded.

On my way to Algebra, I hurried up the stairs and dashed into the restroom on the second floor. Dabbing lip gloss on and running my fingers through my hair, I frowned at my reflection, unsure what he saw.

The bell rang as I stepped into class; the only seat available was next to Grant. Musical chairs had somehow played out during the past twenty-four hours because Zach sat behind where I'd sat yesterday and Estelle had taken my seat. Figures. I liked the back though, full view. Estelle sat cockeyed, blabbering to Zach. I forced my eyes away.

"Hey. What are you doin' Friday?" Grant asked.

I shrugged knowing what I hoped to be doing. "I don't know. Why?"

"Some of us are headed to the beach. Didn't know if you wanted to tag along."

Tag along? That sounded third wheel-ish.

"Tag along?"

"I mean like ride with me," he explained.

"Really?" The astonishment was apparent in my voice and I wondered if this would at least get me there.

"Yeah."

I couldn't respond at first. In fact, I'm sure I looked like an idiot with my mouth hanging open and a vacant expression on my face. This was the second time in two days that Grant surprised me. Yesterday—the reference to my body and today—asking me out? Was he serious? I couldn't begin to compare to Chloe Burkenkamp, the girl he dated until her family relocated to Okinawa. This summer was his summer to bust loose at the beach and he and Ryan had done exactly that, but I never saw *this* coming.

"Um…who's all going?"

Mr. Bowman came through the door and went to the front of the class.

"A bunch of us. It'll be fun. Katie loves me. She won't care." He was right—my mom did love him.

Hmm. I laughed under my breath as Mr. Bowman began explaining the assignment for today. I figured mental math in my own head. What was the probability of me—Runt—being asked out by two guys? No, scratch that, two hot guys. Fractions, probability, even a linear equation wouldn't help me figure the odds.

Mid-way through the hour, Estelle passed a note to Zach making sure I saw. My teeth clenched as jealousy shot through me. Zach watched Mr. Bowman from his desk as he opened it, read and responded. Her hair flitted over his desk as she glanced at me through her long lashes when she grabbed the paper back. My throat tightened and I finished my work, hoping tears didn't come. *Crying is for babies Emma-* I heard Ryan chant in my head.

When the bell rang, I exploded out of my chair and flew down the hall hoping to make an unnoticed exit. Someone knew what had transpired this summer in my absence and I was hell bent on finding out.

"Em!" I heard Zach shout from behind me. I acted like I didn't. "Em!" he shouted again much closer. I think he was running. I had to turn around. I didn't have a choice.

"What?" My voice cracked. Damn it.

"What's wrong? I thought I'd walk you to gym?" He seemed disappointed.

I flipped my hair behind my ears—a nervous habit I'd had for years. A few strands fell back, and as if it were no big deal, he slid them back into place. It was a huge deal to me. I caught a whiff of his hand and my stomach quivered. It was going to be more difficult than I thought to ever be angry at him.

"Oh. Well. I didn't know. You were late yesterday and…Well, Estelle." My babble stopped there. My mouth failed again and blood invaded my cheeks.

His features softened. "I would like to walk *you.*" He gestured down the hall, his chocolate brown eyes sparkled.

It hurt to look at him. I wanted this so much. I nodded. He moved next to me and the funny feeling in my body was there again—an overwhelming desire to bury my nose in his T-shirt and sniff so I would keep the smell in my memory forever.

"I brought something for you."

"What?"

"Repayment for yesterday. I'll have it for you after gym."

"OK. Well, thanks for walking me."

"Wait for me next time," he ordered then headed down the hall.

When P.E. was over, I purposely kept my stride slow as I met him outside the door. He stood with broad shoulders against the wall, talking to Connor and Brett, two of Ryan's best buddies. I hesitated then went out. Zach winked at me as both boys turned and saw me.

"Hey, Runt." Brett said with a shocked tone, his smile fading as he turned back to Zach.

"Hi, Brett." I cringed at my nickname then watched as Brett's eyes darted from me to Zach then to Connor.

"Hey, Runt? Does Ryan know about this?" Connor asked, and jetted his thumb toward Zach.

I pursed my lips together and narrowed my eyes glaring at them. "This is none of Ryan's business or yours."

Both boys stared at each other then rotated back to Zach.

"Dude," Connor said.

Zach shrugged. "I have no obligation to him."

"Man. She's fifteen. Runt is—tiny. You hurt her and…"

"Connor!" I shouted.

Zach's eyes scanned all three of us stopping on me. "I'm seventeen. That's two years difference. If her parents are okay with that then it still isn't Ryan's business. And I have no intention of hurting her."

I didn't know if my heart could physically melt but the heaviness in my chest increased with each of his words.

Connor wiped his palm down the length of his face stopping on his chin. "O-K." He patted Brett's shoulder. "Let's go. See ya, Runt. Zach." They clasped Zach's hand, bumped shoulders then left.

Zach dismissed them easily with a chuckle and shook a brown paper sack.

"What is it?" I don't know how I spoke but I did. All I wanted to do was jump in his arms. No one had ever stood up to my brother's posse before. Ever. He was my own personal savior.

"I've got peanuts, crackers, beef jerky and drinks. The best a gas station has to offer. I stopped on the way to school. I haven't eaten a school lunch in several years. So, this is the best I could do. Shall we?" He motioned toward the cafeteria.

"You're eating lunch *with me?*" I couldn't hide the surprise in my voice. The thought of me eating in the cafeteria with Zach—a senior—it was almost unfathomable.

"Would you rather I not?"

"No. Yes. No!" I paused trying to gather my scattered thoughts. "Yes, I'd like that." Oh my God. I sounded like a blubbering idiot. I scratched my head.

"Good," he said grinning. I think he was laughing at me.

Ali and Lauren weren't in the cafeteria yet. He picked a table on the far wall and sat next to me. I didn't know if I'd be able to eat and breathe at the same time.

"So, Runt, is it?"

I released a tremendous sigh and closed my eyes. "Please don't." Not him too.

"Annoying?"

"You have no idea. I have been Runt for six years to my brother's friends. It's a nickname I hate."

"Where'd it come from?"

"Look at me," I said, then felt stupid because he *was* looking at me.

"You're not a runt." He opened my can of Dr. Pepper. "Here."

"How did you know I liked Dr. Pepper?"

"You downed two cans at your house—in May."

I nodded my head and smiled. "That's right. Good memory." I opened the nuts even though I wasn't hungry.

"OK. Back to Connor and what he said. *Does* Ryan know about this?" he asked.

I examined and fingered the nuts in my palm. "When you say 'this' you're referring to you and me?" My face flushed just saying the words.

"Yes." He took one of my hands in his. I couldn't look at him and kept my eyes focused on my lap where his hand held mine. I was terrified to look in his eyes, afraid of what I wouldn't say and deeply concerned with what I would.

"He knows…" I swallowed hard. "…that I like you." I hoped the words were audible because I didn't think I could speak them again. I chanced glancing up.

A soft, gentle grin crossed his face.

"I think you know that already. Right?" I wanted to clarify.

A small chuckle slipped from his mouth—his perfect mouth. "You know, back in May when I met you, you were one of the first people to really *talk* to me. I hated being here. I didn't want to leave San Francisco. No one, and I mean no one, really asked me about me. Do you remember what you did for me?"

Was he talking about the song? "You made me sad that day. You seemed so unhappy and…" I chanced looking at him and our eyes met. I was suddenly embarrassed because for the life of me I couldn't remember what we were talking about. "I don't remember what I was saying." I rubbed my forehead trying to jar a thought.

"I asked if you remember what you did. Do you?"

His other hand rubbed my back. I had a feeling everyone in the lunchroom was staring at us but I didn't care.

"Are you talking about the Journey thing? That was pretty cheesy."

"Yes!" He laughed out loud and it sounded musical. "When I heard that song, *Lights*, come over the speakers through your house—you made me smile and I hadn't smiled in a while. You know that song was written about San Francisco, don't you? Anyway, I don't care how cheesy it was. It made me feel good. *You* made me feel good."

I longed to say something but didn't want to ruin the moment, so I just looked at him.

"Emma?"

"What?"

"You OK?"

"Uh, huh." I wasn't though. "I have a question for you and I don't know how to ask it."

"Just shoot."

"I'm not as good with words as you are." I was already struggling.

"You're fine."

I hesitated. If he only knew. "Why…me?" I asked reluctantly.

"What do you mean?" He seemed confused.

God! He didn't understand and I knew I couldn't explain it. He was one of the hottest seniors in the school and here he sat in the cafeteria with me. He had girls ogling and it didn't seem to faze him. I knew they all were thinking the same thing as I was. Why her?

Thankfully, the bell rang.

I stood. "I'll explain later," I said.

"OK. Do you want a ride home after practice?" he asked.

I always rode home with Ryan and today I wasn't going to rock the boat. "Um, I'll probably just ride home with Ryan. But thanks."

"OK. See ya." He squeezed my hand before disappearing in the mix of kids.

After school, Ali was down with a sore throat so she punted cross country. It was lonelier today but I was certain I earned a better time even though we ran the three miles on our normal cross country path behind the school rather than the track. After I changed and left the locker room, I found Grant waiting outside.

"Hey, Runt."

"What's up, Grant?" I asked shocked to see him.

"Ryan took Claire home after cheerleading practice. He asked me to tend to you." Grant laughed.

"Nice. 'Tend to me?' Like it's such a chore."

"Come on." He threw his arm around my shoulder and dragged me toward his pickup.

"Claire and Ryan?" I was confused. "When did that happen?"

"Today, I think."

"Claire?" I repeated.

"Shut up. She's hot."

"She's a fake bitch." I acted like I shoved my finger down my throat. "I thought it would be Estelle, again."

"Nope. She blew it. Apparently hooked up with some other dude this summer."

It was as if he'd knocked the wind from me. I fought for breath and felt dizzy for a second. I wasn't sure if I wanted to scream, cry, run or hit Grant for saying it. But jealousy burned inside of me, and I shook my head trying to get rid of the thought.

"Who was it?" The words were barely spoken.

"I don't know. Ryan does. What a bitch." My slow pace must have annoyed him because he grabbed me, threw me over his shoulders like a sack of potatoes and ran to the truck dumping me on the hood.

Laughing, I shouted, "you punk!" and slid off till my feet hit the ground. He had opened my door and moved around to his side. I used the running boards to boost myself up and once in the truck, my dinky little legs dangled over the seat and my feet barely touched the floor. I slammed the door and smacked his shoulder. The smell I'd loved for the past three years—his smell—saturated the inside of the truck. He laughed and started the engine. As he reversed out of his spot, I glanced out the front windshield. Zach stood about fifty yards from us and stared. Grant waved and I sat frozen.

TEN

The moment I got home, I texted Zach. Nothing. I slept with my phone that night.

The next day, I was anxious at school. I watched the clock and though texting wasn't allowed in school, I kept a close eye on my phone—hoping. No messages. I ran straight to Algebra eager to be in my seat before Zach. Being the first to arrive, I had my pick of seats and chose a back row.

I tugged my homework assignment out and pretended to recheck as voices of kids began filling the room. Zach breezed through the door the moment I looked up and I could see the questions in his eyes. I didn't look away. He gave me a casual nod. How could someone that beautiful worry about Grant? But it gave me a hint of satisfaction knowing Grant bothered him.

With my pencil, I pointed to the desk next to me. He pushed the desks apart to get through and slid in.

"Hey," he said.

"Hey. Did you get my text?"

"I had a crazy night. Sorry."

I studied his flawless face wondering if I'd blown things yesterday. He kept his eyes down. How was I supposed to know Grant would show up to take me home?

"Zach." I touched his hand but he didn't look at me. "Zach." My voice more forceful. I scooted as close as I could get without tipping off everyone in the room.

"What?" His one word was abrasive but his eyes seemed confused.

"It's not what you think." I needed to speak fast or I wasn't going to get it out. "Ryan took Claire home and left me. He asked Grant to do it. I'm sorry."

He nodded.

"He's like my brother." I frowned just thinking about Grant. And of course he strolled into Algebra at that second.

"Why didn't you call me?"

The thought never actually occurred to me. Grant was always there to pick me up when Ryan couldn't. It was a given. Grant was not just another brother; he was my best friend, the love of my life, until now. But I couldn't say that. I had to make him understand.

"Like I said…"

"Hey, Runt." Grant reached over and smacked the back of my head, whiffing my hair.

"Stop it, Grant," I said annoyed and rubbed my head.

Zach's brows raised and his jaw tightened.

"Hey, Owens." Grant greeted Zach.

"Meiers."

Grant plopped next to me on the opposite side. Then Estelle danced through the door. She did a rolling finger wave to Zach. *Ho Bag!* No seats were available except for the one in front of Grant—diagonal from me.

"Hi Emma," she said.

"Hi Stelle."

"Grant." She acknowledged him by sticking her tongue out.

"Keep the tongue in your mouth Stelle. I've heard it's been getting around lately."

She gave him the middle finger behind her back where Mr. Bowman couldn't see. "You're just jealous because you haven't seen it," she seethed.

"I've seen it one too many times. No interest here." Grant looked at me and winked.

"Kiss my ass." She was pissed and I tried to hide my smile.

"Been there. Done that sista."

"Open your books to page 19," Mr. Bowman ordered. I wish I could have seen Zach's face during that interaction—to know what he was thinking. She was a 'ho and he needed to know it. But then again, he may already. The bell rang and Zach met me at the door.

"I can't walk you today."

My throat tightened. *Crap.* It was SO over. "Why?"

"Last night I needed to do an Anatomy and Physiology report and I didn't get it done. I need to do it now. I'm ditching Spanish."

"Why didn't you get it done?" I questioned. I had never ditched before.

"I had a meeting and some other things on my mind." He ran his fingers through his hair and wouldn't look at me.

"Like Grant?" I asked quietly, scared of his answer.

I wasn't sure he was going to answer. "It doesn't matter." He paused. "I really wanted to punch him when he hit you in the head."

A smile swept my face. "Thanks, but they all do that."

"Yeah. Well. They need to stop." His tone was serious and his eyes still weren't happy. "Do you have practice tonight?"

"Yes."

"I'll drive you home, if that's OK."

I nodded biting my lip and rolled my eyes as the bell rang. "That would be great," I yelled over my shoulder and darted for gym.

On Friday, Zach picked me up at the house. This was our first official date and the butterflies eating away at my stomach were irritating. We were getting a later start than the others because he had another meeting to hit. Not sure what the meetings were about but he said that a lot.

I had a feeling Ryan was taking Claire but because we still weren't on speaking terms, I wasn't sure. Mom and Dad approved me going with Zach, but I had to be home at a reasonable time because of cross country. They had tickets to the Shakespeare Theater and would be home late anyway. Grant didn't seem too bothered when I said I was riding with Zach. In fact, he said nothing at all.

Zach wore khaki shorts and a USC sweatshirt, and as we walked to the unfamiliar car, I noticed the blanket, jackets and cooler in the back seat. Cooler? I wondered what was in it.

He wasn't driving his Jeep. "Sweet car. Whose is it?"

He opened my door and closed it after I slid in, then went to his side. "My dad's."

"Is it a mustang?"

He rubbed my knee as he chuckled. "No, it's a '72 Chevelle." His touch sent chills up my leg.

"I like it."

He reversed and backed out of the drive. "Good."

"North to Grants Pass, my dad said and then take the Redwood road?"

"Yes. You've lived in California your whole life and never seen the Redwoods?" I was appalled.

"I've been through 'em, just usually asleep. Besides. Where I come from, we have Sequoias," he boasted.

No matter how many times I'd been through the Redwoods, they were still incredible. On Zach's side of the car, a rushing stream wound through a massive rock gorge. Cars were parked at every lookout taking pictures and I was grateful that he didn't pull off. Though it was breathtakingly beautiful, it was gut-wrenching for those of us with height and motion sickness issues.

"Wow. This is awesome," he said. "Call me stupid, but these trees don't seem that big."

"Well, Stupid…we're not to the Redwoods yet." I smiled

"I knew that." He quickly lied. "And remind me, *how* are you getting home?"

I flipped back around to him and pouted. "You wouldn't."

"I wouldn't." He winked.

I didn't like it when he took his eyes off the road, let alone closed one, even if it meant he was looking at me.

"So does your family come this way a lot?" he asked.

"No. Not really. I've been on this road maybe five or six times. But that's it. It's not like an annual thing or anything. How about you?"

"I have an uncle that lives in Brookings, Oregon. We've been up there, I think twice maybe three times. We drove through then."

"Yes but *you* slept." I reminded him.

"I did." He acknowledged. "They're trees." He shrugged.

I rolled my eyes. "That's like saying a tsunami is just a wave. Wait till you see them." I wouldn't have admitted it but the winding roads were upsetting my stomach. The radio hummed in the background and I thought nervously for something to talk about.

Relieved, he started. "Tell me something- about you."

"Like...?" Where would I start? I didn't want to bore him.

"Favorite music." He suggested.

"I like a lot of different kinds. Kid Rock. Nickleback. Drake. Dave Matthews."

He nodded as I spat off a few.

"You?" I asked.

"I'm old school, I guess. I like the Stones, Aerosmith, ACDC...you know. Journey." He grinned on the last one. "OK. Favorite food."

"Hmm. That one's tough. I think I was born to be Mexican...or Italian or a sea gull."

His brows rose. "I followed the first two but you lost me on the sea gull."

"They eat crab."

"OK. Note taken."

"And you?"

"Well, ditto on the crab but I'm a meat and potato kind of guy. Give me a steak any day and I'm good."

We nearly passed the National Park sign. "Wait. Stop here." I shouted and he hit the brakes and swerved. "I know we don't have a lot of time but quick pic?" I laughed. The view was perfect with the setting sun slicing through the enormous trees. We got out.

"Go stand over there. Oh. By the way, *now* we're in the Redwoods," I joked.

He nodded slowly and deliberately. "OK. All right. I see. They are a wee bit bigger. But I'm not in the picture alone. Here." He took my camera from me.

"Ma'am. Would you mind?" he asked an elderly lady who smiled at us.

"Just point and shoot," I explained and he grabbed my hand as he walked past.

He stood with his arm wrapped around my shoulder. The sudden closeness sent shockwaves through my body. I forced a smile and the flash went off. I quickly moved away from him afraid of what was happening between us. I'd never felt what I felt with him. I walked unsteadily toward the lady.

"Thank you," I said. I was scared to look back at him—afraid of what he might see in my eyes. I was afraid that I was already madly in love with him. I studied the picture on the screen.

"Emma!" Zach shouted but was nowhere to be seen.

He obviously ducked behind a tree. I stood staring at the overwhelming height of lumber that surrounded me. "Marco?" I yelled and held my breath.

"Polo," he hollered with a chuckle.

I busted up laughing, not because it was funny, but because he got me and this thrilled me to the bone.

Crescent City wasn't a particularly pretty town but the ocean it rested against was breathtakingly beautiful. I was glad Zach knew where he was going because the car wound around so much I would have been undoubtedly lost. Dusk was settling in the east and the sun was melting into the water above the ocean in the west. We parked next to about fifteen cars. My stomach twisted when I saw Ryan and Grant's truck.

Zach carried everything except the blanket, which he handed to me. I saw no one around so I imagined we had a bit of a jaunt ahead of us. My flip-flops slid in the sand, and as coordinated as I was, walking in them down the hill was a challenge. I took them off and held them between my fingers.

"Here, get on." Zach hunched down insinuating a piggyback.

"No! You already have the cooler and the jackets." I walked past him.

He grabbed my arm and jerked me back behind him. "Emma. Get on. You're not gonna walk barefoot through here. There could be glass and the grass is sharp."

"Fine." I gave in. "But only until we get to the good sand. Once we are out of this grassy, dirty stuff, I am so down." I hopped on his back wrapping my arms around his neck. God he smelled good.

"UGH!" He groaned. "Baby, you are heavy," he teased. "I'm not sure I can manage this."

"Shut up!" I tried to knee him in the back but he held tight to my legs.

"What do you weigh? Like seventy-five?"

The ride was rough and I bumped up and down on his back. I couldn't stop thinking about him calling me baby. "Eighty-four—thank you very much." I was relieved I'd chewed gum because though I was behind him, our faces were close. The feelings my body was experiencing were becoming more and more frequent and foreign.

"Hold on. We're goin' downhill." He leaned forward and my body tilted with him. It felt like I was going to go head first off his back. But, I didn't budge. I closed my eyes and could hear the underbrush as he kicked through it. Then, his feet thudded a few times in the sand and we were on even ground again. I opened my eyes and saw the fire maybe a hundred yards in front of us and lots of people sitting around.

I felt nervous. "Put me down, please." I flapped my legs to break free, fearful he might not oblige. He did.

"Hey, Owens!" Brett yelled and threw a football toward us.

Zach dropped the cooler and the jackets and caught the ball with a thump to his chest. I loved watching him. Ryan, Grant and Connor all turned after Brett pointed in our direction. I offered a smile and Ryan spun back to the fire without so much as a nod. Jackass. Grant stood and stared with his hands in his pockets.

"Great. Meiers is here," Zach whispered.

I smiled at his protectiveness.

"Hey Ru...Em." Grant changed his greeting. I acknowledged everyone I knew and they were nice enough. Except for Ryan. I had a feeling freshmen weren't allowed, especially freshmen sisters. As I sat on a piece of driftwood, I counted only seniors. Until I saw *them* walking up from the beach...Estelle, Claire and Jaycee...the queen bees of the junior class...they certainly wouldn't be happy to see me.

Claire plopped next to Ryan who didn't seem over enthused to see her either. Plus the threatening glare he was shooting Zach was less than friendly. Estelle squeezed in between Connor and Brett but definitely kept her lurid eyes on Zach. I couldn't look. I felt sick as my stomach growled.

"You two want a drink?" Jaycee asked and poured what looked like punch from a cooler.

"Sure, thanks." I took two Styrofoam cups for Zach and me and handed one to him.

"Em!" I heard in unison and glanced up after swallowing a mouthful to find Grant, Connor and Ryan shaking their heads at me. About that moment, my gag reflex activated and the bitter taste of the drink made me shiver. Zach casually took the drink from my hand as he sipped his. Great, Zach wasn't a boyfriend but a fifth brother. He opened the cooler and handed me a soda. The girls giggled at what they saw and my back stiffened angrily.

The night grew cooler as the evening passed. Estelle began to act silly, laughing non-stop and dancing around—maybe one too many drinks. She pulled off her shirt and exposed a swim suit top, skimpy at best. It was freezing. Zach was making a point not to look and offered me a smile. I think Connor was the only one who didn't look away and I almost shouted at him—'close your mouth Con'— but Ryan's nudge in the side did the trick.

I hadn't even considered a swimsuit and wondered if anyone else had. Claire had gone up to a crate of items and brought down a portable MP3 station and flipped on music.

A shiver rippled through me and Zach grabbed one of his jackets and draped it over my shoulders. It was huge but smelled like him.

"Thank you," I whispered and smiled.

"Oh. That was sa-weet." Estelle remarked then sat next to Brett laying her head on his shoulder but still staring at Zach.

I pulled my knees to my chest trying to ignore her comments. The wind picked up and sparks from the tipi fire followed the breeze landing in the sand.

"Let's go for a walk." Zach spoke softly in my ear and pulled me to standing.

I nodded and we headed toward the ocean as he took my hand in his. I walked away from the circle feeling proud but sure seven sets of eyes were on us.

It was romantic and perfect and I feared I would wake up and it would all be over.

"Sorry about the drink. I didn't know it was spiked until your *guardians* spoke up. Then I tasted it."

"My guardians?" I knew who he was talking about but wanted to hear his theory.

"Your brother and his buddies. They are quite protective of you." The sand squished up between my toes as we strolled. It was soft and cold. I think he was jealous.

"I told you. I've known these guys forever." I glanced up at him. His height had to border six feet something. I felt like a shrimp.

"Yes. But what you don't understand is they've known you forever as Ryan's little sister or Runt—as they choose to say. And I think they are beginning to see that you aren't so little anymore. You're *not* a runt, Emma. Just like Grant said the first day of school. He saw you this summer—I mean really saw you." His words seem to insinuate something and I didn't like it.

"I don't like Grant," I explained.

He faced me and tilted my chin up. "I'm not certain they trust me with you."

"I trust you." And I did. I trusted him so much. I wanted him to kiss me. The moon, the ocean... "Did you date in California?"

"Yes."

That wasn't what I was getting at. "I mean. Did you. Like...you know." I held my palms open hoping they might catch the words that were not coming.

"Did I have a girlfriend?"

He figured it out. Maybe he understood me more than I realized.

I nodded though I wasn't sure he could see me.

"There was this girl, Brandy, I dated for a while. We were *supposed* to date. I was the quarterback. She was the cheerleader. But it never clicked. I think we both played along."

"So why not a cheerleader here?" My feet kicked the sand around.

Suddenly, he knocked my legs out from under me and caught me in his arms. "I don't know. I'm kind of partial to cross country runners." He spun me around.

"Stop," I giggled. And, he did stop. But he didn't put me down. He stared at me. His eyes searching mine, and I could feel my heart pulsing in my head. His eyes flickered from mine to my lips and back to my eyes. This was the moment I'd been waiting for. I watched as his tongue brushed his own lips. My heart fluttered, maybe even skipped some beats, as he leaned in to me. His breath was warm and when his lips touched mine, I thought I'd come out of my skin. I took his face in my palms and held it—his skin as silky as his lips. Our tongues touched briefly before he pulled back and stared at me.

My hands were in his hair and I don't know what came over me, but I pulled him to me again—unable to resist. Thankfully, he didn't hesitate. He slowly and cautiously moved to his knees and laid me in the sand. His kiss was more forceful than before as he tucked me under him. I felt warm and safe. I could taste the drink from earlier on his tongue.

He kissed me softly, pecking my forehead, nose, cheeks and chin. A funny feeling stirred inside—one that was new to me. Then, suddenly my body betrayed me as a shiver ricocheted through me from head to toe.

He leaned away. "You're cold?"

"No." I lied, but chatter rattled my teeth.

"Em. Why didn't you say something?"

That was the first time he'd called me Em. He rose off of me and I was sad. No! I didn't want this to end. I didn't care if I froze to death. He easily pulled me to my feet. It wouldn't have mattered had I resisted. The glow of the fire was farther away than I expected, and now that his body wasn't protecting me from the wind—my body shook uncontrollably.

"I am so sorry. I should have had you dress warmer."

"I should know buh-buh-better. I spent the last two months on the oh-ocean." My words were jerky as my body trembled. We rejoined the group and he made me sit directly in front of the fire between his legs as he rubbed my arms creating friction. The fire popped and it frightened me to be so close.

"Well…how was your little *walk*?" Estelle chimed.

My chin rested on my drawn up knees and I didn't look at her. He chose to ignore her too.

"We've been for walks, haven't we Zach?" I looked this time, her eyes centered on him.

His rubbing stopped for a moment then started again—his strokes faster.

"ZAAACH…" she sang his name and I felt tears brim in my eyes. I looked at Ryan who would be so angry at me for crying.

"Shut-up, Stelle." Ryan warned. He shook his head as his eyes met mine. Then he winked, which I assumed was a surrender to the fight we'd had. Finally. Thank God.

"Oh, Ryan. Silly boy." She moved close to him, her navel next to his nose. He shut his eyes and twisted his neck sideways away from her, but she still managed to run her fingers through his blonde hair. Claire sat quietly, as she too watched Estelle. "You're just jealous, Ry. You're jealous that Zach tapped into what you left behind this summer."

"You're a bitch," Ryan gritted through clenched teeth.

So. They had been together—Zach and Estelle. My chest was caving in or so it felt. I was so scared my tears were going to deceive me and boil over my lids. Zach held my arms now and the rubbing had stopped. I felt his head rest against the back of mine or maybe it was his chin. His breathing was heavy in my ear. I stood abruptly never taking my eyes off Ryan. He'd always been there to protect me and there was nothing he could do. Nothing.

"Em." He mouthed slowly before his lip pulled into a fierce snarl. "Zach!" Ryan shouted and spit the name off his tongue like it was poison.

Before he could utter another word, I sprinted from the circle. Away from them all.

ELEVEN

"Emma!"

I could faintly hear Zach holler.

I wanted to turn and run straight back into his arms but I knew I couldn't. I also knew, without a doubt, that I could out run him long distance—but damn my short legs—I didn't stand a chance in a sprint. But I tried. My feet dug into the cold sand and burned with each step, tears falling freely. *Hurry and get them cried out before he sees. Never cry in front of a guy.*

I knew it. I knew it. I knew he had been with her. I felt sick and dizzy and thought for a second I would vomit. *Crap!* I heard his footsteps behind me.

"Em! Wait!" he shouted gasping for breath.

My chest was tight and my lungs felt ablaze as I sucked in the cold air. I stopped running as I approached the foot of a rocky cliff where I couldn't pass. Tide was in and salt water sprayed against the rocks then splattered my face as I got too close. With the dangerous rip tides, it was not passable.

When I spun around, he had decelerated to a walk. My tears were dry, thank goodness, and my breaths were manageable, but I could hear the whistle coming from my weak lungs. He bent down, his palms resting on his knees, his back arched. "I am sorry." he puffed. "So sorry." His labored breathing concerned me worse than mine.

I stared at him my eyes unable to hide the hurt. My brow creased, then I tried to step around him. I couldn't do this. He'd chosen her over me and not even given me a chance.

"Don't run, please," he begged, his breathing still uneven. He gently gripped my arm.

"Let me go, Zach."

"No. I won't. Because you'll bolt up the beach." He released me anyway, I guess taking his chances, and intertwined his fingers behind his head, still trying to catch his breath.

The bitter wind whirled around me, and I wiped my runny nose on the shoulder of my shirt. "You and Estelle? You were with *her* all summer?" My voice was faint; I wasn't sure he could hear me over the roar of the waves. It wasn't even clear to me what I was asking—maybe clarification. Though my eyes stung—I refused to cry again. That would just make him want me less.

His cautious, measured steps in my direction sent me backward without hesitation. The frigid water rolled over my heels reaching the arch of my feet, then receded, but not without stealing my breath. He held his hands up, surrendering, and stepped back.

"Answer me." My small voice sounded weak even to me. My teeth came down hard on my lip. I wasn't sure I could handle the truth.

"Please, let me hold you. I know you're freezing." The butt of his fist rested against his mouth.

"Zach—answer me, please." The water this time surrounded my ankles causing me to gasp as a shiver rippled through me.

He pressed his hands together and rested his chin between his thumb and index finger. He was stalling.

"Yes," he conceded. "Estelle and I were together this summer."

Childishly, I swirled around and headed down the beach, my feet splashing carelessly in the icy water as I kicked at the waves soaking my legs.

"Baby, please talk to me."

Damn it. There was that baby thing again. I couldn't sort my racing thoughts. I wanted to hold him, to kiss him, but at the same time I wanted to slap him and be mad at him. I resisted both impulses.

"What does that mean…together?" I couldn't feel my numb feet.

"Em. I am begging you. Let's go to the car and warm up. *I'm* even cold."

"Please, tell me what that means," I asked calmly, but the restriction of my chest was becoming painful. I needed my inhaler.

"It means what you think it means." His sympathetic voice annoyed me. "I was stupid. I didn't know anybody. You had left…"

"Oh! This is my fault?" I screamed then regained control. "I've been around too many guys to see how you all always manipulate the story to be the girl's fault. And they take it. They somehow believe they did something wrong. Dumbass'!" I was pissed and turned to walk away.

He grabbed my shoulders with force. "I'm not blaming you. I own this."

I tried to pull away and suddenly he yanked me from the water and carried me to dry sand. "At least get out of the water." His words were stern.

"So you… you two…" I covered my eyes with my fingers like that could prevent the images from coming. "…you two…" I was stuttering—again.

"Yes. We hooked up." He grimaced as the words came out.

My knees wobbled beneath me then buckled and I fell in the sand. It hurt—the words—the thoughts—the images. I didn't want to picture it, but I did. I saw it in my mind, play out over and over. His tan hands in her onyx hair as his lips kissed hers.

"I'm truly sorry," he murmured in my ear, and I realized he'd knelt next to me. Before I could shove him away, he'd wrapped me in his arms tucking my body into his chest. He was so warm.

"Why are you sorry? You don't owe me anything." My body stiffened.

"Listen. If I thought it would have made a difference, I would have told you. I would *not* have lied about it." He stared at my face. "You're breathing funny."

"Em!"

From up the hill, I heard the voices of Ryan and Grant who had parked themselves about thirty yards away. When I tugged my body, Zach withdrew his hold from me immediately. I dashed to them burying my face in Ryan's ribs.

"Tell me—you didn't cry," he asked, pecking my hair with a kiss.

I stared up at him and shook my head. I wasn't sure if he believed me. My shallow half breaths were coming quicker.

Grant pulled his sweatshirt off and nestled it down over my head—the strong smell of campfire smoke permeated the material but it felt warm.

"Are you OK? Ryan asked.

"You knew?"

He nodded. "She told me the minute we got back from Cannon, trying to make me jealous. I didn't give a shit, and I'm sure that pissed her off even more. So, I think she went after you."

"Does he like her?" I asked.

Ryan shrugged. "I can't answer that one. Only he can. I could beat it out of him." Though he grinned, there was a shard of sincerity to his words.

My eyes moved from Ryan's to Zach's, who'd wandered toward us.

"Em, where's your inhaler?" Grant asked.

I shook my head. "I don't know," I whispered.

"What inhaler?" Zach asked.

"Zach, did she bring a bag with her?" Grant's voice was tense.

My eyes closed as I fought for air.

Suddenly there was cold on the right side of my body as Ryan's arm abandoned me. I heard the jingle of keys. "It doesn't matter. There's one in my truck. Go fast, G!"

"Ryan! What's going on?" Zach's voice brought my eyes open for a moment.

Ryan held me close. "Don't go to sleep, Runt." He patted my cheeks harder than normal.

"It's her asthma," I heard him explain.

"Asthma? I didn't know."

This time Ryan's touch was a simple, soft caress. "She's gonna be OK. Aren't you, Runt? Look at me. Look at me, Em!"

I opened my eyes to the urgency of his voice. He smiled at me.

"Faster!" He yelled.

"Ryan, is she gonna be all right?"

TWELVE

Zach

"Shut the hell up, Zach." Ryan shouted.

Emma's lids came only to half mast but her hand made it to Ryan's mouth. Her tiny little fingers barely grazed his lips. "Don't," she said in a forced breath. "I like him," she panted.

I knew that it was physically impossible for a human heart to ache but the pain echoing from under my sternum was like no pain I'd ever experienced. I raked my fingers through my hair, pulling it slightly, feeling a different pain. This was my fault. She lay in her brother's arms fighting for breath and yet she still tried to protect me? What the hell?

"Emma!" Ryan shouted.

"I got it," Grant's yell resonated over the sound of the waves. Brett and Connor were running behind, and past them Estelle walked with Jaycee and Claire.

With my hands shoved deep in my pockets, I moved closer to Emma refusing to allow them to shut me out. Grant tossed the inhaler to Ryan.

"I already shook it," Grant gasped and rested his hands on his knees.

Ryan maneuvered the opening between her lips and gave her a puff. Her breaths so shallow, I didn't see how it would work.

"Is it working?" I didn't even realize that I'd said something until Grant glared up at me.

"Em, come on," Grant said, tapping her cheeks harder than I liked. "Come on, sweetheart, breathe. Do it again."

Ryan did, puffing the air again into her mouth.

"Ryan, should I call 911?" Connor said falling knees first into the sand next to them.

"No. She's gonna be OK, aren't you Em?"

My eyes roamed from Conner to Brett to Grant to Ryan. All of them standing over her, protecting her, taking care of her. I thought about the wall of pictures in their living room, each with her and the boys around. I didn't fit in this picture at all. I seemed to hurt her with every step I took to get closer to her. This girl truly needed taken care of. She could barely breathe on her own and her stubbornness only put her more at risk. This circle of heroes seemed impenetrable.

Grant's hand slid under the sweatshirt she wore—his sweatshirt. Though I knew it wasn't sexual, jealousy consumed me. I wanted to touch her, to help her, to protect her.

"It's working," Grant said. "The breaths are deeper."

"Is she OK?" The words whispered in my ear and the smell of alcohol accompanied the breath.

My quick step away should have said enough but Estelle stepped closer.

"Seriously, is she OK?" she asked again.

My hand kept her at arms distance. "What do you care? You got what you wanted. You told her. You're such a bitch."

"Stop being mean. Besides, you need to know, I'm late."

"What?"

"My period. It's late." Her hair blew so I couldn't read her expression. I swiped my hand down my face. The hits just keep on coming.

"You think you're pregnant?" I questioned.

Suddenly, her eyes seemed to focus behind me. I spun around and the whole crew stared at us, I'm guessing digesting everything Estelle and I said. Emma's eyes were fully open and she was sitting upright. The anger I fought so hard to control was at a boiling point. I hated this town. I hated the people in it. With one exception.

"Are you OK?" I asked moving toward her.

Her little shoulders jetted up then down right before Grant stepped in front of her.

"I think we've got her from here. Looks like you got bigger problems to tend to."

Not engaging with him would be the biggest obstacle I'd overcome since I'd been here, but punching him would only get me more jail time. My eyes stayed focused on hers.

"Is that what *you* want?" I asked her directly.

Grant threw up his arms. "It doesn't matter what she wants."

If I'd have been in Vegas, I would have bet a million dollars on her next response.

Her little elbow jabbed into his side and I hid my smile and focused on those baby blues. BINGO! She was becoming more predictable to me. As weak as she seemed at times, the girl had spunk. I liked that.

"Come on, Em. Just ride home with me," Grant encouraged.

Being this vulnerable was killing me. I wanted to shout 'screw it' and leave everyone standing there; yet taking even one step away from this girl was freaking impossible. I needed her to say yes.

"I'll take you home," I said matter of fact.

Ryan whispered something to her I couldn't hear but she nodded.

"I have some questions," she said.

"I'll answer any question you have as long as you ride home with me."

"Come on, Em. Are you crazy? Estelle just said…"

"Stop, Grant. Estelle said the same thing to me and you know it. They need to talk," Ryan said.

Wow! To what do I owe this honor? I was too guarded to ever take this act of kindness as such. There had to be a hidden agenda. My eyes left Emma's and found Ryan's.

"Thanks, Man," I said.

"I'm not doing this for you."

Whatever. She was going with me, that's all that mattered.

She slid around in her flip flops trying to make it up the hill. I was starting to find her stubbornness and independence humorous. The harder she tried, the more she seemed to fail. I stayed behind her and watched as she took her flip flops off and attempted the hill barefoot.

"Ouch!" She winced lifting her right foot.

That's it. I lifted her and the battle started immediately.

"Put me down, Zach."

I didn't respond.

"I'm serious. Put me down." She angled her body away from me, pressing the heel of her hand into my chest. I chuckled, which I'm sure only infuriated her more, but she so wanted to be strong.

"I will put you down in about forty yards."

Finally, I sat her on the hood of the Chevelle, handing her the flip flops.

Once in the car, I tossed the blanket at her.

"Wrap up."

The quilt landed on her lap then slid to the floor. She left it.

"Come on, Emma. Get warm." The heater was blowing cold air.

"I'm fine."

"Great, then take off the Oregon Ducks sweatshirt." Disgust was thick in my voice.

A smile touched the corners of her mouth. She knew I was as jealous as she was. "So, let me make sure I've got this straight. You can scrog Estelle but I can't wear someone's sweatshirt."

"Scrog?" I asked with raised brows.

"Sex…scrog…hook up…same thing. Whatever."

Now these people had their own language.

I started the car. "You said you had questions. What do you want to know?"

"Why are you so angry right now?" she asked softly.

"I'm not angry. Let's just get this over with. What do you want to know?"

Those words didn't come out right.

"What if she's pregnant?"

The thought made me sick but I knew there was no way. "I used protection. Every time."

"Every time, how many times exactly have you done it?" she whispered.

A groan escaped my throat. "Are we talking ever or with Estelle?" I hated these types of conversations and girls were notorious for instigating them. It brought no good.

"There must be a huge difference. Let's start with Estelle."

I shook my head from side to side and took a deep breath. "Probably five times."

"Where?"

"Em, don't do this." I reached for her hand but she pulled away.

"I have to know."

"Why? So you can think about it? It meant nothing." I found myself shouting and didn't like it. I didn't want to frighten her.

"Why did you do it then?"

I sighed. "Because that's what guys do, I guess."

"Believe me. I know that. I see that all the time." Her fists were clenched. "Is that what you want from me?"

"No!" I said instinctively then regretted it the moment I saw her face crumble. It was if my words slapped her. Her head fell back against the headrest.

"Where'd you scrog her?"

"Emma. You took that wrong. All I meant was…you're fifteen and…"

Her teeth snapped together. "Where?" she interrupted.

This girl was infuriating. The truth is the last thing she wanted. "Fine. Let me think—her house, her cousin's, her car and the Jeep. You want positions?"

Her brow furrowed. She didn't have a clue what that meant.

"That's four," she pointed out.

"The Jeep twice," I admitted reluctantly knowing this would come back to haunt me.

She wrapped her arm around her gut as if she were in pain. She slid down in the seat and laid her head on the blanket, pulling her knees to her chest.

"Emma, I'm sorry. I can't say it enough."

Girls were so confusing. I wasn't even with her at the time. We had kissed. That's it. Nothing more and I'm apologizing. I was so far ahead on the scoreboard with Will and Travon that I didn't regret it. But why the hell do I care what this girl thinks?

"I know."

"Emma. I had just met you. You left. I didn't know if you even liked me. Then, I met her and…" I didn't say anything else.

We rode in silence for awhile; my hand never left her back.

"Zach." She reached and clutched my hand. "We weren't together. I can't be angry. You had every right." she sighed. "But it still hurts."

I lifted her hand and kissed it.

She continued, "And, it's obvious she still wants you."

"I don't care what she wants. There is only one girl I want." I squeezed her shoulder and when I saw her smile and heard her breath of relief, I knew she was once again mine.

THIRTEEN

Emma

     Saturday morning, as the clouds blocked the sun's way into my room, I woke to a throbbing head. My eyes were swollen and red and I didn't want to go down for breakfast but I hadn't eaten anything since yesterday at lunch. I was starving.

     Ryan's door was shut. I smiled as I passed it. He'd been loyal to me last night. I remembered the look on his face when Estelle said the words. He knew I'd be hurt and he tried to prevent it. He always had.

     I remembered when I was six and woke up from my heart surgery when the doctors had closed the hole in my heart and he was lying on my bed with a big stuffed hippo. I thought that he'd had surgery too. The doctor had assured Mom and Dad before the surgery that this would be my last time in the hospital, God willing, and Ryan took it that it would literally be my last time…ever…that I wouldn't be coming home. He was a permanent fixture at my side. He was there when I woke up, when I went to sleep, when I ate and when I went to the bathroom—until I was able to be wheeled out and put in the car to go home.

It started with me weighing only three and a half pounds at birth, hence the name Runt. I didn't remember any of the stories, just memories of being told so many times how I'd been more like a pet to him rather than a normal sibling annoyance. He'd always taken care of me, seeing me as fragile—breakable. I guess that's why I'd been off limits to all the guys. I don't know that he ever voiced this. It was just sort of unspoken.

I trotted down the stairs. Mom sat at the kitchen table with her mug of coffee and newspaper and Dad was mowing.

"Good morning sweetheart."

"Hey, Mom." I poured water in a glass and washed down some Tylenol, then got out a small skillet to cook some eggs.

"How was the beach?"

"Cold. I should have dressed warmer."

"Was your brother upset you went?" She asked with a raised brow.

"No. I don't think so."

"And Zach? How was that?"

Hearing his name caused a heavy sensation in my chest. I shrugged. "It was fine."

She stood abruptly and hustled through the kitchen. "I have a showing at 11:00. I hope to be home for lunch." She rushed out. "Oh." She was back. "I have that bridge and those booths from the carnival a few years ago. Mrs. Redd stored them at her house and now wants to get rid of them. Any ideas?"

"I'll give it some thought," I replied with the start of a smile. She was gone again. I already had the perfect idea, if I could work it out.

"Hey Runt." Ryan shuffled into the kitchen, his eyes barely open, a couple of minutes later.

"Morning."

"Breathing ok?"

"Yes. Thanks."

"For what?" he poured cereal sloppily into a bowl and doused it with milk.

"Last night. You know." I was embarrassed. My first real boyfriend and he'd already slept with my brother's ex. That should make for interesting Sunday dinner conversation.

He sat his bowl on the table and ruffled my hair. "Estelle's a bitch. She's pissed at me and lashing out at you."

"Why is she pissed?"

He garbled something I couldn't understand through the cereal and milk. A pink piece of half chewed Fruity Pebbles flew out of his mouth and landed in front of me. My lips pulled up and my tongue darted out. He laughed.

"Sorry. She likes to think she broke up with me. It started after prom. Long story. But I dumped her before we left for Cannon. You know the stupid shit we do there. I wasn't going to go up there with a chick back here."

"That's nice. Break up with a girl you like *here* so you can go have sex with someone you don't know *there*. Hmm. Classy, Ry."

"I ain't tryin to be classy. And I didn't like her that much. I'm leaving for college next year anyway."

I carried my plate to the sink, rinsed and put it in the dishwasher. "Remind me never to date someone of that mentality. Do you think she's really pregnant?"

He shoved another bite of cereal in his mouth as I left the kitchen. "You don't need to be dating at all," he mumbled.

I rolled my eyes as I walked out.

"Runt!"

"What?" I stopped in the hallway.

"I'd put money on it that she's not pregnant. I've heard that one before. But, don't you see, he's just looking for someone to nail?"

Wincing, a wave of nausea rushed over me. I knew better. Last night, had he said yes to wanting that with me, I was ready to offer myself to him—like a sacrificial lamb—and yet he refused me. That's not what he was looking for, clearly. After all, I was just fifteen…

"You're wrong," I said faintly with my back to him.

"Emma. I'm a guy. I'm not wrong. Trust me on this."

I swallowed hard and walked away.

FOURTEEN

Zach

Even the water in this town tasted funny, I thought as I downed a full glass. It was clear Emma loved this place, but even now, I racked my brain trying to think of something I liked. Nothing…outside of her. Sweat ran down my temples and I dabbed it with my shoulder. I needed a shower after my workout at the gym. My phone vibrated. Estelle again. Twenty-one texts since last night. Not one from Emma. When I walked her to the door last night, I felt confident. But today, I was iffy again. I hated iffy.

Mom's laptop was sitting on the kitchen island and I clicked on Facebook. I never posted much, if ever. Wow, 49 notifications. Estelle had tagged me in a dozen pictures from over the summer. Shit! She was not going to make this easy. I unhooked the laptop from its cord and nestled myself into the recliner. Then I removed the pics from my page and untagged myself in the photos. After a quick search, I found Emma. Her page was set with private settings but I studied her profile picture. Her and Grant. What the hell? I decided to text and friend request her at the same time.

Hey send

Hey back

How r u feeling today? Send
I feel good. You?
Me? Well, I wasn't the one who couldn't breathe.
I'm good too busy day? send
No.   You?
Not too bad   Movie tonight? Send
I can't. Family night :(you can come. I understand if you don't want to. It's ok.

Family night? My head rested against the back of the recliner. Oh, how the thought made me...shudder. But if this was going to go, I don't know where, working things out with her brother and father were going to have to happen.

That should work what time u thinking send
6? My house
See u then send

FIFTEEN

Emma

"Ry?" I banged on his door.
"What?"
I opened it and stepped in.
"Hey. I'm asking...begging for a favor."
He was cleaning and twisted his Chicago Cubs baseball cap on my head. "Like you've ever had to beg for anything."

His words should have made me feel more hopeful but they didn't. He didn't have a clue where I was going with this; if he did he wouldn't agree. "It's about Zach."

He stopped picking up the dirty clothes on the floor and glowered at me. "It's not open for discussion."

"I like him. Really like him. Why can you not do this for me?"

He shook his head. "Runt. He is too old for you." He threw the stinky clothes in his hamper.

That was it. I'd had it and the conversation had just begun. As I took in a long slow breath through my nose and my chin lowered to my chest, I scowled. "Benjamin Ryan Hendricks," I yelled with my hands on my hips. "I am fifteen and he is seventeen and this means a lot to me. For years, I have dealt with all the girls that you have dated. Being polite, defending you when I shouldn't, listening to sob stories and worst of all becoming friends with someone that you dump and I usually lose the friendship. Now! I am asking you. No, I am telling you, to be nice to someone that *I* like. Do you understand me?"

The corners of his mouth twitched into a semi-smile and he stared at me. I kept my jaw tight.

"WOW! This must mean a lot to you. I don't think you've gone off on me like that since—well—maybe never. OK."

My arms fell limp and my eyes widened. "OK?" I asked.

He shrugged. "OK," he repeated. "But…"

I knew there was a 'but.'

"If he hurts you, I will break his neck." He batted his eyes a few times but didn't smile.

"Well. Maybe not his neck." I smiled jumping on top of his mattress and throwing my arms around his neck. "Thank you. Thank you. Thank you."

"One more thing. I'm not willing to listen to his sob story if you dump him, got it?"

Little did he know, I would never dump Zach Owens. More like the other way around. I feared for the safety of Zach's neck. "Deal. By the way, he'll be here at six," I laughed as I ran from his room.

The doorbell rang at 5:55 and I beat my dad to the door. Zach's tan face greeted us both with a warm smile. His tattered khaki shorts rested low on his hips and his polo shirt hid the muscles I knew were underneath. His chest was broad and my heart fluttered just thinking about how perfectly I fit between his arms.

"Zach. You remember my dad. Matt Hendricks."

"Yes. How are you sir?" He extended his hand and my father shook it.

"I'm great, Zach. Nice to see you again. Awake, this time." Dad grinned.

Zach nodded and studied his feet for a quick second. "You too, Sir." I could tell he was nervous. "That won't happen again."

My dad grinned. "I'm sure it won't. Call me Matt."

"Yes, Sir." His eyes flashed to mine.

"We're leaving. Hope you're hungry." I spoke softly.

"Ryan!" my dad yelled up the stairs then stepped out of the room; Zach captured me in his arms. He buried his nose in my hair and I was glad I had just washed it. My insides felt like they'd burst.

"Hey, when is your birthday?" I asked.

"November 23rd. Why?" He rocked me back and forth not letting go.

"No reason. Just curious."

"When's yours?"

"May 20th. I think it's the day of your graduation."

He rubbed my back with his hands. "So we'll have two things to celebrate." He bent down and brushed an unexpected kiss across my lips. It didn't go unnoticed that he said 'we' and insinuated we'd be together in May. I bit my lower lip to hide my smile.

Before I knew it, he distanced himself quickly.

"Hi, Mrs. Hendricks."

"Well hello, Zach. Glad you could join us."

"Thanks for having me."

Ryan pounded down the stairs.

"What's up, Zach?" Ryan gripped his hand and they bumped shoulders. I smiled at their sudden camaraderie.

"Hey, Ryan," Zach responded and glanced suspiciously at me.

"Let's go, Runt." Ryan shoved me playfully.

Zach grabbed my hand. "What the heck is up with Ryan?" He whispered shocked.

I shrugged.

After dinner the boys engaged in a friendly backyard football game while I watched from the deck. Several times, I caught myself staring at Zach—I'm not sure I'd ever seen someone so handsome.

It was seventy-five degrees today and though it was cooler with the sun meeting the western horizon, the guys worked up a good sweat. When Zach tugged his drenched shirt off his broad shoulders and tossed it to me, I giggled and draped the wet material over my lap but felt goofy when my dad shook his head and rolled his eyes.

My body had become foreign to me, acting on it's own in ways I couldn't explain. Just watching Zach—sweaty and shirtless stirred up feelings in my body that were a little alarming. After a bit, we moved inside to catch the Oregon/Arizona game. More football. Not that I was all that interested in the game, but it meant time with him.

Mom and I chatted in the kitchen while I threw break and bake cookies on a cookie sheet and tossed them in the oven. While I waited for the timer to go off, Zach's phone vibrated on the counter next to Ryan's, where they'd left them before going outside. I peeked at the cookies. Not close.

I snatched his phone off the counter to run it to him. The screen showed that he had a new text message. *From Estelle.* Obviously, she was in his address book for her name to appear. My body felt like it was imploding and my shoulders slumped. I stared at the view button as my finger hovered over it for the longest time. I clenched my fist. *Don't.*

In the living room, they were all three absorbed in the gripping zero to zero game but Zach smiled as I came in. I held out the phone and his brows rose.

"It vibrated," I said innocently.

He took it from me, glanced at the screen, slid the phone shut without responding then patted the empty spot next to him on the sofa. I shook my head.

"I'll be back," I said. "Come on Reesy," The dog leapt from her bed and toddled behind. Jealousy crept into every bone as I moved away from him and up the stairs. I felt sick. From my bedroom window, I stared at Zach's Jeep parked next to Ryan's truck in the driveway. I thought about the time last spring, I'd seen Ryan and Estelle in the truck making out, from this very window…something I'd never told him. But today, as I looked at the Jeep, I pictured Zach and Estelle. His hand on her knee and her beautiful ebony hair blowing in the wind. The bow-tie pasta I'd eaten earlier crept up my throat. I tried to shake it off…think of other things. But then last night at the beach replayed in my mind—her singing his name—telling everyone that they'd been together. She was so beautiful and a junior and could have any guy she wanted—well, she'd had most of them.

The Jeep was narrow, not like Ryan's truck and I wondered when he and Estelle were together how they fit. What was it like? Did he kiss her the way he kissed me? I imagined their lips pressed together. His hands on her body. *STOP!* I could never compete with her. I sprawled across my bed next to Reesy, frantically shoving my Ipod ear buds into my ear, listening to Nickelback. I closed my eyes trying to slow my breathing. It wasn't working.

Finally, I grabbed my Ipad and tapped my Facebook app. Two friend requests. I smiled instantly when Zachary Owens was one and I accepted immediately. Going straight to his wall, I was excited to see any piece of him that was foreign to me. His friends from San Francisco, his parents, anything…but I hadn't expected this. Forty-two pictures of him and Estelle and the group that she had posted. Today! Torturously, I clicked my way through them. They were in front of the drinking fountains downtown. In his Jeep with the top down. In a house with a painting of a mountain behind them. I tried to place the painting, his house?

"What's going on?"

I flipped completely over, startled by his voice and presence in my room.

"I, uh."

He glanced at the screen and his shoulders fell ever so slightly.

"Emma," he said softly.

Needless to say, I hadn't expected him in my room today. My bed was only half made and dirty clothes were scattered around. Reesy met him, wagging her tail as he got closer.

"Those were a long time ago." He was upset, but there was tenderness in his voice. I untagged myself today but she must have retagged me."

"I'm sorry," I said gazing down at my lap.

He knelt on one knee in front of me. "For what?"

"You can sit on the bed." I patted a spot next to me.

He pulled his saturated shirt away from his body. "I'm drenched and I stink. I'll stay put." His smile was beautiful.

He was quiet. When I glanced up at him, his eyes were patient

"I know that message was from her," I whispered clearing my throat.

He nodded. "Yes. It was. She texts me about twenty times a day."

"Why?"

My words hadn't angered him and I was relieved. "You can read any of them. All of 'em. She asks me to call, text back, you name it...I don't."

It was silly after last night and after being with him today that I felt the way I did.

"Look." He switched knees. "This Estelle thing is going to pass. I know it hurt you and I regret ever doing it. But I can't take it back and I can't take away your pain. I wish I could." Remorse was thick in his voice.

"Why did she just now post the pictures?"

Sweat beads trickled down his temples and he dabbed them with his shirt. "Why do you think? To upset you. To upset us. Estelle doesn't bother me. I understand and respect that it concerns you...but it is *not* a concern for me. What concerns me is that you don't give *you* credit. You are a beautiful girl and you can't understand why I'm attracted to you. I like you. I like spending time with you. Is that OK?"

I nodded as he uncrossed my legs. Just him touching my leg blasted a shot of adrenaline through me. I swallowed hard trying to ignore what my body was saying. He took my hand and pulled me down to rest on his one knee then kissed the tip of my nose. "If I wanted to be somewhere else right now, I would be. But I don't."

He left me speechless.

The next couple of weeks went by in a blur with football and cross country. Quality time together usually came only on the weekends and either after games or meets. But, I couldn't remember the last time I'd gone a day without seeing him. He had been amazingly attentive to me and in overdrive at distancing himself from Estelle. Our conversations were different now and centered around us and getting to know each other. We would talk for hours in his Jeep or on the sofa.

I wasn't sure if Ryan was just playing along or if he and Zach were really becoming friends. Somewhere along the line, Zach stepped down as secondary quarterback and the coach put him in as a tailback, which could have something to do with Ryan's behavior. I wondered if either of them did it for me.

It was Friday night and Homecoming. With every ounce of my attention focused on the love of my life, I'd been slacking at home with dinner and laundry, school work and definitely cross country. I needed to make adjustments.

Mom said I could go watch the football game if I got my chores done. Ryan and Zach had to be at the school early, so I worked hard and fast. By the time Dad got home, I'd washed, dried and folded three loads and put my own stuff away. The dishwasher was empty and, because Mom had a late night, I'd talked Dad into grabbing something at the game. He agreed. Thank goodness. I left the trash for Ryan and I was good to go.

I changed and threw on my AHS sweatshirt and a pair of ripped jeans, one of Zach's favorites, dabbed on some perfume and headed out.

Dad and I picked up Ali and arrived shortly before kick-off. Zach was number eighteen and I spotted him immediately. The band was playing the school fight song and the cheerleaders were doing their thing on the track in front of the stands. Looking as great as ever with her mile-long legs sticking out from under her short uniform, Estelle flashed me a lazy smile.

Though Ryan had played football for as long as I could remember, I'd never been as psyched about games as I was now. About two minutes before half, we had the ball. Ryan took the snap, handed it off to Zach and he rammed through the center for a touchdown. I screamed, of course, like a maniac. His first touchdown of the year. I was so proud. He was at the bottom of a dog pile getting up way too slow for my liking. Finally, the guy on top of him, rolled off—he pounced up, tore off his helmet and body slapped Ryan. He searched till he found me in the stands and pointed at me. Ali nudged me in the side.

"You are so lucky."

I pointed back at him doing my own little victory dance and his smile sparkled from the field. My dad glanced at me and rolled his eyes then took a seat with his buddies.

"Hey Mr. Hendricks." I heard the voice. People were everywhere but I knew that voice addressing my dad.

"Hellooo Gorgeous!" The voice was behind me and deep. I spun around, nearly losing my balance on the bleachers, but he caught me. "Whoa, easy Runt," he said.

"Austin!" I threw my arms around his neck. "What are you doing here?"

"Oh, some buddies and I came down to watch your brother kick some ass." He shot his thumb in the direction of four other guys. College guys. They were hot and the girls in the stands were checking them out.

"He's doing great," I bragged.

"Austin. How's it going?" My dad stepped up a bleacher and shook his hand.

"It's good. We made the trip down from Eugene to watch Ryan."

"How was the drive?"

Leave it to my dad to ask about the drive.

"It was fine. Do you all want to catch some dinner after the game?"

My dad eyed me and nodded. "Sure. Em and I haven't eaten at all and I'm sure Ryan will be famished."

My spirits sunk as he spoke. It was my evening with Zach. Austin was a family friend and I didn't think I'd get out of it. I turned around to see Ali glaring at me with her jaw clenched. Then I spotted Zach on the sidelines—unnecessary questions in his eyes. I winked but wasn't sure he could see.

"You know. You could introduce me," Ali seethed through gritted teeth.

I laughed. "He's a college freshman, you dork."

"I know! I recognized the name. Introduce me, please."

Austin was engrossed in trivial conversation with my dad so I waited. Finally, they broke.

"Hey, Austin. I was kind of rude earlier and didn't introduce my friend, Ali." I pointed to her. "Ali, this is Austin."

Ali extended her hand. He shook it. The corners of my dad's lips twisted into a smile.

"Nice to meet you Ali. Em's mentioned you. You are more than welcome to join us for dinner as well."

Great. Austin was flirting and Ali would be in love in two seconds.

"OK. Thanks," She whispered and stared.

I turned back around. "OK, Ali. Just casually turn your body back toward the game and act like you can breathe."

"Em. I can't breathe. He is SO cute."

"He's in college, silly."

After the game, Ali and I waited for Zach at my usual spot by his Jeep. Dad, Austin and his college friends had already headed to the pizza place. Zach and Ryan came out together and separated as Ryan neared his truck. I heard them talking but couldn't make out the words.

"Ladies," Zach greeted.

"Congratulations on the touchdown." I smiled and moved toward him. He gave me an awkward hug.

"Thanks." He kissed the top of my head.

We squeezed into the Jeep. "I hear I'm losing you tonight." My heart fluttered until I realized Ryan must have told him about Austin.

"We have some friends here from Cannon. It was a surprise. I'm sorry."

"Don't be sorry. I'm sure you'll have fun." His eyes left the road and met mine for a second.

"Can I call you after dinner?"

"You better."

We were at the pizza place and he parked next to the curb. Ali climbed out first and I took the opportunity to lean over and kiss him quickly.

"Thanks for the ride. I'll call you in a little while." I headed in.

The pizza place was jammed with celebrating fans, and Ali and I had seats at the end of the table out on the patio. I could tell by her expression she was a little disappointed. The older guys were playing a beer drinking game. I knew Austin wasn't of age and assumed the others weren't either so I wasn't sure how they were served. Fake ID's? We watched as they bounced the quarter off the table and into a small glass of beer. If you made the quarter, you got to pick who drank the small glass.

"Where's Dad?" I asked Ryan.

"Mom's car wouldn't start after showing a house. He thinks she left the lights on," Ryan laughed.

"Can Ali and I play?"

Ryan pursed his lips and didn't respond.

"Hey Austin. Give us a try," I tried.

He furrowed his brow. "You're dad would kill me."

"So would her brother," Ryan added with a serious look.

"You wanna drink beer?" Ali whispered just to me.

"Not really. But it beats watching." I had tasted my father's beer when I was a kid though he never drank all that much. I didn't like it then but the game did look fun.

Ryan's phone rang. He plugged one ear with his finger, then obviously unable to hear, he took it outside. I slid into Ryan's chair. Ali followed me over.

"OK. Give me the quarter…what's your name?" I snapped and pointed to the hot blonde.

"Vince." He eyed Austin who nodded his approval then handed me the coin.

"Thank you, Vince," I said and bounced the coin off the table. Swish!

Both my fists shot straight in the air—first time success.

"Who's gonna drink?" Austin prompted.

"You!" I shoved the glass toward him and a little sloshed outside the glass.

"All right. I see how you are." He swallowed and slid it back. "You're up again." They didn't fill the glass as full as they had before.

Bounce. Swish! "SWEET!" Ali and I laughed. "Vince!" I said.

He laughed as I shoved the glass in his direction. Back to me. Pour.

Bounce. Swish! "You've got to be kidding me," Austin shouted. Ali and I cracked up knowing our fun would end when Ryan rejoined us.

"What's your name?" I pointed to the guy next to Vince.

"Kyle."

"Kyle...Drink!"

It was fun, playing the game, fitting in with the group. Then I missed and it was Ali's turn; she didn't make it even once. Kyle's turn.

Bounce. Swish! "Ali." He pushed the glass her way. She blushed and chewed on her lip.

"It's a small glass." She shrugged, too the glass and swallowed with a grimace.

Pour. Bounce. Swish! "Emma."

I smiled unwilling to feel intimidated. "I know. I know. Drink!" I downed it quickly and shivered with the bitter aftertaste.

We played for a good forty-five minutes before Ryan returned spoiling the fun. It never got back around to us. Ryan took one look at us and shot Austin a glare. "What the hell?"

Austin laughed and shrugged his shoulders. "She was very persuasive."

"They are fifteen and my dad's gonna have my ass."

"They didn't drink that much. We weren't filling the glass," Vince added.

"Where'd you go anyway?" Austin asked.

"Had to run my dad the jumper cables. He said sorry for bailing on you."

Ali and I giggled. We couldn't defend what we had done. And we were lucky we hadn't been caught. Ryan opened his phone and dialed. *Crap.* I was toast. My folks loved Austin—maybe they wouldn't be that angry. My bladder was full, and when I stood, the room titled. I giggled and Ali followed.

SIXTEEN

Zach

"Thanks for calling me, man. Has she ever drank before?"
Ryan shook his head. "No. Never."

The pizza place was busy and hearing the congratulations from the fans was nice but knowing Emma wasn't ok, made me uneasy. Dick measuring was never a good thing, but I sized up Kyle, Vince, Cole and Austin as I waited for her. They had shown poor judgment in allowing this and the more I watched them, the less I liked them.

Her laughter was infectious and when she saw me, her little lips rolled inward. Damn she was cute...drunk but cute. Someone whistled and she swayed her hips in an exaggerated manner from side to side. Though the corners of my mouth turned up, there was no doubt I'd hurt someone that tried anything.

Ryan took hold of Ali's arm. "I'll take *her* home. You've got Em." He led Ali out.

"That is so sweet." Emma reached up and touched my cheek. "Babe...you've got me Babe." She sang, off key, and she had the tune but couldn't recall the words. "How does that song go?"

"Let's go." I smiled.

"Austin—bye. I'll see you in Ju Juuune!" Her arms wrapped his neck and I stood by patiently.

"Bye—Emma," He chuckled and met my glare.

She crinkled her nose and snorted. "See ya, Vince...Kyle. Wait." She held up her index finger to me. "I am so sorry. I forgot your name." She spoke to the ginger next to Austin.

"Cole."

"YESSSS! Cole...it was snice meeting you."

"You too." He laughed and they waved as she and I walked out.

"What a great group of boys," she complimented.

"They're men, Emma. Men who got a couple of young girls drunk in record time."

She missed entirely the two cement steps outside the pizza parlor and fell, ironically landing on the 'watch your step' words. I lifted her, not just to her feet, but into my arms.

"Look at that, Zaaach. It says 'Watch your step.'" Then she busted up laughing.

At the Jeep, I slid her across to her seat and got in twisting the key.

"Where are we going?" she asked.

"I'm not sure." I reversed the jeep. "You can't go home."

"Are you mad at me?"

My eyes found hers then returned to the road. "No. I'm not mad," I said, unsure if my voice was convincing.

"What are you?"

"I wish I would have come with you tonight. What happened to your dad?"

"Why? Why do you swish..." she slowed her words. "Why...do...you...wish you'd comed?" She shook her head knowing it still didn't come out right.

An unexpected snicker came from my mouth. "If I would have been there...never mind."

"I was naughty?"

Naughty? This girl had never been naughty a day in her life. Trying a drink at age fifteen was far from naughty. I pulled into a spot at the city park. I didn't want to be angry at her for trying something that I had already done myself.

I smiled at her. "I believe you were naughty." I agreed eager to lighten the mood.

The giggles returned and I couldn't help but laugh with her. "I can be naughty," she said as she unbuckled her seat belt and leaned toward me. Before I realized what was happening, her sweatshirt was up and over her head, exposing a white cotton tank. No bra underneath.

"Em. Stop."

"I'm hot," she complained.

Yes you are. I scratched my head with both hands. The straps of her tank rested on her upper arms and I gently lifted them back on her shoulders. What was I doing? This was the chance I'd wanted. I could take her right now. So easily. Suddenly, she crawled over the center console to my seat and crept onto my lap, straddling me.

"Em," I said weakly, my body responding to her.

Her lips found my neck and my head relaxed against the headrest. Caught between stopping her and wanting her to never stop was the most tangled line I'd ever walked. But, when she whispered "kiss me" in my ear, my thoughts went down a dark path. The hands that held her protectively, now forced her back against the steering wheel. Questions about her innocence assaulted me. Her actions screamed experience to me and identifying the feeling that festered inside me was impossible. Anger? Jealousy? Sadness that I wouldn't be her first?

The moonlight touched her cheekbone and I traced up and down her jaw. Her head turned to my touch. I liked this. Not waiting another second, I raked my fingers through her hair and pulled her close to me, my mouth wanting to make sure that if she had done this before, mine would be the mouth she remembered. Her tiny little tongue stroked my upper lip and when mine reciprocated, a whimper came from her throat that brought my eyes open. It was as if I'd hurt her.

Her eyes fluttered open and, she panted. The smell of beer on her quick breaths pushed me back over the waffling line. A smile touched her lips when her hands maneuvered under my shirt and touched my chest. Her fingertips then grazed down my abdomen. What was she doing to me? I wouldn't do this, not with her virtually drunk. With a force I shouldn't have used, I gripped her upper arms and yanked her hands out from under my shirt.

"What?" she asked. "You dont twant me?" Her words jumbled no matter how hard she tried.

God, how could she possibly think that? What was wrong with this girl? Was this a joke? Frustrated, I pinched the bridge of my nose and laughed out loud.

She fell over the console, moving away from me, and fumbled for the door handle. I locked the door. She pulled out her cell phone and texted someone. I wanted to know who.

"Just say it," she hissed. "Jush shay you don't wan me."

I hit the steering wheel. She really didn't get it. "You…" I said softly "…have no idea how bad I want you. I…can't think of one thing in this world I want more." I couldn't look at her.

"Then why'd choo stop?"

He bent forward and rested his forehead on the wheel. "Because I'm an idiot and because 'choo' are buzzin or drunk and a definite lightweight."

"Please," she hesitated. "Kiss me again."

She was begging. Who was I to say no? My lips mashed against hers and when she gasped, I breathed into her. I kissed her long and hard and I wanted her more than I'd ever wanted anyone. I didn't fight this time when she lifted my shirt over my head and stroked my chest. But then that whimper came again snapping me back like a rubber band. What was that? Was this noise of hers a good thing or bad? This type of noise was foreign to me. I'd had girls that intentionally moaned before, bordering on annoying but this was different. Involuntary. Pleasurable? Painful? Confused, I pushed her away once again.

"We *have* to stop." I unlocked my door and stepped out.

She got out on her side. Silence loomed between us. My body, shaking with desire, needed tamed. There were two ways to do that. Take her or leave her alone. I wouldn't take her. I couldn't. Damn my stupid feelings! Why did I have to care so much about her? I needed out of this town.

Car lights hit me. Ryan stepped out of his truck and approached the Jeep. Self-conscious, I retrieved my shirt.

"What's going on?" Ryan asked looking from me to Emma.

"No-thing. Ab-so-lute-ly nothing," Emma said angrily.

"Why are you here?" I directed at Ryan.

"Em, texted me. Said she needed a ride home. Told you all were here." Ryan seemed just as puzzled.

Pissed, I spun around. "You what?"

She avoided looking at me which pissed me off even more. Frustrated, I jammed my hands in my pockets.

"I'll take care of her." Ryan said and slugged my shoulder.

My eyes never left her as she stumbled into the truck and parked herself in the seat. Her eyes never found mine again.

SEVENTEEN

Emma

The Earth's rotation halted or so it seemed. The minutes passed like hours and the hours passed like days. We hadn't spoken since the night I'd drank too much. Not since rejection night in his Jeep. The same Jeep that he and Estelle scrogged in. Twice!

Ali and I walked up the school yard and my eyes focused on the grass after I'd spotted his Jeep in the lot. I was nervous. Embarrassed. The inexplicable hurt of him shoving me away from him hadn't gone away.

"I have to tell you something," Ali squealed full of energy.

"What's that?" I asked acting interested.

"You aren't going to believe me."

I was not in the mood. "Try me."

She took a deep breath and held it. "I think I have a crush on Ryan." Her words were giddy. "Who'd have ever thought? I've known him for like…what it's been…my whole life. But, Emma. You should have seen him Friday. He was so totally awesome. He wouldn't take me home even though I said it was OK." She slugged me in the shoulder. "Oh my God, I still can't believe we drank that beer." She shook her hands in front of her trying to get back on subject. "Anyway, I was goofy…I mean really goofy. He took me to Starbucks and we ordered a drink and we just sat and listened to music and talked. He knew I had to be home by midnight and around 11:30, we took off in his truck. I think he got a text from you."

My expression soured as I recalled the text.

"But Em…" she looked at me dead in the eyes. "Do you think??" Her words stopped, finally, and I didn't know what to think. Ali was beautiful but she was fifteen like me. Ryan had never…. My thoughts stopped. I couldn't go there, not right now.

"I don't know. I'll see if he says anything." I wanted the conversation to end and fortunately we'd entered the school.

Third hour was here before I was ready and I hustled up the stairs hoping to beat Zach to class. I sat in my regular seat and opened my Algebra book. I started copying today's word problem from the smart board. As people made their way in, I forced myself not to look up. The problem was easy but I took my time writing it out slowly and neatly re-tracing numbers I'd already written. Unaware of who had come in, I lifted my head when the bell sounded. Mr. Bowman was not in class yet.

"Hey, Runt." Grant was behind me. When I turned to say hi, I realized Zach was sitting in his normal seat to my left with his head down. "Want a beer?" Grant chuckled under his breath.

I stared angrily at him. "You're funny."

"I heard *you* were funny. I'd like to see you drunk."

I swear a low growl came from Zach. I casually glanced in his direction and his jaw was set tight as he fingered his pencil.

"Poor Ryan, straddled with two drunk chicks. What I wouldn't give?" Grant seemed amused with himself.

"Ryan is a gentleman, Grant. He took great care of us."

"I know. I'm only kidding. You were lucky. I'm sure one of the frat boys would have loved to nail ya."

"Grant, you're such a douche. Austin would never hurt me and you know that more than I do."

"Emma, the other four guys there didn't give two shits about you." Grant's tone became serious and I noted that he called me by name. "Guys don't get girls drunk just so they can laugh a little." He took a deep breath and shook his head from side to side. Zach's pencil hit the floor and as he picked it up—his unsympathetic eyes met mine for half a second.

"We weren't even that drunk." I whispered.

Zach cleared his throat purposefully, in a lame attempt to negate my words.

"It doesn't matter, Em." Grant seemed angry. "What if they put something in your drink? What if you wake up and don't know where you are and… Besides, we both know I'm going to be your first anyway and…"

"Meiers!" Zach barked, and Grant giggled.

My head snapped toward Zach. Blood simmered through my own veins, and I wanted to scream. *What are you upset about? You didn't want me!* What difference did it make? I slammed my book shut, squeezed past the front of Zach's desk and ran out of class.

Before I could breathe, I was down the stairs and sitting behind the stairs of the bottom stairwell letting my irritation subside. With my legs drawn to my chest, I rested my forehead on my knees. I heard a noise. Zach was there.

"You OK?" he asked flatly.

"Fine." Did I friggin look fine?

"No you're not."

"Fine." I shrugged.

He exhaled. "Are you angry with me or Meiers?"

"Both," I pouted.

He chuckled. "That poor boy."

I narrowed my eyes as anger crept into me again. "Poor boy? What's that supposed to mean?"

He relaxed with his back against the wall and stuck out his lower lip. "It's clear he's in love with you and you don't even see it."

My mouth hung open at his ignorance. "What are you talking about?"

He smiled. "Clean your ears, Em. He went nuts when he thought about those men…" he took a breath. "…touching you." His words were broken. "He couldn't take it. He loves you."

Rage brought me to my feet. "He loves me…like a *sis-ter!* But even if it was more…" I contemplated my words. "I have to believe if I asked *him* to touch me—he wouldn't hesitate."

My heart thudded hard against my chest. Zach's adam's apple jetted out as he swallowed hard and tried to compose himself. Suddenly, he lunged at me grabbing my wrist and pulling me down the hall.

"What are you doing?" I hissed under my breath.

"You can make a scene if you want or you can come peacefully. But you're coming regardless."

His pace was too fast for me to plant my feet and I knew he'd pick me up if I fought. Within a minute, we were at the Jeep and he heaved me through his door. He didn't speak and there was a small piece of me that was afraid. The Jeep screeched to a stop in front of a house. The house was a three-story home built into the side of a mountain. His house?

"Where are we?"

He was suddenly at my door, opening it and taking my hand again, with not as much force. We walked past a trail of wildflowers as he fumbled with the key. It *was* his house.

"What are we doing?"

The warning alarm beeped as he opened the door then punched in numbers shutting off the sound. He tossed the keys on a table, and with me still in tow, stomped up the stairs. I struggled to keep up with him. We passed two doors before he opened one and went in. Obviously his bedroom. This was the first time I'd been in his house—let alone his room. Trophy's. Posters. Pictures. A blown-up picture of the lit-up Golden Gate covered half of a wall. I smiled. On his desk sat a picture of me on the beach this summer. Books. Magazines. CDs. The room was tidy for the most part. It felt right here. I turned to him.

His shirt was off and in a pile at his feet. His bare chest was tanned and perfect. I gave him an awkward smile. Then he began working on the first button on his jeans, his belt already unfastened. My heart fluttered—he was scaring me again. He took a measured step toward me, and I instinctively back stepped.

"What are you doing?" My voice quivered.

"I'm gonna have sex with you." His expression was indifferent.

My eyes bulged. "What?"

He pointed to the bed. "Lie down."

EIGHTEEN

ZACH

"No!" she shrieked and I hated the panic in her eyes.

"Go ahead. Lie down." There was no meanness in my words—they were simply emotionless.

"Stop!" She folded her arms across her chest. Guess she was going with the pouting.

Typically, her pouting would work, but if sex is what she wanted, sex is what she was going to get. She attempted to walk around me.

When I grabbed her arm, I was careful not to use force. "Isn't this what you want?" I asked mockingly. I reached for the top button on her shirt. She swatted my hand away. "What's wrong? You want me right?" I mimicked.

"You're being a jerk."

Inside, I flinched at her words. She was right. Surely, she knew I wouldn't force this.

"You want to be touched. You said so yourself. Even Grant would have touched you—but *I* didn't. Wasn't that your point?" At that moment, I lifted her easily in the air and placed her on my bed like a doll, positioning myself beside her. Before giving her the opportunity to speak, I smashed my mouth to hers. The powerful kiss gave way to a whimper resonating from her throat. Instinctively, I reigned in the aggression and opted for tenderness by sliding my hand under her shirt making contact with her stomach. Her skin quivered. I was back to believing she hadn't done this before.

"Stop!" She ordered with the fierceness of a rolly polly insect.

If that small touch unsettled her what I was about to do was going to rock her world even more if she was indeed what I thought her to be. Her blue eyes held questions, concerns and I held on to that look as my palm wrapped her knee and slowly inched up her thigh. Immediately, the blues I was falling for filled with fear.

"Zach, please stop." Her voice shook.

I gently removed my hand and buried myself next to her. Besides disappointing myself, I confirmed what I suspected. She had to be a virgin. Several long minutes passed in silence. She sniffed and I feared her tears.

We lay there in silence for a few more moments. I would have given anything to know what was going through her mind.

"Why do you want this so bad?" I finally asked.

"What exactly do you mean by 'this'?"

I propped myself up on my elbow and faced her. "Sex."

Her face flushed. "I don't want sex." She spoke firmly. "I just want you."

"You *have* me." I lifted her chin so I could see the truth in her eyes. "Why don't you get that?"

Her eyes flickered away.

"Emma, have you ever—been with anyone?"

"I've dated."

I kissed her forehead. "You know what I'm asking."

Baam! Question answered the moment she looked down. When her tiny little hand rested against my chest, it nearly robbed me of breath.

Finally, she shook her head no. I clutched her into my chest and her cheek rested against my skin. When the softness of her lips brushed over my chest muscle, I vowed at that moment to never hurt this girl, I knew I had to be honest about some things.

"Zach…" her breath skimmed over my skin and an unspoken invitation lingered.

A low groan came from my throat as I rotated her away from me. "I would be honored to be with you, Emma. But not like this or like Friday. Why do you want to rush it?"

"You rushed it with Estelle."

"Is that why you want to do it?"

"You touched her—everywhere—and you won't even touch me." Her voice cracked.

I tucked her head into my chest again and pressed my lips into her hair. "Don't you see, that meant nothing. That was just a quick…" I stopped myself watching my word choice. "It was sex or a quick 'scrog' as you would say." I paused. "I didn't love her." The words came out before I could think. Her eyes darted up to mine.

"Zachary?"

We heard the soprano voice and within two drawn out seconds, we both flipped up and off the bed.

NINETEEN

Emma

A tall, stunning redhead in a pale green dress suit stood in the doorway. I was certain my face matched her hair.

"Mom. Can you please give us a sec?" He immediately buttoned his jeans.

"Certainly." Our eyes locked for a moment and she smiled then pulled the door shut behind her.

"Oh my God! Your MOM!" I quietly mouthed the words.

He chuckled, which infuriated me more. "Would you stop?" He snickered.

I paced the floor adjusting my skirt then examined my face in the mirror by his door. My hair was tangled. Smoothing it, I eyed the window for an easy escape.

"Don't do it," he laughed donning his now wrinkled shirt and running his fingers through his shiny hair. He looked as good as new as he sat on the bed and pulled me next to him.

"We have nothing to be ashamed of." He brushed a kiss over my lips.

"She doesn't know that. All she knows is we were on the bed, shirt off, pants unbuttoned, my skirt hiked," I groaned.

His aggravating smile was still there. "We're going to hold our heads high, walk down the stairs together and go back to school." He stood and offered his hand to me. I squeezed it tightly and he opened the door.

He took the stairs slowly hauling me behind. My heart pounded like never before. What was I going to say? *'Hello Mrs. Owens, I am Emma, the girl who was on the bed with your son, half-naked, nice to meet you.'*

His mom sat in a chair in the living room with a book in her lap. I doubted if she was reading. She raised her head.

"Zach...and Emma, I presume."

"Yes, ma'am." There was a frog in my throat, but I smiled when she said my name.

"I am very sorry for interrupting. I thought Zachary was sick or something. You are very little and I didn't see you behind him." Her words were kind and truthful.

"Mom." He rubbed my hand. "You didn't interrupt anything. I promised Em I would explain that in front of you. I know it didn't look appropriate up there but nothing happened, at all."

She sighed. Zach resembled her in many ways. Her eyes were soft and met mine.

"It's nice to meet you, Emma. We've heard very good things about you and your family. Your brother is a wonderful football player."

Zach winked at me.

"Thank you. It is a pleasure meeting you too."

"Zach says you're a sophomore. Have you grown up in Ashland?"

Sophomore? I was sure I flinched at the word but not enough for her to notice. "I was born in Portland. Lived there for a few years before my dad became partner in a firm here. Been here every since."

"Mom. We need to get back to school."

"Yes. You do. And we will address *that* this evening." She forewarned.

He kissed her cheek.

"It was nice meeting you," I said.

"Please come over again. Maybe *after* school some day." She smiled. "Zachary, don't forget your meeting tonight."

I beat Zach to the Jeep, shut the door behind me and turned cockeyed in my seat shooting daggers at him.

"What?" he had the nerve to ask.

"What? Are you kidding me? You told your mother I was a sophomore."

He frowned. "Buckle up."

I buckled but stayed cockeyed. "Why…why…"

He drove in the opposite direction of the school.

"Where are we going?" I asked.

"One question at a time, please." He seemed amused.

"You're embarrassed of me, aren't you? You're embarrassed that I'm a freshman." My feelings were hurt.

He hit the brakes and my body jerked forward. His finger jetted in front of my face and he scowled. "Don't ever say that again. I am *not* embarrassed of you. You being a freshman doesn't bother me a bit." A horn honked behind us and he glanced in his rear view mirror, waved and started moving again.

"Then why?" I asked more calmly. He was driving out of Ashland, but I knew he wouldn't miss football practice and I had a state qualifier meet in two days so I couldn't miss cross country. He seemed to be thinking, maybe contemplating his words, as I stared at his profile, which was perfect.

He swerved around almost doing a complete U-turn and darted down a dirt road that led to a small creek. He cut the engine. The water ran low but I could hear the trickle of the creek moving and I closed my eyes and listened. He took my hand in his.

"I need you to listen."

I nodded.

"My mom," he paused. "She was a hot-shot defense attorney back in San Francisco—under a lot of stress. She started having some health issues the doctor believed were stress-related." He paused again. "Then came the talk of moving." He lay back against the headrest. "I was pissed. I was going to be a senior in the only school I'd ever known. I didn't want to leave." He took a deep breath and blew it out slowly. "I didn't understand why she couldn't just switch jobs. But my dad applied for his job here. Mom decided to do part-time *stress-free* work as a paralegal and boom…we're here." He intertwined his fingers and wrapped his hands behind his head.

"I'm sorry." That was all I had to offer and it didn't feel like enough. I couldn't imagine leaving everyone behind.

He untwined his fingers and they fell to his lap. His posture made me nervous. "I started doing stupid shit. Drinking. Smoking weed. Getting in fight after fight. " He looked at me out the corner of his eye.

I tried desperately not to react.

"I dabbled in other stuff too."

"Like?"

He hesitated. "Some illegal. Some prescription."

I suddenly felt sheltered and innocent and naïve. I had no idea what he meant. "I'm not sure I know what you mean," I admitted.

He snickered. "Why would you?" he asked under his breath facing me. "Drugs. I bought stuff from kids who were selling their own meds." He rubbed his eyes. "I was out of control. I hurt my parents. I hurt myself." He dwelled on his thoughts for a minute or two. "I was arrested, Em."

I felt like I'd been kicked hard in the stomach. I remembered one time in fourth grade, falling off the jungle gym when I was a kid and landing smack on my back—unable to breathe. This felt exactly like that without the dust and kids staring at me. His words literally stole the air from my lungs. "Why?" The word barely came out but he heard it.

His brown eyes were bigger than I'd ever seen them and held a fear that scared me. "I was driving under the influence."

"Influence of what?"

He paused. "Alcohol. And drugs."

My brow creased. "Did you hurt someone?" My voice broke before the words came out. *Don't cry,* I thought trying to fight the emotion. I unbuckled and I don't know why. I felt scared—not of him—but of losing him. My parents…if they found out—oh God. I felt sick and raked my fingers through my hair. He grabbed my wrists.

"Em?"

"Did you go to jail? Do you still use drugs? Why…are you?" My words were rushed and not coming out right.

He squeezed my arms. "Please. Just listen to me. That's not who I am. I wanted to tell you before but I was afraid."

"Afraid of what?"

"Of losing you." He frowned.

My eyes bore into his. As thrilled as I was to hear his words—my thoughts were too scattered. "So, what happened?"

He released his grip. "I spent two nights in detention. My folks were pissed and made me sit there."

"Detention? Like jail?" Maybe he wasn't the prince I'd made him out to be. "Why did you do it?"

"I was so screwed up. When I got pulled over…" his words trailed off. "There were drugs in the car." I stared at him and knew he was measuring my responses. I lifted my chin a little higher. "When I got out of jail, my mom made a deal with the juvenile judge, that if I went into treatment, some of the charges would be dismissed."

"And were they?"

"Yes. I spent ten days in an inpatient center for kids. Then the deal was…upon completion, I was sentenced eighteen months of probation. He allowed us to move and have a courtesy supervision here. Well…Medford. The judge knew my mom so I think that helped. He let me keep my driver's license."

"So…you're on probation right now?" I couldn't help my voice from squeaking.

He nodded. "Em. You have to believe me. I'd never even tried drugs before. It was a really bad time and it all happened in a short period. Things spiraled fast. Suddenly I was arrested, released, in treatment, out of treatment and in Ashland. I'd never felt so alone in my life." He traced the steering wheel slowly then shifted his body toward me. "Then when I came by your house to pick up the football stuff, you were so nice to me. I'd never seen you at school. We laughed. We talked. You asked me about me and about San Francisco. And suddenly you made me remember how wonderful it was there and for a minute, I forgot about the shit. When you played that song for me, well, I just felt this incredible connection. When I decided to try and kiss you, I had no idea how you felt or if you felt what I did. I was so nervous that night. Then, when I felt the way you kissed me back."

The way I kissed him back? Was that a good thing?

"The next thing I know, you're gone, you left for Cannon Beach." He smiled at me.

"Sorry." Somehow with all of his honesty and sincerity, my one little word didn't manage to cover it.

"It didn't make sense to me. I spent four or five hours with you and you were all I thought about over the summer. I waited for you to get back to see if…I don't know what."

I thought about Estelle and the five times he spent with her.

He winced. "I know what you're thinking and that was stupid of me. I will live with a planet of regret on my shoulders forever on that one. You know, she and I—we never even talked. We'd see each other out and…"

I plugged my ears. "OK…let's not go there."

"Sorry. I asked *her* about *you*."

"You what?"

"I did. She blew it off because you were a freshman. And mentioned something about Ryan killing anyone who touched you." He laughed at his words.

"So, explain to me…why am I a sophomore?"

He raised his brows. "Oh that. There's this law, statute, something—that my mom knows about. It's this Romeo and Juliet thing, seriously. Depending on the state, if you are more than two years older, in some states it's three but you would have to be at least sixteen for us to—you know… or I'd get in trouble. So when I mentioned you to my mom, I knew you were fifteen but I told her what I thought she wanted to hear about your grade."

"You can't have sex with me because of a *law*?"

He nodded. "Kind of. I mean, I can, but with already being on probation…it's risky. I was kind of unofficially diverted the first time through the court and I'd be officially charged if something happened." He shook his head. "And as much as I know you hate hearing this…" He swallowed and hesitated. "You *are* young…er."

I processed every word he spoke and hung onto the part of him not wanting to lose me. I knew the other parts were more important. My parents would find the words like arrested…drugs…probation much more relevant.

"So…sex is off limits?" I raised my brow as a part of me was relieved.

He wrapped his arm around my shoulder and pulled me over to his seat. "You know what, nothing is off limits. But, no matter what, I want it to be for the right reasons. Not because I did it with someone else or because you think you have to do it."

I nodded. "I know. But." I paused. "I'll be sixteen May 20th." I chewed on my cheek waiting for his response.

He grinned. "In March, I'm off probation." He winked.

Blood rushed to my face as he started the Jeep.

TWENTY

I was grounded for skipping school and grounded from Zach for a week, which was a load of crap. I'd never ditched class a day in my life. To be honest, I'd never even faked being sick. Well…maybe once in sixth grade when Jennie Stewart wanted to beat me up for liking Wolf Belford. I'd held the thermometer under hot water to prove to my mom I had a fever, realizing later one-hundred-six was pretty dang high for a temperature.

This by far ranked up there with the worst week of my entire life. Zach was feeling guilty because he literally dragged me from the school. The brooding expressions he wore around the halls worried me. This was so not his fault. We were at least allowed to text and talk on the phone. The short two minutes before and after third hour was all we had.

Zach never said whether he got punished, but given his mom's demeanor that day and her obvious disappointment, my guess was he had. He and Ryan seemed to be hanging out more, which made me a little nervous. I certainly didn't want some mutual alliance with my brother to drive a wedge between me and Zach.

Ryan was getting ready for school, and I caught him in the bathroom gelling his hair.

"Ry?"

"Yeah?"

"I'm supposed to ask you something. I already know your response but I promised I'd ask."

"What?" He rinsed his hands.

"Ali likes you. Apparently, you were too nice when you took her drunk butt home."

"We went to Starbucks," He explained like it wasn't that big of deal.

I laughed. "Yeah. Well. I guess us freshmen are pretty easily entertained. You really swept her off her feet, bro." I sat on the edge of the tub.

"Ali…little Ali?" he questioned, then added a, "hmm," which confused me cause it was as if he was considering it. "Maybe Zach has the right idea. Maybe freshmen are easier to deal with than the catty, bitchy shit we deal with." He slid his shirt over his head and smacked me on the shoulder nearly knocking me backward into the empty tub. "Come on. We gotta go. I'll give it some thought."

Paralyzed from shock, I gave no response.

The guys were decked out in their new football jerseys for the big game, and Zach, of course, looked incredibly handsome. We both knew I'd miss the game because I was grounded and he seemed more bummed than me. We walked quietly to Ryan's truck after school; I spotted three guys leaning against the roll bar on his jeep, five stalls down from the truck. I pointed.

"Who's that?"

He glanced up and a broad smile swept across his face. "You've got to be kidding me."

He abandoned my side and jogged to the Jeep. "*What* are you doing?" he yelled. The three guys jumped out of the Jeep and body bumped him.

"What's up, Big O?" One of them hollered.

I slowed my pace. Ryan wasn't there yet anyway. I watched Zach from the corner of my eye.

"Hey, Estelle." The taller, thin guy said. "Where's Jaycee?"

Estelle had passed me from behind and was closer to them than I.

"Hi, boys. Long time no see." Her seductive little finger wave made my skin crawl.

The blood drained from my face. She knew them. I looked away as she joined their group.

"Em," Zach shouted immediately.

Relieved, I glanced over as he motioned with his hand for me to join them. I walked toward them, purposefully standing away from Estelle.

"What's up?" I asked casually.

"Em. These are my boys from San Francisco." He laughed. "Will. Jackson. Travon. This is Em." Finally, when his arm wrapped around my shoulders, I breathed.

"M...like the letter M?" Will asked confused.

Jackson shoved him against the Jeep. "You dumbass. He told us before her name was Emma. Hi, Emma." Jackson smiled, a perfectly beautiful smile with dimples at the corners of his mouth. I didn't miss that Zach had told them my name.

Travon acknowledged me with a simple nod. He was by far the hottest black guy I'd ever seen. His velvety skin, short cut hair and a small goatee covering his chin beneath his full bottom lip were sexy. He had a Michael Jordan smile.

Will was the thinnest and the tallest of the three and I wondered where they grew these boys. California, obviously. They looked like city boys. Metros.

"You all coming to the game tonight?" Zach asked.

"Hell, yeah!"

Jackson nodded at Estelle. "You all gonna be there?"

"Of course." She smiled, fluttering her eyes and twisting from side to side in her cheerleading skirt.

Zach's palm rested against my back.

"Meet me at my house," he called over his shoulder as we started walking to the truck where Ryan waited.

"Call me after the game?" I hoped.

"You know I will. I gotta go though. We have to be back here in just a little bit." Bile rose up the back of my throat as he jogged to the Jeep.

Folding laundry, I listened to AHS win the game on the radio. Knowing Ryan had a good game, I hoped for good moods. I wasn't disappointed. Mom and Dad ungrounded me early. I flew ecstatically off my chair and hoped I wasn't too late. I texted Zach immediately.

When his soft tap graced our door, I shoved my Dad out of the way to get there first.

I flipped on the porch light and opened the door. "I'm free!" I shouted and threw my arms around his neck. His wet hair was cold from his shower and he smelled like soap. He kissed my forehead and allowed my feet to touch the floor.

"Hi. Mr. Hendricks."

"Zach…it's Matt remember."

"Yes, sir." He responded. I knew he'd never call him Matt. "May I take Em out to get some air?"

Dad looked at Mom who shrugged in approval. "Have her home in an hour. Oh, and Zach, no more skipping."

"Yes, sir." He tugged my arm. "Let's go."

"No. Wait. Look at me. I can't go anywhere." I wore baggy sweat shorts and an old tank. My hair tied in a ponytail.

"You look fine and we have less than an hour. Just come on." He nearly yanked my arm out of its socket on the way to the car.

He reversed the Jeep and tore down the street.

"Zach, slow down!"

He hit his brakes at the end of our street. My heart thudded against my chest.

"I haven't kissed you for a week and I couldn't kiss you the way I wanted in your driveway, so…" He grabbed the back of my head shoving his lips to mine. His breath hit my face exciting me. My lips parted when suddenly headlights shined brightly on us and he pulled back. Ryan's truck idled next to the Jeep.

He stared at us and didn't say anything. I was suddenly nervous. "Did you escape or were you freed?"

"Freed." I smiled.

"That never happens to me, you know." His truck revved as he began pulling away.

"You aren't as good of a kid as I am. They like me better," I joked. He spun his tires.

Zach's eyes closed and I rubbed across his forehead. "You OK?"

"It's been a long week and I just got my fix."

I lowered my head not liking his analogy.

"Bad choice of words." He turned right at the stop sign. "Are you worried about that?"

"About you using drugs again?"

"Yes."

I knew it would bother him if I said yes. "Do you miss them?"

He took a left turn. "I wish I never would have done 'em."

"That wasn't an answer."

He watched the road ahead of us. "Do I miss them?" he repeated…stalling? "No. They brought me nothing but trouble." He rubbed his forehead.

"Aside from trouble…did it feel good?"

He squirmed and I could tell my inquisitiveness troubled him.

"What do you mean?"

"I wonder what it's like."

His foot came off the accelerator and he scowled. "Em. Don't ever, ever go near them."

"Well now, that's a double standard isn't it?" I winked at him

The anger didn't leave his eyes. "I'm serious."

"I won't. I was kidding. Where are we going?"

"The top was already off the Jeep when I got your text, I thought we'd just drive around."

"What happened to your friends?"

There was a slight hesitation prior to his answer. "Oh, they hooked up with some other people. I'll catch up later."

I knew what he was hiding. "You'll catch up with just the guys?" I rolled my eyes the moment the words came out. Could I have sounded more insecure?

His eyes flickered away from Main Street and found mine. I had to do something to prove I wasn't insecure. Brett and Josh went honking by in Brett's truck. When he waved, I waved too then brought my hand down resting it on his thigh, not looking his way. His muscle tensed under my hand.

My brain did somersaults trying to determine what to do next. As he turned on Oak Street and drove by the brewery where adults drank liquid courage, I saw this as a sign and found some of my own. In one swift move, my hand moved off the khaki colored cotton, skimmed over his knee then back up his thigh under the material.

This time, I dared glancing at him and his eyes were dark and held a warning. My upper teeth came down on my lower lip. With my fingertips, I began to lightly graze his thigh. I closed my eyes, forcing myself not to look at him, but my eyes bulged open when he reciprocated the touch to my upper thigh. Every nerve ending above my knees sprang to life.

"What's wrong?" he asked.

"Nu…nothing."

The corners of his mouth twitched upward and the Jeep suddenly came to a stop in a parking lot. He unbuckled and leaned into me forcing his hand upward another inch. In all the truth or dare games, this was as far as a guy's hand had been up my thigh. I wondered what underwear I had on.

"How about we make a deal?"

I nodded. "Kay."

With his other hand, he fingered strands of my hair. "I believe turnabout is fair play. You touch me, I touch you. Sounds fair. Yes?"

I nodded again, and, testing his theory, I inched up a wee bit further on his thigh. He reciprocated. My mouth fell slightly open and his sexy lopsided grin appeared.

"I don't think this is a game you'll win, Emma."

A little woozy in the head from the barrage of hormones flying through my body, I took the challenge.

"It's a deal," I said short of breath. Having him touching me, I'd already won.

He pecked my lips softly at first then his mouth parted and he kissed me fully. His tongue was warm and soft, and slowly reacquainted itself with my tongue. After the kiss he buckled his seat belt again. "Let's get you home on time."

This challenge and newly found courage made me smile. I touched his knee. He touched mine. I touched his fingertips to my lips and traced the tips with my tongue. He groaned. I smiled when he jerked my hand toward his mouth performing the same. Except it was obvious his touch was WAY more effective on me.

"Zach," my voice was barely a rough whisper with a slight warning attached.

He lowered my hand but held it, and I realized we were back in my driveway.

He jumped up and over his door and came to mine. "This is going to be fun."

I was already sitting sideways thru the open Jeep door. He backed up to me and I got on his back. He sat me on the hood of the Jeep. It was warm. I leaned in and kissed his neck before he turned toward me with a cocky grin.

I shrugged my shoulders up to my neck and kept them there as I giggled protecting my neck from an oncoming assault. He leaned in, and then with his fingers tickled my sides until I lowered my shoulders in an attempt to stop the tickling. As soon as my neck was fair game, he swooped in and showered it with kisses.

"I'm gonna win," he nearly sang. "If your noises don't kill me first."

My noises? "Good luck with that." I grinned and moved in for a kiss.

TWENTY-ONE

It was Saturday and time to make the call. I was a bundle of nerves but had procrastinated long enough. This half made me the most nervous.

"Hello?"

"Mrs. Owens?" I heard anxiety in my voice.

"Yes."

"This is Emma Hendricks."

"Hi Emma. How are you?" Zach's mom was always kind.

"I'm fine."

"Sweetheart, Zach's not here."

"Yes ma'am. He's with Ryan. I kind of planned this out. I'm wondering if we could meet later this morning, if you have time. I have a favor to ask of you." I got that much out and breathed.

"Is something wrong?"

"No. It's about Zach's birthday. I would just need maybe a half hour."

She didn't hesitate. "That would be lovely. Where would you like to meet?"

"My mom and I could meet you at Greenleaf."

"That's fine. I can be there in a half hour."

"Thank you, Mrs. Owens."

"You're welcome Emma. I look forward to seeing you." Half over.

Greenleaf was a quaint little eatery downtown. It was quiet when we got there, and Mrs. Owens smiled at us from a wrought iron table in the corner. Her eyes were warm and inviting; I wanted to hug her.

"Hi Emma, and you must be Mrs. Hendricks." She nodded.

"Please. Call me Kate. It's nice to finally meet you. We have come to adore your son." My mom shook her hand.

"Thank you. I'm Lisa. Our son is quite fond of Emma."

We all sat.

"Emma," My mom addressed. "You called this meeting."

"Yes, I did." I took a deep breath. "Mrs. Owens. I'm sure I'm not telling you anything you don't already know. But Zach misses the city terribly and…" Spit it out. "I know taking him there isn't so much an option. But, I was wondering if I could borrow him for a few hours on November 15? What I have planned, I will need to do at night."

I went on and told her my plan and gathered the information I needed to pull this off.

"Emma." Her hands touched mine, and I stopped talking. "I can see why Zach worships you. You are very thoughtful. No one has ever been so kind to him."

I smiled and exhaled air I didn't realize I was holding. "Thank you. I hope I can pull it off. I'm probably more excited than he will be."

She shook her head. "I doubt that."

"It's the next best thing to being there…maybe." I shrugged. "Remember, it's a surprise."

She smiled and pretended to zip her lips. "Thank you for doing this for him."

Her tender smile was a reflection of Zach's. She hugged me before we left; it felt nice.

By the time Friday came around, I was busting at the seams with excitement. Zach didn't have a clue. I couldn't wait for him to see the work I had put in on this. All I'd told him was to be at my house at 7:00pm. With the time change, it was dark like I needed.

I heard his Jeep from the back patio, then I heard my dad welcome him and tell him he needed to go through the back gate. I heard a chuckling 'uh-oh' and the front door close. Perfect. My cue for the music.

He knocked and I opened the gate slowly.

"Welcome to San Francisco." I couldn't help but smile wide. His brows pulled together. "Huh?"

Stepping backward, I hoped his questions were answered. I took his hand and we started our tour of the make shift city. The only thing I didn't paint, build or create was first up on the tour. Pier 39. We stepped up onto the pier; an actual wooden pier that my father made. When he stepped over the three stuffed sea lions, he chuckled.

"They don't smell like the one's there," he whispered. "Come here, I can't believe you did this."

"No!" I swatted his hand away. "We have a city waiting for us."

"Please show me the way."

About halfway down the lit up wooden walkway hung my homemade sign for Fishermans warf. Plastic crabs and octopus hung in fishermen's net along the walkway.

I watched him, measuring his response. *Sittin on the dock of the bay* echoed over the speakers. Confusion masked his smile.

"What is this?" he asked slowing to examine the intricately made signs. He looked at the map, indicating China Town was straight ahead, Scoma's to the left and Ghiradelli square to the right.

"Scomas?" he asked.

I nodded. "Your mom said it's your favorite."

"My mom was in on this, eh?"

"Which way?"

He looked again at the map smiling. "Let's see how Scomas measures up."

We walked to the left and white lights lit up around the area. My mom lit the candles on the tabletop and poured our water. My dad suddenly appeared with two bowls.

"Please sit," I gestured at the chairs.

He did while my dad sat the bowls in front of us.

"Clam Chowder for the lady and the Lazy Mans Cioppino for the gentleman."

"Dad!" God, he was dorky. Couldn't he just set the soup in front of us and walk away.

"Thanks, Mr. Hendricks."

Zach's eyes widened as he picked up his soupspoon. "Is this really..?" He tasted the soup and smiled...big. I was happy.

I'd saved my money for weeks to pay for the soup to be overnighted from Scomas.

He reached across the table. "Emma. Thank you."

After dinner, we headed to Chinatown. First up, were press-on tattoos. I had no idea what they said; I'd only ordered them a week ago special delivery so they'd be here. Ryan frowned behind the table.

"Which one do you want?" He asked with the world's worst customer service. Mom was making him do this, and it was clear he wasn't going to play the part well. When Zach broke into laughter, Ryan threw the sponge he was holding and stormed off.

"At least he tried," Zach said still laughing. "What do they say?"

I shrugged. "I don't know really."

He leafed through them then pulled his phone out and took a picture of one of the tattoos.

"What are you doing?"

"My app translates. I want this one."

I moved quickly behind the table to the small Tupperware bowl of water. I found the sponge Ryan threw and dipped it. "Where?"

Unbuttoning his shirt, he pointed to just above his right pec, right below his shoulder.

After getting him wetter than intended, I peeled off the backing and it stuck to his beautiful skin. This time, I pulled out my phone and took a picture of the lettering.

"What's it say?" I asked.

But he didn't answer; he simply ran his fingers the length of my face. It must have been something he missed from the city.

"Next stop, Ghirardelli Square."

"Let's go," he said with enthusiasm.

Ali's area lit up with lights and I'd made the sign above her, an exact replica of the sign in San Francisco. She retrieved what I'd put on ice earlier, lit the candles and walked away.

"Happy Birthday," I semi whispered.

The ice cream cake from Ghirardelli's read "Happy 18th Birthday Zach." It was starting to melt so I cut him a piece quickly.

His spoon slid easily thru the beautiful confection, and the first bite came my way. I opened my mouth and the cream, and cookie crumbles and fudge, WOW, they were awesome.

He took the next bite and smiled.

"I can't believe you did this." He paused and just stared at me. "For me."

Goofily, all I could do was smile. This was SO worth all of the trouble I went to.

"You've done your homework young lady," he said taking me into his arms.

"Yes sir I did."

"Up for a quiz"

I shrugged. "Sure."

"Name of two bridges there?"

I snapped. "The Golden Gate!"

He pecked my lips. "That's one."

"The Bay Bridge?"

He nodded and pecked me again. "Good girl. Name the prison sitting in the bay."

I knew this but couldn't think of it. "Um, can I get a life line?"

"Fair enough. There was a movie made about it."

"Escape from Alcatraz!" I shouted. He reared back then pecked me again while chuckling.

He released me and rubbed his hands together. "Ultimate San Francisco question. Name the most used mode of transportation by visitors."

"Bus?"

"No."

"Those electric thingy like trains."

He smiled. "Electric trains, no again."

"Oh!! The Trolleys!"

He turned on his heels and walked away from me.

"Where are you going?"

He shook his head. "I must break up with you over that one. I'm sooo disappointed!"

If it wasn't for the smile that I loved inching across his face, I think I may have vomited right then and there.

"I don't know the answer," I whined. "So I don't get a kiss?"

He shook his head. "Nope."

"Consolation prize?"

"Huh-uh."

"Zach! Just tell me!" I shouted moving toward him and he back stepped. "Kiss me."

"Not on your life," he grinned.

I knew he was joking but the thought…oh the thought. I had always been protected. My whole life surrounded by guys who would keep me safe. But Zach was different. He was mine. There was no obligation to my brother. He liked me. And even though I loved him, his liking me was enough.

"I'll reconsider when you can answer it correctly."

He must have noticed by inability to focus. Immediately, I darted toward the house. It only took a minute for me to get the right answer.

I confidently strolled toward him. His brows arched.

"Well?"

"You best pucker those lips. Because the answer is…cable cars…"

He grabbed my face and cradled it for the longest time.

"You're right, cheater." Then he kissed me long and soft; and it was by far the best kiss yet.

The last stop on our tour was the hardest thing I'd had to build. It started from a cardboard bridge my mom scored from an empty house. The bridge had been used in a vacation bible school and carnival as were some of the booths I'd redecorated.

Our hands clasped tightly as we walked to the east side of the house. As we rounded the corner, his eyes shot upward toward the lights and his mouth hung open.

"Em-ma."

I loved when he drew out my name and a shiver rippled through me. The homemade Golden Gate was pretty stinking good. Didn't really look like the real thing but the gist was there. My dad had unhappily dug three holes in his manicured lawn for this. The tall PVC pipe wrapped with lights was his brilliant idea and it worked.

"I know that it doesn't look quite like…"

His fingers hushed my lips. "It's perfect." With his hand still over my mouth, he unbuttoned his shirt and my heart skipped a beat. He pulled out his iPhone and took a picture of the tattoo.

"Click on the translation app," he directed. I did. Then he clicked on the image of the tattoo and the phone was loading. My eyes looked up to his and he slid his finger over the V between my eyes.

"Relax your face," he whispered.

He smiled at his phone then turned it to me. The image had been translated. The screen read: 我爱你 / I love you.

The V was between my eyes again. I could feel it. I didn't understand what that meant.

"The phone translated your tattoo?"

His wide smile forced me to smile. After sliding his phone into his pocket, he placed my hand over his tattoo. His heart pounded beneath my palm.

"I love you," he said.

I nodded. "Yes, that's what the tattoo says?" I asked again.

"Yes. That's right. And that's what I'm saying to you."

"You love me?" What?

A chuckle shook his chest, and I realized my hand seemed glued to his skin.

"Me?" I asked again.

"Very much," he added.

"I love you too!" I nearly shouted, hoping his mind hadn't changed in the fifteen seconds I'd hesitated.

When his lips met mine, on our very own Golden Gate Bridge, I didn't dare close my eyes. This memory would be mine forever.

TWENTY-TWO

I was shocked to find out that Ali and Ryan had gone out that night. Shock would be an understatement when Ryan admitted to actually having fun. Evidently, the verdict was out on the whole freshman thing…but Zach warned him not to knock it. Ali banked on the thought that because things were going so well with Zach and me, she and Ryan would follow suit…I wasn't that optimistic. I knew my brother too well.

A week prior to Christmas break we planned a movie night for the four of us, and Ali's excitement level was bordering on obnoxious.

"So, what are you wearing tonight?" she asked.

"Jeans and a shirt. Why?"

"You aren't going to dress up?" She acted appalled.

"Ali. We are going to a movie." I spoke like I was talking to a first grader.

"I KNOW! This is going to be so much fun." Her squeal shocked me.

Zach's arm wrapped around my waist from behind and I smiled without looking at him. I faced him with my back to her. "Ali is excited about tonight." I spoke with my teeth tight then crossed my eyes.

He picked up on my irritation. "It *is* going to be fun! I am SO excited," he laughed sarcastically.

"I KNOW!" Ali added.

He patted my back and hurried to his next class. "Good luck," he whispered in my ear while Ali and I made our way to Advanced Biology.

"You know," Her voice was hushed. "we kissed the other night and…"she glanced around to guarantee no one was listening. "He touched me."

My response couldn't have been positive because she closed her mouth in a little pout. "What do you mean he touched you?"

"Nothing. It's no big deal."

I grabbed her arm. "Ali. Don't do anything stupid."

"I won't," she defended and entered class.

I followed and pulled my lab stool next to hers. "I didn't mean to make you mad. We are both in the same boat. We should take it slow and make sure it's right."

"Oh, Em. It feels so right."

I knew what she meant; I'd felt the same way. But I was scared she'd jumped into this too fast.

My gut told me I needed to have a talk with my brother.

Zach picked Ryan and me up before Ali, and, as we got to the car, Ryan lifted the front seat so I could get in the back. I frowned and started to speak when Zach interrupted.

"Ryan. Not trying to piss you off dude but that's Em's spot."

Ryan looked back at me, rolled his eyes and squeezed into the back. "Fine."

I smiled at Zach, who winked at me, and I slid in to my shotgun position.

We drove to Ali's and she bolted from the front door like the house was on fire. Zach had gotten out, lifted the seat and helped her in. Her perfume was strong.

"Hi guys." She chimed and took Ryan's hand immediately. I wished I could see his face…his reaction. But I couldn't.

We voted for the scary movie, which I wasn't psyched about but made for a good excuse to have Zach's arms around me. Not that he needed an excuse. We all sat together with a seat between

Zach and Ryan. I wasn't sure why guys did that—but I'd seen it a lot.

The movie was terrifying with a guy running around with a chainsaw trying to kill only the, hot young people; I spent half of it with my hands over my eyes. Zach chuckled if my screams actually escaped and would grip me just a little bit tighter. I heard a moan come from Ali mid way through the show and glanced over to see them making out. Please. Are you kidding me? Good thing we sat two rows from the top; no one was behind. I elbowed Zach in the side and he shook his head. I was embarrassed for them. Zach tugged on my hair till my head titled back, then he kissed my lips. When the credits rolled, we made our way back to the Jeep and stopped off at Starbucks and got a drink.

"Do you guys want to head back to our house?" Ryan spoke up. He looked at me. "Mom and Dad are gone to Roberta and Mo's till who knows what time."

I shrugged. "Sure." It was ten o'clock and Ryan was right, Mom and Dad would play pitch there till at least midnight or after. Ali was all about doing whatever Ryan wanted to so she eagerly agreed. Zach seemed to approve as well.

The house was cold and Ali and Ryan hung out with us for a bit before he asked if she wanted to see his room. Ali had been to my house a thousand times and seen it all, including his room. She bit her lip and smiled as he held her hand walking up the stairs.

"Hey, Ali," I shouted after.

"Don't. She's going to do what she wants," Zach responded.

"I know." I gave up. "Whatever. Want a drink?"

He shook his Starbucks glass.

I threw a quilt over our laps and he flipped channels. I tried to get my mind off what was about to happen upstairs. My hands were cold and he rubbed his on top of mine creating friction. My head rested on his chest as we watched TV. His heart beat slow and steady and I paced it to mine. I closed my eyes hoping to stay in this moment forever.

My cheek fit perfectly into the crevice between his chest muscles. With my fingers, I traced the outline of his face, feeling where he had shaved. When I touched his mouth, he held my hand and kissed each finger. I giggled, stole his hand for a moment, and reciprocated his action. Then, he lifted me by my underarms and pulled me up until our lips met and mine melted into his. His breath, intoxicating.

Supporting my neck like a baby's, he rested my head on the sofa as he twisted me around lifting me 'til my legs dangled behind his knees. He brushed the hair from my face and swept his thumb across my cheekbone till his fingers reached my hair. Wrapping his hand around my head, he crushed his lips to mine then moved to my ear and down my neck. He treated my throat to small kisses as his hand rubbed down my sternum and over my stomach. My left boob was bigger than my right, though neither were big at all. And I didn't have cleavage, not really, so I tried to push myself together with my arms as he lingered near my bra. This was the furthest I'd ever been with a guy. A dull ache built in the pit of my stomach.

"Zach." I'm not sure why I whispered his name. I wanted exactly what he was doing. Being a gentleman, he raised his head and stared down at me.

"What?" I barely heard him but knew he spoke when his mouth moved.

"I so want to be with you," my voice whimpered. I wasn't even sure what I meant.

Reflections from the TV flickered in his eyes; they were as hungry as mine. I watched as his tongue moistened his lips and he searched for the right words.

"I want to be with you too." Then he kissed me and sampled every inch of my lips. His palm cupped my **left** breast, thank God, as his other hand moved over my jeans to my upper thigh where I'd never been touched. My body quivered and, as hard as I fought, I couldn't keep the moan from coming out. It seemed loud.

Your noises… I covered my face. "I'm sorry," I panted. My breaths were coming in short gasps and I was embarrassed.

"Don't be sorry." His voice was low and rough and he lifted his leg trapping mine between his. I was on my back and he rested on his side. His rubbing hadn't stopped and my head spun. I found it easier to keep my eyes closed. On an impulse, I moved my hand to touch him down there. Through the denim I could feel him respond. I pulled my hand away. I had never touched a guy before, not like that.

"Now, you can be sorry," he growled between kisses.

The blood running through my veins burned my insides. It felt trapped and ran crazily through my body. Air hit my stomach as he lifted my shirt and brushed kiss after kiss across my abdomen. I trembled with each breath of air that I inhaled. The small of my back rested in his palms.

"Are you OK?" he asked with a trace of concern.

"I...I'm per-fect. W-why?" the broken words mumbled out.

"You're shaking. Am I hurting you? Are you cold?"

I rubbed my thumb over his soft lips as I looked down at him. "No." I yanked at his shirt.

He didn't take his eyes off of me, but with one hand pulled the cotton up and over his head. The feverish skin on his stomach touched mine as he pressed his body to me.

"We can do this. You know, I would never tell a soul." I could barely speak.

He snickered between kisses. "So, it would be our little secret?" he teased.

"Ab..so...lute...ly." the syllables matched his kisses and my gasps.

"Maybe we should work something out. Five months *is* a long time." The desire in his eyes hadn't faded. "Though it will *so* be worth the wait."

"I don't want to wait." I pouted. My body had never—felt this—responded like this. My mom had warned me about hormones but not this...this internal plea...a longing I'd never experienced.

"Oh, Em. My hot, adorable freshman." He nibbled at my ear.

"I'm supposed to be a sophomore. You know that, right?" He hesitated for a second then proceeded down my neck stopping in the tuck of my collarbone.

"I did *not* know that."

It was hard to concentrate on my words with what he was doing. "Born premature. Docs thought it was a good idea to wait to send me to school though I exceeded all their expectations." I smiled.

"You're exceeding mine right now." His groan was satisfying.

"So, there is really only two years between us." I arched my body toward his.

"Please, two years is nothing," he was teasing me.

"Exactly. Then let's not wait," I begged, goose bumps covering my body.

"You have a legitimate argument." He glanced up at me and nodded. "I'll tell you what. I'll be with you as soon as my probation officer gives me the green light." Then he unsnapped my jeans and I sighed.

"Probation officer?" I heard the deep voice of my father and was taken back by Zach's reaction. He flew off me, pulled my shirt down and grabbed his within less than three seconds.

"Mr. and Mrs. Henricks. I'm sorry. I…" His words trailed off as he shoved his shirt hard over his shoulders. His jaw tight.

I slid my shirt over my unbuttoned pants hoping my parents didn't notice. Zach extended his hand to me. I accepted his offer to help me, but, once up, he dropped my hand.

My dad took his jacket off tossing it into a chair. "Zach, did you say probation?"

The look on Zach's face was full of shame. "Yes, sir." His words were strong.

"Dad! Stop!" I cried. "I'm just as much to blame probably more."

"Emma, get to your room." My father ordered.

"NO!" I shouted knowing I'd regret it later. "You don't understand. I wanted to be with Zach and he told me no. He knew we shouldn't."

Dad's face was tight and rigid and I was scared…but not of my dad…of what he was going to do.

Mom moved toward me. "Emma, honey, you should go to your room."

I jerked away from her and stood by Zach. "I won't. I won't let you persecute him." I held his upper arm and he gave me a tight smile.

"*He* is eighteen and an adult and *you* are fifteen and still considered a child. Now, go to your room."

"I am not a child, Dad. Please…he's good, and honest, and everything I need him to be." My dad's anger wasn't subsiding no matter my words. I felt sick.

Zach gripped my shoulders and his eyes bored into mine. "Do as your father says, Em. Go to your room so we can talk." He was trying to be strong but I could tell by his eyes that he was worried too.

I shook my head. Tears streamed down my cheeks. He wiped them with his thumbs and nodded toward the stairs. "I love you." I choked out. He kissed the top of my head and smiled.

My mom's face was sad as I rounded the corner.

"I suppose it doesn't matter that Ryan's up here with a fifteen year old. That's different...right." I spouted off before my assent up the stairs. I slammed my door before falling onto my bed feeling like my heart would burst.

Thirty long minutes ticked by on the clock before I quietly opened the door and tip toed down the stairs. I heard my father's voice and I didn't move.

"Zach, this is nothing personal."

"I understand." Just hearing Zach's voice soothed me.

"Emma will accept this in time."

What? Accept what? My world was crashing down around me. I couldn't take it. I flew down the stairs.

"Accept what?" I demanded to know.

Zach glanced at me for a second. His eyes were dark...expressionless. He blinked away.

"Tell me!"

"Emma Nicole. I will tell you when he leaves. Get back to your room." Dad said harshly.

"No. I want to hear it from him."

Dad stared at Zach then nodded as if he approved the conversation. The hair on my neck stood.

Zach's shoulders slumped as he faced me. His chest moved up and down slowly. I smelled his breath as he exhaled and I inhaled the air he blew, knowing I wouldn't be doing so for a while. His eyes couldn't find mine and he struggled to find words.

I broke the silence. "I can't see you anymore, can I?" My tear ducts ran dry. This wasn't happening. My parents knew I loved him. They wouldn't do this.

He closed his eyes. "It's just for a little while." His lips were tight. Even a little while would be too long.

He reached for my hand, which shook uncontrollably. "'Til you're off probation?"

He nodded and his eyes fell. "It's just 'til March." I shook my head until I was dizzy. He grabbed my cheeks. "Em. We can do this. I should have been honest with your folks. This is my fault." It was so not his fault. I'm the one that pressured him. Always the gentleman. He would never hurt me.

I sniffed. "OK. So, what. I can't see you but we can talk on the phone…text…what?"

I watched him swallow hard and I knew I wasn't going to like what was coming. My chin quivered and he touched my face. "It's going to fly by. I'll see you at school. Don't be angry at your folks. They're only doing this because they want to protect you."

My eyes about came out of my head. "Protect me. From you? This…this is crazy. And you agreed?"

He nodded.

I swiveled around to face my parents. "I can't believe you are doing this!" I glared at my father as my mom rubbed her forehead. "This is ridiculous. I love him! You can't keep us apart."

My dad dismissed my words. "Why don't you go ahead and leave," he directed.

Zach grabbed his keys off the sofa table.

"NO!" I caught hold of his arm. "I'm going with him!" I screamed. "Take me. Take me with you, please," I begged.

His eyes were sad. A 'no' was coming.

"Please," I cried as tears streamed down my cheeks. "Please," I whispered.

He glanced toward my parents. "May I hug her?"

"Yes." My mom spoke before my father had a chance.

"Don't leave me."

He pulled me into his chest rubbing my hair. My arms didn't go fully around him but I held on as tight as I could.

"I love you," he whispered so only I could hear, then tried to break my hold but wasn't forceful. "Em. Please. Help me out." His voice was quiet.

I shook my head.

His body stiffened and his strong hands gripped my arms and pushed them to my sides. He bent forward and kissed my forehead. I didn't look at him…I couldn't. I heard our front door open and shut.

I walked to the stairs.

"Emma." My father's voice was soft and I glared at him.

"I'll never forgive you for this," I said flatly, and took one step at a time. As I reached the top, I heard his voice again.

"Katie. This is nuts. This relationship has gotten totally out of hand." He was angry.

"Matt. It's her first love. The more we fight it…the worse it's going to get."

"Did you see what they were doing?"

"Yes. I'll talk to her."

"You better."

I went into my room and slammed the door.

TWENTY THREE

I texted Zach immediately.

Call me. Send.

Fifteen minutes passed. My stomach hurt. I texted again.

Zach please! Send.

My head hurt as I lay and watched my ceiling fan rotate. I tried to listen to music but every song reminded me of him. I couldn't do this. I texted again.

What day in March? Send.

I was desperate for a response. But...nothing.

A little after one o'clock in the morning, there was a tap at my door and my mom stepped in.

"May I?"

I shrugged.

She sat on the corner of my bed. "Honey. How ya doin?" Her voice was sticky sweet with sympathy and instantly annoyed me.

"How do you *think* I'm doing, Mom?" My tone was bitter.

"That first crush is so hard to deal with."

"It isn't a crush, Mom. I love Zach. My first crush was Nate Wiley or Grant. This is nothing like that." How dare *she* belittle this.

She moved closer. "Did he tell you and Dad why?"

Her brow's raised. "Why he's on probation?"

I didn't look at her.

"Yes. I believe he told us everything. He was very honest."

"Then how can you do this?"

"Emma." Her tone of voice distracted me. "Your father wanted it to be *over.*" I glanced up at her threatening eyes. "Over." She said it again and waves of fear rocked me. "As we talked with Zach, and I watched him struggle with telling us, we became aware of how much he cares for you, darling. Add that to what we walked in on." My face flushed. "Then, your father hears probation. It wasn't pretty. Like it or not, you will always be our little girl. We know that in five months you will be sixteen. But no matter how old you are, there are certain things your father doesn't want to see. AND a grown man on top of you, kissing your stomach is one of them."

I couldn't respond and buried my face.

"I think you should know how hard Zach negotiated. That takes a lot of nerve and guts to go head to head with the fifty-year-old father of your girlfriend."

She rubbed my back. "Your dad is angry right now. I don't know if he will rethink this and change his mind. Until then, you may see Zach in March."

"That's three months!"

"Not quite. And don't think that we won't be addressing the protection thing again." Her eyes were firm. I knew she was right. She stood to leave.

"Mom?"

"Hmm?"

"Why is it OK for Ryan?"

"Sex?"

I nodded.

"It isn't. He's in trouble too. You just missed that encounter." She pulled my door closed.

I woke up the next morning, my eyes almost swollen shut. I hadn't slept most of the night…checking my phone every half-hour. The sunshine breaking through my window was hot and I felt like I was baking so I kicked the covers off. I reached for my phone on the nightstand. No messages. The clock read 10:45. I scrolled through

some old texts reading them one by one, stopping on my favorite—
'love you baby!'

My pillow was hot so I flipped it. The cold cotton was comforting to my cheek. I scrolled through the songs on my MP3 then hid in the quilt again. I decided I was staying here for the next two and a half months.

There was movement in my room and I tossed the covers down. Ryan stood at the corner. I paused the music.

"I knocked."

"What do you want?" I growled.

He sprawled across the bed landing on my feet. "I'm sorry. It was my stupid idea to come back to the house."

"So, what happened to you?" I propped myself on the pillows.

"Ali and I were on my bed. We both had ear phones on listening to music and kissing. Then I felt a tap on my leg. It was Dad. Poor Ali freaked." He chuckled in amusement. "She'd given me a back rub so my shirt was off."

My eyes were wide. "That's all? You were up there a while." My accusatory words didn't go unnoticed.

"What do you think we did? Give me some credit, Em. She's fifteen."

I offered him an apologetic smile. My brother had more heart and brains than I'd thought.

"Sorry." I elbowed him in his side. "Are you grounded too?"

"No more girls in my room…"

"That's all?" I interrupted.

"*AND*, I'm grounded for a week."

My lower jaw suspended in air. "A week? Whatever!"

"Why? What'd you get?"

"I can't see Zach for two and a half months."

'He shoved me back. "Bullshit."

"It's true." I went on to tell Ryan about Zach's probation and what happened in San Francisco, swearing him to secrecy since no one around here knew. I explained how difficult the move was for him. Then I told him about getting busted making out on the sofa. He laughed, of course.

"You gonna be able to do it?" His tone was hopeless.

I shrugged. "I have to. And I know *he's* going to. I've texted him four times and nothing back." My throat tightened just saying that.

He rubbed my head. "I'll see what I can do."

"What do you mean?"

"I'll talk to Dad. Zach's not a criminal."

"You'd do that? I didn't think you even liked him."

"I like the way he treats you. He defended you—against me—but he still defended you." He closed the door and I fell back across my bed in disbelief.

Three days till Christmas break. Finals were over, progress reports would be sent home tomorrow and we had three days of nothing. Initially, break meant more time with Zach, but now…I hoped for a quick break then back to school.

My chest tightened as I thought of third period and I contemplated skipping. I didn't know how much longer I could endure looking at his perfection with no hope of touching. This wasn't the longest I'd gone without him but it was close.

I stopped at my locker to get my book. My mind wasn't in it as I twisted my combination three separate times before it finally unlocked. Next to my locker hung a fluorescent flier advertising Christmas break extra credits through online courses or night classes. I read it over carefully then ripped the flier from the wall and shoved it in my backpack, running to third hour.

I was late and breathing hard when I entered the class. Zach was already working. The seat next to him was open, which wasn't surprising given most people knew we dated. I slipped into my seat. Mr. Bowman had written the assignment on the blackboard and he didn't notice I was late, thankfully. My heart beat erratically against my chest and I wondered if Zach could see it pulsing against my back. I could smell him.

"When you're done, please bring your paper up for me to check, then you may talk quietly in your seats." Mr. Bowman announced.

When I finished, I moved to his desk and handed him the paper, which he skimmed. Without moving my head, I peeked up to see Zach. His eyes were on me and he offered a tender smile. Don't cry, I told myself. Be strong.

"Good work, Hendricks." Mr. Bowman marked my work and handed it back. On my return trip, Zach's head was back down.

"You look beautiful," he murmured into a whisper.

I twisted my neck around. "Thanks," I mouthed.

"Hey. Did I hear right? You two are kaput?" Grant asked inquisitively his sun touched hair darkening to its natural color as always during the winter.

The words stung as I processed them. I didn't look at him and I listened to see if Zach did.

"Hmm. No response from either party. It must be true."

"Meier's shut up," Zach jabbed as he walked past me to the teacher's desk.

"Em. What's the deal with you and Owens?" he whispered.

I shook my head. "I don't want to talk about it, Grant." I feared my tears had restocked.

"Did he hurt you?" he asked, his voice full of accusations.

"Stop! It's none of your business." I gathered my books and Zach stepped past me.

"Owens—did you hurt her?"

The bell sounded and I hurried out.

"Answer me!"

I jerked back around when I heard Grant's gruff tone and Zach weaved around him.

Suddenly, Grant shoved him from behind and Zach nearly fell into me, his chin was tight with anger. He glared at me.

"I can not fight him. You know why." Zach grimaced.

His probation. A school fight wouldn't be good. I threw myself between them. "Stop, Grant." I saw Ryan running up from behind; my eyes wild with fear. Grant's chest puffed out and his upper lip was tight. He looked more like a snow boarding surfer than a fighter.

"Move, Em," Grant ordered.

Zach grabbed my arm and yanked me behind him. "Yes, please move."

Ryan was finally there tugging Grant to the side and I gripped Zach's hand taking him in the opposite direction. Within one long second, he dropped my hand, caught my eye, whispered "thanks" and walked away. Feeling rejected, I spun around to see

Estelle in front of me with a glimmer of hope twinkling in her eyes. My stomach knotted and I headed to gym.

I skipped lunch altogether which upset Ali and Lauren. Ali—cause she wanted to talk about Ryan. Lauren—cause she wanted talk about why we broke up. Selfishly, I couldn't handle relationship talk right now. I headed to the counselors office.

The room was hot when I arrived, and I ditched my sweater. Ms. Trudeau came from her office and greeted me with a smile. "Hello, Emma. What can I do for you?"

I retrieved the crumpled up flier from my backpack.

"I'd like to do this."

"Earn some extra credits? Are you not doing well in a subject?"

"No. I'm doing fine. I just want to earn a few more."

She seemed suspicious. "Are your parents on board with this? Most of your classes are already advanced."

"They are fine with it," I lied. But why would they care if I studied more.

"Very well." She handed me a sheet of paper. "Here are the classes available. I need your parents to sign off on that release. We have a class online and a night class you can take. Do you prefer one?"

Pretending to contemplate the thought, I answered, "I'll do both."

"That's a lot to take on over the two weeks of break. It requires a great deal of time."

Time is all I had at this point. "OK. Thanks. I'll have it back to you tomorrow." I knew her eyes followed me out of the room.

Later that evening, after we'd cleaned up dinner, I approached my dad who seemed the easier target.

"Dad?"

"Yes?" He removed his bifocals and gave me his attention.

Waving the piece of paper, I said, "I need you or Mom to sign this."

He reached for it. "What is it?"

"It's an approval for me to take a class over break. Seeing how I will have nothing to do." My words held blame. "I was thinking I could earn an extra credit for school."

"An extra credit? Emma. You're already ahead of credits. Why don't you take the time to spend with friends. Maybe some sleepovers, going to movies…you know."

I nodded with fake excitement. "That's sounds awesome, Dad. Maybe I could do both. It'll keep my mind busy rather than thinking about…" my words trailed off but I figured he got the gist.

"You're right. What am I talking about it? Nothing wrong with a little extra education." He smiled apologetically. The guilt trip had worked.

SWEET! "Thanks, Dad."

"Emma?"

"Yeah?"

"This time will go fast honey, you'll see."

I think I smiled.

TWENTY FOUR

Christmas break started, which meant my fourteen days of learning were underway. I was swamped with homework, but to say I didn't have time to think about Zach was the overstatement of the century. I thought about him every minute of every day. I had to believe that Zach thought of me too, that there was still a future waiting for us...and he was counting down the days till March. My life had become a lingering moment in time where nothing mattered over the duration of this extended time apart. I felt empty at times, wondering what I had done before Zach. Dad was right. I'd kind of dumped my friends to spend time with him. For now, the task was to stay focused on my studies.

The online courses were a joke and I knew by day seven that I wouldn't get lower than an A. How this justified an education was beyond me. My night class on the other hand was more of a challenge. Held on campus at Southern Oregon University, not only was I a runt in with college kids, but I was smarter than half of them, which didn't go over well. So—I played the part of the dumb high school freshman the best I could.

Three days before school was to start, Ryan clued me in on an impromptu skiing trip to Mt. Shasta. My first and only question was who? Specifically Zach…and Ryan wasn't sure. He didn't know who was going and didn't particularly care. He and Grant were headed down and Ali was tagging along with me. I'd been pretty disengaged since 'the break' and the Ryan/Ali status seemed to be on track, which unnerved me just a bit. My folks basically packed my bag and nearly kicked me out of the house once they knew there was adequate adult supervision. I wondered if they knew there was a possibility that Zach would be there.

We headed out at 6:30 the next morning though the trip averaged less than two hours. It would give us two full days of skiing. Grant opted for the back seat allowing Ali to sit with Ryan. Figures. The last hour, I buried my head in my pillow as Ryan took the twists and turns of the Siskiyou Mountains. On a good day, Mt. Shasta was easily seen from Ashland but today the skies were overcast. As we got closer, a light snow fell making me more nervous on the roads.

"OK." Ryan tossed a crumpled up piece of paper. "The address is Jefferson Street. But read me the directions."

Grant examined the sheet. "Take a left on N. Shasta Boulevard."

"Where are we staying?" I asked. Typically we stayed at the Woodsman Hotel. Ryan eyed Grant in the review mirror and it didn't go unnoticed. "Ryan? WHERE?" I felt anxious.

"Take another left on East Ivy." Grant squeezed my knee. "It's fine," he soothed.

"OK. Now I'm getting pissed. Whose house are we staying at?" I gritted.

Ryan sighed. "Em. I didn't tell you because you would not have come."

"Right, onto Rockfellow," Grant said softly then looked at me. "I'm sorry. Ryan said I couldn't tell you," he whispered.

"Whose?" I mouthed.

"Estelle's cousins," he said ashamed. "She said you could come. Well…we weren't coming without you…so *then* she said you could come."

In a very childish act, I threw myself back against the leather and scowled.

"Turn left on Jefferson and we're there." He hurled the paper on the floor and rubbed his brow.

"I'm sorry. You needed to get out of the house. And besides, last time we snowboarded, you kicked my ass so I needed to seek revenge."

I managed a slight smile. "Is he gonna be here?"

Grant's elbows rested on his knees and he stared into the gap between his legs and nodded. "Yes."

I appreciated the honesty. It was blatantly obvious Grant's feelings had shifted somewhere along the line. I remembered the time Ali, Lauren and I played truth or dare with Ryan, Brett and Grant during a sleep over. The disappointed look on Grant's face when we had to kiss had angered me.

When we arrived at Chez Estelle, I studied the enormous rustic looking A-frame. It gave me the willies thinking about staying here. Connor and Brett were already here. No Jeep. Ryan spotted Claire and groaned. Ali bit her lip. *Welcome to my world...Ali.* Claire waved us inside.

Grant grabbed my bag and we trudged up the sidewalk into the beautiful home. The front room was open and woodsy, perfect for a mountain hideaway. Gigantic wood beams shot across the ceiling and the A-frame was solid glass in the back of the house. Mt. Shasta graced the breathtaking view.

The Oregon mountains were odd as far as mountains went. I'd been to the Rockies, twice—a massive mountain range spanning several states—but in Washington and Oregon there are several colossal mountains surrounded by a few hills out in the middle of a plain. Maybe that's why our mountains are known by name— Ranier, St. Helens, Adams, Hood.

Claire continued the tour.

"There are three bedrooms. Each room has a sleeper sofa so four can stay in a room. Connor and Brett already called this one." She pointed to a hallway off the living room. "You all can put your stuff in that one over there for now till we figure things out."

"Let's roll out. Snow is movin in and I want to hit the slopes," Connor alerted us and slid over the back of the sofa already in his ski pants.

"All right. Let's hit it." Ryan agreed and clapped his hands.

We changed quickly and loaded back into Ryan's truck, our skis and snowboards still on the car rack, and headed to the slopes.

The resort was busy and we parked near the back of the lot. Most of us had our season pass lift tickets and rode on up. The bitter cold wind bit my cheeks and I pulled my goggles down to protect my watering eyes.

I hated the ride up. My fear of heights and dangling feet bothered me. My parents had Ryan and me on skis by the time we were five. We'd been to Utah, Tahoe and Mt. Ashland. Snowboarding was my game. Grant and I were both boarders and my runt size helped me whiz in and out, annoying the crap out of skiers.

Ryan and Ali slid off the lift first and Grant and I followed behind over to Telemark slope. Ryan's choice would be to start with the most dangerous black slope but I preferred a warm up. At the top of the slope, we fastened our boots, engaged the board and took off. Fresh snow meant a softer ride.

The temperature was always colder at the top unless the sun was out—and today it was lost in the clouds. Helmets weren't our thing, which ticked off my mom. I never understood what a helmet would prevent if you hit a tree. But, I was glad I had on my stocking cap. The storm moving in had dropped the temperature and with the blowing snow, I wished I'd worn my face mask.

Half way down we stopped at a boarders break area behind a barrier.

"Crap it's cold," Ryan complained. "You OK?" he asked Ali. I was glad I had goggles on because his demeanor around her surprised me. I hoped my eyewear hid my shock. He *could* be nice to girls.

"I'm fine."

"Aaah. You big wienies!" Grant scoffed and I laughed. He looked at me and nodded down the mountain…tempting me.

I stood stretching and shook my head. "Nope. I need to rest for a second."

"Fine." He sounded disappointed and kicked off his board.

"I'm rested!!" I shouted, pointed my board vertical with the slope and cackled.

"You cheater!" He yelled as he frantically tried to reengage his boots. I rounded the first curve by the time he hit the run. I could see his determined smile. I flew unsafely past skiers, probably bordering on dangerous—to beat him, though I'd have beaten him fair and square anyway. I knew the slopes too well to lose. As I reached the bottom I slowed and waited smugly.

He soared around a corner and spotted me but didn't slow. My board was parallel with the mountain as he got closer, his speed making me nervous. All of a sudden, he popped his board horizontal and threw a heap of snow directly into my face. The force from his speed propelled him my way and he toppled onto me as I reacted with a somewhat surprised and painful scream.

"Oh shit! Em. Are you OK?" He knocked the snow from my goggles. "I'm sorry."

My head was cold lying in the snow. His face inches from mine. The closeness made me nervous. I was sure he could see my anxious eyes through the yellow-tinted goggles. To look at him was unavoidable. The wet snow stuck to my face and I spit it back at him.

"You never call me Em." My voice came in a whisper.

"I'm sorry…God, let me get off you." He kicked off his board and helped me stand. "You all right?"

I nodded, still at a loss for words.

He reattached his board. "Shall we?" He motioned to the bottom of the slope.

"I won, you know." I finally managed to speak.

He popped vertical and started moving. "Whatever…cheater." Then he shot me a smile.

Ali and Ryan weren't far behind and we met up by the lift. After another less aggressive time down, we all agreed to call it quits until the blizzard passed. We hit the lodge at the base of the mountain. Brett and Connor lounged by the fireplace with Jaycee and Claire.

Hmm. Jaycee had made it. No sign of Zach.

We hung out for a while and the older kids harped on homecoming, which was two weeks away. Ali and I couldn't go as freshman, unless we were invited. Envy settled over me as I presumed Ryan would be escorting Ali. I tried to smile. It was painfully obvious there were two people missing from our little tribe—and that made me feel sick. I hadn't eaten since this morning in Ashland. The only thing in my stomach was bile. It was now inching up my esophagus burning as it moved. Three weeks had passed…had Zach moved on? Tears stung my eyes and I was determined not to cry.

"Ya'll ready to head back?" I proposed, prodding Ali.

"I'm ready. Whenever everyone else is," she agreed. I wasn't sure if she was aware of my motive.

Ryan stretched back to catch a glimpse through the windows. Near blizzard conditions swirled outside. He shook his head. "We may as well."

I breathed a sigh of relief as everyone rose to their feet gathering their things. The return trip took longer because of the snow. Ryan drove cautiously and concentrated on the road. The only thing I concentrated on was what I'd find when we got back to the house early.

TWENTY FIVE

Zach's Jeep was parked in the drive with a two-inch accumulation of snow. So, it had been here awhile. Everyone piled out and proceeded to the door. I lagged behind, my feet heavy in the snow.

The house was warm and we ditched our coats in the entryway. The fire was blazing hot and as I came around the corner, my eyes casually scanned the room. Damn. Where was he?

Estelle's mom was in the kitchen and the house smelled of food. My heart raced and the deep breath I took was loud enough to catch Grant's attention.

"You OK?" he asked and moved close to me.

I nodded and swallowed when I spotted Estelle come from the hallway laughing, Zach directly behind her. My fists instantly clenched. He laughed at something she said. God, I'd missed his smile. He looked exceptional in his sweat shorts and long-sleeved USC hoodie. Estelle's eyes narrowed when she saw me.

"Em? What's wrong?" I heard Grant vaguely and I was afraid I was going to cry.

"Get me out of here," I gritted through clenched teeth.

"All right." He agreed. "RYAN?" he shouted.

Zach glanced up when Ryan did.

"Your keys?" Grant held his hand out and Ryan tossed them without question to his buddy.

Zach's perfect smile crumbled. I froze until Grant spun me around and pushed me out the door; then I ran to the truck. He opened his door and I slid across while he started the engine and we were gone.

The silence in the car was unbearable. I couldn't manage my own thoughts let alone conversation and I think he realized that because he parked at a Taco Bell.

"Let's eat," he said and grabbed his door handle.

"Wait." I held onto his forearm.

He glanced at my hand touching his arm then to my eyes. "What?"

"Thanks."

His eyes were confused. "For what?"

"Getting me out of there."

He acknowledged my words with a simple nod. "Let's get inside and we can talk. You gettin' out on my side or yours?"

"Yours." I slid over.

After ordering, he waited for our food and I got our drinks from the fountain. We were the only two customers and we sat in a corner booth. Once we sat, I took a bite of my taco though I wasn't hungry.

"So, what upset you? Was it Owens?" He bit into his burrito.

I hesitated until he threw his napkin in my face. "When I saw him with Estelle…" my words trailed off.

"What? They hookin up again?" He asked curiously.

His words beat the breath from my lungs. The thought…ugh. I tossed my taco onto its wrapper. "Maybe." I answered and took a sip of my soda. "I don't know."

"He's an idiot."

"Grant, you don't understand. We're kind of—taking a break."

He held up his index finger. "See. That's where you're wrong," he mumbled with food in his mouth. "I do understand." He chased the burrito with a drink. "Ryan told me he couldn't see you right now…you two were grounded from each other or some shit. But when you care about somebody, you make it happen."

"He promised my parents." I defended.

"AND?"

He didn't seem to understand Zach's position but how could he? He didn't know about the probation…no one knew.

Grant wadded up his wrapper. "So, are we going back?"

I scratched my head. "I think we have too." I lowered my head.

"We don't *have* to do anything. I have my credit card if you want to go to a hotel or something."

I pursed my lips and scowled.

"Please." He got angry and slid from the booth. Then turned back to me. "Give me more credit than that," he said with dark eyes.

He waited at the exit until I got close then pushed open the door. The snow was deep and I was glad we had Ryan's four wheel drive. I went to my side this time and got in looking straight ahead.

"I'm sorry. I didn't mean that…"

He interrupted. "Forget it." His tone was cold and I'd known him for too long to let something like this come between us.

Trying to find courage, I thought before I spoke. "You know what, Grant Meiers. I have loved you for four years and you wouldn't give me the time of day. Suddenly, someone else expresses a tad bit of interest in me and BOOM…there you are." He abruptly veered the truck to the curb and shifted into park focusing on me. "Hey, Runt." I continued mimicking his voice. 'I noticed you this summer.' 'She ain't a runt anymore.'" I watched as he smiled, which infuriated me. "'Hey…I hear you and Owen's are kaput,'" I continued.

Unexpectedly, he grabbed my jaw with both hands, one hand on each side, and pulled my mouth to his cutting off my words. At first, I kissed back…his lips soft, mushier than Zach's, then I realized that this wasn't OK. As his hand touched my cheek, I drew away. I heard him exhale and his hands gripped the steering wheel.

"It happened this summer. I didn't see it comin' either." He stared out the windshield.

"You know when you and Chloe broke up and you were so down in the dumps? You crashed with us for a couple of days and you didn't think there'd ever be anyone else. Do you remember that?" *I* remembered it clearly. I saw it as my chance to have Grant.

"Yes." The heater was on high and I barely heard him.

"I wanted to scream at you…pick me. Me! But you waited until…" I shook my head.

"You know what…it's OK. You like Zach."

I lowered my head. I couldn't recall a time in my life where two guys liked me at the same time and now, Zach *and* Grant. Unbelievable. Why was this happening?

"Let's get back." He broke the silence.

"Fine," I squeaked out. I didn't know how to respond to my brother's oldest and best friend. He squeezed my hand as he steered back to the house.

TWENTY-SIX

I didn't know what to expect when I walked through the door. Grant and I'd only been gone about an hour, but night had fallen, and I'm sure dinner had been served. The front door was unlocked. Everyone was crashed in the living area around the giant flat screen television. Zach and Brett lounged on the sofa while Claire and Jaycee sprawled out on the loveseat. Ali sat indian style between Ryan's legs. No Estelle.

Still in my ski pants, I went directly to the bedroom, showered quickly, pulled on some sweat shorts, towel dried my hair and ventured back out nervously. Everybody was still in their spots, so I plopped down on a step leading down into the living room and stared at the TV. No one spoke. They seemed either annoyed or exhausted.

Zach hadn't acknowledged me…even with a look. My lip burned from where I'd chewed too deeply and I tasted blood. I glanced at him out of the corner of my eye. His face was serious…tight…angry. He stared at the TV as well, but I knew he wasn't watching. His eyes weren't focused.

Grant dumped his body next to me. "You doin OK?"

Hell no! I shrugged getting angrier by the minute. He poked his index finger into my side and tickled. I giggled out loud. "Stop," I whispered.

He kissed my forehead and I laughed, but my smile faded and I swallowed hard as Zach's eyes rested on us. His brown eyes glowed red. I had never been scared of him, but he scared me at that moment. He stood and stalked toward us. Grant rose gracefully to his feet. With urgency, I glanced at Ryan, whose eyes were on all three of us.

Zach's hands were in tight fists. "Meiers? May I speak with her?"

"Why are you asking *him*?" I blurted out angrily.

Grant grinned obviously pleased that he was consulted with the request. "If it were my say, the answer would be no." His voice was flat. "But, it's not. She's a big girl. I can vouch for that." He winked at Zach.

A growl ripped through Zach's chest. He shoved Grant violently backward jarring him against the wall and a picture clattered to the ground.

"ZACH!" I screamed and lunged toward him.

Ryan tossed me to the sofa and Brett bear-hugged Zach from behind heaving him in the opposite direction. Estelle's mom peeked around the corner then ducked back into the kitchen when she saw it seemed under control. Grant chuckled as he got up and picked up the picture, hanging it back in its spot. Brett whispered something to Zach, who snarled and glared at Grant who made his way to Ryan and me.

"That was mean," I accused Grant.

"Whaaat?" he laughed.

Zach broke away from Brett and bolted to me. He offered me his hand politely though his eyes were cold and hard. I hesitated for a moment. Grant waited too. My hands were freezing, and, when I touched Zach's, his heat sent a warm tingle through my body. I stood and he guided me to a bedroom. As he shut the door behind us, I heard someone ask, "Who wants to get in the hot tub?"

His eyes still frightened me and he dropped my hand after the door was closed. I heard him breathing…in and out…his fingers intertwined and locked behind his head as he paced. I sat on the corner of the king-sized bed. Suddenly, he moved toward me, took my hands in his and rubbed them between his, blowing into his palms to warm them. He didn't look at me.

With the door shut, the room didn't get the heat from the fireplace and I shivered. He finally positioned himself on the opposite corner of the bed, his elbows resting on his knees. "I'm sorry I scared you." I loved hearing his voice.

"It's OK." I wondered if I'd get the chance to hold him.

He slapped his knee. "It's not OK," he disagreed. He shook his head at an apparent bad thought. "When you left tonight with— with your boyfriend…I went nuts. This is not…"

"He's not my boyfriend and you know it." My words were hateful.

"Where did you two go?"

"What difference does it make? You spent the day with *your* girlfriend." Finally, eye contact, though it wasn't what I was hoping for. His eyes were full of disappointment.

"Her mom was already here and Claire and Jaycee thought she'd left and they took off without her. She apparently tried Ryan but he didn't get the call because you all were already in the mountains and didn't have reception. So…she called me. Brett and I hadn't left so we picked her up. I AM SORRY. Given that we were staying at her place, I figured it was the least we could do."

My heart raced. "Yeah, but…"

"When we got here, everyone was gone." His tone was harsh and his words articulate. "We decided to punt skiing for today because of the storm. So we hung out here…all *three* of us. So, I wait all fucking day to see you and you walk in the door—give me the benefit of the doubt….oh wait, no you didn't…then you run off with Meiers. Nice."

My eyes lost their battle with my emotions and tears swelled. I couldn't breathe and I made a dash for the door opening it slightly but he wrapped one arm around my waist and pushed the door closed with the other hand. His breath came in short bursts through my hair. It had been so long since I'd smelled him.

"Zach," I cried. "I thought that…"

"I *know* what you thought." His words were soft and his eyes turned gentle.

"When I saw you two…" My throat tightened. "Come from the hallway…" I sniffed. "I panicked and I had to get out." He kissed my head and sat me on the bed, his arms still around me. My crying bordered on sobbing and I was embarrassed. With his thumbs, he wiped the tears and held my cheeks.

"Then…I turned around to escape and Grant was there and I knew he'd help me and I…" He tucked my head into his chest where it had belonged for the past few months. I missed it. I missed him.

He whispered. "Grant helped you because he's in love with you."

"I know." I sniffed again and his body stiffened beneath me. He pushed me away and took hold of my shoulders, his eyes penetrating mine.

"For six months, I've tried to get you to understand that he likes you and you've fought it. Now you're agreeing. Why?" He wanted an explanation.

My tears ran dry and my emotions seemed more under control. But I feared saying too much. "He told me."

"Told you what exactly?" His tone was casual.

I cleared my throat. "I asked him." Zach's eyes were soft. "I asked him, why now?"

"And what was his answer to that by the way?"

"He said that it happened this summer. He was surprised by it too. But he said that he knew I liked you and wouldn't push it."

"And did he?" he asked.

"Push it?" My heart skipped a beat. I could be honest and trust that he wouldn't get angry at me or I could lie. I detested lies. "Maybe a little." I heard him inhale. My lips pursed and I gave him a squinty look. "He was a gentleman. As much as you don't want to hear it…he was."

"Mmm," was his only response.

"He kissed me." I whispered the words but he heard them clearly and shot up off the bed.

"And you allowed that?"

"No." I explained. "I pulled away from him." I watched as he rubbed his eyes with the heels of his hands. He blew a long breath out and walked to the door. I jumped up. "Where are you going?"

"I need to talk to Meiers." He appeared calm.

"Oh no, you don't." I waved my head from side to side and blocked the door as if that would keep him from getting out. He picked me up and I sighed, resigned to my second defeat when his lips met mine gently. Finally, the only thing I'd wanted since I'd gotten here. Weeks had passed since I tasted these lips. His breath the same as I remembered. His legs moved beneath me…he was walking as he held me suspended. Then our bodies tipped and I fell onto the bed. He landed near me but used his arms to prevent falling on me.

"You know what makes me the saddest?" he asked.

His eyes looked tortured. "What?"

He pecked my nose. "You didn't believe in me…in us. I don't know how to make you understand that I want to be with you, Em."

There was no limit to what I would do to make him happy—to see his beautiful smile. But, didn't he see how perfect he was and how weak and insecure I was? He was strong enough to endure this break and I wasn't sure I'd survive. We had tonight though and I refused to waste any more time. I finally answered. "I do believe in us. I'm sorry I was…" the word sounded too immature to say. "…jealous," I sputtered out.

His lips brushed across mine so softly I wasn't sure if they really had.

"Well. I've wrestled with my fair share of jealousy tonight too. So don't be too hard on yourself." He kissed my fingertips and up my arm, smiling as a shiver rippled through my body.

"Don't be jealous of Grant." I hoped he believed the words.

He snickered. "Right." He nuzzled his lips near my throat and kissed. "The guy who stole you away tonight, kissed you the second he got the chance, then goads me out there in front of you. That shouldn't bother me a bit."

His breath tickled my neck and I giggled. "Yes, but who's lying on this king size bed with me, with his lips pressed against my neck?"

"Hmm. *That* would be me. And the reason I know that is because if he got this close to you, I'd break his neck."

"Someone's not playing well with others." Then I easily shoved him backward onto the bed and crawled on top of him, straddling his waist, which wasn't an easy task. I'd never straddled him before. "Dude. You are big!"

He laughed. "I'm only an entire foot taller and hundred pounds heavier than you. You are way too far away from me at this moment."

"Do you remember the turnabout is fair play conversation?" He had kissed my neck and touched me over and over again in the past ten minutes and…turnabout…

I lifted his shirt and rubbed my hands across his tapered torso. His chest rose and fell with a slow breath, and I leaned in to kiss the soft skin. "Em." A warning was attached to his tone.

"Hmm?"

"Why do you always have to test my strength or this *mutual* agreement?" His words blew out of his mouth.

"Is that what I'm doing? Testing you? Believe me you passed the test long ago."

He wrapped his arm around me, held my hips in place and twisted me over till I was on the bed and he was on top. Brushing the hair from my face, he smiled at me. "I believe someone wants me to fail the test." He pressed his lips to mine, the familiarity of his kiss so distinct after the kiss with Grant. I felt his body's response as he rubbed against me. My head spun as his tongue delved into my mouth for only a moment, then he brushed a soft kiss over my lips and arched his throat. I kissed his Adam's apple, then his chin, then our lips met again—the kiss was much more powerful this time. He reached down and grabbed my knee and pulled it up to his hip and his body fell deeper between my legs. I lifted my T-shirt over my head exposing my single tank nightshirt. My cheeks burned with the blood that raced to them.

"Emma." I heard the more formal warning.

I smiled. I wanted to please him, didn't he understand?

"Zach." I mimicked him with a deep voice. "How strong are you?" I slid my hand down his back below his waistband. Boxers?

He gripped both my wrists with one hand shoving them over my head. "Not strong enough, apparently. Especially if you keep taking your clothes off." He raised my tank exposing my stomach and he kissed it softly, rubbing his nose across the pale skin. He inched upward closer to my breasts and his nose brushed over the top of my bra and a shudder rippled through me.

"Oh, Zach." At the same time, he traced under my waistband with his finger. No one had ever touched me like this. I couldn't breathe or I was holding it—I didn't know which. Nothing was clear—except that I wanted him. Finally, his thumb replaced his nose on my bra and his other hand went farther south brushing over my cotton Jockeys.

There was no room for my mother in this bed but she was with me in spirit. As I was touched down there for the first time over my panties, I heard her saying things like: 'when you're caught in the moment, you'll do anything,' 'hormones are a powerful thing,' 'Emma, you won't want to stop.' My mother couldn't have been more right.

I breathed or tried too—a long, heavy, broken breath that resembled crying, I think. He took his hand away and stared at my face. My expression must have been miserable because his eyes widened with concern.

"Are you all right?" he asked, his tone colored with worry.

I couldn't breathe right—a quivering pant mixed with a sob came from my mouth. What was happening to me? I couldn't control it. I was so scared of what was happening between us. He released my wrists immediately and propped himself on his elbow at my side.

"Em?"

Your noises... I hid my face with my palms embarrassed at my body's lame reaction.

"Please don't stop." My voice was weak and I'm sure unconvincing. It sounded like I was crying, but I wasn't.

He turned me onto my side and pulled my body snugly into his—one spoon much larger than the other. "I'm sorry. I let that get too far. I should have known better."

My breathing still hadn't returned to normal, but I thought I could speak. "Why are you so afraid to be with me? I'll be sixteen in a little over four months. Most other girls have done it before now."

He was quiet and I couldn't see his face. But I could tell he was contemplating his words. "Well, outside of the statutory rape thing…"

His words made me feel sick. It would never be rape, unless I was the perpetrator.

"What if it was *me* that raped *you*?" I tickled his under arm.

He chuckled and hugged me tighter. He started to speak and then stopped. He seemed to struggle with the words, which made me anxious. I broke the silence. "I am too young?" If he agreed with my assessment, I thought I would be sick.

"No. Not in May. But that's not all."

"OK, what else?" I didn't like not being able to see his face. His beautiful brown eyes told me so much.

"You know earlier, when you straddled me, and I think your words were 'dude, you are big.'" He paused and kind of laughed. But I couldn't respond because I didn't understand. "*You* are so little and I don't mean that to be mean, Em. But you are in fact tiny."

"Zach, when you are on me, I don't even feel you." I was going to make him understand. I had all the confidence in the world that he wouldn't hurt me. He closed his eyes and shook his head like I didn't understand. I didn't.

"OK." He let out a frustrating sigh. I bit my lip. "You—are littler and I—am bigger and you've—never done this and…I don't want to hurt you."

I felt like a first grader and the story problem just made sense after being explained by the teacher. He was afraid of hurting me with his…body. I shuddered and he buried his face into my hair. I pulled his hand up and kissed it. He was worried about physically hurting me when we made love. I couldn't argue with that one, but it also never crossed my mind. And I didn't care. I would be fine. How bad could it hurt?

"I think I'll be fine," I whispered.

"You will be when the time is right."

We lay there for the longest time not talking. Just the two of us. I remember looking at the clock at 1:15 the last time. And then I must have given in to sleep.

The sun came through the window and I squinted and glanced at the clock. It was 8:15. Zach and I had slept through the night on the king-size bed and hadn't moved. He still slept. His deep breaths behind me were slow and relaxed. I limboed under his arm that held me hostage to escape from the room before others woke.

When I freed myself, he muttered something, then rested peacefully again. I opened the door and snuck out.

By 11:00 everyone was up, dressed and ready to go. Zach and I rode the ski lift together and I felt restricted as I sat on the bench. I was going to be too hot…I could barely move. We were headed to Coyote Butte, which meant two lifts, certainly not my favorite thing. Ali and Ryan were in the seat in front of us and Grant and Claire were behind. Now that Claire had given up on Ryan, I think she'd set her sights on Grant, which I didn't like.

I'd never been boarding with Zach but was relieved he was a boarder too. I'd slow down or do what I needed to keep pace with him.

"Hey Em!" Grant yelled from behind.

I turned around in my seat. Zach grabbed onto my arm. "Yeah?"

"What're ya gonna take? Diamondback or Black Bear?"

"It doesn't matter, Grant, she'll kick your ass either way," Ryan shouted from in front of us.

"Notice how Meiers doesn't call you Runt anymore. Guess he thinks Emma is more endearing," Zach added. I nudged him in the ribs.

"I was thinking of Sticks and Stones," I responded to Grant.

"That's not funny," Grant said seriously.

"What's Sticks and Stones?" Zach asked.

"It's just a tricky black."

"Do you think that's a good idea?" His tone was concerned.

I shrugged. "I'm not worried about it. But please understand, for Grant and me, it's all about competition. It's been this way for the past six years and he hasn't beaten me yet." He wouldn't win either. I smiled just thinking about it. He knew it and I knew it.

"Believe me. I like the thought of you beating him but don't do something foolish. I'm a surfer turned snowboarder so I'm not quite as good as you. But, I'll try and keep up."

Ryan and Ali had gotten off the lift and it was our turn. We slid off the ramp, joined my brother then waited for the rest of the crew. Zach carried my snowboard as we walked to the slope.

Grant came up on the opposite side of me. "Hey."

"What?" I asked a little annoyed. I didn't want to hassle with jealousy today. I could feel Zach's eyes on us, though it was kind of funny knowing he didn't want Grant around.

"You were kidding about Sticks and Stones, right?" His goggles rested on his forehead and his eyes were serious. He was really bothered by this.

"Why? You nervous?" I winked at him, trying to keep the competition real.

He grabbed my arm and spun me around to face him. "Em!" He barked. "Don't!"

"Let her go!" Zach snapped, dropping our boards and wedging himself between Grant and me. "Now." Zach's jaw was rigid. His nostrils were wide and his lips were tight. My heart pounded and I was suddenly frightened for Grant's safety. I shouldn't have joked about it. Grant released my arm and started on Ryan.

"Ryan. Do not let her go down *that* slope."

"Runt. Stick to one of the other three. OK?" Ryan requested. Uh-oh. Big brother intervention. It must be serious.

Zach's face was still tense with anger. I reached up and touched him with my gloved hand. "Relax," I tried to laugh it off. "He wouldn't hurt me. You know that." I certainly knew that.

Zach released a breath and a puff of steam came from his nose. "He's getting on my last nerve."

"I told you…it's kind of a competition thing."

"I'm starting to see that. I'm not sure *you* are." He handed me my board. "So what's the deal with this slope that's got him all worked up?"

"See ya at the bottom!" Ryan hollered as he and Ali started down. I waved.

"It's rocky on one side. Kind of dangerous. But with the snow that fell, it'll be fine." I rolled my eyes.

He took my gloved hand. "Let's just say for the sake of safety, stay away from that one."

"OOH. Siding with Grant?" I teased. That was a shock.

He nodded. "Maybe. No need to tell him that." Zach winked at me and lowered his goggles. "He is waiting for you though. As much as I'd like to smack him with my board."

I waved my finger at him. "Now. Now." I glanced over my shoulder and Claire was with Grant. "Looks like you're going to have a partner...so...keep your eyes on the slope." I bit my cheek. Why was it OK for me to head down the mountain with Grant but jealousy oozed from my body at thinking of Zach boarding with Claire?

He propped his board in the snow, raised his goggles back up, wrapped his arm around my waist and pulled me in. "Let's make it clear to both of them then." He lowered his mouth to meet mine and his mouth was on fire. It was hard to kiss him because I was smiling so wide.

"You're being mean," I mumbled.

"And?" He laughed and dislodged his board. I glanced over at Grant.

"You ready?"

"You're not going with loverboy?" Grant's goggles were down so I wasn't sure if he was eyeing Zach or me.

I shook my head. "Nope. He understands all about friendly competition." The wind was cold but the sun was making me sweat under my layers.

Grant engaged his board. "I'm not racin'. I've lost the mood."

My boots were on my board and I was ready to go vertical. "OK...loser!"

A grin touched his mouth. But he still didn't give in.

"I'm going in 10, 9, 8, 7," I counted.

"OK! I'm in!" Grant shouted and went vertical. I bent my knees low and went straight staying right on his tail. The fresh powder was awesome and sprayed up as we swayed. I glanced back to see Zach and Claire following behind. Grant didn't turn around. He didn't have too. He knew I was there without looking. We had to veer right up ahead and I saw the sign for Sticks and Stones. Diamond Back continued down and I spotted Ryan and Ali taking a break. If I was going to take it—I had to do it now. I would undoubtedly beat him. Grant shot his head around to measure my speed. I think he could tell I'd slowed and he brought his body upright. I looked for Zach and didn't see him. At that moment, I darted right, changing slopes and leaning back on my heels. Zach would never know. Grant shot right and made the turn too, barely, almost taking out a tree. He shook his head, disgusted at me, and I knew he was pissed.

TWENTY-SEVEN

I wafted through the powder giggling to myself. We would laugh and have a competitive race down the hill then fight later. He'd never be too mad at me. Confident, I slowed and watched as he pulled up and lifted his goggles glaring at me.

"Seriously?"

I grinned.

He was on the farthest side of the mountain. We both heard the scrape against the bottom of the board indicative of rock. He leaned away from the sound edging the board down and I swerved his direction.

"Emma, take it slow," he cautioned.

"I am." *Crap.*

"I need to get right," he said studying the slope for a good path.

He was right. Rocks poked out of the snow all around him. Gravity, along with the incline, kept inching my board away from him, as much as I fought to get to him. I tried to sit but even then the slope was too steep.

"Grant. Kick off your board and walk it over."

He nodded and tried to gain leverage, then his foot slid and he biffed it. One foot still engaged on the board.

"Shit," I hissed beneath my breath. Still creeping down the slope, I forced myself to inch left.

"Don't EM! It's fucking ice over here."

A wave of nausea swarmed over me.

"Why wouldn't they have this blocked off? Closed it? Anything!" I shouted and my chest tightened.

I glanced up at Grant, he had disengaged his board. The altitude had never really gotten to me even with my asthma, but today, I struggled. He held onto his board as he maneuvered over the rocks. Snowboard boots were not easy.

The sun hadn't touched the side of the mountain Grant was on. It didn't make sense.

"There was…" I inhaled. "…a freaking…" breath "…blizzard last night…" Breath. "…this is crazy that…." Breath. "…that there's no snow…" breath. "right there!"

Grant stared at me as if I was the one in trouble.

"Em. Do you have your inhaler?"

I nodded.

"Get it out, sweetheart."

To prevent sliding farther down the mountain, I decided to kick off my board. As I did, I realized I was now in the shade, and, when I disengaged my foot, my other foot slid out from under me. The slope was coming toward my face and I landed hard on my arms.

"Em!"

My breaths were coming quicker and he was right, I needed my inhaler.

"Ryan. Get back up here. We need help."

Was Ryan here? I stared up at Grant. He was on the phone. Talking to Ryan?

"Sticks and Stones." He grinned. "Hey, I knew she would." His smile disappeared. "Stop, don't be mad at her. Listen. She just lost her board and she's whistling."

Was I whistling? I was whistling. And my board was gone! I didn't remember that happening.

"Em. I'm coming down."

After unzipping my front pocket, I searched for my inhaler.

"Shiiit!"

My head jerked instinctively at the shriek and Grant was falling or sliding feet first.

"Aaahh!" The painful scream echoed off the mountain then suddenly, his scream stopped. His board reached me first and I stopped it.

"GRANT!"

Working my way toward him while holding onto his board was hard.

"Grant…" I panted reaching him and wedged the board horizontally at his feet.

My stomach twisted when he didn't move. *No! No! This can't be happening. Why?* I studied his chest as I got closer. He had on too many layers. That was a good thing…right? It would be harder to get hurt. Too many layers to get through. I dug my boots into the icy snow as I grew closer. I unzipped my coat trying to relieve the increasing tension in my chest. It hurt. I hurt. I couldn't breathe.

Gradually, edging my way up to his face, I lifted his goggles and allowed them to rest on his forehead. His eyes were closed and his lips slightly parted.

"Grant." My voice broke. No response. "Grant, can you hear me?" I could barely hear myself. I took off my gloves and raised his head. *Oh shit!* Blood. There was blood on my fingers and on a rock beneath his head. I was SO wrong. I thought the fresh snow would have been enough to cover the rocks. Why wasn't the slope closed??

I laid his head down gently on my gloves and found my phone three layers deep. I had only two bars and prayed for reception. I dialed.

"Where are you?" Ryan demanded angrily. Not even a hello.

"Ryan. We need help. Grant's hurt." I started to cry.

"Grant? We are almost off the lift. We called it in, so ski patrol may be there first."

" It's bad….Ryan. When you make the cut…veer as far right on the mountain as you can." A wheezy breath interjected itself between words. His phone disconnected. I stuffed mine back into my pocket. I closed my eyes and recalled slowly all the things my dad taught Ryan and me over the years. *Never panic.* TOO LATE! With my eyes still closed, I assessed my surroundings. I could hear people through the trees on Diamondback—laughing and chatting. I could hear skis and boards wafting through the powder. They were close but they didn't realize we even existed. I thought about the three climbers on Mt. Hood and how'd they'd never been found. The cold air burned my throat as I inhaled.

Opening my eyes, I knew I needed to gauge Grant's injuries. I had a feeling he'd broken something by the pain-wracked scream. I peeked gently into his left glove. His wrist was swollen. Broken bone, possible fractured skull. I shivered at the thought. I rubbed his forehead. He was cold and that frightened me, maybe even clammy, or was I making that up? Cold was beginning to seep through my layers as well and I shivered.

I ran my fingers through his shiny long curls then kissed his forehead. "I am so sorry." I wiped my tears and bent over him resting my cheek against his—rubbing them together—creating friction. "Please be OK." Then I pushed my cheek firmly to his nose trying to keep him warm before moving to the other cheek. I smelled his shampoo or soap or something that smelled good.

"Could you please get your hair out of my mouth?" he spoke in a monotone.

I reared back and gasped. "Grant?" I wailed. "Oh my God. Don't move."

He blinked his eyes and stared at me—confused. He didn't smile.

"Do you know where you are?"

Without moving, he swiveled his eyes in their sockets. Tall evergreens hovered over him. He was on a bed of snow, I hoped something would click. "Mt. Ashland?"

I swallowed. Oh, this was so bad. We were miles from Mt. Ashland. He raised his head and cried out reaching one hand to his head.

"Please don't move." I warned. "What's your name?"

"Grant." His words were soft.

"Do you know who I am?" My pulse raced as I waited for the answer. I kept glancing up the slope. Was there a friggin closed sign that I didn't see up there?

"Don't be stupid, Chloe," he answered and I'm glad he'd closed his eyes because I couldn't hide my shock. Chloe had been in Okinawa for twelve months now. It had to have been my voice because I certainly didn't look like her. She was beautiful.

His left wrist was two times its normal size and was turning purple by the minute. I felt his right hand in my hair and I turned to face him again. "Did that make you mad, babe?" he asked quietly.

Mad? How could I possibly be mad at him right now? He should be the furious one. "Why would I be mad?"

"That I said don't be stupid. I'm sorry."

"No. I'm not mad." He was always so good to her. What I wouldn't have given to be her a year ago when I'd watch them hug and kiss. My heart broke as I snuck peeks of them. I ached to be in his arms. What a twist of fate.

"Good, then give me a kiss," he requested tugging my head downward. I took a quick glance up the slope then guiltily, touched my lips to his. His breath was cold and made me shudder as it blew into my lungs. His tongue touched my top lip then withdrew and he closed his lips and pushed me away. The kiss was different than last night. Better. "I've missed you," he whispered. He seemed out of it. Loopy.

Where was everybody? His eyes closed. I was wiping my bottom lip when finally, I saw them come out of the break. Two ski patrol, pulling their carrier. Relief washed over me. I patted Grant's shoulder. "They're here. You're going to be OK."

Suddenly, behind ski patrol, Ryan took the corner followed by Zach then Brett...*crap*...then Connor. My face flushed. Why don't we bring the whole crew? Now, if anyone else got hurt I would carry that burden too. Great. All five of them maneuvered toward us.

The ski patrol pointed to the right. "Stay—right face," he yelled back at them and all five stayed right of us and stopped parallel.

"Em, you all right?" Zach hollered. I sat back on my bum, suddenly feeling weak.

"Ma'am? You OK?"

He confused me. Why was he asking me that?

"Dude," he shouted toward the guys. "Did they say what happened to her?"

"What do you mean?" Ryan asked.

The guy took my wrist and pressed his two fingers on the underside then spoke into his hand held radio. "Patrol—we have a betty respirations are slow, eyes darkened, lips blue, conscious."

Suddenly, Ryan was next to me unzipping and rummaging thru my pockets. He rested my head against his shoulder and puffed the inhaler in my mouth. "Breathe it in, Em."

"Asthma?" the ski patrol guy questioned.

"Yep. She'll be ok. Just give her a second."

The other ski patrol guy spoke into his hand held radio. "Patrol—we have a bro—down. We will be transporting. Looks like a broken wrist and possible concussion."

They unrolled a neck brace and wrapped Grant's neck. As I felt oxygen make its way into my lungs, I wasn't sure if it was relief that Grant was going to be okay or the inhaler.

"What's his name?" they asked.

"Grant," Ryan said.

"One, two, three," they said in unison lifting him to the carrier cage. "Transporting." One guy spoke into his radio again. They weren't wasting time which was definitely good.

"You OK?" the ski patrol asked.

I nodded.

"You certainly look better," he smiled and they took off with Grant in tow.

I swiveled back to my five brothers who stared at me. "I don't care that you can't breathe right now, I'm pissed at you. You just couldn't not do it, could you?" Ryan asked bitterly. He moved away from me, re-engaged his board and tossed my inhaler to me.

"How many of us begged you not to take it? AND, I might add, you still did it," He added.

"Leave her alone, Ryan," Brett said calmly.

"Yeah Ry. Leave Runt alone," Connor echoed. "Let's hit it."

Ryan turned his board and took off. It was obvious Grant and I had cut the corner too short and ventured into a rougher terrain because where they boarded from, there was no problem. The guys followed Ryan except for Zach; he waited patiently for me. He didn't say anything. He didn't ask anything. We boarded down slowly in silence.

TWENTY-EIGHT

My hands were frozen by the time we reached the Jeep. I couldn't remember what happened to the gloves once I slid them beneath Grant's head. The dizziness from forgetting to use my inhaler still hadn't subsided. My thoughts were scattered as well and Zach still wasn't speaking. He was angry—I think. He was something. I needed him to hold my hands, to help me get warm.

The radio played inside the Jeep, thankfully filling the void. I guess it was for the best because, like usual, the mountain roads made me nauseous. Regardless, I didn't like either feeling.

He pulled in and parked by the entrance of the emergency room at the clinic and my eyes widened.

"Why are we here?" I asked. Ryan's truck was three stalls away.

Zach stared out the windshield. "Tell me you *don't* want to be here."

Couldn't he have asked a different question? One that I could answer without hurting him. Of course I wanted to check on Grant. Make sure he was OK. I was, after all, the reason he was here!

"I just want to make sure he's OK." I feared saying Grant's name.

He jerked the keys from the ignition and opened his door. I grabbed his arm and held on when his eyes met mine. "Are you angry?" I asked.

"We'll talk about it later." His tone was flat.

"Well, you're something. I can tell."

He pulled his arm from my grasp. "We'll talk about it later."

168

Feeling sicker than I did a few minutes ago on the curvy roads, I stepped out of the Jeep too.

The ER was quiet and we were pointed in the direction of the waiting room where we found the crew. Zach slapped hands with a couple of the guys and I plopped down in a chair next to Ali.

"Hey," I said. "You mad at me too?"

"Don't be stupid," she said. "I think Ryan's kind of mad but not because of Grant. Because he asked you not to do it. How's Zach?"

"What do you mean?" She knew something.

She shrugged. "I don't know. He was so upset when he got down the mountain. We were all waiting and hanging out." She was whispering. "Then you and Grant weren't down yet. Ryan kept telling him that he didn't need to worry about you but you never came. And neither did Grant."

I glanced at Zach across the room, next to Ryan, and his head was back against the brick wall with closed eyes. The older girls sat down by the TV but Estelle's legs were pulled up to her chest and she rested her chin on her knees. She looked worried. What was that about?

"Anyway—then Grant called from the slope and they took off. Zach led the pack sprinting to the lift. You are so lucky. He really likes you."

Her words were comforting at that moment given he wouldn't speak to me, or worse, look at me. That was the hardest of all. Usually, I could see him across a room and know what he was thinking by the look in his eyes. But as I watched him now, his lids blocked my access.

I continued to stare at him. His black ski pants rested low on his hips and his Under Armor was tucked neatly in. The thin material lay perfectly over each ripple of his abs. My stomach tingled and my breathing quickened just looking at him. I shook my head trying to clear the thoughts. His hands were in tight fists resting on his knees. I wanted to go to him and open his hands. Rub his palm on my face. White rings circled his eyes from where his goggles sat and his face was tanner from the wee bit of sun today. He looked relaxed, but I could tell by his jaw line that he was tense.

"Emma?"

I heard my name but didn't respond. Ali elbowed me in the side. A nurse in turquoise scrubs scanned the room. Zach's eyes snapped open. I raised my hand like we were in school.

"I'm Emma."

She offered a warm smile. "Grant's asking to see you. Will you come with me?"

Crap. Deeper trouble. Grant was smooth. I had to hand it to him. He knew I'd be sitting out here with Zach. I eyed Zach, but all I saw were his lids and his head against the wall again. I walked down the quiet hall, boots clunking on the tile floor.

The nurse directed me to the room. I tried to step lightly in case he was resting. A curtain hung between us and I took a deep breath.

"Chloe?" he asked and I stood frozen, confused. The nurse had asked for Emma so he must have used my name. Why would he have said Chloe now? Oh My God!!!!

"You are a jackass," I jabbed, yanking the curtain back and narrowing my eyes. "I can't believe you tricked me."

"Whatever." He held up his newly casted wrist. "And, I can't believe you risked my life." His words cut deep and my eyes flickered to the floor.

As angry as I was, he was right.

He sat up. "Em." He reached for me…I was too far away. "Come here."

I took two steps closer to the bed and he took hold of my hand.

"I'm kidding. This wasn't your fault."

"It *is* my fault. You wouldn't have made the turn if I hadn't."

"That's true. But I'm the one that crashed and burned!" He seemed embarrassed.

Our hands together, intertwined, it was odd how right and wrong it could feel in that one moment. How could I feel so crazy in love with Zach but still respond to this one person, my oldest friend, my longest crush, the first guy to touch my heart.

"I knew you'd take the turn, Em. That's who you are. I knew before we got off the freakin' lift. I wasn't going to let you do it alone." He laughed. "I bolted over there to make sure you were OK and now here I am." His sheepish grin made me smile and when he looked down at his cast, his blond curls fell around his face. "Broken wrist and concussion. So much for saving the day."

I pulled my hand from his and pinched the bridge of my nose. "Grant."

"I know." He ruffled my hair, which made me seethe. He was retreating…I could feel it coming. "You like Owens." His voice cracked as he acknowledged the truth.

I nodded. "But…"

He held his palm up. "No. No buts. I'm not sure if I can be good. But I'll try."

"You won't."

"You're right." He grinned. "Do you know I stared at that bedroom door all night last night praying it would open and you would come out." He cleared his throat. "You didn't. I think about you—*being* with him. You're too young, Runt."

Oh here we go with the too young bit. AND—we're back to Runt. I couldn't keep up with him. "You know, I could ask fifty guys at our school to sleep with me and forty-eight would say yes. Leave it to me to find the two saints who want me to keep my virginity."

His eyes widened. "You and Owen's haven't…or didn't…" His words broke off.

I shook my head.

Suddenly, he popped off the bed and did a gyrating dance rotating his hips and flapping his arms in the air. "Now we're talkin'. So—you, are still a weirgin."

Before considering the consequences, I lunged and shoved him as hard as I could which amounted to him falling back a couple of steps. He snickered. "Em. I love ya, Sweetie, but game on! Admit it baby. It's me you've always dreamed about losing your virginity to—not Zach."

My chest swelled with anger. "I hate you sometimes." I wanted to slap the smile from his face.

"No you don't. And that's the problem. You wish you could, but you don't." He grinned as I bolted from the room.

I walked slowly trying to reconcile the love/hate feelings brewing inside of me. Why was I so angry? Because he was so cocky…or could it be because in a way he was right. That made me hate him more. I wanted to nark Grant's remarks out to Ryan—who would break both his legs…no make it Zach—Zach would kill him.

Guilt stung every nerve ending. I trusted Grant. He was my best friend...*was* being the operative word. I was SO done with Grant Meiers. This would certainly make Zach happy. I focused, putting one foot in front of the other to find the waiting room and as I rounded the corner, I saw Ali and Ryan sitting together.

"Where is everybody?" I asked.

"They went back to the house." Ryan stood. "How's Grant?"

My teeth clenched at the sound of his name. "He's an asshole."

"Well, I'll take that as a fine," Ryan quipped and Ali giggled next to him, which annoyed me.

"Where's Zach?" I asked.

Ryan flung his arms out to his side implying I hadn't followed the conversation.

"I told you he went back."

"Well, let's go then!" I demanded with a scowl. Unbelievable! Zach freaking left.

Ryan bobbed his head up and down sarcastically. "Oh, yeah like I'm going to leave Grant here."

"He's riding with us?" I fumed.

"Of course," he answered and tossed Ali the keys. "I'll get Grant and we'll be out in a minute," he yelled as he moved down the hall. I glared at Ali and she offered me the keys without hesitation.

Ali swapped the front seat with me, putting her in the back with Grant. The ride back to the house was quiet, thank goodness. In the driveway, I immediately hopped out of the car and beat it inside.

I froze in the living room staring out the windows at Claire, Jaycee, Brett, Estelle, Connor and Zach in the hot tub. Josh slept on the sofa. A powerful surge of jealousy burst through me and I couldn't see straight. Zach was wedged between Jaycee and Claire and through the steam bubbling up, he looked friggin hot. Both girls sat a little too close for my comfort.

I looked away only for a moment then back again. Droplets of water fell from his dark hair and he was laughing and smiling—the smile that caused my body to react in funny ways and it *was* doing just that. I rubbed my neck, stretching it from side to side while I watched him. Thoughts of losing him made my gut wrench as I watched the older girls, the more mature girls. Blonde ringlets, black manes, tan skin, big boobs, skimpy bikinis, drinking beer. Jaycee laid her head back against a headrest and closed her eyes. A hint of a smile touched her lips and she glanced at Brett. Something stirred inside of me when I realized he was touching her under the water. I watched for only a minute before Ryan darted past me and out the door. When Zach spotted him, he looked at the wall of windows behind him but he couldn't see me. I bolted to the bedroom.

In SFA class during eighth grade, we learned about masturbation. Suddenly, I had never been more intrigued. I could still picture the animated brochure that I threw away before my mom could see it. MASTURBATION: rubbing of genitals until orgasm. There had been no real interest in trying this before, but I would try this when I got home. I now wanted to know my body. I wanted Zach to know my body. If these older girls could do this, so could I.

I couldn't think straight. My weird thoughts tormented me as I pulled my sweatshirt off deciding to leave on my sports bra and throw on a T-shirt. Where was my T-shirt? I was suddenly hot. I threw myself across the bed beneath the ceiling fan, trying to sort my thoughts. Lying there in only a sports bra and my ski pants, thinking about that eighth grade class, my fingers traced over my stomach….

"Need some help?"

I flew off the bed wide eyed. "Zach!" My face must have turned purple. He stood smiling…*not the smile…please, not the smile*. His hair was still wet and his body…his body wrapped in a towel below his waist. This was not good.

TWENTY-NINE

ZACH

Relief muddied with a bit of excitement, forced a slow wide smile across my face.

"You OK?" I asked.

She nodded too quickly and my smile only broadened.

"When did you get back?" I asked taking another step closer. Given where her fingertips were only a moment ago, gracefully flitting over her stomach, I had a feeling my presence was intimidating to her.

"Um…we…" she shrugged. "When they did." She pointed out the door.

This time I fought the oncoming smile and stayed put. I didn't want to intimidate her or make her to feel threatened in any way. This little innocent creature had placed every ounce of her trust in me and I would not let her down.

"Are you OK?" I asked and watched as her eyes scanned down the front of me in a hypnotic gaze. Was she breathing? Did she need her inhaler? "Em?"

"What?" She sounded angry and defensive and I hated that. So, I quickly closed the distance between us. She was sweating and hot when my hands touched her face and she suddenly unfastened her ski pants and shoved them over her tiny hips working them off with her legs and kicking them aside. Her long underwear was the next remaining layer. She was clearly flustered.

"Emma." My hands now held both her cheeks and she rested her hands on my shoulders; then she balanced and lifted herself onto the bed. We were almost nose to nose. Almost.

Without hesitation, she rubbed her index finger over the length of my bottom lip and her baby blues darkened with desire. Aggressively, she pressed her lips to mine with an uncontrolled force. I retreated, broad eyed, for only a second—hesitated—then my mouth took hers, fully. Her mouth was hot and wet and everything it should be and her kiss, damn, her kiss was like no other. My hands met behind her and it wasn't until her legs wrapped around my waist, that I realized I had lifted her off the bed.

"Wow. What happened at the clinic?" I joked.

She didn't laugh or even smile. For being just fifteen, this girl could be sexier than any other girl I'd seen. I also knew she'd tremble and cave when pushed, which made her cute and sexy at the same time. I decided to test the waters and pressed her body up against the wall and kissed down her neck. Within a short three seconds, her predictable panting had begun. She kissed my shoulder.

"What's gotten into you?" I whispered.

"The girls need to keep their hands off of you," she said between kisses.

I grinned, where she couldn't see of course. "Damn! You saw that?" I kissed her harder and she squeezed me with her legs. I leaned back and looked at her. "I have *one* little girlfriend, Silly. And she should *never* be jealous."

"I'm not jealous," she lied.

I wasn't done trying to rock this boat, and I slid my hands down her back between her long underwear and Jockeys. "Well. In that case, she and I are running to Taco Bell in a few minutes. Do you want anything?"

Her eyes fluttered just a bit before she twisted a little bit of my chest hair in her fingers.

"Ow!" I laughed. "Come get in the hot tub."

Her brows furrowed causing that cute little V between her eyes—the V that I wanted to smooth away with my finger because she only had it when angry or stressed. What had I said that upset her? The hot tub? That upset her?

She released her legs from my waist and I sat her gently on the floor. My fingers trailed down her neck, along her back and came to rest on her hips. My eyes took in every inch of her causing *my* breaths to be uneven.

She bit her bottom lip and blushed, hot with desire. Screw the hot tub.

"You are so beautiful," I whispered and leaned into her, as there was a knock at the door.

"Emma. Can I come in?" Ali asked.

"Yes. Just a minute," Emma answered and I couldn't read if she was disappointed or relieved. I kissed her forehead, then quickly grabbed a T-shirt from my bag and tossed it to her.

I opened the door and Ali stepped in.

"Sorry. I need my swimsuit." She scurried around the room.

"Do you want to get in the hot tub?" I asked again.

"Sure." She nodded and searched her bag then pulled out a bikini.

Not wanting her to lose the vibe between us, I winked. "Hurry."

THIRTY

Emma

Ali started to change. "Did I interrupt something?"

I chuckled. "It was probably a good thing you knocked." I fanned my face and smiled.

"Oh, well, then you're welcome."

"Ali, how far have you and Ryan gone?" I removed Zach's T-shirt only long enough to tie my suit around my neck, then slid it back on. It was his USC shirt, one of his favorites, and I knew right then and there, I wouldn't give it back.

"Well. Are you wanting details?" There was an embarrassed look to her face.

I shrugged. "Just wondering, I guess." They had dated about two months and Zach and I were going on five.

"It's kind of embarrassing to talk about," she stalled. "I guess if you compare it to baseball...you know the whole first base, second base thing?"

I nodded uncomfortably because Zach and I were hanging out on first with thoughts of stealing second but not really budging. I wanted to budge.

"We haven't made it home." She said under her breath.

I analyzed her face. Was she saying they'd made it to third? My body shuddered at the thought. "So third then?" I inquired nosily.

"Pretty much."

OK...she was holding out. "You *have* gone all the way!" I exclaimed.

She shook her head denying the accusation. "No, we haven't. I swear." Her soft words led me to believe she was telling the truth. "But." She bit her cheek.

I raised my brows...waiting...anticipating...jealous...

"He like—did the oral thing...kind of...down there." She closed her eyes obviously trying to hide her awkwardness.

I smacked her shoulder. "Oh My God! When?" I was so freaking jealous. Zach touched me down there once through my underwear for like ten seconds before I freaked out. I was never going to freak out again.

"Last night," she giggled. "Don't say anything."

"Please, you know me better than that. What was it like?" Curiosity was worse than the jealousy—maybe. My insides flipped thinking about it.

"Well...it was soft and Ryan...he..."

OOHH. She mentioned my brother's name. "OK. Stop. TMI. Let's go."

She giggled as we left the room.

Zach and Ryan were already submerged in the hot tub. Two seniors...two freshmen...the other girls were peeved and moved inside almost immediately to help Estelle's mom cook dinner. I-5 had been closed between Ashland and Shasta so we were staying one more night. Mom and dad weren't necessarily upset, but they weren't thrilled. When I spoke with them, they had asked to speak with Ms. Downard and she assured them she was here and adequately supervising us. I'd slept in the same bed as Zach last night so I questioned her judgment as to adequate supervision.

My parents had reason to trust us. Ryan and I had never given them reason not to, and I didn't intend to start now.

I tried to hide my surprise when I spotted the beer in Zach's hand—another good indicator of adequate supervision. I noticed earlier that everyone was drinking. Ali climbed in sitting next to

Ryan. Physically, my self esteem had never been the best and getting virtually naked in front of Zach was harder than I imagined.

"Nice shirt," he smiled referring to his USC shirt I wore.

"I'm keeping it," I threatened.

"You think?"

"I know!"

I dropped the shirt and swung my legs around. The outside temperature was near freezing with snow on the ground and I was in a bikini. The water was hot and it took my breath away as I immersed myself. When I slid into the seat next to Zach, my chin nearly went under. *Crap!* I was too little for the seat. Figures. Not big enough for the hot tub. When the older beautiful girls lounged in the water, they casually laughed and drank beer and I couldn't manage to keep my head above water.

"Come here, shorty." Zach witnessed my personal struggle and intervened. I'm sure he didn't want me to drown on his watch. He positioned me on his lap. Even better. I smiled. Maybe I should play the victim more often.

My legs rested between his and his leg hair tickled. He held me firmly around my waist and suddenly I was happy about the bikini—skin on skin contact.

Grant swaggered out the French doors with his newly plastered arm and a bottle of beer in the other hand. My eyes narrowed as I shot daggers in his direction.

"You are NOT getting in here." My words were angry.

He chuckled. "That's exactly what I'm doing. The doctors said with my concussion—that *you* caused—I should take it easy." He stepped in the water.

Zach readjusted his posture. "Don't blame her for your inabilities."

I offered Grant a smug smile after the remark.

"I will do no such thing." He slid in and his foot touched mine.

"Don't touch me!" I gritted through clenched teeth. Zach leaned forward and picked me up, pulling my knees in.

"Would you two stop? We're trying to relax over here," Ryan complained. "This is a hot tub not a boxing ring." He took a long swig of his beer. Ali rested under his arm.

Zach found my ear furthest away from Grant. "Do you want to clue me in on what caused this tiff?" He whispered. The steam coming off the water was difficult to see through.

"It would ruin the evening." My jaw was tight with anger. That didn't make him happy and he chugged his beer. "Are you supposed to be drinking?" I spoke softly.

"It's one beer and my PO is in Medford." He winked.

My mind jumped immediately to our deal. "So, if we're breaking rules?"

He laughed out loud and I dug my fingers into his side.

"Want to share with the group?" Grant inquired.

"NO!" Zach and I snapped in unison and smiled.

"Grant…go away…you're like a third wheel…look around." Naturally, at that moment, Claire made her appearance in a different bikini than before. I was certain there was less material to this one. I eyed Ali who inched closer to Ryan. Claire was the last chick Ryan had dated. God, the list was long and I hoped Ali stayed on it for a while. Claire floated into the water, her boobs three times the size of mine. I was glad I was down under.

Grant welcomed her with open arms and I thought I was going to puke. I nestled into Zach's arms and kissed his chin hoping to instigate a kiss. He watched me intently but didn't respond. My lips pressed against his and he kissed back emotionless. I moved closer to nibble his ear.

"Stop," he said. As I studied his face, I could tell he was serious and his eyes were stern.

"Why?" my voice cracked as rejection settled over me and in front of Grant no less. I prayed he didn't hear us. The bubbles blowing out of the jets were loud and that helped.

"Because you're doing it for him. And I refuse to give him the satisfaction." He wiped a trickle of sweat from my face.

"I'm sorry." My inadequate words didn't seem enough. I glared at Grant who seemed hell bent on destroying my night.

Grant and Claire were whispering and my eye roll didn't go unnoticed because Grant looked at me and laughed.

I jabbed my finger in his direction. "You're a jackass."

"Look, *Runt*. Just because you've kissed two boys in one day—just like you did yesterday—doesn't mean you need to get all worked up about it. Don't make me out to be the bad guy." His cocky grin was all it took.

I glanced at Zach and shook my head. "He's lying."

"Am I...lying? Choose your words wisely. We know how much dear sweet Em hates liars." His tone was sarcastic and hurtful.

"Meiers. You better back down." Zach threatened, his body tensed under the water.

Ryan spoke up. "Come on Grant. Knock it off."

"He totally tricked me." My voice was loud. "Blood was oozing from his *brainless* head and I was feeling all guilty. Then he was like 'oh Chloe, I've missed you and I need you to kiss me'...so I friggin did...like an idiot."

Zach's nostrils flared. His grip tightened on me. "It's so sad that you had to resort to tricking her."

Grant chuckled.

"Man, just stop. What are you doing?" Ryan asked his best friend.

Grant shrugged his shoulders and kissed Claire's cheek.

"And that's not the worst part. Do you want to tell him about the hospital?"

He rubbed his forehead. "They'd just given me some drugs." He laid his head back and rested it on the fiberglass pillow. "I was so out of it. What are you talking about?" he asked, and when everyone looked at me, he winked.

I surprised myself when I actually snarled and a growl rose in my throat.

"Let's go inside," Claire said in a seductive tone and emerged from the water, her body steaming.

Grant ran his hand up the back of her skinny thigh stopping shy of her butt cheek. She oozed out a suggestive laugh and gracefully climbed over the side—Grant in hot pursuit.

I let out a sigh of relief. "My apologies for my behavior," I said to all three of them. Ali smirked.

"What the hell happened between you two?" Ryan asked with a slight insinuation that maybe it wasn't all Grant's fault.

"He's just an ass," I responded and nestled closer to Zach.

His skin was cold above water and felt soothing to my hot face. I relaxed fully in his arms as his hand raked up and down my back.

Both boys drank another beer offering Ali and me small sips. The taste was repulsive just like before. I didn't like the feeling, but the older girls were drinking, and, well…they weren't legal either. After finishing his bottle, Ryan stood.

"We're out of here. Ali's a raisin," he said holding up the hand he held. She smiled and followed behind him.

"Goodnight, Em," she said.

"Hey. We need to be on the road by eight. Dad's order," Ryan added handing Ali a towel.

I nodded. "I'll be ready." A sudden sadness hit me about saying goodbye to Zach.

"Don't start thinking about it," he whispered reading my mind. In response, I kissed him to stop the thoughts from coming. His mouth seemed as hot as the water and a groan escaped my lips. After a short minute he pulled away.

"Do me a favor?" he asked softly.

"Anything." I couldn't think of a thing in this world that I wouldn't do for him. He swung me around so my back was against his chest.

"Promise me, you'll do it."

"I promise. You have my word."

"Lay your head back."

I did and I felt his collarbone behind my head.

"Close your eyes."

"They're already closed."

"Good, keep 'em closed."

I smiled. "I might fall asleep."

"Then I'll put you to bed."

I giggled.

"Now…don't move…just breathe and relax."

I took a long, deep, premeditated breath and let it out slowly.

"Good," he said. His mouth skimmed my ear as he spoke and his breath was warm. I felt his body slide forward forcing me to lay back. The water inched up the back of my neck. I was really starting to worry about falling asleep.

Then, he kissed the area right in front of my ear. My teeth bit down on my bottom lip as his tongue lightly touched my ear lobe. Both hands circled my waist, then skimmed down my outer thighs. *OH!*

His hands slid easily through the hot water over the tops of my thighs. My breathing was uneven and I gasped as he grazed my bikini bottoms. I jolted forward instantly bringing my legs down off his.

"Ah! Ah! Sit baaack." His arms wrapped my waist tugging my body back. "Put your legs back where they were."

"Zach. What…"

"You promised." He reminded me in a gentle tone.

But I was thinking more along the lines of 'promise me you won't get depressed tomorrow' 'promise me you'll marry me.' This hadn't even crossed my mind. I reluctantly put my legs back on his.

"Now. Close your eyes."

I swallowed hard. My lungs tried to keep up. "Closed." My heart raced at an uncontrollable speed.

"Relax."

"Trying! What if someone sees us?"

He was by my ear again. "It's dark out here and no one is looking. If they do, they're going to see the back of my head."

I took a slow breath. His hands were there again. First my stomach, then my thighs…a nibble on the ear…I rolled my head over and leaned back for a kiss, but he only pecked my lips then turned away.

"You're supposed to be relaxing, not thinking about me." It seemed like an order.

He rubbed across my suit and my stomach trembled. "I can't…" I moaned.

"You can. Please…just…calm…down. I won't hurt you." He caressed my stomach, up both arms, over my throat. My breathing stabilized for the moment. Why was this so hard for me? I didn't understand my body. It craved his hands…his touch… but my mind told me no.

He kissed my collarbone and I felt an overwhelming need to reciprocate so I moved my hands up his legs.

"No," he whispered. "You're being difficult. Please follow directions."

I smiled though I was sure he couldn't see and kept my arms still.

"Are your eyes closed?"

"Yes."

"Do you feel good?"

"Yes...but..."

"No buts. Just let me touch you. Trust me."

I could barely hear his words over the soft roar of the bubbles. I felt my shoulders relax against his chest and my arms floated down in the water next to his legs. I took a long, even breath as I tried to do what he wanted. His hands pressed tenderly against the skin on my stomach and I felt his pinky slide beneath the waistband of my swimsuit. I instinctively began to move but then calmed myself by trusting him. This was one of the hardest things I'd ever done—not turning my body toward him and forcing my lips to his.

His other hand began an upward motion and I knew he was going to touch my breast so I tried to prepare myself, hoping that my noises were contained. I called it. His left hand covered my bikini top on the right side. He had grazed over the top last night and cupped it the night we were busted by my parents. But this...this gentle massaging was not only incredible but second base, right? When his hand slid beneath the material, it was official. I smiled to myself and held my breath.

Before I could fully exhale, his hands ran over the material of my bottoms and down between my legs. My body ached and blood rushed to where his hands touched. I wanted to yell stop because I was scared of what I was feeling, but I knew he would and I wasn't sure I wanted him too. The material between him and my body was suddenly aggravating to me. I brought my hand up out of the water and rubbed my steamed face. Maybe I was unintentionally trying to cover it—embarrassed of the panting that always accompanied this. Could he hear me?

"Lay your head back," he whispered, though I hadn't realized it had come up. I did as he said and he nuzzled his nose into my hair. Then he kissed me softly, tracing the length of my neck with little pecks. I'd never been touched like this and I was suddenly afraid I'd never be again.

"Does it feel good?"

I nodded. I think.

And in that moment, I realized that now there was no material between his hand and me. Third Base!

"Zach. I'm scared…" I whispered as I grabbed his hand and gripped it tightly.

"Don't be," he comforted pulling his hands away. "Em. I need you to trust me and know that I wouldn't hurt you or do anything you don't want to. "

God I loved it when he said my name and this time, his voice was a rough whisper. I couldn't really move or speak.

"Being out here, I knew it couldn't…wouldn't get out of control. I didn't have to worry about it going too far. I just wanted you. You don't know how incredible it feels knowing you want me." I heard a low groan deep in his throat and I draped my hand behind his neck and pulled him to my mouth. His kiss was hungry; mine seemed weak…physically weak…I wasn't sure if my lips even puckered before I rested my head against him.

He massaged my fingers. "You're skin is shriveled up. Let's get you inside."

And, just like that we were up and out of the water.

THIRTY-ONE

Zach

When she stepped out of the bedroom in my USC shirt and her sweats, an instant smile spread across my face. She swam inside the gigantic shirt; it hung past her knees. She met my gaze, blood invaded her cheeks and she looked away. I didn't like that, but I assumed she was embarrassed about what happened in the hot tub.

Never had I been concerned about a girl's feelings before, but I wanted to assure this one that I was going nowhere. Less than an hour ago, she trusted me with her body. And given the way I had violated girls in the past, I didn't deserve her trust. Thank God she didn't know. For whatever reason, she saw the good in me. I wouldn't let her down.

Simply thinking about what happened in the hot tub, made my lower half react more than I wanted, and I was glad a down throw covered me. I patted the pillow next to my head as she approached the sofa. To my relief, she smiled. Her tiny little body curled up next to mine.

The bedroom doors were shut and things were quiet. This was our last night before returning to my own living hell without her. I'd barely made it two weeks without going insane and still had two months left. It had to be done or I'd lose her for good.

Her eyes were my best gauge for her emotions, but she wouldn't meet my gaze. I needed to see in them. I tried to remember this was new to her. No one had ever touched her before and that made my heart tingle.

I lay flat on my back on the oversized sofa, and I wrapped my arms around her, pulling her onto me. Her head rested on my chest and moved up and down with each breath. We watched Sportscenter on ESPN. The muted TV previewed upcoming BCS bowl games.

An anxious, unfamiliar feeling grew inside of me. Another foreign feeling when it came to Emma. Something was wrong. Usually after fooling around with a girl, I found them needy and pathetic for attention. But—she wouldn't even look at me. Roles had been reversed. I was the pathetic needy one! Had I pushed her too far? I only wanted her to know she could trust me. She was one girl I would never push into something she wasn't ready for. My hand instinctively rubbed her back, soothing her? Then I propped my head up with my other hand and purposefully cleared my throat. Finally! She looked up at me planting her chin in my chest. The little V between her eyes was there again, and this time I didn't know why. Shit! I didn't know what to say, and I turned back to Sportscenter.

"I love you," she spoke softly.

Shocked, I glanced away from the TV. "What? Where did that come from?"

She shrugged. "I don't know."

Coming from her, those three words were music to my ears. With my other hand, I ran my fingers through her tangled hair gently working them through. "And I love you baby girl," I whispered as my thumb traced over her eyebrows and softly caressed the V away. Her eyes closed.

"Zach?"

"Hmm?"

Her face turned red before the words came out. "Why did you..." she shook her head.

"Why did I what?"

"In the hot tub. Why..."

The corners of my mouth turned up. She liked me touching her? I stared at her patiently praying for that to be confirmed.

"What made you?" She lowered her head and buried her nose in my chest.

"What made me…what?"

She lifted her right foot and kicked my left shin. "Stop…you know. What made you do that?"

I hugged her tightly. "I'm not sure I had some grand plan to do *that* if that's what you mean."

"I wasn't saying that." She was embarrassed and laid her cheek against my chest. I think I hurt her feelings. "It was a stupid question."

I cradled her cheeks in my palms. "Haven't you ever heard no question is a stupid question?" I smiled. "I don't know why tonight, Emma. I wanted my touch to feel good. Did it? " I whispered.

"You just proved your theory wrong. *That* was a stupid question," she said biting her lip.

So it did feel good. Relief again.

"Maybe. But tell me anyway. Did me touching you feel good? " Her innocent eyes seduced me without her even realizing it.

She sighed. "Well, it was…nice."

"Nice?" I questioned a little too loudly because Brett stirred on the other sofa. "A picnic is nice, Emma. A walk in the park is nice. My boyfriend touching me… *nice?*" I asked sarcastically.

Suddenly, she rose all the way up on her arms and narrowed her eyes. "Are you kidding me? It was…it was…perfect."

I smiled on that one. "All right. Better."

She leaned in and brushed my lips with a kiss. "Zachary Dale Owens."

"Uh, oh. The full name," I chuckled.

"Sometimes…I feel stupid…and young and I feel like I don't deserve you and that you should be with someone who can offer you more."

What?? "Baby. What more could I possibly want?"

"Someone who knows what they're doing."

I positioned my body more upright. "Who's kidding who now? I don't care what you know or don't know. I enjoyed that just as much as you. Believe me."

188

She scratched her head and didn't say anything.

"Listen." I paused. "You wanted to know why tonight. I'll tell you, but you can't get mad."

She pouted and I could tell she was unsure if she could make that deal. "Kay."

I studied her beautiful face. "Every time you and I—touch. I feel so bad. When I touch you…" I stopped and looked at her. Her eyes were scared. I had to soften the words. "You…your body…it's response to me. I don't know if I scare you or if you're nervous."

"I'm not scared."

"Are you sure? Because your quivers measure an 8.4 on the Richter scale," I teased, grinning. Thank God she smiled.

"I'm not scared," she repeated. "I can't help it." She rested her nose on my sternum and I forced her chin up with my finger. When our eyes met she said, "I'm sorry."

"Emma. Baby. Don't be sorry. You have no idea what it does to me when you tremble."

"Well. I'm not scared. It…" She shook her head. "It drives me crazy."

"Crazy?" I asked.

"Wait! Not crazy crazy. Ryan has always said that guys don't like crazy. So, not crazy like that. A good crazy," She corrected quickly.

I understood, and a cheesy smile took over my face. "I *want* to drive you crazy. When I hear just the slightest whimper come from you, I swear to God, I…" Truth be told, I couldn't tell her what those whimpers did to me. They reminded me of her innocence. They reminded me of what I wanted to take from her. But I also knew that it had to be when she was ready. "I just needed to know that you weren't scared."

"Well. Maybe a little," she giggled. "But not of you, and I don't quiver *that* bad."

Her smile was beautiful and gentle and her teeth glistened even in the flash of the TV.

"Yes you do. And it is *so* cute."

"Whatever." She flipped her head over and refused to look at me.

THIRTY-TWO

Emma

He massaged my shoulders. "There is something you could do for me."

This was it. Of course he expected reciprocation. Duh! In twenty minutes, we cruised from first base to second and he tried to steal third before I stopped him. Though he did touch me, I wondered if I could consider that totally third? I wondered what he wanted...a blow job? I knew of girls who had done it and I had overheard Ryan talking about it with his friends but I didn't really know what to do. But, I would try. I'd do anything for Zach.

"What do you want done?"

"If I could have one thing tonight, it would be for you to tell me what happened with Grant."

My smile faded. Not at all what I expected. "Um, OK."

"Em, he upset you. That pisses me off."

"I don't want to think about that. And besides, he's off scroggin Claire somewhere."

He laughed loudly and Brett stirred again.

"Shh." I covered his lips with my index finger.

"Scroggin. Where did that word come from? And if he is, does that make you jealous?"

Was I jealous? "No. I am not jealous. Claire can have Grant."

"Please, tell me what happened."

I sighed. "After the incident on the mountain and the whole Chloe thing," I rolled my eyes, "he asked to see me at the hospital."

"Yes, I know. I was there. And he knew exactly what he was doing by doing that."

"Anyway. He told me he was going to back off. That he knew I liked you." I paused.

"And?"

I took a long deep breath. "He said that it drove him nuts that our—yours and mines—bedroom door was shut all night long and that he waited and waited for it to open last night. That he stayed up and watched it. He said he realized I was serious with you given that we'd slept together. SO…being the idiot that I am, I told him we hadn't *scrogged.*" I giggled then turned serious again.

"And his response to that?"

"Oh my God," I snarled. "He was ecstatic. Said he was still in the game."

Zach's jaw tightened.

"He called me a weirgen."

"A what?"

I shook my head. "It's a stupid name they came up with. If you still have your virginity by a certain age then you're weird. They combine it."

I felt his body tense below me. "Well. Some people can't help their ignorance and he appears to be one of them. *We will* be together someday. I'm sorry he upset you."

"Wow. You took that better than I thought." I yawned.

"You're exhausted. Try and sleep." He brushed his fingertips over the bridge of my nose.

"I don't wanna sleep."

"I know you don't but you should try."

I started thinking about tomorrow, the trip back, Grant, my parents and him leaving for college. Two months of misery left. As we lay there, my eyelids were heavy and I saw his smile before they close.

"What are *you* lookin at?" Zach's chest vibrated under my ear. I was so tired that I didn't open my eyes.

"Someone who didn't get any last night. Is that why you're layin' awake?"

Grant?

"Oh dude. I got exactly what I want right here." I felt Zach's arms tighten around me. Was I dreaming? His arms felt so good.

"Too bad you can't close the deal with her?"

"I could close the deal anytime I wanted. But we'll do it when it's right for her. Somethin' you wouldn't know anything about."

"Zach?" I spoke but was confused. It was impossible to open my heavy eyes.

"It's OK, Baby. Go back to sleep." He kissed the top of my head. I nestled into his underarm. "And you, go back in there to someone you can actually have."

"Bite me, Owens."

I felt Zach's chest shake with laughter.

"What's so funny?" I mumbled.

"Nothing," he whispered. "Just rest, baby."

THIRTY-THREE

Ryan woke us the next morning and he and Ali were showered, dressed and ready to go. The sun poured through the windows and I squinted up at Zach.

"Good morning," I said turning away from him afraid my breath might knock him out.

"Morning," he groaned.

His eyes looked puffy and red and I wondered how much he'd slept. I pushed myself upright.

"Hey, Zach," Ryan addressed. "Before I have to start dealing with her whiney ass." He nodded toward me. "If you want, she can ride with you. Let's just stop south of Ashland."

"Thanks, man." Zach smiled and they bumped fists.

"Two more hours!" I was thrilled. "I'm jumpin in the shower."

"Want company?" Grant asked.

Zach flipped around glowering at him. Ryan quickly stepped between them.

"You…" he pointed at Zach. "Go get ready to go."

"And You." His finger was inches from Grant's nose. "Friends or not…stop fuckin with my sister."

I left the room with Zach but watched and listened to Grant backtracking.

"I'm only kidding. She enjoys it as much as I do."

"I don't think so. She's pretty pissed at whatever you said or did yesterday." Ryan tossed his sports bag to the front door and grabbed Ali's from her. Zach rubbed his hand up and down my back.

"Your brother is good to you," he whispered.

I grinned.

Grant laughed at something and I listened again. "Fine. Runt's off limits but you have no ownership to Owens."

Ryan shrugged. "Go for it. Play at your own risk, though. He outweighs you by fifty."

"Nobody said it would be a physical fight," Grant added with a chuckle.

Zach wobbled his head. "Get your shower and let's get out of here."

Being in the Jeep again felt like coming home. We rode in silence for awhile, listening to the radio. He drove slower than normal and Ryan held pace with us. I wondered if Grant and Ryan were going at it in the truck.

Why was Grant so mad at me though? We had always been buddies. Best buddies long before Zach was around. I stared out at the trees edging the highway. Green mossy trunks with wild ferns growing around them were on each side of us.

Zach leaned over my lap and popped the glove box open and retrieved a small gold foil wrapped box.

"Merry Christmas." He handed the gift to me.

"Zach!" I pouted. "I didn't…"

He squeezed the back of my neck. "I didn't really either. Just open it."

My heart fluttered as I tugged at the tape. Outside of a couple of quick glances, he kept his eyes on the road. I opened the tiny box. Two men's class rings on a silver chain lay on a thin slice of cotton. Two? Puzzled, I peeked at him out of the corner of my eye. I lifted the chain and the two silver rings rested in my palm—one, with a topaz from his high school in San Francisco and the other with an emerald, from Ashland High. Emerald was my birthstone and my eyes met his.

"Two?"

Holding the wheel with one hand, he picked up the chain with the other. "My heart, or at least some of it, is here." He pointed to the topaz ring engraved with his old school name. "So it holds my gemstone. Another piece of my heart is here, NOT at Ashland High, but here…" he patted my chest where a necklace would hang. "…So it holds your gemstone. You can have one or both or whatever you want."

I tried hard to determine what I had done to be blessed with him. And I tried harder to come to grips with the fact that I would probably lose him. It didn't really matter how much I loved him or how much he loved me…we were doomed to fail. And the brunt of the blame would be shoved his way because of his age. I could hear them now—the mean things they'd say. 'He's outgrown her.' 'He has to go away.' 'He's in college now.' The voices made me ache.

"May I have them both?" I'd never give them back if he said yes.

"I didn't order them for me." He winked.

"I've decided something," I said fastening the clasp around my neck and admiring the rings in the mirror behind the visor.

With brows raised, he asked, "about?"

"About you and Ashland. You've shortchanged my city and Oregon. It's beautiful here and there is so much to see—just like in *your* city. Maybe you'll love it so much you'll want to stay."

A deep rough laughter filled the inside of the Jeep. "They're not comparable and I won't stay."

I tried to hide my growing pout and disappointment by examining my fingernails and digging at a hangnail. My hair fell covering my face so he couldn't see my hurt. He brushed my hair back tucking it behind my ear.

"You took that wrong," he said gently.

I rolled the rings between my fingers. "I know you will leave here…leave me." I tried to sound brave like I could handle it but my voice cracked on the last word. He took my hand.

"I'm not going to lie to you, Em. You are right…on one of those."

"Where *are* you going? To college, I mean."

He shrugged. "USC offered me an academic scholarship…or possibly KU."

"KU?"

"The University of Kansas."

"KANSAS!?" We weren't talking hours away—but days.

He smiled. "My grandma and grandpa live in Lawrence, Kansas. My dad is a KU alum. They've offered me academic scholarships too."

"I guess I didn't realize you were so smart." I was the smart one. Never earned a B in my life.

He laughed. "Thanks a lot. I have 4.2, missy." He bragged.

"I figured you'd play sports."

"I'm not good enough to go Division one in sports."

"Ryan is?"

He laughed again. "Emma. Ryan is an exceptional football player. He has that opportunity. I could play Division two…maybe."

"But they're so far away." I couldn't begin to hide my agony at the thought.

He tugged my head toward him and kissed my hair. "I'm still looking. We're not going to spend the next six months worried about this either. Got it?" He pursed his lips and his brows shot up on his forehead.

He veered right onto an exit ramp of a rest stop. A State trooper was talking to some homeless people as we drove past.

I threw my arms around his neck before he'd even pulled over. "Will you at least talk to me at school?"

"Emma. Your father asked me to do this and I'd rather have two months of a break than no future at all. Don't you see that?"

"Yes. But, how will they know?"

He drew in a long breath as he parked in a spot and turned to me—"Is that what you want? You want me to risk us?"

I shrugged. "Maybe," I said selfishly, reaching for my door handle. When I got out, he was there. I stepped into his arms.

"Don't..." he started, then paused. "Nevermind."

"Don't what? What were you gonna say?"

"I was gonna say, don't cry. But, you don't. Cry, that is."

I smiled proudly. "It takes a lot of effort some times."

His brows pulled together. "Effort? Why?"

Was he serious? I shoved him playfully. "Guys don't like girls who cry, silly."

For the longest time, his eyes studied mine, looking, waiting for something. "You're serious?"

"Yeeaah…why?"

His expression softened. "Who told you that?"

"Ryan, I guess. All of them have. The guys."

Zach shook his head and closed his eyes. "I'm afraid you have been misinformed on that one."

HONK! The truck horn startled me.

Suddenly, he lifted my chin and kissed me tenderly. I was thankful his arms were around me as my legs weakened.

"Go. They're waiting."

He hugged me one last time. "We'll be together soon." He walked me to the truck.

As I crawled into the backseat of the truck, I saw Grant walking back from the restroom with Ryan. Zach winked at me and headed back to his Jeep. Ali had just wokeup in the front seat and seemed pretty groggy. I wondered how late they'd been up. I was certain they didn't have as good of time as I did. We were only about twenty minutes from home.

I laid my head back, bummed that our time was over when I heard a thud against the side of the truck. My eyes popped open and Ali flipped around and looked at me. Ryan's door was open and she peeked out the side.

"Oh, shit, Em!" She shouted and bolted from the front seat.

I whipped around to look out the back window and Zach had Grant by the neck in a headlock. I leapt to the door and nailed the front of my head on the doorframe of the truck, shooting myself backward. Jarred and disoriented, I forced myself upright as stars speckled in front of me.

"Zach," I said not sure if it even came out. Squirming from behind the seat, I got to my feet, woozy as I fought for balance.

"No, Zach." I still wasn't sure the words found my lips. My head throbbed as I stumbled to the back of the truck where Ali stood petrified . Ryan grabbed Zach's arms pulling him off Grant.

"Zach. Stop!" Ryan gritted through his teeth, yanking him backward and Zach let go of Grant, who slumped to the cement then staggered resiliently to his feet. He shook his hair from his eyes and glowered at Zach. Suddenly, Grant lunged toward Zach, whose back was to him as he was talking to Ryan. Grant rammed him at full speed forcing Zach to the ground. Zach's cheek bashed against the cement. I screamed as Grant reared his fist back then brought it down pummeling Zach's other cheek. I ran toward Grant but couldn't run straight.

"Get off of him!" I yelled hitting his back with my fist, sweat dripping into my eyes blurring my vision.

"Em, get back," Zach shouted and Ryan pushed me off.

My equilibrium was off and I lost my balance tumbling to the ground.

"Emma?" Ali was at my side. I tried to look past her to see if Zach was okay. Zach was now on top of Grant.

"Emma!!" Ali yelled again. "You're bleeding. There's blood everywhere. RYAN!"

I could hear her muffled scream as things grew foggy. As my body leaned toward the cement, I saw fear register in Zach's eyes. Then from out of nowhere, a highway patrol officer was on top of him. I closed my eyes.

THIRTY-FOUR

I squinted, protecting my eyes from the bright sunrays as I pried my eyes open. Ali was holding my hand and crying. I was lying in the bed of the truck. Ryan's truck I think. Ryan's cell phone was stuck to his ear and I moved to sit upright. My head throbbed and the sky moved all around me.

"Emma, stay down," Ali directed and Ryan jerked his head around.

"Let me call you back. She's awake," Ryan said and slid into the bed. "Runt. What happened? No one knew how you hurt your head."

"Where's Zach?" I didn't care about my head.

Ryan gripped me by the shoulders. "The officer is talking to him and Grant." Ryan's eyes held an unspoken message. He was worried about the same thing that suddenly filled my mind.

I rotated my head to the highway patrol car and Zach and Grant stood at the trunk of the car with their wrists handcuffed behind their backs. A shiver rippled through me as I looked at them. This was all because of me.

"Ma'am. How are you feeling?" I spun my head toward the voice and another officer stood next to the truck. He was tall and thin and young. An additional highway patrol car was parked to the side of the truck with its lights flashing. I tried to remember that but didn't.

"Ma'am? Are you OK?"

I blinked a couple of times trying to make it make sense. "Yes. I'm OK." The officer walked over to talk to his partner who was with Zach and they glanced over at me. Zach hung his head. After a minute or two, the officer walked our way.

"Sir. Here's your license and registration. Thank you for your cooperation." He spoke directly to Ryan. I heard a siren in the distance.

"Get back against the car." The voice was threatening.

I turned and watched Zach shaking his head and back stepping. "I just would like to check on my girlfriend, please. She's hurt."

"Against the car, now." The officer pointed.

"Can I go over there?" I asked the officer with us.

"No, Ma'am. You have a head wound and you've lost some blood. Did one of these gentlemen hit you?"

"NO!" I was mortified at the thought. Wait. How did I hit my head? "The TRUCK!" I blurted the words out remembering it. "I was getting out of the truck and I hit my head on the door." The officer looked at me skeptically. The siren was getting closer. I wasn't sure he believed me.

The officers were conferring again and I watched the tall one move to Grant and unlock his cuffs. Grant massaged his wrists and said something to Zach, who nodded. The officer was talking to Zach now. An ambulance entered the rest stop and stopped at the foot of the truck. Ryan shot me a hesitant look as he bit the side of his cheek.

My eyes darted toward Zach who was being led to the police car. The officer protected Zach's head as he bent to sit him in the backseat.

"NO!" I shrieked so loudly I felt faint. Zach's eyes found mine and the grimace on his face hurt more than my head could ever hurt. Tears swelled in my eyes. "Grant! Please! Tell them. Tell them he didn't do anything."

"I did, Em." Grant seemed sad.

"No. You have to tell them. Please, Grant."

"Ma'am. We need you to calm down so we can treat your head." A female paramedic climbed into the bed.

"Please sir, where are you taking him?" I yelled at the officer.

"We're just questioning him," he replied as he shut the car door.

"But he didn't do anything." The tears were streaming down my cheeks. My heart felt as if it would explode.

"Ma'am?" The paramedic asked, "you need to calm down."

"RYAN! I'm fine. Don't let them take me. Please."

"Em. Mom and Dad will meet you at the hospital and Ali and I'll come straight there."

I looked at Ali who was still crying.

"Ryan, please. Let me ride with you. I'll go to the hospital," I begged and promised at the same time.

He squeezed my hand. "I can't. They said since you're a minor that you have to be transported. There was a lot of blood, Em."

"We aren't going to hurt you but your head needs sutures," The paramedic explained.

"Stitches and an ambulance…it doesn't make sense. I'll go, I promise. But why can't my brother drive me?" I asked more calmly.

She patted me in a condescending manner. "Because you've lost blood and you apparently lost consciousness. Please, don't make us restrain you, sweetheart." Her tone was soothing and I surrendered.

Before I knew it, I was lying on the gurney. I didn't want to do this. I sat up and fought to see Zach. The car hadn't moved and his eyes were on me, his fist resting against his mouth. I quickly flashed the I love you hand sign and he flashed it back. The sadness in his eyes was unbearable. Then, the doors to the ambulance closed.

THIRTY-FIVE

ZACH

When the doors on the ambulance shut, so did the door to my heart. The time had come to end this. I was poison to her. Nothing good could come out of me staying. I would hurt her when I left anyway, so if I stay it's only delaying the inevitable. This commitment thing was overwhelming and she deserved someone to treat her right.

Ryan, Grant and Ali piled into the truck and followed the ambulance. The ache in my chest as they pulled away was nearly unbearable and like nothing I'd ever felt. I didn't like that. I hated it. Ryan would take care of her though. I forced myself not to think about Grant. *Dick.* How did he find out?

The ambulance siren faded. The heater in the Trooper's cruiser was blowing on high and the police radio wouldn't shut up. I banged my forehead on the headrest repeatedly wishing it was me in that ambulance. How the hell did she get hurt? The blood, her face…the images haunted me. I needed her out of my head.

The officer with the stale breath opened my passenger door and helped me out by lifting my tricep.

"I'm sorry, Son. Just had to get an all clear of no pending warrants given your probation. Everything looks good but we will send a report to your PO in Medford."

I closed my eyes, hearing the key unlock the cuffs. The outside air felt refreshing.

"So, I'm free to go?" I asked rubbing where the silver had circled.

He nodded. "Yes, Sir. And just so you know, she made it to the hospital. Still conscious."

Knowing she was safe, in good hands, a relief I'd never known flooded over me.

"Thank you," I said, giving the officer a nod.

"Go to her. She was pretty upset with us for keeping you."

When I got in the Jeep, I could smell her and as soon as I brought the Jeep to life, I knew exactly where I was going. At the very least, she deserved a fair goodbye. Besides, as soon as Grant told her what he knew, she'd end it with me. Either way, we were over; so for now, I'd go to her.

THIRTY-SIX

EMMA

The look on my parents' face was of sheer terror as the paramedics wheeled me into the emergency room. I felt terrible for their worry. My mom looked ten years older as she approached us with my dad keeping pace behind her.

"Emma!" she groaned in desperation.

"Mom. I'm totally fine. I have a small cut on my head," I explained.

"Oh, honey. When Ryan called, you were unconscious."

"She came right to after that," Ryan said running in from the hallway. I was relieved he was there. "She's a tough sister."

My dad stepped to the bed. "How did you hit your head on the truck?"

"Well? Grant…"

Ryan cut me off. "Dad. I told you. We were swapping seats at a rest stop and she jumped up quickly and hit her head. It happened so fast. Knocked her silly. There was an OHP officer there and he thought we should call an ambulance because of the blood. You should have seen Em. She was ticked!" He laughed and winked.

"Please," I started where he left off. "An ambulance? It was so not necessary." Anything to get my folks' mind off of what happened. "How does my head look?"

"Honey. The blood," My mom whispered.

Why did everyone keep saying that? I glanced down at my shirt and saw drips of blood all over the front of it. Hmm. I hadn't noticed before.

"Bring her into this room," A woman in scrubs ordered pulling back a curtain. The door read TRAUMA. This was hardly traumatic. A bright light flipped on overhead and it hurt my eyes. Suddenly three or four people were hustling around me. One washed my forehead and hairline. A stabbing pain was suddenly there as they poked and pulled then warned me of the shots to deaden it. I kept my eyes closed as they worked; the stinging nearly unbearable. The medicine seemed to make my heart race and a funny taste filled my mouth. They talked to me as they worked which was nice. The smell of whatever they used churned my stomach.

I heard my dad's deep voice in the hallway and I heard Ryan. I closed my eyes, and, for a moment, I dreamed I heard Zach. I ached for him and wondered where he was at this moment. Why would they have taken him in? What had started the fight? Grant made the deal with my brother that I was off limits. SO…I figured Grant said something to Zach. The nurse came in and examined the seamstress's performance. Evidently, a job well done though I wasn't allowed to leave. Ryan stepped into the room. Mom and Dad were completing paperwork.

"How ya doin?" he asked with both hands in his pockets.

"Worried about Zach."

"Grant knows. The officer said something about him being on probation. That's what was with the further questioning. He doesn't know why and I played dumb."

"Do you know where he is?"

"No. We followed you here."

"Where are Grant and Ali?"

"In the truck. Grant's face is pretty whacked. None of us thought we needed to address that in front of Mom and Dad or anybody else."

A smile touched the corners of my mouth as I thought about Grant. It wasn't fair and it wasn't nice but it served him right. "So. What happened??"

Ryan shrugged. "Who knows. Grant got an ass whoopin' though." Ryan smiled on that one.

"Was Zach hurt?" The words burned my mouth. I would rather die than have him hurt.

"Sis, he can hold his own. Don't worry about him." His cell phone rang and he muted it then walked to the hall. I laid my head back and closed my eyes but kept picturing Zach in the back of the highway patrol car. His eyes haunted me. I rubbed my neck and instantly realized my necklace was gone. Oh my God!

"Ryan!" My voice was an urgent whisper. No response.

"Ryan!" Louder this time. Nothing. I recounted my steps. Out of the Jeep, into the truck, out of the truck and into the ambulance. Where could it be? It made me sick to think about the chain breaking and losing…I couldn't go there. Where was everyone? Everything seemed so quiet. My heart beat steady in my chest and I could even feel the pulsing in my wound. It was certainly throbbing and seemed to coincide with my heart. I heard someone running in the hallway. It made me sad as I thought about sad scenarios—stroke, heart attack, car accident and the running slowed then stopped. I heard the footsteps come into the room and I opened my eyes.

"Zach!" Nothing could have prepared me for the shock of his face. His lip was swollen and a line of dried blood curved down the bottom lip. Under his eye by his cheekbone, his skin was scraped and raw. Blood ran just below the surface of his skin. I rolled my lips together unsure what to say. In an instant, he was at my bedside taking me into his arms.

"Oh." He breathed as if he'd held his breath underwater for as long as he possibly could stand. He stroked my hair and I heard his heart now beating beneath my ear, pounding under his shirt. "I…am so…sorry." His voice cracked and I pulled away to study his face. Why was he sorry?

His eyes held unwarranted pain and I touched his face. He grabbed my hand and kissed it and tucked it in to his chest.

"Why are you sorry?" I asked.

His eyes closed and he wrestled with what he wanted to say. "I should have controlled my anger. I let him get to me." He paused. The gravity in his tone matched his hardened eyes. "You got hurt because of me." His tightened jaw defined his cheekbones but I didn't like his clenched fists.

"What did he say to you?"

He shook his head. "It doesn't matter. What matters is that you're OK." He gently pushed my hair back and examined the stitches. "Seven, huh?" He pressed his lips against my forehead and I inhaled his scent.

"I can't find the rings. They were around my neck and now they're gone. I can't lose them." I'm sure I sounded panicked. As if trying to calm me, he rubbed my back.

"I'll find them," he said his voice barely audible.

"What happened with the police?"

He answered but wouldn't look at me. "No charges. Thank God. But he's going to report the incident to my PO."

"PO?"

"Probation officer."

"What's going to happen?"

He shrugged and didn't seem to care. Something was wrong. I could tell. Suddenly my dad walked through the door. I pulled out of Zach's arms. He noticed and faced my father, sliding his hands into his pockets.

"Daddy. Please..."

My dad held up his palm to shush me. "Zach called and asked for permission to be here, Emma. I'm not upset. But the doctor's discharged you."

Finally! I swung my legs off the bed and grinned.

"Zach. Would you be willing to bring her home?" My dad asked giving Zach's face a thorough glance over, as he left the room.

"Yes, sir." Zach smiled, but the happiness didn't touch his eyes. The hair on my neck to stood on end.

The Jeep ride home was uncomfortably quiet. I didn't know what to say and Zach said nothing. He put my hand to his mouth repeatedly and kissed my fingers but the words never came. Though I knew he wasn't angry with me, I couldn't put my finger on what upset him. The probation issue was what I came up with. But I wasn't sure and curiosity ate at me. Could he possibly conceive how much I loved him?

In the driveway, he shifted into park but didn't cut the engine. My heart fell into the pit of my stomach. He wasn't coming in. He wasn't moving at all. I finally turned to him.

"You OK?"

He slowly nodded. "*I'm* fine."

I'd never seen his eyes expressionless. His beautiful brown eyes were my personal window to his soul and he wouldn't look at me. Was he implying I wasn't fine? Because I was. Seven stitches. Big deal.

"Come on. I'll walk you up." And just like that, he was shutting his door and around the Jeep at mine. Wasn't it just this morning that he'd given me his class rings? And last night that I'd slept in his arms all night long? I tried desperately to muster up courage and security. He wanted me to feel secure in us. I was attempting it but failing.

Once at the front door, I heard him release a long breath and his eyes flickered to mine for a short second. Then he gripped me tight. My cheek pressed hard against his chest and goose bumps crawled across my skin. Don't leave. Don't leave. Please just hold me forever. I wasn't sure I could breathe without him. Then I felt his embrace release and I held my own breath so my tears wouldn't betray me. His palms were under my jaw lifting my chin and his mouth came down to mine. There was the air I needed to survive another day blowing through my mouth and into my lungs. By the time I had gathered my thoughts enough to return the kiss, he was done and pulled away.

I think my heart stopped. He didn't say goodbye and he didn't wave. He abandoned me on my front porch assuming I could make it in the house on my own. I wasn't so sure and the tears fell.

No one else was home yet. I went straight upstairs and drew some bath water pouring beads into the tub. I threw my clothes into the hamper and pulled my hair up into a clip. The mirror fogged over from the steam and I wiped it with a towel. That's when I saw the image Zach had seen…my face…streaked with dried blood. My mouth fell open and I was horrified. I was nothing short of Carrie covered in pig blood at her prom. It all made sense now, everyone kept saying 'the blood' and I thought they over exaggerated…but they hadn't.

I turned on the water as hot as tolerable and scrubbed at my face, digging with my fingernails at the dried blood. It was matted in my hair and I raised a clump up. I'd had no idea I'd bled this much. The water in the tub was scalding, hotter than the hot tub had been. The heat of the water pricked my skin and was barely tolerable. For some reason I felt like I deserved to be punished—burn and wash away my selfishness. Zach was, after all, defending my honor with Grant. And through all of this hadn't I led Grant on to make him believe maybe there was a chance with me? None of this was Zach's fault.

Zach was so good to me—Grant too for that matter. Perhaps I didn't deserve either. Sweat formed across my brow and I was too hot. I thought about the night in the hot tub. How great it had been to feel his touch. I'd read so many times how a girls first time with sex was nothing like the movies or books portrayed. That it was actually painful, or worse—uneventful. I couldn't imagine it that way with Zach. I wondered if our first would be what I fantasized about.

I heard noise downstairs and decided to drain the water. I remained there—soaking—till the water was half gone. I towel dried, darted to my room, then threw on some sweats and a sweatshirt. The clock read 1:30. One day before Christmas break was over. One afternoon and night to endure before seeing him again. Someone tapped on my door.

"Come in."

Ryan opened the door. "Hey, Runt. How you feelin?"

I shrugged and didn't think he cared to hear how miserable I was. "OK."

He moved closer to the bed with a suspicious grin.

"What?" I asked.

He held his fist out to his side, then something fell from his fist when he opened it but dangled from his finger. My rings! I lunged up and threw my arms around his neck.

"Oh Ryan. Thank you! I didn't know where... thank you." I retrieved them from his finger and held them to my heart.

"I didn't know if you wanted mom and dad to see them or not. They know Zach was at Shasta, though," He warned.

"They mad?"

He shrugged one shoulder and shook his head. "I don't think so. I think you getting hurt helped."

Who'd of thought? I laughed to myself.

I crossed my legs and lay back against my pillows. "Ry. What did Grant say to Zach to piss him off?"

He shrugged. "I tried to get it out of both of them. But neither would budge. They ain't talkin." He scratched his head and I could tell he was mulling over something. I waited. Then he pulled a pillow under his chin. He was ready. "Em." OK, he never called me Em. "Have you and Zach...you know?"

I yanked a pillow from behind my head and hit him with it. "That's none of your business." I blushed. "Have you two?"

"That's none of your business," he mocked me in a girly voice. "Ali wants to."

"And you don't?" I asked in disbelief.

"Hell yeah. But she's fifteen."

"AND won't be sixteen until next September," I added.

"Thanks." He tossed a small pillow up in the air and caught it.

"You're leaving in August. I know you too well. You're not going to want a girl back here to worry about." I tried to rationalize.

He stared at me, maybe surprised by my opinion of him. "You don't think I could do it?"

"Ryan. It's not a dare. Of course you could do it. Do you like her that much?" Now I was surprised.

Wrinkles formed across his forehead as he thought. "I like her. She's fun. What about you and Zach? What happens when he leaves?"

Bile rose in the back of my throat as he even said the words. "I don't know." Keep it brief. Don't think about it, I told myself.

"So why haven't you two done the deed?" He blurted. "Not that I would encourage it."

"I'm fifteen too, remember." I kicked him in the gut with my heel.

"And you don't want to?" he smiled.

"Hell yeah!" I repeated his words and we both laughed. "But he won't."

"That's good." Ryan stood and walked to the door. "I know there's a double standard but hold out as long as you can." He winked and pulled the door closed.

Downstairs, my parents were fixing Sunday dinner together. Odd. Not that we didn't have Sunday dinner every Sunday…but it was usually mom cooking while dad crashed in front of the TV and watched football. I knew it was bowl time and for him to miss that was out of character.

"What's up?" I asked casually.

Both of them looked up and smiled. "Emma. You look better." My mom kissed my cheek as I peeked in the pot. "We're making your favorite."

"Yum. Chicken and noodles, sound good. No football, Dad?"

"Ducks play at three."

Well, there you go. Ten minutes and counting.

"How's your head, sweetheart?" Dad asked.

"I kind of have a headache," I complained hoping pity might come my way.

"Zach didn't stay?" My dad asked like he was shocked.

I raised my eyebrows and it hurt so I tried a different facial expression. "Could he have?" My heart picked up it's pace.

They eyed each other over the steam coming up from the boiling chicken. This was good…they were thinking about it. "You talk to her." My dad said. Oh crap.

"Emma. Sit down."

I was screwed.

"Your father and I have given a lot of consideration to how well you handled your grounding from Zach. We monitored your texts and *he* complied one hundred percent. You tried to text him the first night but not again after that. You both seemed to take us seriously." She glanced at my dad who answered her with a nod.

"Two other things. First, his probation. We believe Zach is a good kid, which brings me to my second issue. We will allow you to start seeing him again, here at the house…"

"Thank you. Thank you. Thank you. Thank you…." I whispered under my breath.

My father cleared his throat. "On one condition."

"Anything." I was so relieved. I itched to bolt from the chair and go call him. "What is it?"

"You will meet with Dr. Erickson to have your first womanly exam and get on the birth control pill," Mom added. It didn't sound like it was open for discussion.

"We aren't having sex." I covered my face with my hands.

My mom chimed in again. "No. Not yet. And you know we have taught you that it is best to wait. The bible references saving yourself till marriage and we believe that is best. BUT…your father and I were also young once and we know when hormones are involved that it is difficult to make a rational decision. We'd rather you abstain. And being on the pill does not protect you from disease. We're not condoning sex. But we think this is a good idea."

"I have no plans to have sex right now. But I hear what you're saying and I'd be willing to do that." I wrinkled my nose at the thought of the doctor's appointment.

"I'll make the appointment tomorrow." Mom added.

"OK." My legs bounced up and down. "Can I call Zach?"

"Yes." My father answered. And I ran to the phone. It was four.

The phone rang six times at his house. No answer. I tried his cell. Three rings. My heart pounded.

"Hello?"

Relief. "Zach?"

"Am I going to be in trouble for answering this call?"

"No." I wondered if he heard the excitement in my voice. "Not anymore at least."

"What do you mean?"

"It's over. My grounding…our grounding." I giggled.

I heard a deep breath. "You're kidding."

"I kid you not. Can you come over?" I wanted his mood to pass with the grounding. But I didn't have a good feeling.

"Um. I don't know. Let me talk to my folks when I get home."

"Where are you?"

"At the school. Lifting."

He'd gone to the school to lift weights? "Oh. OK."

"I'll give you a call in a bit."

"OK." I agreed. "Bye."

The line disconnected and my stomach hurt. Fear pulsed through me and I didn't know why. No. I did know why—he was being distant…aloof and I didn't know why.

THIRTY-SEVEN

The longest two hours of my life ticked past as I waited for the phone to ring. It was after 6:00 and Zach hadn't called back. I pushed my chicken and noodles around in the bowl and managed to get by without taking a real bite. Mom was meeting a buyer and dad never let her go alone on a night time showing so they were leaving, which worked out better for me. I could pout on my own with no one else around.

Around 6:30, I curled up on the sofa with a throw and flipped channels. My heart started beating when my phone vibrated in my hand. It was him.

"Hello?"

"Em?"

"Yes?"

"May I still come by?" Assurance settled over me as his words came out.

"Sure," I chirped out too quickly.

"I'll be by in a little while." He hung up.

I didn't like his tone. What was going on? It had to be his probation. Something had happened.

I opened the door casually when he arrived and wanted to give him a hug but he showed no inclination of returning the favor. So, we sat next to each other on the sofa. Calm on the outside, I was flipping out on the inside. His arms were crossed across his chest and his left ankle rested on his right knee.

"How are you feeling?" he finally asked.

"Totally fine." I lied a little because my head still hurt. "A little embarrassed."

"Why is that?" Still no eye contact. In fact, no contact period.

"Why didn't you tell me I had blood all over my face?" I playfully poked him in the side.

He offered a slight smile. "You looked fine." He studied the TV.

"How were the weights?" I prodded.

He nodded. "Good."

"And your folks?"

"Good, as well."

I tried to suppress the anger that was growing inside of me but I was fighting a losing battle. What the hell? My breathing bordered erratic.

"What is going on?" I asked irritably.

He acted innocent. "With what?"

"With you. You won't touch me. You won't look at me. What did I do? Oh, and I found the rings." My words were pained and I pulled the necklace out from under my shirt to show him.

"Yeah. Ryan said he had them." He paused. "Emma. I'm not going to make out with you right here. This is where we got busted last time." His words were sharp.

"I'm not saying we have to make out. But a simple hug, hand touch, kiss or even a little eye contact would be nice." My voice cracked and I could now check off the eye contact—done. His troubled eyes met mine. "Talk to me."

"Where are your folks?"

"Mom had a 7:00 showing." It was just now seven.

He nodded and pulled me over onto his lap then nestled his nose under my ear rubbing it up and down the side of my throat. It tickled. "Em. I need to tell you something."

"You wanna break up?"

He pursed his lips and glared at me. "Seriously?"

He twisted my hair around one of his fingers lightly pulling it to his nose and smelling it. "I'm sorry." If that wasn't it, what?

I searched his eyes for answers.

"I need you to know I've never been in a relationship like this. With someone like you. You make me feel good about who I am. What I am to you. You make me laugh." He smiled. "I've never really taken a relationship seriously and now this one has blown me away. I think about you all the time. Today…" He struggled to get the words out and kept rubbing his forehead. "That was worst thing I've ever been through. You were hurt and I couldn't get to you. When you left in that ambulance…" his words trailed off.

It hurt me just watching him agonize through this.

"Zach. I'm fine."

"I know." his voice was soft and he pulled me into his chest. "I love you so much. Please. Please don't ever forget that. No matter what."

"I won't forget it. Did you forget how much I love you?" His arms wrapped me so tight; it robbed my lungs of air. Why did it feel like he was saying goodbye? When he released me, I cupped his lower jaw in my palms. "So why are you being distant tonight? And why didn't you come sooner?"

He lay back against the sofa still fingering my hair. "I worry if I'm right for you."

My body instantly stiffened. "What?"

"Forget I said that." He was backtracking.

"No. What do you mean right for me?"

He blew his mouth up like a puffer fish. "You are innocent and sweet and pure and…well…I'm none of those and you got hurt today because…"

"STOP! I got hurt because I'm a klutz. I hurt myself. You had nothing to do with that."

"But you wouldn't have jumped out of the truck had I not punched Grant." He rubbed both eyes with his palms.

"You have to stop beating yourself up. I am fine and I'm going to be fine. As long as you are OK and we're together. Promise me you aren't thinking about walking."

He twisted his neck till our eyes met. "I promise. *I'm* not going anywhere." Then he leaned in and kissed me and my thoughts hung on his slight insinuation.

The next morning was cloudy. I missed the brightness and warmth of the sun. I was back to riding to school with Zach and decided to wear my faded jeans with holes in the knees and my Lake Tahoe sweatshirt. Dabbing a touch of perfume on my neck, I hurried down the stairs to watch for him.

Like clockwork, he was on time and drove straight to school. Though he still didn't seem quite himself, I thought back to our conversation last night and managed to smile. Plus his beautiful rings dangling from my neck brightened my mood.

He kissed me goodbye and we both headed to first hour. US Government was boring as usual and the class was discussing our mock election.

In Advanced English, our test took nearly the whole hour and I was ready and waiting for the bell to ring for Algebra.

I took the stairs two at a time and turned up the last flight and ran smack into Grant. His eye was nearly swollen shut and the white of his eye looked raw and bloody. I swallowed hard and stared at the purplish black bruise around his eye. He didn't look away in fact his gaze was so intense I wanted to look away but felt compelled to maintain the eye contact.

"Grant." My voice broke midway through his name. Even though I was mad at him he was one of my best friends and he was hurt…physically and emotionally. I saw the pain in his eyes and I was responsible. I'd hurt him. My chin trembled and I fought hard to keep back the tears. They came anyway. His left index finger swiped one off my cheek and he flipped a blonde curl out of his eye.

"I'm sorry," I whispered.

He finally broke the eye contact and looked at the stair he was on. "I'm sorry too." His voice was sincere and I knew he meant it.

"What did you say that made him so mad?" I was almost too afraid to ask. I didn't like the sound of the chuckle deep in his throat.

"That's his to tell you, and he *will* tell you." Then the bell rang and we were late.

"Tell me what?" There *was* something.

"Nope. Not my job." He tugged at my sleeve. "Come on. We're already going to be in trouble."

"Ms. Hendricks and Mr. Meiers so lovely of you to join us. Please have a seat and I'll see you both after school as well." Mr. Bowman smiled then turned back to the smartboard.

Zach was in his normal seat and I slid in to my empty one. Grant sat across from him. I opened my book and got started on the assignment. It was hard to concentrate on linear equations when I knew Zach's eyes were boring into my back. I slid a piece of paper out of my notebook.

I want to know what Grant said to you.

I passed the paper back.

When?

Before the fight.

I heard a deep breath as he read.

Why?

I was getting angry.

Because!

I tossed him the paper.

Because why? Is that why you two were late?

I watched Mr. Bowman.

Stop stalling. Just tell me. He will…if you don't.

I heard him laugh under his breath and I felt annoyed.

No he won't. But you can try to get it out of him in detention since you'll be with him. Not happy about that

I'm getting angry. Tell me now what he said.

I threw the paper this time.

Later. Now is not the time.

At the end of the hour, I wadded the paper up and walked to the trashcan. On the way back over, if looks could kill…Zach would be toast. The bell rang and I sprung out of my chair. I almost expected his laughter to continue but his face was serious and his eyes met mine. He was doing it again…hiding it from me…whatever it was…it was eating at him. And, now I was sure this is what had been bothering him for the past two days—something he didn't want me to know. Grant knew.

"Let's go. You don't need another detention," he said firmly and pushed me toward the hall.

"What's the big deal? He said something to piss you off. What was it?" My probe continued.

"Emma. I'm not talking about this right now." He scratched his head the way he did when he was angry.

"Fine." My throat felt tight and we made our way to gym in silence. "Do you want me to ride home with Ryan?" I asked.

"Why would I want you to ride home with him?" he replied.

"Because you're angry at me."

"I'm not angry at you. And I *will* tell you."

"Tonight?"

He blinked his eyes slowly and didn't answer right away. "I have an appointment with my PO at four. I was going to take you home first and then go, but with your detention…I won't have time."

"I'll come with you."

"No," he responded instantly, but then must have reconsidered. "OK, you can ride with me and wait in the Jeep."

"OK."

"I'll meet you at Bowman's room after school."

I nodded and went into the gym.

Ali and Lauren ambushed me at the door.

"What's he on probation for?" Ali asked. "Ryan wouldn't tell me."

Chalk another point up for my brother. I wasn't prepared to answer questions about this. I forgot about Ali learning this information. I laughed. "It's so totally not a big deal. I'm not even sure to be honest. It was like a little misdemeanor." I downplayed.

"Did he steal something? You know, my cousin, David, was on probation in Sacramento for shoplifting," Lauren added.

"I don't think it was shoplifting," I said and heard the whistle blow. The game started and as much as I hated dodge ball, I was glad. Shoplifting would have been easier to explain.

At the end of the day, I closed my locker and headed back to Algebra. Zach was waiting with his backpack at the door.

"Hey," he said.

"Hey to you." I smiled.

"How's your head?" He asked brushing back my bangs to see the stitches, then pulled me forward till his lips met my forehead.

I shrugged. "Fine. I don't really notice it." This wasn't really true. It hurt more today than yesterday.

"Do you want me to wait here or in the Jeep?"

"Did you tell her?"

My head snapped toward Grant, who'd shown for his detention. The day didn't do his face any favors. Zach's face hardened and he reminded me of a male peacock spreading his tail as his chest puffed out when Grant neared.

"I asked, if you told her?" Grant repeated.

"Does it look like I've told her?" Zach's lips pulled back across his teeth.

I wedged my body between them and Zach swiftly pulled me behind without saying a word. "Stop. Both of you," I demanded.

Grant smiled out one side of his mouth. "I have nothing to lose." He eyeballed Zach. "Do you man?" His smile broadened.

Zach's teeth were clenched together and his eyes shot daggers at Grant. "How about your other fucking eye?"

Grant entered the classroom without another word.

"Maybe you should wait for me in the Jeep."

He agreed but stared in the classroom.

I touched his cheek to get his attention. "Tonight? You'll tell me tonight?"

His jaw was still rigid but he nodded.

As I left the school and walked to the Jeep, I shivered. Something was looming tonight that I couldn't control and I couldn't predict. My fight or flight was kicking into overdrive and I considered playing sick. I wasn't sure I wanted to know. Grant wanted me to and Zach didn't…so I knew it wasn't good. Zach's head was against his headrest and I think his eyes were closed but I couldn't tell. I wondered how many people Ali or Lauren had told, and I suddenly felt like I was dating a criminal.

I racked my brain trying to think of what could possibly make Grant happy and Zach not…nothing. Estelle…maybe. That had to be it. He'd been with her again. At Shasta, Grant slept with Claire and she told Grant about Zach and Estelle. Jealousy ran through my veins and before I could calm down, he was at my door opening it for me.

"How was detention?"

"Quiet. Bowman didn't allow us to talk." I rolled my eyes.

"Wow. I like Mr. Bowman." He winked, smiled and shut the door behind me.

I didn't want to admit to him I'd never been to our county courthouse—well, maybe once when my parents paid for their car tags. He seemed agitated and distracted and I had the feeling if he had the time to drop me off at home, he would have. Once we arrived at the courthouse, Zach turned in his seat. "I won't be long. Just leave the Jeep running and stay out here."

I nodded. "Got it."

I watched as he fed the meter then jogged indoors. I smiled watching him and marveled at how he was mine. I felt lucky and blessed. I knew most people had those feelings with their first crush…but this was so much more. He knew it and I knew it.

I opened his center console and rummaged through its contents not really looking for anything. Maybe snooping, but fortunately only found six CDs, a tube of Carmex, some napkins, and a straw. I closed it shifting my focus to the backseat. Immaculate except for a pair of sweat shorts on the seat, which I grabbed and smelled searching for the scent I loved then wished I hadn't.

The Jeep was hot and twenty-seven minutes had passed so I turned the key off. The meter was flashing so I plugged some more coins into the slot. Eighteen more minutes. Tired of waiting, I locked the door and went in. The warmth of indoors met me near the door and the massive metal detectors loomed in front of me. I laid my purse on the moving belt and walked through the detector. Probation was on the first floor so I moseyed around till I found the office. About twenty chairs filled the small room but only four of them were occupied. I sat in the one closest to the door. I fought hard not to make eye contact with the others wondering what they'd done to be on probation. Three men and a woman with a child all waited like me. A door opened and a tall man stepped to the door.

"Andre?"

My eyes darted to a middle-aged man who got up and met the guy at the door and went in. The room smelled funny…musty…not clean and after a while, it burned my nose. The door opened again. Zach stepped out with a heavyset man. Zach's eyes met mine and widened first with recognition then anger.

"Emma. I told you to wait in the car."

"I'm sorry. I got worried. Are you done?" At the moment I asked, I saw the latex gloves on the man's hands and a small plastic container in his other.

"Not yet," Zach's said his jaw tight.

The man two seats away snickered and I looked at him for the first time. He was smirking at me and his eyes narrowed roaming over me from head to toe. His clothes were dirty, and I saw grease spots on his jeans.

"I'll be right back," Zach clarified. "Don't move." And he was gone.

"Thatcha boyfriend?" the man asked.

I nodded feeling an obligation to be nice.

"You can't be but what….how old you?"

"Sixteen," I lied watching the door Zach went out.

He rotated in his seat. "Ahh. To be sixteen again. Enjoy it, Doll."

I offered him a smile and he moved a seat over and sat next to me. "You see that?" He pointed to a pale scar stretching from his wrist to his elbow.

His sudden closeness frightened me and I wasn't sure why, we were in a courthouse full of officers and people. "Yes."

"That's where…"

Suddenly, my arm jerked nearly out of it's socket and Zach was storming with me in tow out the door. "You're hurting me."

He instantly let go and looked at me. "The one thing I ask and you can't do it?"

"What…what did I not do?" He took my hand again. This time more gently.

"I asked you to stay in the Jeep." His words had calmed. "It doesn't matter."

"Then why are you upset? Did you not want your PO to see me?" Zach was at my door. I pulled his keys from my purse and handed them to him. He opened my door and I got in. He closed the door and went to his side. "Did I embarrass you?"

He hit the steering wheel. "I'm on probation for drugs, do UA's, have to go to meetings and *you* think *I'm* embarrassed of you." He shook his head like I was dense. "Don't you see Em. I'm the embarrassment. You would never be in that office talking with those people if it wasn't for me. You should never have stepped foot in there. *That's* why we shouldn't be together. You should never be subjected to this sort of thing. Yesterday when I said my PO…you didn't have a clue what I was saying. Now you spout it off like it's part of your daily conversations."

Another reason not to be together. He made it sound like those outweighed the reason's we should. "Fine. Take me to Safeway, let me shoplift, get arrested then it'll be OK if we're in this together," I scoffed.

He glared at me. "Not funny." His tone harsh. "That was stupid," he said softer.

"No. You're being stupid. So what if you are on probation? Everyone screws up at some time or another."

"Yeah, but, I gave it one hundred percent effort." His scowl twisted upward and I smiled.

"See…you are good at something," I teased. "What did he say about the fight?"

"He's going to talk to the judge. I may get a twenty-four hour sanction." He looked out the window.

"I don't know what that means." I hated saying it, but it was true.

Suddenly, my hand was in his and he kissed my fingertips. "Why would you?" He questioned and I wondered if he meant to say it aloud. "It means I may get locked up for twenty-four hours and…"

"In *JAIL*?" My heart raced. This couldn't happen. I wouldn't let it. This had been my fault to begin with.

He squeezed my hand. "We don't know yet so don't panic. OK?" He must have seen the fear in my eyes. The Jeep was moving slower than the other cars on I-5 and I wondered if he was buying time. I nodded. The thought of him being locked up…away from me…made me sick.

"It was just a fight."

"Em. There are conditions of probation. You can't hang out with people who are known criminals…like myself."

"Stop."

He laughed. "You have to attend school, be on time, keep in contact with your PO, stay clean, and not engage in illegal activity…fighting included." He made the turn on my street. I didn't want to be home.

"When is later?"

He paused trying to decide what to say. "I suppose now is later. But I'd like to tell you at my house."

I wasn't sure if that remark was good or bad news. "OK. Let me go and throw a casserole in the oven then I'll have some time."

In the drive, I reached into the backseat and grabbed the shorts. "May I?"

"Have them?"

I eagerly nodded.

"I don't care. They need washed."

"I know. I smelled them earlier."

His mouth fell open with a repulsed look on his face. "Why does that not surprise me?"

I smiled, shut the door and ran up to the house.

When we got to Zach's, his dad was leaving with his golf clubs.

"Hello, Emma. Zach."

"Hi Dad. Golf? Use a colored ball, there's still snow on the ground." Zach slung his backpack over one shoulder.

"Hi, Mr. Owens."

His dad laughed. "I'm taking them in to get them re-gripped. After that, your mother and I are meeting Dan and Susan for dinner. What are you two doing?" he asked sliding the clubs into his trunk.

"We'll probably eat a bite and then hang out."

His father gave an approving nod but added. "Hang out downstairs, all right?"

Zach held his hand up like a gun and lowered his thumb like he was firing. "Good tip, Dad. Thanks."

I grinned at his dad and I'm sure he saw the blush rushing into my cheeks. Zach shut the door behind us. He watched his dad pull away then set the alarm.

"Is that necessary?"

"If there is one thing I learned from your house. Expect them when you shouldn't. This will let us know. You hungry?"

I was. "A little."

He opened the kitchen cupboard. "Popcorn?"

"Sure."

After grabbing a soda from the fridge, he opened it and handed it to me. He tossed the popcorn in the microwave then grabbed me close.

"So, this is why you set the alarm," I smirked. We hadn't kissed in a couple of days and I'd missed him.

"Maybe. Do you want to kiss a criminal?" His nose touched mine.

"Actually," I brushed my lips across his without kissing him. "it's really a turn on and I was thinking about contacting a death row inmate. I hear they are looking for chicks to e-mail."

"You think?" He hugged me tightly then lifted me and sat me on top of the granite countertop. "I think one criminal in your life is one too many." He maneuvered his way between my legs. We still weren't eye level but closer and my legs dangled at his sides.

"I love my big 4.0 GPA thug," I hazed.

"Your thug loves you too." He laughed quietly then pressed his mouth to mine. I'd never been addicted to anything…but I had a feeling this is how an addict felt. I broke free, which was hard to do.

"What's wrong?"

"When you were using…you know….drugs." I looked down ashamed that I'd brought it up.

"Yes."

"Did you do it because you were addicted?"

"I did it because it made me forget about what was happening. I was reckless across the board. I did a lot of stupid shit." He pulled me close and I leaned my chin against his shoulder.

"Why?" he asked.

"You'll laugh." I didn't want to say.

"Try me."

I couldn't see his face so maybe I wouldn't know if he laughed. "You're my drug," I whispered. "I need you." He didn't laugh and he reared his head back scrutinizing my face then kissed me again. I felt his tongue on my bottom lip and my body became so limp I think he held me up in his arms. What was it about his kiss? I couldn't think straight and his breath was warm and inviting. His hands traced down my back till they met the countertop then he pulled my lower body toward the edge till our bodies met. My legs wrapped around him and I wasn't sure if they were connected to my body anymore because my reaction wasn't conscious. He lifted me off the countertop and turned to walk, his arms wrapped so tightly around me, I knew I wouldn't fall. I wondered if his eyes were open.

BEEP! BEEP! BEEP! I dropped my legs and broke off our kiss. My legs dangled as he held firmly. "The alarm." I informed him, my eyes wide.

Then he swung my legs up and caught them with the other arm. "How about the microwave."

Relief settled over me as it registered that he was right. "Oh." He replaced me in my position on the granite and got a bowl. I hopped off the counter and opened the microwave. Steam billowed out as I poured the popcorn into the bowl smelling delicious.

We flipped the channels and munched on the popcorn. Remembering the casserole at home, I texted Ryan and begged him to tell Mom and Dad that Zach and I were grabbing a bite. Hopefully, he'd comply. I'd know as soon as I got home.

Zach took the empty bowl and cans to the kitchen and as he walked back through the family room, took my hand and led me upstairs. I figured to his room.

"You're dad said to stay downstairs," I reminded him.

"Uh-huh."

"You're breaking the ruuules," I teased.

"Uh-huh."

We rounded the corner to his room and he moved an old popcorn tin next to the desk chair. He sat on the tin and patted the chair. I sat in front of the computer.

"What are we doing?" This isn't what I thought he had in mind.

"It's later…right?" His Adam's apple moved up then down as he swallowed.

I remembered what my mission was and why we'd come to his house. The blank flat screen monitor sat on his desk. He moved the mouse and it lighted to life. Then he clicked on Google.

I put my hand over his on top of the mouse and his eyes flickered to mine. I lifted his hand and pulled it in to my heart. I stared at the Google page and couldn't for the life of me anticipate what was coming. I wondered if he could feel my heart beating against my chest. I closed my eyes and felt the pulse inside of me.

"Em?"

I stood and back stepped tugging his hand till he moved with me. His eyes locked on mine. I moved past the light switch, flipping it down then walked backward till my calves made contact with the mattress. I sat, scooted back and pulled him onto me. He rested his weight on his forearms above me and stared into my eyes.

"I don't want to know," I whispered.

His fingers swept over my cheek. "But you said…"

"I know what I said," I interrupted. "I've changed my mind. I don't want to know."

"Emma. It's not that easy…Grant. He's going to tell you." His words were certain.

I shook my head. "I'll talk to him. I'll make him see." I wasn't as certain as he was. But I was hopeful. "Tell me something though."

"Anything."

"Is it something illegal?"

"No," He answered quickly.

"Have you been loyal to me?"

A growl came from his throat. "One hundred percent."

I inhaled and let out a long breath and sigh of relief. "Then, I don't care."

"Seriously?"

"I mean I care...but not enough to ruin this. We have five months before I leave for Cannon and you leave for God knows where. Tell me then."

He lowered his body to meet mine again. Our lips searched for each other in the dark and his kiss was sweeter than ever. But I again retreated pushing him away.

"Two last things. First, Saturday...can you drive me somewhere? And, second, I don't want your folks to catch us up here. Can we please go back downstairs?"

"Yip." He heaved me up and off the bed with a grunt then sat for a second positioning me between his legs. "I'm good for Saturday. What's the plan?"

"I'm not telling."

His hands cupped my jaw and he grinned. "I love you."

I bit my bottom lip. "And I love you." We headed downstairs.

THIRTY-EIGHT

Friday, my mom had scheduled an appointment for me with her Gynecologist. I'm not sure why they call it a Guy-necologist when they treat girls…women. I had thought about it all week and even researched on the Internet what HE was going to do to an area I could barely look at. I shaved my legs and painted my toenails. Not that I was trying to impress a doctor I didn't know, but I wanted to look like I should be old enough to have this done.

My mom picked me up from school around 2:15 for my 2:30 appointment. I told Zach I had an orthodontist appointment and I did have one coming up just not today. I hated lying to him but couldn't muster up the courage to confide what I was really doing.

I checked myself in at the doctor's office. My mom was already reading a magazine, I think it was House Beautiful or something and she didn't meet my glance. I was certain this was difficult for her as well…bringing her fifteen-year-old baby girl to the gyno for some birth control…a mother's dream. I appreciated that she wasn't mean about it or constantly preaching abstinence—I knew she and dad would rather I wait for that special someone with whom I would marry…but to me…that *was* Zach.

"Emma?" The nurse startled me.

"Yes." I stood with my purse.

"Do you want me to come?" My mother asked.

"No. I'm OK." And I followed the nurse.

After she got my height and weight, I had to provide a urine sample and a finger prick to check if I was iron deficient. Then she escorted me to a room where she took my temperature, blood pressure and asked me a series of questions including my sexual activity, which I could report, was at zero. Though by the skeptical look on her face, I think she questioned my honesty.

She finally left me alone with a blue dotted gown to put on after I'd gotten completely naked. I sat and waited.

At 3:10, my phone vibrated and Zach texted me to see if I was done. I texted back a quick no and that I'd call him when I was. The door opened.

"Good afternoon, Emma. I'm Dr. Erickson. It's nice to meet you." He shook my hand.

"Hi. Nice to meet you too."

He sat on his little round doctor's stool. "So. You are interested in starting to take birth control. Is that right?"

Wow. Let's get straight to the point. "I'm not having sex," I quickly clarified. "I have a boyfriend and we've talked about it but we haven't."

"OK. Has your boyfriend had other partners?"

"Yes." I think I blushed.

"Alright. Do you know if he practiced safe sex? And the reason I'm asking is birth control prevents pregnancy but not disease."

Disease. Nice word choice. "No. I don't know for sure but I think."

"Let's start with you. How long ago did you start your menstrual cycle?"

Some of my friends started in the seventh grade and I seemed to be a slow poke with February of my eighth grade year. I wasn't sure what the norm was...but was certain as with everything else...I wasn't in it. "When I was in eighth grade." My words were soft.

"Are you periods regular?"

I shrugged. "I guess. I mark it on a calendar and it's once a month."

"And what about your flow. Would you call it heavy, moderate or light?"

This had to tie for the most embarrassing inquisition of my life. "Light."

"About how many days does it last?" He was taking notes.

I sighed. "Three or four."

He nodded and laid his pen on the chart and I hoped we were done. He opened a drawer and pulled out a metal odd shaped contraption. "We have two different types of exams we perform. One is a simple exam and the other is a more extensive exam. With the second one, this..." He held up the piece of metal. "Is inserted inside the vagina and opened." He popped it opened and I think my eyes popped out as well. I consciously crossed my legs. "This allows us to view the cervix which leads into the uterus. Since you are not sexually active at this point, we will not do that today, but we will in the future." I breathed a quiet sigh of relief and wondered if my father had paid him to have this conversation with props. "If you'll lie back, I'm going to do a basic exam. I'm sure this is a tad uncomfortable but we'll make it quick."

I didn't move. "Uncomfortable how?" I'm sure he heard the stress in my voice.

He smiled. Why couldn't he have been sixty-five and ugly? I think my mom picked the hottest doctor in town though he was bald. "Not painful. Uncomfortable—awkward. All I'm going to do is use a finger and then also apply pressure outside on your abdomen. It won't take but five seconds."

I swallowed. Great. The first thing inside of me was going to be Dr. Erickson's finger. Ugh! I reluctantly laid back and he placed my heel on top of something cold. My legs spread wider than I wished and I closed my eyes.

Saturday morning Zach was at my house by 9:00 just as I'd requested. I checked the computer to make sure the road I wanted to take wasn't closed due to weather. The day was a go. I'd told my mom and dad my plans the night before and Dad showed his approval by printing me off a map of the trip up and back, telling me the places to stop if we needed. Weather was unpredictable so I packed some essentials.

We headed east out of Ashland and took Dead Indian Memorial Road. Zach had never been on this highway and that excited me to no end. I wasn't crazy about the drive due to problems with my motion sickness, but it was going to be worth it. He'd never been where I was taking him and I was going to make him fall in love with Oregon too.

"So, no clues?" He asked.

"We're going north." I teased.

"Well, it's a guarantee, I've never been there then." There didn't appear to be another car in sight. The forest encroached on both sides of the narrow winding road and massive patches of trees in certain areas were missing where they'd been cut and sent to logging. It made the small mountains look funny when a portion of it was bare. I watched Zach stare at the vacant area.

"It's sad, isn't it?"

I knew that was coming. "Puh-leeeze. Oregon is the most environmentally savvy state in the US. Our tree huggers wouldn't allow that," I laughed.

"What do you mean?"

"Well, not only did we have tree planting expeditions in elementary school but there are so many not for profit agencies and urban forestry groups that plant. Where ever they take out…they put back."

He nodded. "Sweet. That's good."

"We need to get my little city boy out into the country more." I wiggled his ear lobe and he smiled.

"I can do country."

"Oh, please. You have city written all over you."

His eyes bulged out. "What's *that* supposed to mean?"

I giggled because I wasn't sure what I'd meant. "You're like a metro."

"I am not." He refused to accept my stereotype and I slapped his thigh.

I nodded. "You *so* are. Look at your gelled hair and your cologne. " I unbuckled, got to my knees and sniffed from his collar bone up to his ear. Then kissed his lobe. "It drives me crazy."

"Buckle," he warned and I did. "Really, it drives you crazy?" he questioned surprised by my analysis.

"Crazy…" I repeated and rolled my eyes. He had no possible idea how crazy. "Zach, I don't mean it to be mean. But, you wear nothing but Billabong, Hurley, Hollister, and Abercrombie. You're a walking advertisement."

"That's no different than anyone else," he contested.

"Maybe no different than some others. But you look so much better in it."

"Shut Up," he joked playfully shoving my shoulder then held my hand.

"Have you ever been hiking or on a walk through the woods?" This seemed unimaginable to me.

He shrugged. "I guess I was always more the surfing beach guy."

"But it's cold in San Francisco."

"We wore wet suits. I played golf with my dad. Played football. I guess not so much hiking." He smirked. "I have been to Napa Valley several times. It's beautiful there."

"It is beautiful," I agreed. "Take road 140 up here. Look…all I'm saying is there is a big world out there and there are lots of places to love."

"I hear you. I hear you." He turned right and merged into traffic.

About 11:15, we passed the Crater Lake National Park sign and I smiled; plus we hit the snow.

"Crater Lake?" he asked. "I've heard of it."

"Just keep your eyes on the road because once inside the park, you'll drive alongside an enormous gorge. It makes me sick."

He rubbed my back. "Must be fun to come here then."

I pursed my lips. "I'm sure it's like nothing you've ever seen." I felt confident.

"I've been to the Grand Canyon, twice. That's a gorge." He was poking fun.

My shoulders fell in a slump. "OK…you're not going to be impressed. Let's just turn around."

He laughed but squeezed my hand. "I'm kidding you. It's going to be perfect." His smile faded and his eyes were sincere.

"I want…" I struggled with my words. I wasn't vying for his attention with a girl or a sport but with a city…an incredible city…a city where his heart was. Oregon was awesome, but I wasn't sure I could compete with a lifetime of memories. "I want you to love it here." My voice came out whiney.

He lifted my chin as he drove. "I love…being here with you." He brushed his thumb over my cheek. I felt him hit the brakes and I looked out the windshield and saw the entrance to the park. I pulled our National Park pass from my purse and handed it to him. He handed it to the ranger.

"The roads are clear up to the lake but don't get off. We've gotten seventeen inches in the last couple of days. The lodge is open up top. Ask about the weather when you get up there. We have an advisory out."

Zach nodded. "Thank you."

We drove a ways in silence and I feared I was fighting a losing battle. He was going to leave after graduation and there was nothing I could do about it. The only hope I had was his parents were in Ashland. I held onto that.

The Jeep abruptly darted off the road "ZACH!" I screamed. And he hit the brakes as he veered off the shoulder. I hadn't been watching the road and the sudden turn startled me. My pulse pounded. I touched my eyebrows with my fingertips as the thought of flying off the gorge overwhelmed me.

"What did I do?" He had no idea of my subtle fear of heights. I could do roller coasters and ski down mountains, but standing on the side looking over, or the thought of our vehicle taking flight and crashing, was almost incapacitating to me.

"I told you about the gorge," I cried.

"Baby. I just wanted to look at it. I pulled off at a lookout. I'm sorry." He unbuckled first himself then me and pulled me into his chest.

I gripped him tightly and figured he'd have to pry my fingers off. "You scared me," I whispered. He kissed my hair.

"I'm so sorry."

My heart must have started again because I could feel my blood pumping through my body. I sat up pushing him away. "I'm fine."

He touched his door handle. "Come with me?"

I shook my head but not too fast or vomit would accompany the shake.

His face was disappointed and I watched him close his door and walk in front of the Jeep over to the gorge. I swallowed what little regret I had and opened my door, unsure if my legs would hold me up. "Hey."

He looked so handsome in his jeans and North Face Pullover, I was sorry I hollered at him. He turned to me and came back to the Jeep. "Are you sure?" I could see the excitement in his eyes.

"No. Just hold on to me." And he did. One arm was around my shoulder and the other held my hand in the front. It was colder than anytime I'd been here and the tall trees held the sun hostage. He walked slowly.

"Why didn't you tell me you were afraid of heights?"

"I don't want to talk about it right now," I said concentrating on my steps. We were probably about five yards from the overhang. "OK. I'm good." I stopped.

He wrapped his other arm around my shoulder. His warmth felt good but I shivered. "It's cold," he said probably trying to make me feel better. The gorge didn't seem as deep as I remembered—maybe because I'd only seen it in the summer when it was rocky and now it was covered in twenty inches of snow.

Back in the Jeep and driving on up the mountain, we got behind some RV's driving slow and this calmed me a bit; plus he hadn't let go of my hand.

"Can you tell me yet, why you can take a black slope on your snowboard like it's nothing but you can't walk ten feet to look over a ravine?"

I gave him a weak smile. "No." I didn't understand it myself. "It would make me feel better right now if you had both hands on the wheel." He grinned and let go of my hand.

"I don't know why. I feel *safe* on my snowboard. I know it doesn't make sense."

"You're safe with me," he said.

When we made the final curve at the top, I felt the tension in my shoulders release. Safe for the moment. The parking lot was empty today except for a couple of cars. I'd never been here when the parking lot hadn't been jam-packed. I slid my gloves on and opted for beauty leaving my stocking cap in my pocket.

"You ready?" I asked.

"Are *you* ready?"

I rolled my eyes and smiled. "I think so," I said and opened my door. The artic air hit my face and caused my eyes to instantly water. Massive piles of snow had been shoveled off the parking lot and walkways. The trees...I'd never seen them look so beautiful...their limbs hanging low with the weight of the snow. I wondered how they didn't snap.

The air I breathed in was bitter cold and my ears burned as we walked to the massive crater in the earth. I decided I wasn't too vain to put my stocking cap on, so I rummaged for it in my pocket but had trouble getting it on with my gloves. Zach took it from me and slid it over my head after first kissing the top of one of my ears.

"It's red," he said softly. "You should have had it on to begin with."

"Look." I pointed, and there it was…the most beautiful and most majestic lake in the world…at least the U.S., I thought. Snow lay on the outer banks of the crater; it looked like the snow was being funneled into the water. The sun, no longer hostage, shone bright and the glare was blinding.

"Wow." I heard his voice and smiled. Yes! He wrapped his arms around me from behind though it provided little warmth.

"It's the deepest lake in the U.S." I bragged.

"What…I mean how…why the crater?"

I was so ready for this. "Well, it was known as Mount Mazama—a dormant volcano. When it erupted, it collapsed—caved in on itself though first it buried the area in a rain of ash. Then this crater was formed. You know Mt. St. Helens?"

"Yes."

"This made *that* look like a little burp."

He seemed mesmerized as he stared at the gigantic hole. "The water is so blue."

"No water comes into it except for rain and snow, and no water leaves it." I felt like a tour guide. "I wish we could make a trip back in the summer because the snow, as beautiful as it is, is nothing compared to looking down the sheer drop offs on the rim."

He hugged me. "You should be a park ranger." I smiled though I knew he couldn't see. I'd come prepared.

"I'm *your* park ranger," I giggled.

"How long ago?"

"Did it erupt?" I asked thinking about my research.

He nodded.

"I think it was like 8,000 years ago."

"It was. She's good." We both turned toward the voice. A real park ranger stood with his coat and hat on. "Where you folks from?"

"Ashland," Zach answered, and I loved hearing him say it. He reached for the ranger's hand and they shook.

"Nice to have you all here. We don't get a lot of visitors in the winter because of the snow. Unfortunately, I'm sorry to have to ask you to leave, but we have a storm coming and we have to close the roads."

My eyes must have indicated some fear because the ranger patted my shoulder. "You'll be fine. It's still an hour or so out, but we need you to start your descent."

"Would you take our picture?" I asked.

"Sure." I handed him my camera, nestled up to Zach and smiled. He snapped it.

"So, no hot chocolate from the lodge?" I asked, taking my camera back.

"Good stuff, ain't it?" he winked. "Next time. Sorry about that." He turned and I thought I heard a "be safe" as he walked away.

We stood for a few more minutes. I knew it was just as beautiful as the Golden Gate and it was a natural wonder. "I love it," he whispered in my ear, and his breath warmed me to the bone.

We stopped at a hole-in-the-wall diner that had only one car in front figuring we'd be safe to at least get drinks. We shed our layers before going in. The place was dark, which kept us from seeing if it was clean, and we sat in a booth against the wall. Thankfully, the room was warm. An older woman, maybe sixty something offered us menus and ice water in a glass. An RC clock hung above us vibrating with a soft hum, and a juke box lit one corner. A TV played on the corner of the bar.

"What can I get you all?" she asked in a gruff voice.

"How about two hot chocolates for starters," Zach directed. She nodded. "Hot chocolate it is."

He reached across and grabbed my hands. "Thank you."

"For what?"

"For today. It was awesome." The table seemed to be three feet across and my hands could barely reach as he pulled them to his lips. Without letting go, he slid out of his seat and into mine.

"Yeah. Awesome, huh?" I asked with a roll of my eyes. "Which part was awesome…me freaking out when I thought we were toast or the two hour ride for the thirty minutes of a hole filled with snow? You know…in the summer it's beautiful and…"

"Stop." He was chuckling. "All of it. It was majestic and scenic and…" he paused and stared at me. "It was like nothing I'd ever seen."

I couldn't control the smile that broadened across my face. "I'm glad you liked it."

His left arm wrapped over my shoulders. "We'll do it again when it warms up and the snow is gone."

I was happy at the thought but knew the truth. "The snow doesn't melt until at least July." I lowered my head.

His index finger lifted my chin and he kissed me. His breath was warm and soothing. The waitress cleared her throat, and he turned to her. Uncomfortable, I wiped my lips with my hand as she placed the mugs on the table—a giant dollop of whipped cream floating high on top.

"Anything else?"

"In a few minutes," he answered politely.

I wrapped my hands around the hot mug reveling in the warmth. I leaned down and licked the top off my cream. It was so good. Zach was watching me with fire in his eyes. He slowly stuck his finger in his whip cream and pulled it out. I bit my lip as he brought it toward me. My mouth opened just far enough for his finger and he slid it in. I enclosed my lips around it sucking the cream off with my tongue. His eyes and his smile made me want to come out of my skin. He slowly removed his finger and suddenly, I was embarrassed.

"Come on," he said tugging me from the booth.

"Where?" I asked, but saw we were headed for the jukebox. I was shocked to see it was a CD jukebox…this joint seemed more like an old forty-five type place. He fed a couple of dollars in, we made some selections and I turned to go back to the booth.

He grabbed the back of my shirt and yanked. "Where do you think you're going?"

I stumbled back and he caught me in his arms. "What?"

He didn't have to answer. He pulled me into his body and we swayed back and forth to the beat of the music. I didn't mind dancing; I just hadn't done it much. Though I'd been in ballet for nine years that was far from the dancing they did these days. My head hit about mid sternum on his body.

"Do you ever feel like you're dancing with your little sister?"

"I don't have a little sister."

"Well, this is what it would be like, I'm sure." When we were sitting we seemed more on even ground but standing, dancing…we didn't fit. I hated that.

All of the sudden, he lifted me up into both arms. "If I felt about a sister the way I feel about you, I'd be in trouble." He laughed and pecked my lips. "Yuk!" He shook his head trying to rid himself of the thought.

"Put me down," I requested.

"I will. When the song is over." And as the music faded, he walked me back to the table.

The drinks were cooler now, and I could drink it without scorching my lip. My phone, which I left on the table, vibrated. It was a text…I pushed read.

Call me. I need 2 talk 2 U

My smile faded.

"What?" Zach asked.

I showed him the text.

"Don't tell me…Mr. Meiers?" It changed his mood too.

I shoved the phone in my purse. "I'm hungry." I attempted to change the subject. He opened the menu and we scanned it. "Onion strings," I suggested.

"That's what I mean," he said. "Most girls wouldn't order onions on a date and you do."

I was suddenly self-conscious. "Is that bad?"

"No! That's my point. You do it because you want to. You aren't someone else around me. You're you." He motioned for the waitress. "We'd like some of your onion strings."

She nodded and turned back to the kitchen.

"We need to talk about Grant."

Hmm. Not Meiers. "I told you I'd talk to him and I will…today when we get back."

"I don't want you anywhere near him." Zach's tone was flat.

"Well, that's gonna make it a little hard to talk to him now, isn't it?"

I could tell he was mulling over the predicament in his head. "Emma. He does not want us together. You understand that, right? His whole motive for wanting you to know this…stupid shit." He hissed through clenched teeth. "Is to break us up? Do you get that?"

"And whatever it is that you two know…" I swallowed the fear that rose in my throat. "It would break us up?" My voice broke as the words came out. He stared into my eyes. The pain evident in his brown ones.

"I…don't…know. I think you'll be disappointed in me. But no more than I am in myself."

I wanted to know…badly, but was it worth the gamble of losing him? Then again, that was my choice. Forgiveness. Isn't that what life is about? And he was so worth forgiving. My grandma used to say to me—Forgiveness doesn't change the past, but it enlarges the future—I heard her now in my head. Emma Nicole, never forget three powerful resources you always have available to you—love, prayer and forgiveness. I smiled as I pictured her little face, the one person in this world who was smaller than me.

"Here's your onion strings." The woman slid the plate onto the table. "Can I get you anything else?"

"You want a soda?" Zach asked me.

"Sure."

"Two sodas, please."

She nodded and was gone again.

"I can't imagine being angry with you." I dangled a string into my mouth. "Have you been using drugs again?"

He swallowed what he was chewing. "No." He sounded disgusted. "March 4th, I'll be a year sober." He smiled.

"How bad did it get?"

He took in a long deep breath and released it. "Bad." He paused. "I was drunk all the time. In the morning when I didn't drink, I'd smoke a joint. It was whacked. I knew it was hurting my parents. I knew they knew. They tried to talk to me, but I blamed them for moving. I didn't care that my mom's health was at risk." He looked at the table and traced the marble lines in the Formica.

"What happened to your mom?"

"Everything. Her blood pressure was off the charts. She wore a heart monitor for a while because her heart was doing funny things. She had a test to check for blockages and that was fine. But stress was eating her up. I think dad felt their quality of life and marriage was slipping, and he knew…he knew he'd have to get her out of the city to make her change. She was who she was and the city was part of that. Do you remember the pit bull case of the dogs that attacked some lady?"

I nodded. Vaguely.

"That was mom's case. She was top notch and made the money and dad wanted her to walk away. She did. And deep down I know it was right for them and for the family but not for me." As soon as he said it, he eyed me and pulled me close. "You are the best thing that has ever happened to me so don't take that wrong. But imagine, Ryan…right now…in a school where he knew no one and was going to graduate with them instead of everyone who was a part of who he was. Think about it…he wouldn't wear his cap and gown with Grant or Brett or Connor or Josh or any of them." He threw another onion string in his mouth. "Em. I'm ashamed of the things I did. Please know that."

"At Shasta, you were drinkin' in the hot tub. Do you not consider that a relapse?"

He laughed. "No. And, I'm not in denial. But I'm also not an alcoholic. I used it to fill a void…to get rid of pain. I didn't have to have it. It was more…self-medication for lack of a better word. It was stupid. When I say sober, I mean from the drugs." He kissed my fingertips.

I spun a string in some ketchup. "And this thing Grant wants me to know. You did it then…when you weren't sober.

He closed his eyes nodding. "I did."

"So it was like a year ago?"

He'd stopped eating. "It was."

"Let's go." I was done talking about it. I didn't know whether I wanted to know or not anymore and I didn't want to talk about it. Out of the blue, my stomach started hurting. Zach slid from the booth and threw a twenty on the table.

"What's wrong?"

"I think we should head back."

He glanced at his watch and nodded. "OK."

I waved at the woman behind the counter.

"Em?"

I heard his voice and smiled. I was dreaming and I knew it. He was there at my bed. He was sweaty and his shirt was off and I stared. He smiled at me…his killer smile with brilliant white teeth

240

perfectly aligned. He ran his hand up my spine and scratched the back of my head.

"Em." He sang my name.

I giggled and that woke me just a bit. I blinked and it was bright.

"Em." This time he shook my arm.

"What?" I sat upright. We were in the Jeep and sitting in my driveway. "We're home?"

"You were dreaming," he reported and I yawned.

"I fell asleep?" it was more of a question than a statement.

He rubbed my back again. "About half way here."

Disappointment settled over me. I never felt like we had enough time as it was and I wasted nearly two hours sleeping.

"Why the bottom lip?" he asked, obviously noticing my pout.

"I just wasted our time together."

"No you didn't," he said softly. "It was nice having you asleep on my lap. Completely relaxed and carefree." My heart melted as his words flowed so beautifully from his mouth.

I got out of the Jeep and spotted Grant's truck parked behind Ryan's. I knew by Zach's jaw, he'd already seen it.

"You've got company," he commented. "Do you want me to stay or go?"

"Stay silly. That answer will never change." I smiled and held his hand as we entered the house.

We moved through the great room and into the kitchen. No sign of either of them. My stomach growled and I opened the fridge.

"You hungry?" I asked.

"For you."

I was glad the refrigerator shot out cold air so maybe my face wouldn't be as red when I looked at him. "Well. I'm not sure that's something I can satisfy."

His arms moved around my sides and locked behind my back. "You quench it every day." He kissed me.

"Yes, but I didn't realize that my kiss was essential for your survival. That I was meeting a necessity." I giggled as I kissed him.

"Then you don't know…"

"What's up guys?" Ryan asked, grabbing a Gatorade from the fridge.

Zach and he slapped hands. "Hey Ryan."

"How was the lake?" He hopped up on the countertop.

"Cold," Zach and I said in unison, and we laughed. Then Zach added, "It was beautiful though."

"You should see it in the summer," Ryan added.

"That's what I've heard."

"What have you heard?" Grant asked, as he breezed through the door.

My eyes instantly narrowed and I shot him a scowl.

"Nothing," Zach said sourly.

"Did you two lovebirds have a special day?" Grant asked oozing with sarcasm.

Anger burned inside of me. "Grant, Zach kicked your ass once. Your eye is still screaming for help. Don't think I will stop him from doing it again."

"No, I think it's great you had two hours to talk on the way up to Crater and two hours back…did you use your time wisely…Zach?" Grant smirked.

I grabbed Zach's hand and started to pull him from the kitchen. "Come on," I said. "We did have fun Grant. In fact, we stopped at a little motel and scrogged on the way back."

Gatorade shooting out of Ryan's nose and mouth was the last thing I saw when I left the room, but I think a growl came from Grant then a whispered "liar."

Zach was cracking up. "You're good."

"Thank you," I said proudly. "I'm going to talk to him now. I think you should go. I think it'll go better if you are not here. Does that make you angry?"

"Not at all." Then he snatched me in his arms and kissed me deeply and thoroughly till my legs were weak and I wondered if he thought this was goodbye and if he feared Grant would out him regardless of what I said. He pulled back and gazed down at me. "Good luck," he winked. "Call and let me know." Then, he was gone and I turned toward the kitchen.

THIRTY-NINE

Zach

I sat in the Jeep staring at the front of her house. It was no surprise my heart was beating the hell out of my chest; I had just left the girl I loved inside with a guy she once loved. She'd known me nine months and him most of her life. Where would her loyalty lie?

Grant was weak. He never had the balls to go up against his best friend for a shot with his sister. He sat, probably longing for her for years, until I opened the door. He actually thought he had some dibs on her because of their past! Did he?

It wasn't until my hand grabbed the car door handle that I realized I had reconsidered. I would just go in and tell her myself. SHIT! I may as well say goodbye...but at least it would be on my terms and not his. No...not yet.

I shifted the Jeep into gear and forced myself to drive off. The one thing still in my corner was her love for me. If I knew one thing about girls, it's that they love with their entire heart. And when that love turns physical...sexual, that connection becomes even more concrete. I knew that it would take a little bit more time; and time I didn't really have, but it was all I had. I felt uneasy with this line of thinking but contrary to the unease, if she had sex with me, I knew where her loyalty would lie.

In the mean time, keep her away from Grant...impossible. So, keep Grant from talking. The question was how to do that? All I could think about now were his hands on her. Him kissing her. The agony of my jealousy was the most powerful feeling I'd ever felt.

More potent than any drug, drink or emotion I'd experienced. I loved her.

I dialed my cell phone and tapped my steering wheel while the call went through.

"Hey Zach. What's Up?"

"Travon. Talk to me. Did you find Nate? I've got to have this fucking website taken down."

"Dude. I've texted him over and over again. Jackson even went by his old apartment and he's moved."

"Shit!"

"Zach, don't you think that if this prick is willing to tell her that he's probably taken a pic of it or printed it off?"

He was right. That would explain Grant being smug and in no real hurry. He had me by the balls. I blew out a deep breath. I would sit and wait at this point.

"Yep. I know. Later."

I threw the phone in the passenger seat, Emma's seat.

FORTY

EMMA

"Grant Allan Meiers!" I shouted as I stomped.

"Yes, sweetheart." His response made the hair on my neck stand.

I stepped into the kitchen, and they were eating from a can of Pringles.

"May I have a word with you?"

He crunched down on a chip with his mouth open and smiled. I didn't. "I'm waiting." He smiled.

"Not here. In my room."

He threw a chip over his shoulder in Ryan's direction. "I'm yours, lead the way." He raised his brows at Ryan like he stood a chance.

"HEY!" Ryan shouted. "If you mess with her, I'll kick your ass before Zach has a chance to."

"Whatever," Grant said, following me up the stairs.

I opened my door and Grant jetted across the room and sprawled out on my bed propped up on his elbow before I flipped on the light. He was infuriating.

His blond curls and tan skin were hard to stay angry with. Grant knew it, and the twinkle in his eye didn't help my fight.

"You know I like Zach. Right?"

"Well…"

"No. It's a yes or no question." My tone was sharp.

"Yes." He fought a smile.

"Now. I know you have something on Zach that you are dying to tell me…"

"Correction. Something…you need to know." He was matter of fact.

This stopped me in my tracks. Did I need to know it? No! Don't let him steer you off course. "Well, whatever. I'm telling you right now that I don't want to know. Not yet." I watched his face for a response. "I have five months before he moves away and I leave for Cannon. Please, I'm beggin you. Just let us be."

He closed his eyes and laid his head back on my comforter. He was chewing on my offer. Suddenly, he propped his head back up. "You can't sleep with him." He was negotiating, and even though I didn't like it, it meant he was negotiable.

"I've already slept with him." I smiled using the word slept literally.

"Semantics," he whispered then pursed his lips. "You can't *scrog* him."

"Fine. We're waiting till May 20th anyway." That would give me my five months.

"Your birthday? You all actually set a date." His forehead creased and his lip snarled.

I nodded. "That's the plan. He wants to wait till I'm sixteen."

"Oh! He is so noble…and spontaneous." Grant rolled his eyes.

Frustration was setting in again. "What is your problem with him?"

"I don't want to talk about that—BUT I will accept your offer."

"You will?" I was excited. I knew he'd listen to me and understand. I bounced on the bed.

He smiled slyly. "On one condition."

My victory party crashed around me as my heart plummeted in my chest. "What condition?"

He stared at me like I should know what he was going to say, but I didn't, or maybe I pretended I didn't. I swallowed but the saliva didn't move down my tightening throat. "What condition?" I repeated.

He cleared his throat. "I want one date and…"

"You've got to be kidding." I rolled my eyes and he took off his sweatshirt and hung it on one of the bedposts.

"One, Em. And don't pretend like that would be so horrible. Don't forget who held your hair this summer when you had the stomach flu and you were vomiting. Don't forget who held your hand when little Scott Turner broke up with you two summers ago. And shall we not forget who you talked to about Zach, the hot new guy. It was me. And it was me who you were thrilled to kiss when we played truth or dare."

"Right! And I was the one you felt *obligated* to kiss."

"That was a long time ago."

"So. Why would you want to take me on a date when you know I'll be thinking of him?"

He winced at first and I knew the words hurt.

He shook his head and grinned. "You won't be."

"I will be." I was sure of that and wondered if I'd resent him for making me be there. But I knew I'd concede if it meant being with Zach.

"Emma. I'm talking one date." He was talking now like it was a take it or leave it offer.

"That's one too many."

He sucked on his cheek making a "tsk" sound. "OK. Then you won't get the next five months with him."

That pissed me off. "What the hell makes you so sure that what you know will end it?"

The smile on his face faded and was replaced with a sadness. His eyes were troubled and his hands preoccupied. "It…it would hurt you." His voice was barely audible.

"Then why tell me at all?"

He sat fidgeting with my belts around the bedpost. "Because you deserve to know." He didn't look at me.

I stuck my outstretched hand in his face. "Fine. One date. When?"

He shook and pecked the top of my hand then hopped up and off my bed. "Next Saturday. Be ready at 11:00 a.m." He pulled my door closed behind him.

I grabbed my cell phone and dialed half of Zach's number before I stopped and stared at my ceiling fan. He was going to be mad…I knew that much and mad may not be a strong enough word. Angry wouldn't cover it…ticked…furious…pissed off. I couldn't come up with a strong enough word. But, he'd have to understand that I was doing this for us. Grant would leave us alone after this. Nevertheless, it would hurt him, and I didn't want to hurt him. On the other hand, I was going to be hurt by this God forsaken secret and I didn't particularly care for that scenario either.

I ran the options in my head. One—back out on Grant and deal with whatever it is that Zach did. Could it possibly be that bad? Two—go with Grant, make Zach angry and work it out after the fact. I'd been forgiving with Zach…he'd be forgiving with me. I didn't like either option…but it didn't get any better the more I contemplated the thoughts. I wished I could call Lauren or Ali but I didn't want to allude to Zach having something else in his past other than the already known probation. Mom? No—same reason. Giving her or dad another excuse not to like Zach wasn't an option. I needed to call him. I opted for a text

Will I see you tonight? send

Of course. How'd it go?

Successful I think! send

Ill b by around 6. Movie?

Anythings fine. See you then. Send

I closed my phone and lay across my bed. A movie sounded great, but I couldn't imagine we'd make it to one. My stomach twisted and I wondered if I was getting sick.

When the doorbell rang, my pace wasn't as quick as normal to greet Zach. Though I missed him over the past three-hour window…I dreaded what was in store for this evening. He'd want to know what went down between Grant and me. And, I'd tell him. I wouldn't lie.

When I opened the door, the dark green hoodie with the big yellow O on it was hard to miss. No USC, No UCLA, No Raiders, or Giants…but Oregon Ducks! I couldn't contain the smile that crossed my face. I flung my arms around his neck. The material was soft against my cheek and already smelled like him.

"You have somehow inherited a small portion of my wardrobe. So I did some shopping this afternoon."

"You made good choices," I teased, and pecked him on the lips. I needed to get in good graces immediately.

"Emma. We're leaving," my dad said passing through the room and spotting us. "Oh. Zach. Emma said you two were going out tonight. What are your plans?"

He released me instantly, which was customary for him, and turned his full attention to my father or future father-in-law, as I dreamed. "Yes, sir. We'd talked about taking in a movie, something to eat...I'm not real sure. We haven't discussed it yet."

He patted Zach's shoulder with maybe semi approval before lowering his bi-focals and glaring over them. "Zach. I like you. And I trust by now you know what is acceptable and what's not."

"Yes, sir. I do." Zach replied, and I grinned at his confidence. "No confusion."

"Excellent. We're driving into Medford but should be back by midnight," Dad said as he left the room. "But it could be earlier."

Zach and I smiled at his subtle warning and walked in to the family room. Ryan had a controller in hand and was shooting at a German WWII soldier on his XBOX360 game. He darted his eyes our way then back to the game.

"What's up?" he asked leaning his body the way the soldier was leaning on the screen.

"Not much." I plopped down next to Zach who was mesmerized by the killing spree. I despised video games and Ryan was a gameaholic. I needed to act fast or Zach would be sucked into his web.

"We're going to a movie."

"Which one?" Ryan asked.

"Not sure. What's Ali doing?" I asked, wondering why he didn't have a date.

He must have completed a level because he strutted around for a second and high fived Zach. "Ryan?"

"What?"

"Ali..."

"Oh, she's sick. Zach you want in?"

I quickly stood. "Nope. He can't. We're heading out. I talked to Ali yesterday and she was fine. What's wrong?"

He shrugged as he began the next level. The shooting already resumed.

"Ryan!" I shouted.

Finally, he pushed paused and glared at me as if I'd distracted him.

Zach laughed. "Let's go."

"She started vomiting last night and is running a fever."

"OK." Zach was pushing me out of the family room. "I was just talking," I explained.

"Exactly," he said. "So what do you want to do?"

I bounced my shoulders with indifference. "Be with you."

He pulled me onto the sofa in the living room. "That one's not open for discussion." Then his perfect lips parted slightly and came toward mine. I quickly moistened mine and met his with a hunger that hadn't been fed in almost a week. Parents gone—check. Ryan busy—check. Alone for a minimum of five hours—check. The minute I shoved him back, he lifted himself but his eyes were confused.

"What's wrong?"

"Nothing." I thought quickly. My plan had to be strategic otherwise he wouldn't comply.

"I forgot something in my room. I'll be right back." I took the stairs two at a time and went into the bathroom. After I rinsed with some mouthwash, I unwrapped a piece of gum and chewed it all the while checking out my appearance in the mirror. I leaned out the door. "Hey Zach!" I hollered down the stairs.

"What?"

"Can you come here for a sec?" I flipped off the bathroom light and stood in my doorway with my eyes closed listening for his assent. I heard his footsteps and grinned then went into my room. The lamp lit the room and I lay on my stomach across the bed with my face resting on my arms. I smiled when I heard him at the door.

"Em? What's wrong?" The concern in his voice was heartbreaking and a small percentage of me felt bad for my ploy. He slid across the bed and his hand caressed up my back. "Em?"

My body couldn't take it anymore and I shuddered in laughter until I couldn't hold it in and I raised my face to meet his. The confusion was still in his eyes. Then I lunged for his lips. His kiss was the best I'd ever had and though there hadn't been a lot...I knew it didn't get any better. But then he stopped.

"What were you doing?" he asked still confused.

"You never would have come up here if I'd have asked you...so I tricked you." I waited for his reaction. Nothing.

"Come up here for what?"

"For this!" I explained and kissed his ear whispering in it. "I wanted to do this."

"And you are under the impression that I wouldn't want to?" his words were faint.

I moved to the hollow of his neck. "You are just so honest and you try to keep me honest and I didn't think you'd follow me up here if you knew my intentions." I spoke between kisses.

My tongue lightly traced his Adam's apple and I lifted his sweatshirt to expose his remarkable abs. "You know me well," he said. I was shocked he wasn't stopping me...yet. He fingered my hair as I kissed over his abs and with my nose tickled the hair around his belly button. The skin was tight and soft and beautiful.

"What are your intentions?" He inquired softly.

I took a deep breath and inhaled the soapy scent of his skin. His jeans rested below his belly button, and I moved along the waistband feeling tensing muscles in my own pelvis. I didn't have a clue what I was doing. I unsnapped the first button and kissed the area underneath. A small groan came from his throat, and I smiled, excited that his body responded to me. His underwear read American Eagle across the band. Figures. My heart raced as the territory I'd ventured into was completely new. I was certain my inexperience showed, and, as I kissed skin I'd never laid eyes on, his hands suddenly lifted me up to his face. I'd done something wrong.

"What did I do?" I asked.

He was moving in for a kiss but reared his head back. "What do you mean?"

"Well, you stopped me. What did I do wrong?" I was embarrassed.

He snickered. "You think I stopped you because you did something wrong?"

He lifted my chin to meet my lips and smothered me with a deep, hard kiss twisting my body till I was flat on my back. Then he stopped. "I interrupted you because you were doing everything right." And his lips were squashed against mine again and it took my breath away. I broke free.

"Zach?"

"Hmm." He was now at the nape of my neck working his way toward my sternum. Suddenly I was nervous that I'd worn a button-down shirt especially, since the first two buttons seemed to come apart with just the slightest touch of his finger and thumb. "Em?" he asked.

"What?" My voice was weak.

He laughed and I didn't know why. The size of my breasts? "You said... 'Zach'...and I said... 'hmm'... and you said nothing else. What were you going to say?"

The kissing resumed, and I felt the warmth of his tongue touch just inside my bra. I hoped he couldn't feel my heart pounding against my ribs. What was I going to say? Oh, yeah.

"Have you..." There it was again—his silky tongue. He was near but not quite touching my left breast. That one was the bigger of the two anyway. My shirt fell all the way open and he slid it off my arms. I was in my bra!

"Have I what?" he asked with a slight giggle to his words.

"Sorry." I forgot again. Could I make a complete sentence? "I'm sorry, I'm not very big there." It felt weird apologizing for my breast size, but I wasn't big and didn't have much hope for the future.

He moved back up to my face and glared at me. "Don't put yourself down. You're perfect."

I rolled my eyes. "Have you had that...*one thing* done a lot?" I hated that I couldn't bring myself to say the word.

"By that one thing, you're meaning...a blowjob?"

I nodded, but he didn't answer either. In fact, he sat more rigid on the bed. "Emma." Oh great, the full name. "I am three years older than you so I've done some stuff you haven't. Good and bad. But that's history. That shouldn't matter."

I nodded. "Would it matter to you?"

"You mean if you'd been with someone?"

"Yes."

"First of all, I'm jealous by nature. Secondly, what you did before me is your business; I was not a part of your life then." I suddenly felt as if he was presenting an opening argument in a defense case. He twisted some strands of my hair from my face and wrapped it behind my ear. "I won't lie to you. I'm glad that your experiences with me are...new...that you've not been there before."

I smiled, my body still weak from his exploration. I shivered, and he rubbed my arms then grabbed the sweatshirt hanging on the bedpost and tossed it over my shoulders. His eyes shifted from mine to the sweatshirt and he abruptly sat up.

"Texas Longhorns," he said out loud with no indication of a question. "Grant had this on when I left here earlier and now it's hanging on your bedpost?"

"Zach. He and I talked. You knew that."

"In your fucking bedroom?"

God, why did I bring Grant to my room? "Yes. I didn't want to do it in front of Ryan, so I brought him up here." Why did I feel like I'd done something wrong?

Zach sat up, wadded the sweatshirt and threw it at the door, then rested his elbows on his knees. I was getting angry. He knew how much I loved him and the thought that he didn't trust me—hurt. My initial reaction was to cry but I fought hard to keep my emotions in check. How could he not know that I didn't want Grant? I propped my feet up on the mattress and tucked my chin between my knees.

He was quiet, and it was killing me, and I still had the news to break about our Saturday night date. Finally, I sprung off the bed and bolted to the door. As I opened it, the sweatshirt in question wedged between it and the floor and wouldn't budge. I shoved and pulled and I'd gotten it stuck and me stuck in the room. Let the floodgates open…that was the last straw. Then he was behind me and my silent tears fell.

"I'm sorry. I know you wouldn't…" his voice trailed off. "I'm sorry. It's that son-of-a-bitch I don't trust. Please forgive me." His words were sincere, he turned me to face him then leaned in and kissed the tears on my cheeks.

"I would never…"

"I know. I'm sorry for even thinking the thought." He sat on the bed and pulled me onto his lap. "What did he say?"

My hands were folded and tucked between my thighs. I found it difficult to look into his eyes. "Promise me you won't get mad."

His eyes contradicted his smile. "I can't make that promise."

My eyes fell to my lap; his thumb forced me to look up. "I won't get mad at you, how's that?"

It brought some comfort. "I asked him to leave us alone. That we only had months left together and…" my voice cracked at the end. He pressed his lips to my cheek and gripped my hand. "He agreed that he wouldn't say anything until May or June." I watched his face waiting for an expression change that never came. "Aren't you happy about that?" I asked.

He nodded. "I am in deed. I'm waiting for the part that's supposed to make me mad, and I figure you haven't gotten to it. Am I right?"

I nodded in return and wasn't sure I could bring my self to say what I had to. "I love you very much."

"And I love you." He cocked his head sideways waiting.

My throat was dry and all of a sudden he slid me off his lap and stood. "What are you doing?"

"Moving…fidgeting…I don't know. But this can't be good if you're struggling this bad." He ran his hands through his hair. "Tell me it's not about sex. Tell me you didn't negotiate something with him."

Had my lower jaw not been attached to my upper it would have hit the floor.

He quickly interjected. "Of course you didn't. Just tell me what it is."

The suspense seemed to be killing him. I rationalized his thoughts…maybe since it wasn't sex…it was just a date…that would be more acceptable. "Sit by me."

When he sat, I scooted close to him and decided to go for it. "Next Saturday I'm going on a date with him." I breathed. It was out. I watched his jaw harden and a tight smile touch his lips.

"You see. No sex. No kissing. One date and he leaves us alone." I quickly leaned in and kissed his neck right below his ear and moved over his cheek toward his mouth. He kissed me back but with no emotion. My heart beat awkwardly for a brief second and I smiled at him. "It'll be OK. I know it. He promised."

A condescending snort came from the back of his throat. My palms held both sides of his face and my thumbs rubbed his cheeks. Disappointment resonated in his eyes and I wasn't sure I could handle it. I needed him to believe in me.

"He promised?" He chuckled as the words came out, and I assumed he was making fun of me for having faith in Grant. "I'd rather tell you what I did," he said honestly.

"I thought about that when he told me his condition." His eyes flickered with hatred then softened when he looked at me. I couldn't look at him and talk so I stared at my comforter. "But as much as I want to…what if I can't forgive you. If I do this, at least we have several months to spend together."

"You agreed to this?" The frustration in his tone scared me.

"I did." I hoped he heard confidence in my response.

"What if I requested that you not go?" His eyes stayed focused on the ground.

"I hope that you don't. I'm doing this for us."

His eyes found me. "And you think, you going on a date with Grant, will help us?"

I pulled my shoulders slowly up into a shrug then dropped them. "It won't help us if he tells me what you did and it hurts me."

His eyes flickered toward me. "He told you it would hurt you?"

I nodded.

"Did he say anything else?"

"He said that he didn't want to hurt me, but he thought that I deserved to know."

Zach stood and paced the floor in front of my desk and dresser. "That's sweet. I think that's very kind that he doesn't want to hurt you. Although he's going to…hurt you…anyway when the time is right. Am I correct?"

His sarcasm, though on target, was biting. "I suppose," I whispered.

"Let's say for arguments sake that you accept this incorrigible invitation. How long does he give us?" His eyebrows sat high on his forehead.

I smiled. "May 20th." I couldn't help but smile thinking about the date.

He leaned against my desk and folded his arms across his chest. "Your birthday?"

I nodded.

"Why your birthday?"

Crap! My eyes darted around in their sockets trying to come up with the appropriate way to word this. I'd so far been able to leave out the condition of not having sex. But, then again, that was Zach's idea to begin with. "Well. That's the day you and I decided on…the date we picked for…you know." I rolled my eyes, too uncomfortable to say it.

He shifted his weight back to his legs and hovered over me. "Emma. Please tell me. Oh my…" His breathing was erratic. He touched his temples. "Please, Em. Tell me… you didn't tell him that. Tell me…..lie to me…..do whatever you need to….but don't tell me you told him that was the day we'd be together."

"I wanted him to know I was committed to you!!" I screamed and tried to shove him in the chest, but he didn't move—in fact it hurt my wrist.

I'd never seen him this angry. "So now there's a second condition. No sex," his voice was loud but not screaming.

I moved around to the other side of the bed. "Zach. We weren't going to do it anyway…*your* rules."

He drew in a long breath expanding his chest. "My rules?" he smirked, staring out the window. "I think it's *our* rules. I thought you were on board with that too." His words were soft. "I refuse to let him navigate this relationship. And if you allow it, you're doing it without me." A painful grimace distorted his face as he said the words. "Friday, I have to serve twenty-four hours in the Jackson County Jail…"

"What?" My heart stopped beating. No. This wasn't happening. "Because of the fight?"

"I go in Friday at noon and will be released Saturday at noon. My folks are driving me there and picking me up. I guess I'll see you on Sunday after your date." He palmed my cheeks, tilted my chin and forced his lips to mine. His kiss was angry and hard and I felt it held a goodbye. He easily jerked the sweatshirt from under the door and tossed it on my bed.

"Zach wait," I cried, and I heard his feet thumping down the stairs. "Zach," I yelled after him my body frozen. The front door closed, and I watched out the window as his Jeep pulled away.

FORTY-ONE

I suffered through the next few days that held little hope for me and Zach. He went through the motions of sitting next to me in Algebra, walking me to gym, escorting me to lunch, then the obligatory ride home. But there was never an offer of coming in or going to his house or anything relating to the future. I was living one hour at a time or so it seemed.

My ignorance for the legal system in Ashland was limited at best and I discovered, thanks to the Internet, that Zach would be spending his twenty-four hours in Medford. Ashland had a small holding facility but it wasn't utilized for this type of thing. I also learned that because Zach was eighteen he would be in with the adult inmates, which sickened me to the core. Child-abusers. Rapists. Even murderers. I pinched the bridge of my nose as I read. All of this was because of me. He wouldn't have been sanctioned had it not been for me. I hated myself at the moment.

"Emma?" my dad yelled from the bottom of the stairs. I clicked off the computer.

"Coming!" I hollered.

My driving test was today. I was ready. I'd studied hard and driven more than enough hours to pass this. I imagined Mom and Dad were excited too, though it closed another chapter in their life and started the next. Mom was big on talking about chapters. There seemed to be one always closing and, the more I thought about it, I had to give her credit. She was right. Ryan's chapter on high school was closing and a new chapter…a new life was before him. It was sad in a way but thrilling at the same time. I hoped the chapter for me and Zach hadn't closed.

The older female examiner—Doris—is what her badge read, asked me to follow her. I was more nervous now. I drove with caution, utilizing my blinker, abiding by the speed limit and keeping my distance between vehicles in front of me. I even nailed the parallel parking. She finally cracked a smile when we returned and gave my father an approving nod. He winked at me and when directed I offered a broad smile for the camera. I did it! My very own driver's license. I couldn't wait to show Zach. Mom and Ryan too but especially Zach.

"Congratulations Sweetheart!" My dad smiled and patted my leg.

"Thanks, Dad." I paused. "Hey. Would you mind dropping me off at Zach's so I could show him?"

"Can he bring you home by dinner?"

I wasn't sure what to say since he didn't know I was coming over. "Sure." I hoped.

"Be home by six, then." He agreed and drove me by the house. Zach's mom's car sat in front and his Jeep wasn't there. I hopped out and went to the door as if they were expecting me, rang the bell and waved to my dad as he pulled away.

"Emma. What a nice surprise," his mother greeted.

I smiled. "Hi, Mrs. Owens. Is Zach not here?"

"No. But he'll be here soon. He had a meeting today. Please come in." She stepped aside widening the passageway through the door and I stepped in. The house smelled nice.

"Mrs. Owens. May I come with you tomorrow?"

Her eyes were confused. "Where, Honey?"

"To Medford?" Mine couldn't have pleaded more.

"He told you." It was more of a statement than a question, but I nodded. "He didn't want to. He knew you'd worry."

My heart ached as her eyes saddened me. "I am worried and I want to ride with you...with him."

She shook her head. "Emma. He'd be very angry with me if I allowed that. He wants to be done with that piece of his life and certainly doesn't want you to be any part of it. Don't fault him for that."

"I don't. But Mrs. Owens…I love him and want to be there for him."

Her compassionate smile and tender hug was medicine to my soul, though it wasn't clear if I could declare victory. I heard his Jeep rumble outside. She pulled me close again. "I tell you what." She whispered. "Be here at 11:00 and we'll ambush him."

The front door opened and he tossed his book bag on the chair next to the door. His eyes widened when he saw me.

"Hey. What are you doing here?"

His mom patted my back. "I'll leave you two alone," she said disappearing into another room.

"Just wanted to show you something. How was your meeting?" Stupid question. Of course he wouldn't answer.

"Aah." He blew off the question. "Whatcha got?"

A smile broke free and induced a smile from him in return. "Pick a hand," I teased, holding my fists behind my back. He played along and pointed to my right side, which is where the license was, so I switched it quickly and held out my empty hand. So, he indicated the left side and I did the same thing flashing my open left hand.

"OK. I give." He wasn't as playful as usual.

I held up the hard piece of plastic and recognition settled over him. He grinned. "Congratulations. You earned it." He kept the distance.

"Not even a hug?" I asked disappointed, and he cautiously moved toward me as if not to tempt himself. He leaned down, and as he snugly embraced me, we both breathed easy—a relatively simple task—but the air seemed fresher and crisper and I felt like I breathed for the first time this week.

"Let's get you home." He suggested in a hushed tone.

"I still have forty-five minutes."

His mouth smiled, but his eyes didn't and he opened the front door. I stepped out into the cold evening and a sliver of moon hung in the eastern sky just above the mountains. The Jeep came to life and he steered toward my house. I contemplated refusing to get out of the car.

"Forty minutes till I have to be home." I was counting down and hope he caught my drift.

He released what seemed like a held breath. "What do you want to do Em?"

"Talk. I don't like where things are with us." I reached for his hand and held it. He squeezed my fingers and I somehow found relief in that gesture.

He parked the car in the Safeway parking lot. "Let's get through this weekend and then we'll talk."

"What's that supposed mean?"

"It means we'll talk on Sunday." His expression was one of indifference and I didn't like it.

"What time?"

"You tell me."

"Be at my house after church. No. Wait. Go to church with us," I suggested.

He smiled half-heartedly. "Let's say 11:00."

I playfully punched his shoulder. "Really. Our church is totally cool. It's Methodist and we are really laid back and you can wear jeans if you want. I don't even go to Sunday School anymore. I stay with my folks in Church and our pastor talks about stuff that I can relate too. I think you'll like. Please."

"All right," he agreed easier than I anticipated.

"Really?"

"Why not."

I kissed his cheek. "Thank you. Sunday it is."

The Jeep was moving again and we neared my house. Panicked seized me when I spotted Grant's truck. The hits just kept on coming. "Zach. I didn't know. I haven't seen him at all except at school."

"It's OK, Em. It's a small town. He's your brother's best friend. It's gonna happen." He cut the engine and was out his door and at mine.

My pace to the house was unhurried and I prayed for a kiss. "Do you want to come in?"

He shook his head. "No. I don't need to get in any more trouble."

"I understand." I moped. "Will you be in school?"

"For a bit." He swallowed. I wondered if he was nervous. "I better get."

"OK." He reached up and with his thumb traced down my cheekbone and over my bottom lip. I kissed his thumb. He dropped his hand and went back to the Jeep. My eyes stayed on him till he was out of sight.

When I woke, I noticed the weather soaked up my mood. The gray sky held little hope for the day; the dark clouds crept into the neighborhood like an unwanted visitor. I showered and dressed nicer than normal unsure what the required attire was for taking your boyfriend to jail. Mom and dad were still in the dark about my plans to ditch school, and I'd come up with little strategy on how to get away with it. Grounded again?

Zach was there on time with troubled eyes and an unconvincing smile. Silence filled the warm Jeep, and I stayed mum knowing there wasn't a lot to say. He held my hand up to the school. We usually went our separate ways, but today he escorted me to U.S. Government and kissed my forehead at the door.

"I won't be in Algebra?"

"Why?" I panicked.

"Dad wants to get an earlier start what with the fog and all."

I nodded and made a mental note. "OK."

"I'll see you Sunday?"

"Definitely." A smile touched one corner of my mouth and I kissed his fist. He kissed his index and middle finger, touched my lips, then turned and jogged down the hall. My phone vibrated in my pocket—I didn't recognize the number.

Come 15 mins earlier. Mrs. O

I smiled and joined my Government class.

Between Government and Honors English, I spotted Estelle and Connor huddled in the corner. Hmm…that must be new, I thought to myself. Connor's turn. My thoughts were ugly today.

"Hey Runt," Connor greeted first.

"Hi Con. Estelle do you have a sec?" Boy I never thought I'd be asking her for a favor.

She stared at me hesitantly for a moment then caved. "What?"

"I need a favor."

She waited.

"I have to leave for something today and I know you're a student aid for Ms. Copeland. Could you cover me?"

She propped her hands on her hips. "I'm not contributing to the downfall of a Saint, am I?" Her brows rose high on her forehead.

Play nice. "No. It's nothing like that. Just something I have to do. Please."

"Fine."

I was shocked. No thinking about it. No back talk. A simple 'fine'. "Thank you." I leaned in to give her a hug –extra effort— then I bolted for class.

Ryan had agreed to give me a ride and I texted him to let him know it was going to be fifteen minutes earlier. He was clueless as to what it was for and forewarned me of the impending doom when I got home, though he agreed not to tell. He dropped me off about a block from Zach's house and I walked the rest of the way. His Jeep was in the drive and the cold stung my face. I didn't know whether to ring the bell or wait outside. I was freezing so I opted for indoors. My finger trembled as it neared the glowing button and my heart raced anxious about his reaction. I pushed it.

His mom opened the door and greeted me with a wink, pulling me indoors. Zach was just coming down the stairs, with his IPOD in his ears. His eyes met mine and confusion clouded them. Then they darted to his mom's and clarity of our plan hit him hard.

"No!" He shook his head adamantly. "NO!" He yelled and his voice echoed through the house.

"Honey," his mom attempted.

"Mom! I can't believe you…you know how I feel." He was at the bottom of the stairs and his stance was aggressive. He was angry and his lips pulled into a near snarl.

I fidgeted with the zipper on my coat. "Zach. Don't blame your mom," my voice cracked. "I asked. I wanted to be with you."

"You *can* be with me but not like this. Not today." His eyes softened for just a moment as he moved toward me. But then, he grabbed my arm and forcefully led me to the door. "I'm running her back to school. I'll be right back." He was addressing his mom, not me. I felt like a child.

"Honey. There is no time," his mom replied.

He let me go with a slight shove. "Fine. Then we'll all drop her off on the way out."

"I want to go with you, please." Tears teetered on the edge.

"No!" His mom left the room. I felt abandoned in my efforts. "Damn it," he hissed and stomped his foot glaring at me.

I think my heart stopped as I watched him sway his head from side to side then collapse in the chair. I moved to him and the grimace on his face scared me. He hid his face with his palm, and as his chin quivered...an intense pain shot through my chest. I fell to my knees wrapping my arms over his shoulders and cried.

"I'm sorry. I'll leave." I sobbed. I heard a moan rise in his throat and suddenly, his arms gripped me so tightly that he hurt me. He buried his face in my shoulder. My throat tightened; I couldn't breathe.

"I just wanted to be with you. This is all my fault."

His hand tightened on the back of my neck and he reared back and glowered at me. "I did this." He took a long and deliberate breath and his eyes were red. "Not you."

"But you did it because of me."

With his thumbs, he wiped away the tears that had spilled over. "I knew the conditions of my probation."

"I'm so sorry." I moved toward him again and held him. I would do anything to make his pain go away. "Are you scared?" I asked, scared enough for both of us.

He looked at our hands and nodded. "Yeah." He paused. "Before—the first time...I was so strung out...I didn't care. I was also one of the oldest and biggest kids there. Now..." He didn't finish his statement but I knew what he was thinking. I kissed his cheek.

"Zachary. We have to leave." His father spoke from behind me.

"OK," he acknowledged him, then stared at me long and hard. "You ready?"

Relief flooded over me, I took his hand in mine and nodded.

Zach and I slid in to the back of his father's Passat and I buckled the center seat belt so I could sit close to him. Mr. Owens raised the rearview mirror just enough so that we weren't in his line of vision. Zach's arm fit perfectly around me and my head rested against his chest and I listened to his heartbeat beneath his shirt. He slid an ear bud in my ear and he had one in his.

"Another Journey song I like," he smiled then pushed play on the IPOD.

Just a small town girl   living in her lonely world   took the midnight train going anywhere   Just a city boy   born and raised in south Detroit   took the midnight train going anywhere.

I grinned as I listened to the words. I'd heard it several times and never personalized the words like I did now. Song after song, we listened to.

When the lights   go down   in the city   and the sun shines on the bay. Do I want to be there in my city, oh   oh   oh oh oh oh.

I knew the words by heart and sang along to myself. Medford was an easy drive—only about a half-hour. The time would fly; the drive back would be torture. My body couldn't nestle close enough, and I think he was trying as hard as I was. I wondered if he and his folks would have talked had I not interfered and tagged along. His hand rubbed up and down my back. The Journey songs came to an end and I smiled up at him as the next song played and mouthed the words.

Oh, Girl, you stand by me. I'm forever yours…Faithfully

Zach held our palms out and measured them up against one another. His hand was double in size, and he bent his fingers down over mine. I glanced up at the road when the car veered to the right—Mr. Owen's was taking the exit into Medford. My stomach rolled with the turn and I was glad I hadn't eaten breakfast. The digital clock on the dash read 10:40. Lifting my head to look at him, he focused on something out the window—maybe lost in thought for what lay ahead.

He took my hand in his and opened it, laying the IPOD in my palm. He removed his bud and dangled the wire neatly next to it then folded my fingers over it.

"Keep it for me."

I nodded. Be strong, I chanted inside my head. Then he pulled his wallet from his back pocket and handed it to me. The tick of the blinker seemed louder than a siren as his dad pulled into a parking lot and slowed to a stop. Zach unbuckled me first then him and opened his door offering his hand to me. His dad stood next to him and his mom walked around to our side of the car.

"How much time, Dad?"

Mr. Owens examined his watch. "About twelve minutes."

Zach eyed his mom then moved to her and hugged her. "I'm sorry, Mom."

Quiet tears rolled from her eyes. "I am so proud of you and who you are. Never apologize to me. You're a wonderful man with a very bright future." She patted his cheek, and then he leaned in and kissed hers. He swiveled around to me and his parents respectfully stepped away.

"Knock Knock."

I raised my brow. "Who's there?"

"Kermit."

I smiled. "Kermit who?

"Kermit a crime and you go to jail." He winked.

"That's not funny," I pouted.

He grabbed me and pulled me into his chest. "Oh. Come on. We have to lighten this mood up somehow." His lips brushed the top of my head. I wasn't sure I could do this, but I knew I wouldn't cry. He needed strength.

Nothing profound was coming to mind as much as I wished it would. "Your mom is right, you know. You *are* wonderful. You're the best thing that's ever happened to me."

"Well…don't get too down on that fact…you're only fifteen." He smiled.

I playfully shoved him.

"Two shoves in twenty-four hours. I'm not doin so hot."

"Zachary?" his father's voice interrupted, and Zach's eyes met mine.

He quickly bent toward me, brushed my forehead with a kiss, turned and met his father at the hood of the car. His dad wrapped his arm around Zach's shoulder and they walked toward the Jackson County Jail sign and disappeared inside the door. He never looked back.

"I love you," I said under my breath.

FORTY-TWO

Saturday was brighter than yesterday with the sun peeking between the broken clouds. I was shocked to see Ryan and Ali were accompanying us to wherever it was we were going. Ali didn't seem to question that I was with Grant, but I knew she would sneak a surprise attack on me when I wasn't ready. I was exhausted and feared falling asleep in the front of Grant's truck. My night was restless, and though I wore Zach's USC shirt and his sweat shorts the whole evening and then to bed, the distance between us was unbearable. I prayed he was sleeping peacefully and locked in a cell by himself, but I wouldn't have bet on it. I remembered clearly my conversation with his folks on the way back.

"Emma. Please come with us tomorrow." Mrs. Owens had requested.

Sad and feeling as if I'd already betrayed him, I responded, "I can't. I have to do something that I don't want to do but I'm obligated. Can I give you something to give to him?"

"Sure. Honey." Most of the ride was in silence with our hearts and minds elsewhere and they dropped me at home when we returned.

I'd written a note to him and given it to Ryan who dropped it by last night. I knew he was suspicious with what was going on with Zach and Grant, but he seemed to respect my privacy.

The clock on the dash read 12:10. Zach had been released…I was sure. We were on the 5 going north and already passed Medford so there was no chance of passing them. I'd give almost anything to turn around and go to him. But, by doing this…our obstacle was gone.

Grant was allowing me to pout and be stubborn. I assumed he figured I would loosen up. Time would tell.

"So. No hint?" I asked sourly.

He glanced into his rearview mirror and asked our passengers, "Should we tell her?"

I didn't expend the energy to look back at them…just waited for his response. They must have said no because he kept mum. "At least tell me where we're going?"

"Eugene."

The truck was quiet again and I heard Ali giggle, which annoyed me. I racked my brain trying to think of what it could be and outside of a Ducks basketball game…I was clueless.

"Hey," Ryan asked. "Do you remember when mom was in the hospital getting her gallbladder out and the four of us blew up the microwave?"

"That's because some dumbass forgot to take the *metal* lid off the melted cheese," I accused.

Ali laughed. "Yeah. Don't blame Em and me for that. We smelled the smoke and came running."

Grant gave a disgusted look. "I can't believe we still ate the cheese off the microwave glass. It had boiled over and was everywhere."

"It was still good," Ryan added.

"Yes it was," I said.

"That was the first time I ever kissed Ryan." Ali chimed perkily. I heard a kiss echo from the back seat. I made a face to myself.

"That's when Em kissed like a fish."

My jaw fell and I glared at Grant. "I didn't kiss like a fish."

He nodded with wide eyes. "Yes. You did." His lips puckered up tight to prove his point. "I felt like I was kissing a butt hole." All three of them busted into a knee-slapping laugh and as hard as I fought…a smile touched the corners of my mouth.

"Whatever. I was in seventh grade, you jackass. And how do you know what a butthole's like?"

"Ry. Crack the cooler open and hand me a beer," Grant laughed.

"NO! You are not drinking and driving." I jabbed my finger in his face.

He nodded. "All right."

I liked the idea of a drink for myself. Maybe getting drunk was just the thing to make this go faster.

About a mile out of Eugene, I was growing more and more anxious. "When do I get to be in on the secret?"

"Open it," Grant said nodding toward his wallet lying in the console.

I picked it up and followed his instructions. Money and white stubs. "What is it?"

"Pull out the white things."

I did and laid the wallet down so I could examine them. They were some sort of tickets. Kid Rock was written across the top. My mouth opened, but I couldn't respond. My heart sped. I flipped through them again reading today's date. "Are you kidding? Are these for real?" I managed to get out.

Grant nodded and his eyes sparkled with excitement, obviously proud of his choice.

"When did you get them?"

"You'll laugh. About three weeks ago...I won 'em off the radio. Totally lucky. But I knew when I was dialing who I wanted to take but worried I couldn't get your ass to go," he chided.

"So you resorted to blackmail?" I was too excited to be angry with him but jabbed him with the words.

His eyes held an apology. "I saw an opportunity and I took it. I don't want to talk about that right now."

I looked out the windshield and smiled. Grant smiled too. He knew I wouldn't be mad at him for long. My phone buzzed in my back pocket. I knew Grant's deal included no contact with Zach today, so I ignored it for the time being. Kid Rock. WOW.

After grabbing a bite, we headed to the concert hitting traffic on the way. The truck was quiet. It was hard not to feel relaxed with Grant. We'd grown up together. He was as much my brother as Ryan it seemed. And as angry and frustrated as I was with him, I was having a great time. That was the problem...I always had a great time with him…though my phone seemed to weigh down my pocket with every vibration.

"OK. We have about an hour and a half before the concert starts. We'll head that way in about forty-five minutes," Grant said, parking the truck and leaving on the stereo.

I heard the twist of a drink and rotated around to see Ryan handing Ali some sort of drink.

"What is that?" I asked.

"It's like a lemonade. You want one?" Ryan asked.

"Three months ago you won't let me touch a beer with Austin, and now you're handing it to me. What's up with that?" I criticized but extended my hand for the cold drink.

"A couple of reasons," my brother tried to explain. "One, Mom and Dad will be sound asleep when we get home. Two, I trust us. We're not going to let anything happen to you." He twisted my lid and handed it to me.

I swallowed the liquid and was surprised…it was pretty good. We sat and talked and laughed for forty-five minutes talking about good times and bad. I noticed two things. First, Grant seemed to nurse the same bottle of beer for forty-five minutes without finishing it, and the by the time my third bottle was empty, the whole situation was funny to me. Everything was funny…I was sitting with Grant Meiers at a Kid Rock concert, Ryan, my brother, was dating my fifteen year old best friend…Zach had just gotten out of jail and was sitting at home…and this summer….everybody was leaving everybody. Funny. So funny, I figured my fourth bottle would help me forget even that. Maybe Grant would tell me that secret after all.

Once we got into the concert, Ali and I went to the restroom. The guys waited outside. Inside a stall, I secured the door and pulled out my phone. Two texts.

I'm out. Thinkin about U. Hope you have a shitty time

U OK?

I texted back a quick response.

Miss you too. Kid Rocks her send

I used the restroom. It buzzed again before I was through.

Kid Rocks her? Here? Did he take u 2 a kid rock concert?

Yes sir! send

R u drinking?

I laughed hysterically in my stall.
"Em? You OK?" Ali shouted.
"Sure. I'll be out in a minute."
"I'm goin on out with Ryan." Her words sounded funny to me.

I'm keeping well hydrated. No worries. Send

Em. I am asking nicely please stop drinking. Call me.

Can't call. Deals a deal. Its just a lemonade. send

I shoved the phone in my back pocket, opened the stall and washed my hands. I spotted Ali standing against the cement wall like she was sneaking up on someone. Her eyes were big and got bigger when she saw me. She pointed to the wall.

"Some girls are talking to them," she whispered angrily.

"To who?" I was suddenly confused and obviously said it too loud because she shoved her finger to her lips trying to shush me. I listened.

"Well, if the girls you're waiting on don't come back, come find us," A girl giggled.

"What's your name…just in case?" Ryan inquired.

"I'm Lexie and she's Abby and you are…"

Ali and I rounded the corner at that moment and the black-headed girl who was talking had her finger under Grant's chin. "He's staken," I said, glaring at the girl.

"Staken? That's your name?" the girl with a lip ring asked.

Grant smiled at me and I grabbed his hand and jerked him away. "Staken?" he asked laughing.

"I meant taken and it didn't come out right. Shut up." I led him through a crowd of people with no idea where I was going.

I glanced back and Ali and Ryan were far behind and seemed to be fighting. Her arms were folded across her chest and his were shoved in his pocket. Grant led me to our seats three rows from the stage, packed in like sardines.

"So...I'm taken?" he asked with a grin.

"For tonight. Don't read that."

He scrunched his brows at me. "Don't read what?"

I rubbed my face as if that would make the words come out better then tried again. "Don't read *into* that. It was terr-i-torial." Was that a word? I laughed.

His face responded as if he'd gotten it. "Ah. You were marking your territory? Like a pit bull."

"Somethin like that. More like a golden retriever." I smiled.

"Glad you didn't pee on me," he said and we both laughed.

BOOM. BOOM. BOOM. A drum started beating loudly and the lights went down. I felt Grant slide his hand into mine. Why did I feel like I owed him at least that? I tried to untangle my fingers and he gripped tighter. His hands were smaller than Zach's. My heart raced as I kept my eyes on the black stage. The roar of the crowd grew with anticipation and I couldn't help but smile. I knew any minute Kid would be on stage and I was shaking with excitement. Suddenly, an explosion of sparks rocked the arena and lit the stage, Kid Rock appeared holding his mic and broke into song. I let out a scream.

When the concert was over, my throat hurt and we all headed back to the car. The crowd dispersed pretty calmly. Ali and Ryan were still on the outs.

"That was AWESOME!" I shouted lifting my hands to the sky, my ears still ringing from the sound.

"What?" Grant yelled back laughing.

"Hey man," Ryan broke in. "Could you give us just a minute before you two get in?"

Grant nodded and handed him the keys. "Sure. What's up?"

"She's pissed about the damn girls earlier. Never mind that I'm here with *her*." Ryan rolled his eyes.

"I'm cold. Don't be long," I glared at my brother as Grant and I walked toward campus.

"So…Where's Mr. California going to school?"

I shrugged and ignored his remark. "I don't know. California or maybe Kansas."

He nodded. "So what is the plan? You date until summer then it's over?"

I shrugged again. "I don't know. We've never gotten that far." He and I walked for a bit without talking. The streets were busy with college kids darting in and out of places.

"I'm sorry," he said looking straight ahead. "For making you come tonight. That was… desperate…and pathetic…and disrespectful…the list could go on."

My head was kind of spinning. "It's OK. I had fun."

"Forgive me?" His head cocked sideways as he watched my reaction.

I stopped walking and stared at him. "I could never be mad at you." I picked up his plaster cast and read all the signatures…mostly girls. I rolled my eyes at some of the comments.

"I am done. I promise." He held up two fingers like he was a Boy Scout.

"We're you ever a Boy Scout?" I asked skeptically.

He pursed his lips. "No. But…I'll leave you alone unless you tell me not to."

Why did this have to happen? I stared at him my heart aching for the feelings I used to feel. He was my world and everything in it less than a year ago. My eyes searched his for the answer, but it was evident he didn't know how or why it happened this way. With his right hand, he reached toward me and laid his palm against my cheek. His hand was warm. Then his hand slid off my cheek to wrapping firmly around my neck till he pulled me to him.

My heart accelerated as I watched him moisten his lips. I did the same thing and we touched. Our lips were together and Zach's face flashed before my eyes. I knew what I was doing was wrong.

Grant's mouth was always so warm and his lips not as firm. My hands tangled in his hair as I pulled him closer for a second…knowing this was it…acting on past feelings…telling him goodbye. I didn't know why I responded the way I did. But fear consumed me when my body began to respond. Blood rushed through my veins as he kissed me soft and long and my head still spun from before. He pulled my body into his and it felt weird to be this close and I shoved my arms between us and broke the bond. He retreated immediately and wiped his bottom lip.

"I'm sorry," he apologized, shoving his good hand in his pocket.

"I'm cold. Let's head back." I started walking.

He grabbed me from behind, and I was scared my resistance was running low. "This way," he guided, spinning me to go in the opposite direction. I followed him in silence.

"Emma. Don't just blow me off like that. Tell me you didn't feel something back there."

I tried not to look at him. "It doesn't matter what I felt. You stay loyal to who you're with."

He shot me an exasperated look. "Not at fifteen you don't. You date and you find out what fits and what doesn't. You two aren't married. This is the time to date."

He was right. But Zach was my fit and I didn't want anyone else. "Why are you doing this to me? I've wanted you forever. Why do you wait till I find someone to tell me your feelings?"

He turned around and started walking away. "Come on."

"No! Answer me," I demanded, resting my hands on my hips. "Why didn't you do it before I fell in love with Zach?" His back was to me so I couldn't see his eyes. He pushed his hair out of his face and turned around. His eyes were serious.

"Why?" I asked softly.

He moved toward me with his slow swagger that I'd grown to love. "I didn't tell you…because your brother…would have removed my lungs with a spoon. He's my best friend." He sighed. "How do you tell your best friend that you're in love with his sister, when you know he's not OK with that?"

I'm not sure what my expression held but he moved closer. "When I saw how easily he accepted Zach into your life…I was reeling with jealousy. I couldn't wait to see if what you two had was going to work or not…I had to get in there and fight." He leaned into my face, his cheek touched mine. "I knew you loved me once," he whispered. "I hoped…" His words tapered off and his lips brushed across my cheek. I closed my eyes feeling his breath against my cheek. Then unexpectedly, his lips pressed against mine softly.

"Grant," I whimpered and my lips found his. His moan made my body react in a way I knew wasn't good. His tongue was warm and full and it mingled with mine for a moment before he closed his mouth and pecked my lips twice. I opened my eyes and he was looking at me. His blue eyes were beautiful, even in the dark. He stroked my lip with his thumb.

"I'm sorry. In one sentence I say, I'm done. In the next, I'm kissing you."

I shook my head. "Grant…I."

He covered my mouth. "I know you love him. My lips are sealed. This never happened." He took my hand and we walked silently back to the truck.

The truck was warm and it wasn't clear by the looks on their faces if they'd made up or not. Ali's eyes were red and I figured she'd been crying. I'd have to get the scoop later from one of them. Ryan was at least holding her hand.

The clock on the dash read 11:30 and we had a two-hour drive ahead of us. No sleep Friday night and another late night…I would never make it home.

I was too tired to move though the cold air startled my body. My eyelids felt thick and too heavy to open.

"Ryan, get the front door and I've got her." I heard Grant's voice.

"All right."

Grant must have heaved me into his arms and my knees dangled over his elbow.

"Where are we?" I murmured and didn't really care.

Exhaustion had seized my body and I had nothing left to fight. I heard the truck door shut then another door slam.

"What the hell is wrong with her?" Was that Zach? His voice seemed so far away.

"Oh, God. I should have known. Nothing is wrong with her, you douche bag. She's tired. You tell me what's wrong. She said she didn't sleep at all *last* night. What'd *you* do to her?"

"Give her to me." It *was* Zach's voice and he was angry.

"Back off. I've got her and I'm carrying her to bed," Grant tried to whisper.

I could swear I heard Zach growl. This had to be a nightmare. "Grant, I swear to God. Give her to me or I will break you."

"Stop," I mustered enough energy to say. "Stop fighting." And I was questioning if I was dreaming. Zach was here and that was all that mattered. I wrapped my arms tightly around his neck.

"Look. She's yours. OK? Just let me get her inside."

The warmth of the house was welcoming to my body and I could tell we were going up the stairs.

"Mom and Dad are asleep," Ryan said behind us. "Please keep it down."

When my body touched the sheets, I melted into the comfort of my bed. He unclasped my hands from behind his neck. "Don't leave," I whispered.

"That must make you feel good." Zach's tone was ugly. Why was he upset?

"Not really. The words were meant for you." I heard Grant say.

"Grant?" I questioned.

"Yes?" He whispered.

"Thank you."

"Anytime sleepyhead."

"Do I still kiss like a fish?" I moaned and curled up on my side. He didn't answer. "I do, don't I?"

Still quiet. Then finally, "No."

"I've got her from here." Zach's voice barely audible. "Zach. Is that really you?" I was more alert questioning my sanity.

"It's me."

I forced my eyes open and he was blurry and it was dark. "Really?"

"Really, Em. Go back to sleep." He brushed his hand down my face.

I tried to resist. "No. I want to know about your…thing…your sleepover thing." I was confused. I wasn't sure who was in my room and who wasn't and didn't know how to word it.

"We'll talk about it later. I unbuttoned your jeans. You're covered up...now pull 'em off."

I did as he asked and threw them on the floor.

"Here's my shorts you like. Slide 'em on."

They slid up easily. "It was weird. I thought I was dreaming." I laughed. "Why are you here?"

He grinned sheepishly. "I don't know. Just making sure you got home OK."

"I missed you."

"I missed you too." He kissed my forehead. "Sleep tight. Call me tomorrow, OK?"

"Stay."

He shook his head. "I can't. You know that."

I nodded and pulled the blanket to my chin and before I knew it...I was out.

FORTY-THREE

"Emma?" Mom yelled.

I forced my eyelids open.

"Emma?

"What?" I hollered.

"It's time to get up, sleepy head."

I rubbed my knuckles with my eyes and squinted at the clock. Crap. It was 11:15. I shoved the covers back and stumbled out of bed checking my phone before heading to the shower. Ali had texted three times.

8:45—Call me!!

9:30—Please. I need 2 talk

10:40—Have u talked 2 Ryan???

Uh-oh! I walked down the hallway. His door was closed, but I heard soft music through the door so I tapped lightly.

"What?"

I opened it and peeked in. "You up?"

"Yup." He lay on his bed shooting his Nerf ball at the hoop hanging above the bed. I curled up below his feet and looked at him.

"What happened?"

He tossed a pillow across his face. "You chicks suck!"

I kicked him. "Some chicks suck and so do some of you dudes," I teased. "Are you gonna tell me what happened?"

He moved the pillow so I could see his face. "I don't know Em. I can't make her happy. No matter what I do. If we go to a movie, I looked at another girl. Tonight at the concert, I talked to another girl. She doesn't get that I like her and it's a battle I'm tired of fighting."

"Did you break up with her?"

"No. But I told her I was done trying. Then she cried. I apologized for…something. I don't even know what." He scowled as the words came out and tossed the ball into the hoop again.

"Did you all…you know?"

He shook his head. "No. We did everything but that. And *THAT* was an issue too. Why, I wouldn't do it with her." He rolled his eyes and I laughed. "What's so funny?"

I rubbed the sleep from the corners of my eyes. "Wow. What is it with you guys? You scrog any girl that opens her legs but then one asks you to and you don't?"

The nerf ball hit me in the face after it left his hands. "Excuse me. She's fifteen and I'm eighteen and somewhere along the line, Dad taught us that was a noble thing to do."

"Noble? Big word for you and you scrogged Estelle before we left. What was it…four girls in Cannon?" He smiled as I recounted. "Claire when we got back and whoever else before Ali. Show me the nobility. Please tell me you use condoms, you man whore."

This time he kicked me. "That's a stupid question, Runt. I'm not going to get some girl knocked up before college. Do you and Zach use protection?"

I retaliated by throwing the nerf ball back at him. "Dude—we haven't done it. I already told you that. "

"You're shitting me." I could read in his eyes he thought I was lying. "You've been together for like seven or eight months. What about at Shasta?"

I shook my head. "Nope. And it isn't for a lack of me trying. He wants to wait till he's off probation. I thought I told you that already."

"Why are you girls so ready to give it up? Ali was ready too."

Ryan had a great point and I didn't have a good answer. Zach and I had managed to date eight months without doing it and still had it to look forward to. "I don't know. I feel like he's the one."

"Emma, he may be the one. But what happens when we leave for Cannon or worse yet…he heads back south?"

I stood up and stretched my arms high in the air. "I'm getting in the shower."

"Hard to face?"

I ignored him. "I need to call Ali. What do you want me to say?"

He leaned off the bed and picked up the ball to resume his basketball playing. "Tell her the truth. She's got to knock this shit off and enjoy life a little and not always be looking at the dark side."

I smiled and pulled the door closed.

My chest was tight with anxiety as spring break, graduation and summer stared me in the face. Each of them...one at time...leading to our downfall. Time was running out for us and no matter what I did, he was leaving me. Ali must have conceded and adjusted herself accordingly because she and Ryan seemed back on track at least for the time being. I wasn't sure if he'd told her that he and his buddies were headed down to Puerto Vallarta for spring break. Mom and Dad were going for a couple of days too. I remembered when they gave him the trip at Christmas. He was so excited until they broke the news to him. I laughed just thinking about his face. His trip was five days and theirs three. I begged to stay home because at the time, I was broken hearted without Zach and surprisingly, they caved; especially after finding out that Zach was headed to Cancun. But now, three months later, I wished I was going.

Zach and the San Francisco crew were also headed to Cancun for five days, and I secretly hoped that he couldn't go because of his probation. I knew it wasn't fair and tremendously selfish, but I wished he'd stay. His court date was scheduled for March 9th and I, with the approval of my parents and Zach, tagged along. This drive to Medford was much different than the last—with a sense of enthusiasm filling the car.

Once inside the courthouse, we headed to the courtroom. The hallway was full and Zach held my hand as we found an empty bench where we all sat together. His attorney was waiting and pulled Zach aside to talk. Pictures of two of the judges hung in the hallway in thick gold ornate frames.

Apparently, the court docket was running behind, but given that his parents had hired private counsel, he thought we'd get right in. I was certain that would upset the other families in the hallway. Outside of an occasional hand squeeze, we didn't talk much.

"When are you leaving for Cancun," I whispered.

"I'm driving to Sacramento on Wednesday around noon and flying to San Francisco that night. Then Thursday we all fly out…stay Thursday, Friday, Saturday, and Sunday then fly back on Monday. Then staying in the city for a couple of nights." He shrugged.

"So you're leaving before school is out?" I didn't know that.

"Yeah. The place mom reserved was taken that next week starting on Tuesday so we're takin off early. Why?"

"Just wondering." I wouldn't have let him see the internal reaction firing off in my body.

The three days my folks were gone were Monday, Tuesday and Wednesday…two days of which he could be back. I wouldn't sway him. After all he'd been through, he needed this. As much as I hated it…hated being away from him.

"Are you worried?" he asked nudging me with his shoulder.

"Please. Hot sandy beach. Four gorgeous guys. Beautiful, tall, skinny girls flaunting half naked on the hot sandy beach in front of four gorgeous guys. Mix in a little alcohol." My stomach twisted just thinking about it. "Not at all."

His perfect smile eased me. "You're always so cute when you're jealous."

I elbowed him in the ribs hitting his tie. "Maybe you shouldn't drink."

His brows rose high on his forehead. "I won't drink much. You can trust that."

I found little comfort in his words.

He lifted my chin till our eyes met. "You drank with Grant."

I swallowed as he said the words. "I know."

"That was a rotten night for me," he confided.

"That was over a month ago. I thought about you the entire time." I kept my voice low.

He narrowed his gaze. "Even when you kissed him?" His eyes searched my face for a reaction. "Did you know I knew that?"

I shamefully shook my head. "Did he tell you?"

He laughed half-heartedly. "You told me. That night, we were both in your room. You were so exhausted and I don't think you had a clue who was there. You asked him if you still kissed like a fish. At first he said nothing and wouldn't look at me. Then you asked again." He closed his eyes and chuckled under his breath. "He finally said no and stared at me when he said it. You have no idea how that felt."

The side of my cheek hurt from where I was gnawing. "I'm sorry. It wasn't like a kiss that…"

He placed two fingers to my lips to stop me from talking. "Em. You're with me, not him and I know that. If you did it…you had a reason and…"

"Zach. We're up." The attorney pointed at him and he stood taking a deep breath and pressed his slacks with his hands. His dad patted his back and he held the door for his mom.

"Come on." He said looking at me.

My brows rose on my forehead. I never dreamed he'd want me inside. "Are you sure?"

"This is one you can be a part of." He smiled.

I quickly went to his side and we walked in together. The judge already sat behind the bench. This was my first time in a courtroom. It was small and outside of a clock, the walls were bare. Zach sat next to his attorney at a table and we sat behind a small partition.

"Which case?" the judge asked looking at a small table across from where we sat.

"Owens JV4744." She spoke swiftly picking a folder from a stack.

"The court will call the case of Zachary Owens. Case # JV4744—transfer of venue from the county of San Francisco, California. This is a courtesy supervision, correct?

The lady stood again. "Yes, your honor. Our court took jurisdiction in April of last year."

"Fine. Appearances."

The woman stood again. "May it please the court, Midge Harris, appearing on behalf of the state." She sat.

Zach's attorney stood buttoning his suit jacket and Zach stood beside him. "May it please the court; Zach Owens appears in person and with counsel, Jeff Hess." They sat.

"The Court is in receipt of a memo dated today's date from Mr. Owens probation officer. Have all parties had a chance to review the memo?" That must have been what his attorney showed him in the hall.

"Yes Judge." They both answered.

"Any objection to it being placed in evidence?" the judge inquired.

"No." In unison again.

"Ms. Harris?"

"Thanks, Your Honor. The state would respectfully request that Mr. Owens be released of his probation. The memo reflects that he did everything as directed in his original probation agreement and the state would commend him on his efforts." She found her chair again.

"Mr. Hess?"

"Thank you Judge. Ms. Harris is correct. My client has gone above and beyond what he has needed to do to complete his probation. He has certainly learned his lesson and I feel confident, Your Honor will never see him before this Court again. We would ask that the court follow the state's recommendation and terminate probation. Thank you."

The judge lowered his glasses on his nose and looked at Zach. My heart beat hard.

"Young man, would you like to address this court?"

Zach's nervous eyes jetted toward his attorney who nodded at him then back to the judge. Zach stood. "I just want the court to know that I did learn my lesson, and I guarantee—you won't see me back here." He nervously chuckled at the end. "Thank you."

"Thank you, Mr. Owens." The judge said and paused, writing on something. "The court finds that Mr. Owens has successfully completed his probation and will terminate the case. Is there anything further to come before the court?"

"No, Judge." Both parties answered.

"If there's nothing further, the court is in recess."

Zach's attorney stood and gave him a solid pat on the back. The smile and relief on Zach's face was infectious and I smiled too. He turned to us and shook his dad's hand, then gripped his mom in a hug.

"We are so proud of you." Typical mom. He released her and walked around the partition.

"The best for last," he whispered, then hugged and lifted at the same time so my feet dangled in the air. I giggled.

"Congratulations." I whispered.

"No, don't. Don't congratulate me on this. That should come at graduation or a college acceptance but not at this." He kissed my lips quickly before placing my feet back on solid ground.

"You two ready to get out of here?" His dad had one had on Zach's back and one on mine.

Zach sighed and rolled his eyes. "Are we ever." The court room door closed behind us.

FORTY-FOUR

Mom hustled around the house making sure I had numbers to call, food to eat and gas in the car, which was odd because I wasn't allowed to drive anywhere. She'd made arrangements for our neighbors, Bob and MaryLou to check on me daily. I was scared and nervous with them leaving. I'd never spent much time alone and three days was huge. Mom and Dad seemed as nervous as I was. They'd spoken with Ali's folks and Ali was staying with me. I knew daytime wouldn't be an issue but struggled with the thought of sleeping in the house alone or with Ali.

They were packed and ready to go and still had to pick up Grant, Brett and Conner.

"Are you sure about this?" My dad asked with both his hands firmly gripping my shoulders.

"Yes, sir." I saluted him and smiled.

"This is weird, leaving my fifteen year old home alone."

"Dad. I'll be fine. It's three days. AND, I'm almost sixteen."

He hugged me and kissed the top of my head. "I know you will be, sweetheart. I love you. Remember do not text us because it costs a fortune down there. OK?"

"I remember. You'll have your PC so I can e-mail."

"Good girl. Katie....Ryan....let's go." As they moved out the door and waved, a loneliness like I'd never known settled over me.

I had rented five movies and decided to start with *The Breakfast Club*. John Hughes was my mother's favorite filmmaker and director. I heard a lot about these movies growing up and decided it was time to watch. It was well into *Pretty in Pink* a few hours later when my phone buzzed. It was Zach!

Hey baby. Back n SF! Ill call u later. Love.

I actually hugged the phone.

Miss you so much! Love to you too. Send

Huge pet peeve when people didn't just spell right on a text. It doesn't take that long to type you over u. Or see over c.
My phone buzzed again. This time it was Ali.

Doing OK?

Fine. You? Send

I miss him.

I knew how she felt because I hadn't seen Zach in almost five days.

I know. It'll go fast. Send

Call me later.

OK send

A few hours later, I took a long bath with candles and music. As much as I tried to relax, I felt paranoia creep into my mind about the upcoming night. With every minute my body soaked in the hot water, the house creaked and moaned. I'd told Ali the first night I'd do fine on my own. I wasn't so sure. Thank God Reesy was here.

When the water turned colder, I blew out the candles and pulled the plug. Never having the time to lotion, I slathered my body and stood in the bathroom naked allowing it to dry. The reflection in the mirror brought a smile to my face. The person standing before me was becoming a young woman. I embarrassed myself and grabbed my fluffy robe.

The phone rang and, of course, the phone for upstairs was down. I ran hoping to catch it before it went to voicemail. The caller ID read, Matt Hendricks.

"Hi, Dad."

"Hey sweetie. How's it going?"

"Fine. Just got out of the bath. Where are you guys?" I plopped down on the sofa.

"Well. We're in Portland getting ready to take off. We've boarded. Just wanted to let you know. Is the alarm set?" There was a lot of noise in the background.

I smiled. "Yes, Dad."

"OK. Well sleep tight and we love…" the phone went dead.

"Dad?" Nothing. I hung up.

My hair was wet and I headed back upstairs to blow dry it. The phone in my hand rang again. I laughed when I answered. "I know…you love me right?"

"Yes, I do."

"Zach?" I asked.

"Hey, baby."

"Zach!" My voice was shrill even to me.

"You sound surprised. Who else loves you?" He laughed.

"My dad. What are you doing?" I sat down midway up the stairs.

"Oh. We're at Travon's house hanging out."

"When are you coming back?"

He hesitated. "A couple of days. Travon and I are going to hit some old hot spots down here tonight. I'll touch base tomorrow."

HOT SPOTS? I felt sick. I didn't want him going out down there. "OK. Be good." Disappointment settled over me. I hoped he didn't hear it in my voice.

"You all right?"

"Yeah. Have fun."

"I did have fun and I miss you."

I was quiet. I couldn't help it. "I miss you too."

"Em. Do you want me to drive home tonight? Because I will."

YES. I wanted to shout. "No. Just be good." That's twice I'd said that.

The doorbell chimed. "Crap. Someone's at the door."

"Well. Answer it." He said.

"No. It's dark."

"Get your dad to answer it."

"They're gone. I'm by myself." My heart beat frantically in my chest.

He cleared his throat. "Where are they?"

"I'll explain later. What should I do?"

"Let me call my dad." I liked this suggestion.

"OK. But, wait. Maybe it's MaryLou from next door. Let me try and peek."

"Em. Be careful."

I inched down the stairs and lifted my finger to slowly pull the material back.

"Em?"

"Just a minute," I whispered, trying to make out the figure in the light. Suddenly, I saw his face through the window. He smiled. The phone fell from my hand. I unlocked the dead bolt, turned the knob and threw open the door.

"ZACH!" My scream was muffled by the alarm echoing in the night. Crap. I entered the code as quick as possible and disarmed it. "Oh my God! What are you doing? You lied to me." I threw myself into his arms which wrapped tightly around me.

"I tricked...not lied," he corrected stepping inside with me in his arms and shut the door behind him.

I tightened the ties on my robe. "You said you were in San Francisco."

His smile was big and proud. "I wanted to surprise you. I didn't want you to know I got off the plane and drove straight here. In fact, if you give me a second, I'll be asleep."

"Come sit." I motioned to the sofa. His skin was tan from the Mexican sun and he looked unbelievably beautiful. A small shell necklace hung around his neck. His knees cracked as he sat. "Nice necklace."

He fingered it. "Mercy purchase."

"What do you mean?"

"Oh my God. There were tons of little Mexican kids selling stuff on the beach. It's sad. Guilt won over several times." He laid his head back against the pillow. His eyes were tired and white circles surrounded them where his sunglasses protected his eyes. His arm wrapped around my waist and pulled me to his chest. "Man. It feels good to be home." He sighed. "You said your folks were gone, where?"

I closed my eyes as his fingers pulled through my wet hair. "They went with Ryan for three days." I smiled to myself waiting for his reaction. He was home and I wouldn't be alone after all. My parents would be pissed. They knew Zach was gone too or I'd be on a plane to Mexico right now.

"When did they leave?"

"Today." I chewed on my thumbnail.

"So, I have three days to spend with you?" His voice perked up a bit.

I nodded, my head still on his chest. He was warm. I had a feeling our thoughts were in the same place. "I hope it's more than three days."

"You know what I mean."

I giggled. "Your parents may not be OK with you being MIA for a couple of days," I whispered.

"They don't know I'm back." His voice was low and full of insinuations and my body tingled as he spoke. "I have something for you in the Jeep. Let me run out and get it." He lifted my head and slid out from under me.

"Wait."

His glance held questions. "What?"

"Are you…staying?"

He pushed a strand of hair behind my ear. "Do you want me to stay?"

Oh My God! No way. This was going to happen. Another set of implications saturated my mind as I contemplated his offer. Nothing was there to stop us tonight. No probation. No friends in the other room. No parents. I wanted this more than anything, but I was suddenly scared shitless. My eyes flickered to his and away. I nodded since whatever was wedged in my throat wouldn't move.

He spun his keys around his finger and the corners of his mouth turned upward in what seemed an understanding smile. I had a feeling, he'd read my mind. "I don't have to stay."

"I think you should move the Jeep into the garage," I suggested.

He smiled bigger. "OK," he said, and went back outside.

For a short minute, I had to concentrate on breathing before I went to the garage and opened the door.

When he came back in, he had a small bag in his hand and he held it out to me.

"What's the code?" he asked as he shut the door.

"6151" I answered, opening the sack.

"It's nothing big."

A tiny, delicate bracelet…maybe macramé…with a tiny shark tooth attached lay in the sack.

"It's an anklet."

"I love it. Thank you." I leaned up and kissed him and he swooped me off my feet and carried me to the sofa. "Did you guys have fun?" I held my robe closed.

"We did. There were so many people."

"People—girls?"

He smiled. "Yes, there were girls."

I chuckled nervously.

He squeezed his lips together. "I told you I'd be good and outside of seeing a lot of naked boobs…it was a piece of cake."

I breathed a sigh of relief. "Why do girls do that?"

"Usually because they're drunk. It gets them attention."

"Hmm."

"Come here," he said. I was already on his lap and about two inches from his face.

"I'm right here," I explained.

"But that's not close enough." His fingers wrapped around the back of my neck pulling my face toward his, and he smiled just before our lips met for the first time in nearly a week. His breath was sweet and warm. I was hungry for his taste, so I pulled him as close as I could. As one kissed turned into another, he laid me back on the sofa and I was careful to hold my robe closed. His eyes smoldered and when his hand slid between my skin and the fuzzy material then traced down my back, the coolness of his fingers took my breath. I gasped as he rubbed from my shoulder blades, over my ribs and down to my…he stopped short of where my panties typically bordered my hips and his eyes popped open. So did mine. I was embarrassed.

"I'd just gotten out of the bath tub." My words were choppy as I tried to explain.

He breathed heavier than normal. "It's OK. I just wasn't…" His eyes took in every square inch of my face and I outlined his lips with my index finger. His grip around my waist tightened again and I loved feeling his bare skin against mine.

"Maybe I should check out your tan. Why don't you ditch your shirt?" It was more a suggestion than a question.

Keeping his hand on my waist, he pulled behind his neck with the other hand and the shirt came up and off. His sun-touched skin made each muscle more defined than ever before. Five days in the sun did him well. My little hand ran up his arms, across his chest and to his ribs. He wet his lips and kissed me again. His hand skimmed over my hip and down the side of my thigh.

"How's your self control?" he asked.

I laughed quietly and fought for his lips again. "Why?"

He rubbed over my knee then up my thigh and my heart fell into my stomach. "I have no reason to stop any more."

I knew he was right. Nothing stood in our way now…except my sudden fears. My stomach quivered as I thought about it. "We're on the sofa," I complained. And he immediately lifted me and started up the stairs, kissing my neck as he turned in to my bedroom. My heart accelerated as he laid me on the sheets and I knew this could be perfect. I just wasn't sure I could follow through. What was wrong with me?

His kisses were soft and long and deliberate and it was difficult to concentrate. "I love you." His words were strong.

"Zach…do you think…" I stopped short of finishing as he located my collarbone with his lips.

"Hmm?"

"Do you think that…that…maybe…"

He straightened his arms lifting himself over me and stared down. "Do I think what?" He paused searching my eyes. "Do I think you aren't ready for this?" He was barely audible.

"I am ready," I lied. "I've even been on the birth control pill for three months."

"What?"

"I just didn't expect you tonight and I…I'm scared." My voice trembled and he nestled on the mattress next to me and chuckled. "Don't laugh at me."

"I'm not laughing at you, Tiger."

"What's so funny? Tiger?"

He rubbed my stomach. "You. For the past eight months you have tested my self control like no one ever before. You knew I wouldn't give in so you pushed it and teased and played and now it's my turn. I knew when I asked if you wanted me to stay and your entire body tensed up…" He laughed harder. "I know what went through your mind. It's OK, Em. I'm not going to push you into doing anything you aren't ready for. My little tiger turned into a kitten, though."

"But I am ready."

"No. You're not, baby. Some day. And never as long as you're scared." His lips pecked the end of my nose.

"Don't you want to?"

"Oh my God." He rolled on his back. "I feel like I'm going to explode."

I sighed and pouted as he twisted me to my side and pulled me back in to his stomach draping his arm over me.

"I'm trying to remember that you are only fifteen so help me out just a little."

The hair on the back of my neck stood. "I knew that would come up."

"Emma. It is a fact that we can't ignore," he whispered into my hair.

"So. We wait till May…two more months. Scrog the night before I leave and you leave and never see each other again." I said bitterly. I hated that I couldn't see his face.

He inhaled deeply and released it. "If that's what you want."

"What I want?" I rotated to my back. "What do *you* want?"

He rose to his elbow. "I want *you* more than anything. I want you more than college, more than my family, more than any other woman I've ever known. And that's not OK. Because I know that in three or four months I have to walk away from a small town that I swore I would never like, and it kills me to think of doing it. I'm already thinking about what college breaks I could come home to see you. And that's not fair because you have three years left here and you deserve to live it and not wait it out. I've been where you are. I've done the things you're wanting to do and I won't take that from you. So…what do I want? If we make a choice in May to…be together then I'll take it. But I *will* give you proper warning. If you ever ask me to make love to you or tell me that you want me, I will never deny you again."

I wasn't sure if in the darkness he could see the single tear falling down my cheek. There was nothing more to say. "I love you." My voice was softer than a whisper.

"And I love you." He nestled close and I found comfort in the closeness.

The clock read 10:53 and as my eyes closed, I'd never felt safer in my own house than I did at this moment.

I woke up sweating and gasped for a breath. I was so hot. Zach's arm was snuggly wrapped around my waist and I lifted it trying not to wake him before I slid out. The robe was suffocating and I grabbed his USC shirt off my bedpost. The green digital numbers read 3:37.

After untying the robe, it fell to the floor and I slid the burgundy shirt over my head. The cold air was refreshing and I pulled my hair out from under the shirt. Now underwear.

"You are so beautiful."

His voice startled me and my face flushed. "Zach." I didn't know what to say. I was afraid he had seen me naked. "I'm sorry. Did I wake you?"

"No. Come here."

"Just a sec. I don't have…" I took a step toward my dresser before he caught my wrist and held it. In the moonlight his eyes were serious.

"I know what you don't have." His voice was low and rough and he pulled me onto the bed.

I tried to swallow but my mouth was dry. I prayed the thumping of my heart couldn't be heard or felt. At that moment, he rested his palm against my sternum seeming to read my mind again.

My breathing was sporadic and as he gently pushed against my breastbone, I fell backward on the bed holding on to the T-shirt that was thankfully too big and was able to cover my underwear-less bottom half. He was on his knees staring down at me, his chest still bare. With his fingers, he intertwined our hands then raised them above my head. This was playing out like a movie in my head and I worried I couldn't live up to what he expected.

He kissed my forehead and I closed my eyes as he moved to my cheek, chin and hollow of my throat. He lifted my shirt…his shirt…and the cool air hit my stomach and other parts that were exposed and he released my wrists but I didn't move them. I lifted his chin wanting to keep his eyes on the upper part of my body and he smiled.

"Trust me," he whispered between kisses across my ribs, inching toward my breasts.

"I trust you more than anything in this world," I said and brought my hands to his head running my fingers through the softness of his hair. At the moment, his mouth covered my breast. And as small as they were, the warmth of his mouth produced a mighty big feeling. His contact seemed to have a direct line to my lower half that squirmed a bit beneath him. When he found my hipbone and kissed it, I shook with excitement. But he was too close for comfort.

"Zach…I."

"Trust me." His words were so soft. I was surprised I could hear him over my panting. His kisses moved down my thigh, then slowly back up, leaning inward, and I covered my face with my hand trying to ward off the awkwardness.

"Zach."

"Yes?" The breath from his mouth sparked goose bumps as he wedged himself between my legs. "Do you want me to stop?"

I knew what he was getting ready to do. My hands, tangled in my own hair, balled into fists as I considered his suggestion. My body ached. And as his mouth touched my body where no one had ever touched, I released a whimper and closed my eyes. "No."

FORTY-FIVE

A storm moved in overnight and the sky looked gray and dreary when I woke. Wet droplets hung on the window and thunder rumbled in the distance. His breathing was deep and heavy behind me and the clock read 11:20. Crap. I needed to check my email and respond to my parents or the police would be here any moment. His arm rested on my hip and I lifted it laying it on the bed gently then moved away. He didn't stir.

I pulled the door almost shut and bolted to the bathroom where I quickly jumped in the shower. As the water washed over my body, I thought about what he'd done to me last night. I'd never experienced anything like it and I embarrassed myself remembering what I, in turn, did to him. I'd never done that either and wondered if I'd done it right. Pushing the thoughts from my mind, I got out, brushed my teeth and dabbed a bit of make up on before I headed downstairs. A cold bottle of Dr. Pepper was waiting patiently for me in the fridge and I grabbed an orange that mom had bought when she stocked the house for me. As I walked back through the living room, Zach's phone vibrated on the coffee table and the screen indicated two new messages. I held the phone in my hand and curiosity burned into me as I stared at the read button. I glanced up the stairs and pushed it.

*Call us, honey.   M—*I smiled as I read the text from his mom. He needed to call them.

Second message. I pushed read.

Dude- pics r on website. Did u make it home 2 ur girl? U whipped bastard   c ya!   The message was from Jackson.

Uncontrollable thoughts bounced around in my head and I sat on the coffee table. Website? I smiled about the whipped part. At least he was excited to get home to me. I stood gathering my thoughts and walked up the stairs with his phone, my orange and Dr. Pepper in hand.

His body lay still on the bed and his legs were tangled in the sheets. His skin so dark against the pale sheets. His lips were slightly parted and his bare chest moved up and down with each peaceful breath.

I slid into my chair at the desk as quietly as I could. After jiggling the mouse around, the computer came to life. My gut, churned as it hit me that this website was what Grant had somehow become aware of and warned me about. The Google screen popped up and the cursor blinked waiting for my command. I slowly typed trying to make little noise.

Zach Owens Enter. The hourglass spun and as I waited, the different sites popped up.

Zach Owens—who's who among students, Zach Owens—Zimbabwean tour, Zach Owens—NASA instructor, Zach Owens—scoreboard, Zach Owens—entertainment daily. Seven more pages were available. I moved the mouse to Zach Owens—entertainment daily and clicked. Some paparazzi page came up with pop ups and downloads and I quickly clicked back and rocked in the chair. What I was doing wasn't honest or good and I disappointed myself.

"Zach?" I spoke above a whisper.

It was weird. He instantly opened his eyes and glanced around my room. "Hey. What are you doin?" He stretched and rubbed his eyes then ran his fingers through his hair. "Have you already showered?" He seemed surprised.

I nodded. "I need to talk to you."

He scooted to the edge of the bed. "OK. Can I shower or brush my teeth first?" he laughed.

I handed him his phone and his brows lowered. "It was vibrating downstairs and…I checked the messages. I'm sorry." I hung my head. "I wasn't trying to be nosey and I do trust you." I paused and he smiled at me. "Maybe a little nosey."

"Em. You can check my messages any time. I have nothing to hide from you. Who were they from?"

"Your mom. You need to call her by the way. And…Jackson." My eyes watched him for a reaction. His shoulders fell slightly and I think he was watching his own reaction.

"OK. What did it say?"

"You read it." I nodded toward the phone.

He pushed some buttons and smiled once. He shrugged. "That's just my friends. They made fun of me because I wanted to get back…to you. The whipped remark was them being stupid."

"I know. But…what website?"

He closed his eyes, and took a deep breath in and opened them as he released the air. He must have noticed the computer screen behind me because he tilted his head looking at it. "You looked it up?" His voice cracked when he asked and a panicked look crossed his face.

"I tried. I don't know which one it is. I'm guessin the Who's Who you'd be proud of so unless you went on a Zimbabwean tour, work for NASA on the side or are a scorekeeper then I haven't found it yet."

He cleared the frog in his throat. "I thought we agreed to wait until May. Am I wrong?"

He was right. "I think I'd like to see these pictures."

"I can't show you *just* those pictures, Em. Let's wait. We have so much to look forward too—your track meets and prom and graduation. Remember, you wanted to take me down the Rogue River on that jetty."

He really didn't want me to know.

"If you want to jump in the shower and brush your teeth, that's fine. I'm going to peel this orange and drink my soda. I'll wait for you."

He stared at me—a quiet surrender—and his jaw locked. He stood and walked to the bathroom and closed the door. I opened the soda and took a swig closing my eyes as it fizzed in my mouth.

About ten minutes passed before the shower went off and the door opened. He wore a pair of shorts with no shirt. His hair was wet and water droplets still ran from his shoulders. The thought of making love to him before finding out his terrible secret crossed my mind especially given the way he looked at this moment.

"Can I say one thing before we do this?" he asked.

"Of course."

"Everything you're going to see or read happened before I met you. I've never been disloyal to you and I never will. We were stupid and out of control. I was drinking a lot." He released a long breath.

"I don't know what to say because I don't know what we're talking about. I'm assuming it has to do with girls." He looked away from my eyes.

"Promise me…one thing…that's all I ask." His eyes were on me now.

"I'll try." I hoped I could.

"Don't kick me out of here, don't make me leave…I swear, I'll give you space. I'll leave you alone, but let me stay."

I shrugged. "OK. I don't want you to leave." I smiled.

He moved the mouse to the one that read www. scoreboard or something or other. He clicked on it and took my hand in his firmly. I smiled when I saw all four of their pictures pop up. Travon. Will. Jackson. Zach. Each of them distinctively different, but all of them hot. Zach was the hottest by far.

SCOREBOARD
The race is on!

Under Zach's name, it read Playa 1. He moved the mouse over his picture and stopped.

"Can I just tell you? Would you take my word, if I just told you what we did?"

"You can tell me, but I still want to see it."

He suddenly shoved his lips to mine, kissing me more forcefully than ever before. His lips, tight at first, then softening as he slowed and the kiss came to an end. Then he softly pecked me three times before pulling away. This wasn't good. He clicked on his picture. A list of names popped up. Girl's names.

```
Jessica— 11/21   16   BJ
Marley— 11/23   15   BJ
Lisa— 12/4   16   VS
Susan— 12/17 puma   BJ, S
Kristi— 12/17 puma   S
Madison— 12/31   16   VS, BJ
Mindy— 2/7   15   S
Jenn— 2/14   19   BJ
Taylor— 3/8   MILF   BJ, S, M
Carly— 5/26   16   VS
Maria— 6/10   23   BJ M
Kathleen— 6/29   17   VS
Paula— 7/4   17   S
Abby— 8/16   17   S,BJ
Olivia— 9/19 Cougar—S, BJ
Rachel— 11/22 16 BJ
Brandy— 12/17 15 BJ, S
Erin— 12/19 19 S
Lauren—12/20 16 BJ
Mackensie—12/21 22 BJ
Estelle— 7/17   17 S, BJ
```

What? A list of girls names who I knew nothing about except the last one. "Tell me what it means. Explain it to me." I whispered the words.

His eyes were closed and he shook his head. "It means nothing. Literally."

"Tell me," I gritted through clenched teeth.

"The BJ stands for blowjob," he said matter of fact and his hand tightened on my wrist.

"What I did last night?" I questioned.

"Yes," he spoke softer than a whisper.

I'd never done that before and he's had it done...1, 2, 3, 4, 5, 6, 7, 8, 9, 10, 11...no wait...he had had it done...by 13 girls?? I was fourteen? Instinctively, I put my palm over my mouth.

"And the S—that stands for sex?" I was going to cry. There was no doubt about it.

"Yes." His voice was a little louder.

"Yes? Like you *scrogged* all these girls?" My voice raised and I locked my fingers behind my head.

"Uh-huh."

I felt like I'd been kicked in the chest. His hands were suddenly on my shoulders. I flinched away from his touch and he retreated. "What's a cougar?" I couldn't look at him.

"It's an older woman."

I felt my face contort into an awkward expression. "Older? What does that mean?"

He covered his face with his palms and breathed heavily. "It's a woman who's at least forty."

I rested my forehead on my fingertips as my head spun and vomit seemed to work its way up my esophagus. "Oh my God. That's like my mother!"

"Emma. Listen to me." He grabbed my shoulders.

"What's a MILF, a puma? What's the M stand for?" I caught myself shouting and tears pooled as the words came out.

"Emma, Please."

"Tell me!" I yelled, slapping his hand away from me.

He fell back onto my bed. "A MILF is a mom I'd like to fuck, a puma is a late twenty, early thirty."

"And the M? Is that a mom?"

"No. It's married," he whispered.

"Oh God," I shouted and grabbed the trash can next to my desk, and it came, the Dr. Pepper mixed with bits of orange and maybe bile from my stomach. I hung my head over the plastic can with spit dangling from my mouth. He grabbed my hair and pulled it back. My throat constricted and I couldn't breathe.

"Breathe, Emma," he whispered.

"I can't."

"Yes. You can." He rubbed my back and I dry-heaved once more wrenching my gut before I could sit up.

In and out, I thought to myself sitting back in the chair. I wiped the tears from my cheeks. "Tell me the V. I think I know, but I want to hear you say it." I feared I'd vomit again. I could hear myself whistling.

A long minute passed before he answered. "A virgin." His voice trailed off.

"You…had sex….with four virgins?"

He stood up. "Not one of them was under sixteen."

I chuckled sarcastically. "Did you love any of them?"

His eyes narrowed. "No."

My chest was constricting at the thoughts going through my head. "How could you do it then? You went after girls because they were virgins? Oh my God." My lip trembled. He'd been with so many women. Nothing I did was new to him. I was a conquest for his scoreboard.

"No! That's not what it was like."

My body felt weak. I felt weak, pathetic. He'd experienced the world and I'd experienced nothing. He'd had twenty-something women…married women and ugh. He moved toward me. He felt sorry for me. I was the girl who could barely breathe on her own.

"Don't touch me," I warned and he took another step. "Get out of my house."

He retreated. He was leaving. That was for the best. He stopped at my desk and snatched up my inhaler then turned toward me shaking it.

"NO!" I hit his chest with my fist and he didn't flinch. "I hate you," I said coldly and tried to shove him.

"No. You don't. You hate what I did. Now use the inhaler."

My teeth clenched together and I refused. I was being stupid. I knew I needed the albuterol. My breaths were short and coming quicker.

"Come on Em. Take it."

Being stubborn was one thing, being this stupid was another. I'm not sure I was done making my point, but my chest was about done. I knew this because the lack of oxygen had left my arms limp and light-headedness had crept into me.

His arm wrapped around my waist and moved me to the bed. My head rested on his shoulder for its final time; as he slid the inhaler between my already parted lips, I wondered if he saw the irony in what was happening. As he compressed the tube and the mist entered my mouth providing my lungs with relief, he was essentially giving me life. But it was a life that I knew I would live without him now. The irony of this situation was that he was saving me and emotionally killing me all in a few moments.

A long, slow breath came to me on its own. The revelation came to me all at once too. Maybe it was the suddenly clear mind.

I plopped down in front of the computer. "How do I add a name?"

"What?"

I hit the computer screen with my finger. "Add my name. Do it now. Type in Emma...March 17...15...BJ."

"Stop," he said dryly.

"When I see it again...I better be on there." I walked out of my bedroom and down the stairs.

FORTY-SIX

ZACH

After she left the room, I fell back onto her bed and stared at the ceiling fan circulating the air. As the breeze blew over me, I prayed. I hadn't prayed often. I prayed that night in juvenile detention. I prayed the day we moved. I prayed the day I saw blood coming from her head and I couldn't tend to her. I prayed the night I sat in jail. I prayed now. I prayed for God to make things right, not even knowing what that meant.

Deep down, I'd known all along I wasn't good enough for her. The things I'd done. The things I'd seen. The things I'd been a part of. I wanted to change. I wanted her to see that I was everything she needed and wanted me to be. I didn't think that would ever happen, not now.

The little red inhaler in my hand gave her life. I simply wanted to make her smile. To make her feel safe. To make her feel special. I had failed miserably and done none of the above. God, if she only knew…

Forcing myself up and off the bed, I stared at the messed up sheets from the night before. I'd never slept with a girl, I mean actually slept. Never had a desire to stay with one. The thought of never sleeping with her again… I shook away the thoughts. What I did last night was downright playing dirty. I knew she wouldn't stop me from going down on her, and I never predicted she would reciprocate, but there was no way in hell I was turning her down. The innocence in her touch, the passion in her kiss, the love in her eyes…I'd never felt any of that before. She believed in me. She believed in me more than I did. Maybe more than anyone else.

I had to find a way to let her know how much I cared. How much she meant to me. I wouldn't let go. Not yet. I needed her and I believe she needed me too. I had two more days to prove my love, gain her trust back and beg her forgiveness. I'd never done these things either…but I would give this my best effort.

FORTY-SEVEN

Emma

The agonizing ache ripping through my chest was unbearable. I fell on the sofa and pulled my knees to my chest. The fetal position was comforting. As tears streaked my cheeks, my nose swelled inside making it impossible to breathe. I lay with my mouth open to get air then finally tried to blow. I tossed the tissue onto the coffee table and saw the shirt he'd worn here last night. I remembered him tossing it. Was that just last night? I pulled it close and smelled it, then wiped my tears before I threw it across the room, and then the tears came again in sobs.

I'm not sure how long I lay there before he came down the stairs. He picked up his shirt as he crossed the floor and I know he looked at me but I didn't look back.

"Emma. All of that was before…"

"Did you add my name?" I cut him off. My eyes were swollen and I couldn't fully open them.

"Stop that. I'm not going to add your name. I don't know how to get you to understand." He sounded frustrated.

"Understand what? That if we ever scrogged, you'd of scored big points. How can I even compete with all those women? How was my first blow job by the way? I sat up and my head felt fuzzy.

He didn't answer any of the questions.

"Oooh. That bad, huh." I shuffled to the kitchen.

He stood and followed. "I'm not going anywhere. I'll be here when you're done being mad."

"Did I even do it right?" Still no answer. I opened the fridge, got nothing out and shut the door, going back to the living room. "OK then. That would be a no."

He grabbed my shoulders and stopped me. "Em. It was perfect. But not because of what you did, but because it was *you*. Don't you see the difference?"

"Get your hands off of me!"

"Why? Cause I'm dirty? Is that it?" He stepped in front of me when I tried to walk. "You think I'm dirty now?"

I shoved my finger in his face. "NO Zach! I'm the one who's dirty. My mouth where…oh my God. I can't even say it." The tears were back.

"Emma. You aren't dirty."

"Did you even wear protection?" I wiped the tears away.

He pursed his lips. "I never did NOT wear one during sex."

"Please leave, please," I cried, and sat where I had been standing in the middle of the floor.

"No. We have two days to get past this." He sat next to me.

What was he thinking? Get past this? Grant was right. I couldn't get past this. I stared at his pleading eyes. "I won't get past this. How could I ever be with you, knowing I'd be a name on a list."

He balled his hands into fists. "You are different. You wouldn't be a name on a list. You're the girl in my heart."

I stood and ran up the stairs.

My bedroom clock read 4:10 when Zach knocked at the door. I lay across my bed and determined that my body couldn't stop producing tears. There seemed to be an endless reservoir.

"Em. I'm setting some food out here. You need to eat. I won't be out here but please open the door and get the food."

It was quiet again. After a bit, I peeked out. He'd made a peanut butter and jelly sandwich with chips and a Jell-O. I shut the door and went straight to the computer and found the web page this time clicking on Travon's picture—his list was much the same with twenty-three girls. I clicked back and moved the cursor to Will's—twenty-six, which surprised me because he wasn't as good looking as the rest. Jackson sat at twenty. I clicked back to Zach…he was the lowest in points and had gained zero since Estelle.

I stayed home on spring break for a reason…I had to study…so I got on my CD drive and opened the material. Today was the Vietnam War and I listened intently to the narrator and followed by taking notes. My test was Monday at the school in the counselor's office. I hoped I could be ready.

I read until I couldn't see straight but still wasn't sure if we lost or won the war. It was 6:30. I walked down the stairs quietly and he was asleep on the sofa. I stood and stared at him, lying on our sofa, bare chested and beautiful. No tears came. Finally. I wondered if that was a good or bad thing. I wanted to go to him to hold him and to tell him how much I loved him, but I couldn't bring myself to do it. The TV was on Sportscenter but with no volume. His phone lay in front of him on the coffee table and I picked it up. He had phoned his mom earlier and I smiled replacing it in its spot. A spiral notebook was across his stomach and I tilted my head trying to read it. Scribbled on the paper was Ryan, Grant, Estelle. Hmm.

I grabbed a bottle of water out of the fridge, headed back up the stairs and stepped over my delivered dinner and shut my door.

After staring at the computer until my eyes grew heavy, I lay across my unmade bed; his smell inundated the sheets. I buried my face in the pillow inhaling the scent that I'd grown to love. Maybe this was for the best. We break up now and then I wouldn't have to endure the pain later. I couldn't imagine never holding him again, never kissing him again, never feeling his breath against my skin. I wasn't sure I'd ever love again. No one could compete with what he'd given me…with what he was to me. His USC shirt was at the foot of my bed. I grabbed it and shoved it over my head then collapsed onto the pillow.

It was 1:15 in the morning when I woke up to find Ryan's Ducks blanket over me. Zach had visited sometime during the night. I moved to the edge of the bed unable to go back to sleep and noticed my tray of food was gone. My heart ached, my body was numb. I didn't understand this inexplicable feeling inside. Why did I want to forgive already? I needed to be angry. I wanted to be angry. This was not okay. I needed him and his arms and his smile.

The house was dark as I moved quietly from my room and down the stairs. The TV flickered against the wall and splashed across his face. The ache grew as I stepped closer to him and watched his chest move with each breath. I knelt next to the sofa. He had one hand behind his head and the hair under his arm was dark. I cautiously laid my head against his chest and felt instantly soothed by the rhythm of his pulse in my ear. His body jerked and his heart rate accelerated when his eyes opened. He raised his head and looked down at me lowering his arm and touching my hair.

"What's wrong?" he whispered as if someone else was in the house.

I didn't want him to know that I missed him…that I wanted him…or that I needed him. My body reacted on its own by pulling away. He stopped me.

"What?" His eyes were dark and concerned.

"I had a bad dream," I lied.

"Do you want to talk about it?"

I shook my head. I didn't know what I wanted anymore. Except that I wanted to rewind yesterday and start it over. I wouldn't have looked at the messages and I wouldn't have looked at the stupid computer.

His eyes bore into mine, and I surprised myself when the invited tears didn't come. He lifted the quilt that covered his legs extending an offer for me to join him. Not wanting to be too eager, I hesitated then slid next to him. I kept my arms between my body and his chest, my head nestled just below his under arm. My body relaxed regardless of how hard my heart pelted my chest. One of his arms held my shoulders securely so I wouldn't fall off and the other brushed through my hair. I suddenly remembered how he'd told me about the illegal drugs and how they made him forget about the pain of leaving. As if he was a syringe himself…he'd just done that for me. I closed my eyes and allowed my body to succumb.

I must have slept like that for six hours because when I woke up at eight something, we hadn't moved. His eyes were open and ours met for a second before mine flicked away. I pushed myself up.

"Sorry. I shouldn't have wakened you last night," I said, trying to not breathe my morning breath his way.

He didn't try and hold on. "It's OK. I'm glad you did. Do you remember what it was about?"

I knew he was referring to the nightmare that I'd claimed I'd had. The nightmare that I was living as we spoke. "No."

"Do you want some breakfast?" He asked.

"No. I have some reading to do." I started up the stairs.

"Em. You're gonna have to eat. You had nothing yesterday."

I kept walking. "I'm not hungry," I said over my shoulder.

His footsteps padded up the stairs. "What are you reading? You did it yesterday too."

I flipped on the bathroom light and put toothpaste on my toothbrush. "Well. I had a great idea over Christmas break and NOW, it doesn't seem so great but…I earned credits over Christmas during our parental enforced break, and I'm earning enough this week that I will be close to being a junior when I graduate this year." I began to brush my teeth.

"Are you serious?" He stepped in further.

I nodded unable to answer, finished brushing, rinsed and dried. "Not sure what the point in all that is given that…" I couldn't finish the sentence and flipped on the water in the shower.

"You're doing this for me?" His eyes were serious.

I threw his USC shirt in the hamper making a mental note to do laundry today and exposing my tank underneath. I shrugged acting like it was no big deal…but he was right…this was all for him. The bathroom collected steam from the hot water. I started to pull my shorts down and stopped above my hipbone staring at him acting like I'd go further, but knowing I didn't have the courage.

"Excuse me. I know you've been with lots of chicks…women…whatever and I'm sure you've seen them naked, but this is new and a little awkward for the fifteen-year old. So if you could cut me some slack and…"

He shut the door before I could finish, and I smiled before undressing completely and stepping into the hot water.

The day was virtually a repeat of the one before and, as angry as I was, I was sad it was our last. I read today about the Iranian Hostages in 1977 and the Gulf War and Sadaam Hussein—learning more than I would ever remember, but it was credits none the less.

My lunch was delivered again, and to be a bitch and make my point, I refused to eat. I e-mailed my parents to let them know things were great here needing to keep up the façade hoping they'd never find out anything different.

My stomach growled ferociously around four and I headed downstairs again. He was watching some poker tournament on TV. As I passed through to the kitchen, his eyes followed me. I heard him behind me. Crap. I couldn't eat in front of him. That would blow my plan to be on a hunger strike.

"We're running out of time to talk," his voice was flat.

"What's to talk about?"

"I'm glad you asked," he said smugly. "Tell me what bothers you most. You knew I'd slept with other girls."

"Women," I jabbed.

"OK. You knew I'd slept with women before. What upsets you the most? That we documented it?"

"No. That's just stupid and immature. Why would you have scrogged a married woman?"

"I told you and I'm not sure if you heard me…this was all before and during the really bad time. I was drunk off my ass." His lips were tight across his teeth.

"Drunk? For *both* married women?" I brought my brows together ready to prove him wrong.

He hesitated, then raised his brows. "Same time. Same place." He stared at me waiting for me to get it. I didn't and I'm guessing my vacant expression gave it away. "We were drunk, Will and I, at a bar, where we knew we could get served and drinks bought for us. A cougar bar. Will went home with one. I went home with two."

My mouth fell. "You…"

"Yes I did. And don't think for a second that I did the seducing. They came after me."

"And that makes it OK?"

He stepped closer to me. "Em. I didn't care at the time. Asking me now, sober, later…it was stupidest thing I ever did. And if I could take any one of them or all of them back to fix what has happened, I'd do it in a second. There was never a relationship or a commitment or love. It was sex."

"What about the virgins?" My tone was hateful.

He shrugged. "What about 'em? There was no force. It was a decision they made. I wasn't out searching for them. I was a guy presented with an opportunity and I took it. No one was hurt."

I walked from the kitchen. "Just like me. I was an opportunity and you took it."

"That's bullshit and you know it. If I was after your virginity, I could have had it six months ago. Hell, playing my cards right, I could have had you that first night at your house." He was angry.

He was probably right. I fell in love with him the moment he stood in the doorway asking for Ryan. I started up the stairs.

"Think about Ryan, Em. Think about the number of girls he's had. Think about Grant, Estelle…any number of people my age. And I hate to say this but the city is even worse than this place."

Halfway up the stairs, I turned and stood face to face with him. "Oh. I'm sure anything is better than this God-awful hell hole you've been in for the past year. Just leave. No one wants you here. *Leave*." I shouted and ran the rest of the way up.

Something jolted me from a sound sleep. I opened my eyes and lay there. A loud noise echoed through the house. The clock read 11:20. What was that? I sat in bed listening for it again. *THUD*. I concentrated trying to pinpoint where it had come from. I swallowed hard as I opened my door. "Zach," I yelled down the stairs. No answer and my heart started to race. I glanced at the framed family pictures as I took the stairs slowly. "Zach?" Still nothing. Once at the bottom, I noticed the green light on the security screen. The alarm had been disarmed and panic settled into me. "ZACH!" I yelled louder. I walked into the living room and flashes from the TV flickered against the empty leather sofas. Where was he? Tears began to swell in my eyes.

The lights in the kitchen were off. My heart skipped a beat as the thought of him leaving crept into my mind. I had shouted it at him, repeatedly. "Zach." My voice wasn't as loud and the hair on my neck stood. I suddenly bolted toward the stairs. "ZACH!" I screamed running up the stairs straight to Ryan's room. Empty. My feet were moving before I realized and I threw open the spare bedroom door. Nothing.

"ZACH!" I grabbed my cell phone from my desk and dialed his, barreling down the stairs again to check my parent's room. I threw open their door and now every light in the house was on. Nothing! "Zach," I sobbed and sat at the foot of their bed. He'd left. The phone continued to ring then went to his voicemail.

"EMMA!" He yelled. "Where are you?" His urgent tone scared me as he suddenly rounded the corner. When I saw him, I buried my face in my hands and couldn't control the emotion. He was instantly at my side.

"Baby, what's wrong?" He cradled me in his arms.

"Where were you?" I cried.

"I took a shower."

I shook my head. "No. I looked in the bathroom and you weren't there and there was this noise."

He gently stroked my head. "I went to the garage to get stuff out of my bag. I knocked over the coat stand by the garage door, twice. I'm sorry."

I sniffed and wiped my face with my shirt. "The alarm wasn't on and I was screaming for you."

He kissed my forehead. "I didn't hear you. I had to have been outside."

"I thought you left."

"I wouldn't leave you," he whispered and kissed the tip of my nose. Before he could pull back, I grabbed his face and pressed my lips forcefully to his, kissing him hard. His lips returned a kiss just as powerful, hungry and mashing mine. I fought for a breath but refused to break free when his tongue softly met mine and a whimper resonated through my throat. His hands gripped my back and my face, crushing me into his body. I was a part of him, I wasn't sure I could get closer. There was an unspoken urgency between us; as quick as it happened, the urgency disappeared and a loving gentleness took its place. His lips softened and though still eager, a more patient kiss replaced it. He finally did break free and stared at me. Eyes…searching for a sign…any sign that things would be OK. His eyes in return seeking forgiveness…a forgiveness that I couldn't give him. I pushed him away and stood.

"Don't go," he pled, and his words tugged at my heart.

"I have to," I whispered and didn't know if he could hear me.

Up in my room, I tossed and turned unable to give in to sleep. My mangled thoughts shifting between forgiveness...anger...love. I knew without a doubt, Zach Owens was the man I wanted to spend the rest of my life with. But what did I have to offer him? I was a scrawny, miniature fifteen-year-old from a crappy little town in Oregon who, prior to him, had only been felt up by Doug Harvey in the eighth grade. Zach *was* my sexual experience...inclusively. He was all I knew and all I wanted to know. It didn't matter to me who he'd been with or what he'd done with them. It didn't matter that he had just gotten off of probation for drug and alcohol charges. What mattered to me was that I could never be the girl...the woman he deserved. He deserved someone just as perfect as he was and who was worthy of his love.

My back was to the door and when the crack of light shone through, the thumping in my chest escalated. I closed my eyes and tried to take long breaths, which would indicate sleep. His body slid between the covers and pressed up next to my back. My muscles tensed and I tried to relax my rigid posture. I could feel his breath on my neck and I tried to regulate my pulse and breathing. This unexpected visit was more than I'd anticipated, and I wasn't sure my faking sleep could go on much longer. When I felt him lightly shove something in my ear, I jerked around to see what he was doing. He held up the earpiece to his IPOD and stared at me. I relaxed my head on the pillow, now facing him and allowed him to slide the earpiece in.
Don't look at him. Keep your eyes closed. The music was soft and slow and everything I needed it to be to fall right back in love with him.

When morning came, he was up and showered by the time I came around. His bag was in my doorway, and I could tell by his stance he was leaving this time.
"You OK?
I nodded sleepily.
"Well then, I'm out of here."
I fought the urge to beg him to stay.

"Emma. I've told you before that when I came here…I didn't care about much. I didn't care if I fit in, who liked me, who didn't. I didn't care who I hurt. I felt like I'd been banished to a year of hell. I spent three months in school, going through the motions and basically not giving a shit. And no one gave a shit about me. Except for the girls, and as you know, I've been there and done that." He took a deep breath. "Then I met you. You asked about me and about my life and where I was from and genuinely seemed to care. You weren't all about you which made me want to find out about you. But you left and Estelle unfortunately came into the picture when my buddies were up one weekend. They knew about her and one night we added her to the list." He shrugged. "I don't know which one even told her about it but she's on their list too. It was stupid. We were seventeen and stupid." He shook his head and crossed his arms then continued.

"I'm not ready for this to be over. You're everything that's good and I… am so not. You deserve better and I'll leave you alone. I thought given the three days we had that we'd work this out. But I know I hurt you and I'm sorry…God am I sorry." He took two quick steps forward and kissed my forehead. "I love you," he whispered, picked up his bag and left. From the pain that suddenly enveloped my body, I think he ripped my heart from its cavity and took it with him.

FORTY-EIGHT

Mom and Dad made it home and Ryan and his friends followed a few days later. It was agonizing not seeing Zach, but I dreaded seeing him at school even more. After a few days, my brain seemed to slowly begin functioning again. Maybe Zach was right…I was too good, too pure and too innocent. I had nothing to offer him. So I thought long and hard about what my options were and I had a plan. My mind was made up and I was going to do a list of my own of sorts. I didn't want to be a virgin any more. But, no married men! I loved Grant and hoped I could start there, though I refused to hurt anyone in the process. If he was willing to do it…so would I. I knew Doug Harvey would be a willing participant, but I gagged at the thought. Brett? Connor? Josh? I had a feeling they'd all say no. It suddenly hit me…who to call.

He answered on the third ring. "Hello?"

"Austin?"

"Emma? I thought that was your number. What's wrong?"

"Nothing's wrong. Why?"

"You never call during the school year."

That was true. "Oh. Well. I need a favor." I crossed my fingers.

"OK. What's up?"

I knew I couldn't come right out and tell him what my plan was so I manipulated the story a bit.

"I need a date. Grant is turning eighteen and we're having a party."

"A date? Me?"

"Don't say it. Don't tell me I'm too young. You know me. I'm fun…" I paused. "Well…I can be. You haven't been down for a while."

"Runt, who are you trying to make jealous?" He laughed.

I sighed. Was it that obvious? "Nobody. Well, that's not entirely true."

His laughter moved to his chest. "Is this the guy that picked you up from the bar when we were there? He didn't care for me then."

"Austin, please. It's two hours down here. I'll pay for your gas."

"When is it?"

" SWEET!" I tightened my fist. "Saturday night. You can stay at the house if you want."

"Will your folks be there?"

"I'm not sure yet?"

"Fair enough. Can I bring a buddy?"

"Yes. Make *him* cute too."

"Oh. So I'm cute?" He questioned.

"Oh, shut up. You know you're cute. One last thing, dress hot, smell good and you have to do whatever I ask."

His laughter made me smile. "Oh shit. Why am I already regretting this?"

"Thank you. Thank you. You're the best. See you Saturday— be here around nine."

"Bye, Runt."

I closed my phone. One!

Saturday, Mom and Dad agreed to give Ryan and Grant from eight to midnight for their little party and I was thrilled. All keys had to be collected at the door and Dad would determine who left, who drove and whose parents were called. Dad said Ryan was to provide no beverages outside of water and soda. He placed a basket by the door and told Ryan keys needed to go in the basket when folks arrived then locked up until he and mom got home.

Austin had called my dad to let him know he was coming and they were going to dinner first. He assured me he'd be there at nine. Ali was the first to arrive. I was still shocked that she and Ryan were still dating. Grant followed soon after. I think he could tell something was wrong but kept busy opening snacks and getting the music loaded.

I went up and changed as the time drew closer and chose a short skirt with a double tank, brushed through my hair and dabbed on some perfume. There was a knock at my bedroom door.

"Come in."

Grant peeked in. "Did you guys break up?" He lowered his brow.

"Wow," I grimaced.

"Did you?" He stepped in.

"Kind of."

"Why?" He asked suspiciously.

I shoved him in the chest. "Don't act like you don't know."

"He told you?" His eyes almost bugged out of his head.

I nodded and swallowed the lump forming as he grabbed me and pulled me into his chest. "When? When did you find out?" His tone was softer now, more caring.

"Spring break," I whispered the words. "He spent the night here and I found out the next day."

He shoved me backward and glared at me. "Did you two…"

"Nooo." I rolled my eyes. Of course we didn't.

"Well, don't sound so disappointed. I'm sorry you're hurt."

I shrugged. "Whatever."

"Don't whatever me. I know you want to be with him. I should have just kept my mouth shut."

"No. I'm glad I know." I eyed him skeptically. "How many girls have you been with?"

"Not as many as he has."

"How many?"

"Emma," he discouraged.

I shoved my finger in his face. "Grant Meiers. You are a hypocrite. You made him tell me about himself but you won't tell me about you."

He laughed. "You were going to sleep with him. You needed to know." He suddenly raised one eyebrow high. "Do you need to

318

know about me for a reason I'm not aware of?" His tone was hopeful.

I shrugged and started to walk from the room.

"Wait a minute." He grabbed the waistband of my skirt and held me in place. "What are you up to, Emma?"

I couldn't hide the smile. "Nothing."

"Let me have it. You suck at lying."

I laughed. "I was thinking...about having my own list."

"List of what?"

I stared at him waiting for it to click in his brain. He stared back trying to put the pieces together then suddenly his jaw fell open.

"BULLSHIT! Does he know about this?"

"No! And he's not going to...yet."

Grant raked his fingers through his blond curly long hair. "What are you thinking?"

"I'm not going to mess around with just random strangers—I'm choosing people I know and trust. You, maybe. If you can do it without being a jackass." I elbowed him.

"Emma. It's not that easy. You want me to have sex with you and walk away?"

I pursed my lips. "You friggin do it all the time with other girls."

He shook his head as the words came out. The doorbell rang and he stared at me. "Please don't do anything until we can talk about his...OK?"

"Fine." Maybe.

We both shuffled down the stairs and I think I heard an "Unbelievable," beneath his breath.

By 8:40, the house was full. I knew most everybody, and Grant kept staring daggers into me. His protectiveness was endearing so I tried to offer a smile in return. With Estelle and Claire actively pursuing the single guys, Ali kept close to Ryan. I wanted Austin to get here and when the doorbell rang before nine, I bolted to answer it.

Zach and Josh stood in the door; my eyes never found Josh's. "Hi." Zach smiled. "How are you?"

"Great," I lied too quickly, my heart dropping into the pit of my stomach. "You?"

"Not good." His somber expression made me sad.

God dang it! Why does he have to be so honest?

"Would you like to go for a drive?" he asked.

Did I? I wanted to go with him so badly. I wondered if he saw the agonizing streak of pain that shot across my face. "I can't."

"OK. Will it bother you if I stay?"

I shrugged and he finally stepped past me. I closed my eyes and took a long slow breath after I shut the door. He went to the family room and joined whoever was playing the XBOX 360.

Around 9:15, Austin arrived with Vince, the same smoking hot college guy from before. It was amusing to watch Estelle and Claire flit around the room vying for attention. Austin winked at me from where he stood as the girls ogled and asked questions about college making sure the guys knew they were going to be seniors. Ali and I both rolled our eyes at each other. Finally, after plopping my hands on my hips in exasperation, Austin smiled and made his way to me.

"Sorry. I got distracted," he whispered as he neared me. Estelle shot me the evil eye from across the room then turned and stared at Zach. She wouldn't, I thought to myself. Who am I kidding...yes she would.

"That's OK. How was dinner?"

"Good. I saw your boy in there playing the video game."

I felt my eyes narrow and shot a glare at Austin. "He's not my boy."

He chuckled. "So, what's the plan?"

I took the opened long neck from his hand knowing I wouldn't drink it but it would serve as a good prop. Zach didn't like me drinking. "OK. I was thinking. I'd go in and sit down and watch them play, and you could come in and sit next to me. We could whisper and giggle and hold hands."

"Does he know I'm nineteen?"

I shrugged.

"Runt. You..."

"NO! No Runts. Not tonight...got it?" He opened his little cooler and retrieved another beer.

"Got it."

"After that…just follow my lead."

Vince joined us. "Hey Emma. Long time, no see."

"Hi Vince."

"Do I have a job like my buddy here?" he winked and his eyes sparkled with charisma.

"Stay away from the tall, black-haired girl," I warned.

"I can do that," he said as I left the room.

Zach was playing Black Ops and his eyes met mine when I moved through the room. Jaycee sat next to him rambling and the loud music from the other room made it difficult to hear. In all my scheming for tonight, I had never planned for him to be with someone else, and a wave of nausea swarmed over me. From the family room, I saw Grant dancing in the living room where the music played and I laughed. He dashed to my side and I braced myself for his landing next to me.

"What's uuuup?" His breath already smelled of liquor. I wonder where it came from.

"Not much. You look like you're having fun, birthday boy."

"How about a birthday kiss?" he asked pulling my head toward his.

"I'll give you a birthday spankin," I teased, pushing him down on my lap then rolled him to the floor.

Grant laughed and stood. "Don't tease me."

"Excuse me, Grant," Austin said, stepping past Grant and sitting next to me.

"What's up, Austin?" Grant bumped fists with him and stepped back looking at me curiously as Austin touched my bare leg. He obviously wasn't drunk enough to let this go and I panicked.

"No," he mouthed and with two fingers pointed at his eyes then pointed one finger at me.

"Grant. Take a picture," Jaycee said tossing her little pink camera to him then grabbing Zach's bicep as she squeezed him closer. He didn't resist either. He smiled without looking away from the TV. Unbelievable.

Austin leaned over nuzzling his nose into my hair. "Is it OK if I do this for a second and pretend I'm whispering my undying love for you? Because without you even looking over, I can tell you he is checking us out." He leaned back against the sofa and I giggled. I rubbed my neck like it tickled. He pulled me back against the sofa and his arm was around me.

"Who's the chick hitting on him?" Austin asked leaning into me.

Though tension swelled in my body, I managed a smiled. "Her name is Jaycee. I was thinkin' we sick Vince on her."

Austin frowned then touched the end of my nose. "No can do. The tall girl cornered Vince in the kitchen."

"Damn!" I said. "Lay your hand on the inside of my knee."

He did and I pretended to watch the game. "Like that?" he asked cozily.

I nodded. His hands seemed the size of Zach's.

"You owe me so big. I can't believe I'm stooping to this. You have got to tell me what's going on with this guy?"

"Kiss me."

"Where?"

"On my lips, dummy."

He smiled and batted his eyes. "I got that much. My question is here or where?"

"Here. Now." I rested in the pit of his arm and he gently lifted my chin and bent down and pecked my lips softly then pulled away.

CLANK! I opened my eyes in time to see the XBOX controller bounce off the glass coffee table onto the ground.

"Zach. What's wrong?" Jaycee squealed as she went after him toward the kitchen.

Austin's finger was in my face this time. "You are dangerous little one. Why are you trying to hurt the guy?"

A dull ache ricocheted across my chest as Austin's words came out. Was I trying to hurt Zach? "Take me up to my room. I'll tell you there."

"Are we still playing mean?"

I didn't answer. He held my hand as we left the family room. As he walked up the stairs he held both my hands behind his back, and I trailed after him. Zach eyes followed us up the stairs from the kitchen.

I closed the door and smiled at Austin. "Thank you."

He pounced on my bed curling a pillow under his head. "Talk to me."

"OK. He hurt me." I paused because I said it in past tense and the pain was very present.

Austin rose up, his body more alert.

"How?"

I flipped my computer on and waited for it to boot up. "We've been going out for a while and…we haven't…" I bobbed my head from side to side.

"Haven't what?"

"Haven't done it."

Austin grinned. "OK…and?"

"Well, he's done it a lot."

This time he chuckled. "What's a lot to you?"

I held up my index finger signaling him to wait as my fingers typed frantically on the keyboard. I didn't really want to see the site again today. Since we'd broke up, I'd gone on every day to check and see if I'd been added. I knew *he* wouldn't add me but wasn't sure if his buddies would if he'd told them what we'd done. I also found the link to their pictures in Mexico and they made me less angry. If there was a girl in the photo, Zach seemed to be on the other end of the lens. If Zach was in the photo, then it was just he and the guys. Some of the pics were pretty disgusting—wet T-shirts, no T-shirts.

"Here it is." I pointed to the screen, Austin came off the bed to look at it clicking on each of the guys.

"What's the M?" He asked.

"Married," I said under my breath. "Have you ever been with a married woman?"

"One," he said, holding up a finger and still reading.

"Austin! Why? Why do you guys do that?"

"It's safe. They don't want a relationship. Usually just sex from a young virile stud like myself." He glanced at me and winked. "Did he tell you what a cougar is?"

"Yes."

He swiveled in my chair. "So, this upsets you?"

I nodded.

"And you're trying to make him jealous in return?"

Austin was bright. I didn't have to explain anything at all. He'd put the pieces together. "I thought I'd try to get some experience myself...maybe my own list and I don't necessarily mean something like this." I pointed to the computer. "But so I know something about something."

His shoulders fell and I could tell by the look on his face he was feeling sorry for me. "Emma. Don't go out and have meaningless sex just to have sex. Make it with someone you care about."

I took a step closer to him and touched his chest. "OK. Then maybe you and I...maybe you'd show me."

He stared at me as he processed my words then his brow furrowed. "You and I," he repeated.

"I know I'm a little younger. But I trust you."

"Em. Have you ever been with anyone?" He touched my cheek in the kindest, gentlest way.

I shook my head as the tears swelled. "Why does everyone ask that?" He wasn't going to do it either.

He pulled me in for a hug as the warm tears spilled over.

"I am flattered and I'll make you a promise. If by summer, you still want this...we'll *talk* about it again. At least then, you'll be sixteen."

I sniffed and nodded embarrassed.

"If you're so crazy about this guy, why not be with him or wait...that would be the fatherly thing for me to say."

I closed my eyes. "Fatherly? Let's go with brotherly, shall we?" I smiled. "I think I need more experience before I'm with him."

His face scrunched with confusion. "Why?"

"I don't know anything and you just said it yourself, those other women teach you things."

"I promise you, and I'd even bet a million dollars, that Zach would rather you *not* be experienced."

"I think you're wrong."

"Emma." He shook my shoulders. "Listen to me. I'm a guy and I got a woody with you just asking me to be your first."

My face flushed and I flipped off the computer. I didn't respond.

"That's a big deal to a guy. I could have any girl downstairs I wanted right now, but I'm not all that interested because outside of you and Ali, most of them have probably been with multiple guys."

"It shouldn't bother me...all the girls he's been with?"

He shrugged. "That's up to you. I'm guessin the older you get, the more of that you're gonna find. I think it was shitty for him to write names, and I'm glad your name's not on there cause I don't want to have to kick his ass." He winked. "I'm sure he's going crazily insane right now, don't you think?"

"Probably."

As I moved to the door, he stopped me. "I'm glad you chose me for your little experiment. But don't ever make me kiss you again," he warned and opened the door.

"Ok....why?" I said, following behind feeling guilty.

He took my hand and led me down the stairs. "Cause I don't think I'd ever stop." He smiled and we walked to the kitchen.

FORTY-NINE

Ryan sat on the counter and Ali stood between his legs facing out. In the hour Austin and I had spent upstairs, more people had arrived. It was hard to hear myself think.

"Do you want a drink?" Austin asked.

"Yeah. But just a soda. I don't want to do anything stupid tonight."

"You mean stupid…er, don't you?" He elbowed me and handed me a can of soda. Austin scanned the room. "I don't see Vince."

I laughed. "Please. He's somewhere scroggin Estelle. I'd bet money on it."

He slapped his knee. "Damn. Why do I always get the virgins?"

I playfully shoved him, and he wrapped his arm around my neck laughing. I saw his face begin to twist into a scowl. His eyes turned serious.

"Come on." He rotated me so I couldn't see whatever it was. But I felt my face start to crumble before I even saw it. I pulled my head from between his chest and arm and turned around. Zach's arm was draped over Jaycee's shoulders; her head rested on his chest…my chest…as she walked. He stumbled, and they both nearly fell, but of course he caught her…that was so like him. By the unfocused look in his eyes and his seemingly uncontrolled mannerisms, I guessed he had been drinking.

Austin cupped my face in his hands."Let's go for a drive. Let's just get out of here for a bit," he suggested.

I bit my lip unwilling to let the tears come.

"Em. Take a deep breath. Act like it doesn't bother you," he said.

"But it does," my voice cracked and my leg trembled up and down on the floor. Ryan had to have seen what was happening because between the time I looked at Austin and glanced back, Ryan had Jaycee's bicep in his hand.

"What are you doing?" Ryan asked her.

"Get off me Ryan. Zach and Emma are history," Jaycee said hatefully.

Ryan let her go and looked at Zach. "Zach. Come on dude. Be smart about this."

Jaycee flicked Ryan in the head with her thumb and middle finger. "HE-LL-0!" She said loudly. "He's our salutatorian. He is smart." Her words slurred as they came out.

The room had quieted and Grant stood behind Ryan.

"Look. I have no quarrel with you, man," Zach said looking at Ryan. "My fight is with you." He pointed at Austin and everyone turned to look at him. Oh God! Austin was just as big as Zach, if not bigger, and I feared to venture a guess at who might win. Zach wouldn't even look at me.

"Please, Austin. Don't." I begged.

He reached up and ran his thumb over my cheek. "I won't. But he is eighteen." It was a statement, which I confirmed. Everyone waited for Austin' response. "This isn't gonna happen, buddy."

"Don't call me buddy. I am not your buddy. And don't touch her again." Zach took a step closer to us, and Austin casually pulled me backward.

"Look." Austin held his hands up. Vince came into the room and moved toward Austin and me. "I am not here to hurt Emma."

"Zach, stop," Jaycee demanded, and he brushed her off his arm.

Vince was next to me. "What's goin on?"

"Zach." It hurt to say his name. "Wants to fight Austin," I whispered.

"Ohh. This should be good," Vince laughed.

"No." I hit Vince in the arm.

"This isn't going to happen, Vince," Austin echoed my thoughts.

Suddenly Connor, Brett and Josh bolted into the room.

Zach's face contorted with anger. "You call taking advantage of her, not hurting her?'"

The remark made my chest swell. "That's my choice!" I screamed. My face froze and for the first time, his eyes found mine. He seemed confused that I was there. His eyes softened for a moment as I stood between them.

"She's right," Vince laughed. "She's a big girl."

Zach's eyes hardened and left me to find Vince. His nostrils flared and he took a step toward Vince. Ryan crammed his fist into Zach's chest and Connor and Brett helped him.

"Zach. You know Emma loves you, man. What's the big deal? Austin is a family friend," Ryan said.

Zach's lip pulled into a snarl. "Grant told me about your plan. I know what you did upstairs." He stared at Austin.

"What plan?" Ryan asked, and grabbed the front of Grant's shirt.

Grant shoved Ryan's hands away. "This isn't the time to talk about it. OK?" Everyone in the room stared at me and Austin waiting for an answer. I thought I was going to burst in humiliation.

"The plan was for college boy to…" Zach's words trailed off as he shook his head in disgust.

Austin spoke up. "Zach. I believe you've been misinformed."

I quickly turned to Austin and glared at him. "Stop. It's none of his business what happened between us. That's between you and me."

I saw the doubt in Austin's eyes as he looked at me. He thought we should tell Zach the truth. I could see it on his face. I moved closer to Austin and spun around to Zach.

"He's only one. I have seventeen more—then we call it even."

Zach winced as the words came out and lowered his head. Jaycee was right there to console him. Stupid bitch. She whispered something to him. His head rose and the beautiful brown eyes that I'd grown to love were hard as stone. His eyes roamed from my feet up to my face and he shot me a revolted look. He grabbed Jaycee's hand. "Eighteen," he laughed and turned to leave.

When they rounded the corner, I ran toward them with my hands balled into fists. I was going to hurt Jaycee. Ryan stopped me in my tracks. "No," he said, and I took a couple of steps backward. I was glad a barstool was close because my wobbly legs gave out. I fell onto the stool beside me as I buried my face into my hands.

"Dammit!" Ryan shouted moving toward me. "Everybody out of the kitchen."

I looked up at him. His eyes were furious.

"Ryan." Austin patted his back and Ryan shoved his hand away. "Hey. Easy. I was just gonna say…"

"Tell me you two didn't…" Ryan didn't finish the sentence, but his finger was an inch from Austin's face.

Austin stood with his mouth open. "Are you fucking kidding me? You're seriously gonna ask me that?"

Ryan shook his head. "I'm sorry." He held his hands out to the side in an apology.

"Dude. She's a beautiful girl that is going to have sex someday. Get a grip."

Ryan gave him a confused look. "It's not about sex, Austin. I want her treated right. Respected. He did that for her. I don't know what the hell is going on tonight, but that wasn't the Zach I know." He rubbed my back and glared at Austin and Grant.

I grabbed Ryan's shirt. "He's going to be with Jaycee tonight, isn't he?" The words came out in gasps. "I mean. That's what he was insinuating when he took her."

Seven guys—Ryan, Austin, Grant, Brett, Connor, Josh and Vince stood staring at me with Ali at my side. I had to go after him.

On my way to my room, I grabbed Ryan's truck keys out of the basket and slid them in my pocket. I snuck out dad's office upstairs and onto his deck outside. I looked over and even the one floor down made my stomach roll. I could land it. I knew I could. I climbed over the railing, balancing myself on the two by four, then propelled myself off the wood and landed hard on the grass. A stick jabbed into my hand. "Ow." I pulled it out and tried to shake off the pain. I ran behind the house and spotted Ryan's truck parked on the street. I unlocked it and scrambled in starting the engine. I waited to turn on the lights till I was down the street.

I buckled and drove cautiously toward Zach's house, my heart pounding as I drove. What I was doing was illegal. I had my permit to drive to school or work but that was it…this was neither.

The downtown lights in Ashland were beautiful at night. My eyes searched the streets for the Jeep. I pulled down a road leading to the park. We'd been there several times and I wondered if he took her there. Tears surged in my eyes as I felt sick at what I might find. Two cars were in the lot—a blue mustang and silver Volkswagen. I did a U-turn in Ryan's truck and kept making my way toward Zach's house. It was 11:30.

The house was lit but his Jeep wasn't in the drive. I parked the truck and walked up the path glancing in the window. His folks were on the sofa watching TV. I hesitated but rang the bell. Mr. Owens answered.

"Emma. Honey, what are you doing out so late?"

"Hi, Mr. Owens. Is Zach here?"

Mrs. Owens came to the door. "Hi, Emma. Please, come in."

I shook my head. "I can't. I was just looking for him."

"You've been crying. I can see it in your eyes," she said in a soothing voice. "Did you two break-up?"

I covered my eyes so they couldn't see me cry and I nodded my head.

"Oh, sweetheart. Please sit."

Mr. Owens turned off the TV and left the room.

"I'm so sorry. I shouldn't be here. I need...I need to find him...to talk to him...to stop him."

"Stop him from what, Emma?" Concern touched her tone.

"Being with her."

Zach's mom wrapped her arm around my shoulders and hugged me. "Oh. Honey. Love hurts sometimes."

"I do love him. I love him so much."

"He loves you too. No matter what's happening right now. Would you like me to text him?"

I shook my head. "No. I should go." I stood and I didn't want to leave. I felt closer to him being here. I wanted to go up and crawl in his bed and wait for him there so I could hold him. No one understood me anymore. Maybe no one ever would again.

"Emma. When we moved here, Zach was...less than thrilled." She smiled. "He struggled and you know what I'm talking about. But for whatever reason, he took an instant liking to you and it has grown into something bigger than both of you. I don't know if either of you knows what to do with the emotion you feel. He's leaving. You're leaving. He's scared. You're scared. Love is a powerful thing. We will always be grateful for what you did for him. *You* brought Zachary back to us at a time we weren't sure we'd get him back. Thank you."

A twinge of pain shot through my heart as her words sounded more like a farewell. I nodded. "You're welcome. Take care of him for me."

"We will."

"Bye."

My phone was lit up on the seat of Ryan's truck. Seven new texts. I scrolled through them and not one was from Zach. I didn't care about the rest. A car honked behind me and I glared into my rearview mirror. The light had turned green and I hadn't noticed. I suddenly turned and headed to the creek Zach had taken me to when he told me about the probation. Maybe that's where he'd taken Jaycee.

I was driving faster than I should as the city lights faded behind me. I knew the turn was a dirt road, so when I passed one on my left I did a U-turn in the street and went back. I pulled off, following the gravel road for a bit which came to a Y. I closed my eyes and thought back to that day trying to recount his turns. I recalled one for sure, but I know we didn't go right, so I took the left. Gravel turned to dirt and it curved around, but I didn't see a creek. There weren't many trees at all and I couldn't see any lights from the city.

My phone buzzed—it was Ryan. I knew he'd be pissed so I didn't answer. Finally, another left that should take me back to the road I came in on. I breathed a sigh of relief. This road was narrower, more winding than the last and seemed darker but probably not. I decided to turn around on the single lane road and a sense of urgency overwhelmed me. I put the truck in drive and reverse almost ten times before I was going the opposite way. Then before I knew it, a right turn was there. That was too soon…I chewed on my cheek. Keep going it couldn't possibly be that one. Then within a few minutes, I figured I'd driven too far and turned around again. I started to panic. I couldn't remember now which way to go or turn. I stopped the truck and texted Ryan.

Help me! I'm lost. send
Where r u?
Good question dumbass send Seriously, Ryan??
Which way do I go???
South of Ashland—dirt road. send
What?
I'm scared. send
Don't panic
Too late send

Ryan's tank was half full and I left the engine idling and in park with the lights on. I'd tap my brakes from time to time, lighting up the area behind to make sure nothing was behind the truck. Dad had always taught us not to panic in a time like this, but I was failing miserably. I kept the radio loud to drown out any wolves or coyotes that maybe circling. Twenty minutes had passed when my phone rang. I was down to two bars on my battery.

"Ryan?" I answered.

"OK. Where are you? We are south of Ashland on I-5."

"No, go over toward the vineyard and winery. I was on that road and then turned left off that." I knew that much but it was more vague from there.

"OK. We're headed there now. Are you alone?"

"Yes. Hurry. Who's with you?"

"Everybody. We're in Grant's truck cause someone took mine."

I smiled. He wasn't as angry as I thought. "Sorry."

"Let us get over there and I'll call you back."

"Bye."

I decided to turn off my lights to see what I could see. The intimidating black night surrounded the truck and I tapped my brakes again. Only a sliver of moon hung in the sky and stars dotted the orbit. I couldn't see the city lights or the mountains. I could see a red tower light blinking in the distance that might help. Ten minutes had passed since the last phone call. I flipped the car lights back on as a raccoon crossed the road in front. I shivered to think of what other creatures might be smelling this foreign object polluting their air with exhaust.

The phone rang.

"Where are you?" I asked desperately.

"We're on the road. But Em. We have no idea where you turned. Where were you going?"

"Zach took me to this creek once off that road and I was looking for it. You kind of have to do a U-turn to get into it."

"Turn around." I heard him say. "OK. Grant's turning around right now and we're looking for the turn. I'll call you in a minute."

The phone disconnected. I contemplated trying to find my way out but thought about dad's words. 'If you get lost, stay put and stay with the car.' Well, that wasn't going to be a problem. I certainly wasn't getting out.

I listened to music while I waited and every song reminded me of Zach. I pictured him with Jaycee in his Jeep—the top down, her curly blond hair blowing in the wind. The image of them kissing clouded my mind. I felt repulsed and jealousy crushed my chest till I couldn't breathe. They were having sex right now as I sat here.

"Come on, Ryan." I turned off my lights again watching for any flash of light coming my way. Nothing.

The phone rang again. Zach?

"Hello?"

"Where are you?" His voice was short.

"Why?"

"Because I'm at the creek and you're not here. Where did you turn?"

I struggled to answer. How did he know? Ryan had to have called him. Though I sat alone, I was embarrassed. I rubbed my forehead with my fingers.

"Emma?"

"I don't know where I am. I thought it was the right turn and obviously it wasn't." My anger toward him resonated in my words. "Is Ryan with you?"

"No. They took a different road to look."

I wanted to know if Jaycee was or if he'd taken her home already. I heard a door slam and a grunt.

"What are you doing?" I asked.

"Climbing on top of the Jeep. Turn your lights on and off." He paused. "Em. Turn your lights on and off."

"I am!" I turned the switch repeatedly.

"Shit."

"What?"

"I don't see your lights. And you're sure you turned left?"

"Yes. Just past the Vineyard and Winery."

I heard him take a long breath. "You doin all right?"

"I suppose."

"What's your battery look like on your phone?"

"I have two bars."

"OK. Use it sparingly. Does Ryan have a blanket in the truck?"

"I'd have to get out to get it."

He paused. I knew he was going to ask me to get it and I didn't want to. The thought of getting out…

"Em. Doesn't he have a rear sliding window?"

"Yes." I was relieved.

"Climb back and get it then lock the window." I could hear the Jeep through the phone shifting gears and I wished he was closer than what he was. I did as he said and climbed back, opened the window, lifted the box lid and pulled the quilt out. A skunk was close and I shivered at the smell.

"Got it."

"Good. It could get cold tonight."

"Zach," I whimpered. He was starting to scare me.

"We'll find you but at least you'll be warm. Why were you going to the creek?"

I didn't want to say, but Austin was right…I shouldn't play games either. "I was looking for you."

My phone beeped and the screen showed Ryan calling. "Zach. Ryan's calling."

"Call me back."

"OK." I clicked over. "Ryan?"

"Jesus, Em. I think *we're* fucking lost. We took some road but we're heading up a mountain."

"Turn around. I didn't even go over a hill. I'm on totally flat land. Why did you call Zach?"

"Because he at least knew what turn you were talking about. He obviously hasn't found you either?"

"No. Is Jaycee with him?" I inquired.

"I don't know. Em. It's after midnight. I'm going to have to call Mom and Dad."

That scared me more than the dark night. "No Ryan. Give me a while longer. Make something up...lie. But please don't call them yet," I begged.

"OK. Grant turned around and we are heading back down. There is only one more road for us to take." He was exasperated I could tell.

"Well...try it." I suggested.

"We will." He hung up.

My battery bar was down to one. I was nervous and called Zach.

"Hey," He answered.

"No luck?" I asked disheartened.

"Maybe. Tap your brakes."

I tapped them repeatedly.

"Houston. We have a problem." He chuckled.

"What?"

"I see you. The problem is I don't know how to get to you. Stop turning your lights on and off...you'll run down his battery."

I stopped. He could see me and that made me feel better but I was stuck, alone, in the dark, in the middle of nowhere. The thought of something other than an animal getting me entered my mind.

"Zach. I'm getting scared." I huddled down in the seat.

"Don't be scared, baby. We're gonna get you."

Hearing him call me baby was like music to my ears. He always called me baby, which was funny because any reference to being a baby would have infuriated me, but I wanted to be his baby. I felt comforted if only for a minute. My phone beeped.

"Zach. It's Ryan again."

"I'll hold on. Click over."

"Ryan?"

"We're on the last road we know to take. It's gravel."

I got excited. "Yes. It started out as gravel."

"OK. Are your lights on?"

"They are now," I said turning the dial.

"Hopefully we will see you in a minute."

"Bye." I clicked back over. "Zach."

"They're comin' baby. I see the lights getting closer to you."

I took a deep breath and let it out slowly.

"You're gonna be fine, Em. Start flashing your brights."

I saw the lights too and felt relief. "I see 'em Zach. I see 'em."

"Good girl. You did well. They'll get you back, now." I heard relief in his voice too.

"Zach?"

"Yeah?"

"Thanks."

"It looks like they are on top of you. Do you see them?"

"I do and..." Beep. My phone was dead.

Ryan, Austin and Vince followed Grant out of wherever we were and drove me home. It was ten after one. I figured I'd gotten everyone in trouble and would be grounded indefinitely. I desperately wanted to talk to Zach.

"Can I use your phone?"

"He's behind us," Ryan said.

"Who?"

"Zach. He was at the corner when we turned back on the road and he's behind us. Did you go looking for him?"

I was thrilled to the bone that I might get the chance to talk to him tonight. "Yes. I did something so stupid. And you're going to be mad."

"Austin told me." Ryan said.

My neck hurt as I snapped it toward Austin. He shrugged.

"He did?" I glowered at him.

Ryan glanced at me. "Don't be angry at him. I forced it out of him and Grant. Grant's so pissed at himself for telling Zach."

"I screwed up big time."

Ryan patted my leg. "You'll make it right. He seems to be following us home, so you may get the chance tonight." His smile made me smile.

The house was well lit and Dad was on the front porch when we pulled up. Crap. This was going to be bad. I worried more for Ryan with it being only a short time till graduation. My dad's long legs only took a couple of strides before he was at the truck. I was more interested in what Zach was doing than my dad. I knew where I stood with my dad. Zach had parked the Jeep and met my dad at my side of the car by the time I got out and Austin slid out behind me.

"Do one of you want to explain why it is almost two in the morning and my children are just getting home?" He was angry. Worry lines etched across his forehead. Ryan slammed his door and joined us.

"Mr. Hendricks. If I may, sir." Zach spoke and all eyes turned to him, especially mine.

"Zach. I like you. But Emma's not been herself the last couple of days or so. I'm telling you right now, do not try and protect her."

My eyes fell to the ground. Not been herself? Go ahead and tell him that I can't function without him. Get a flashing sign for the front yard!

"Emma and I broke up." He paused and it pained me to hear his words. I closed my eyes. "And tonight we needed to talk, and well…we went for a drive because the house was loud…and I remembered driving past this creek one time and was going to take her there. Well, sir, somehow I missed the turn, took a different one and we were out in the middle of nowhere. Ryan and Grant finally found us when we told them where we were, but not being from here…I wasn't sure which way to go. I'm sorry, sir. But it was not their fault."

My dad scratched his head. "Hmph. Well I certainly didn't hear the phone ring."

"Dad," Ryan said. "We should have called. We were kind of freakin out when we couldn't find them."

My dad finally looked at me and I wondered if he could see the tears welling up in my eyes or my chin quivering. "It doesn't look like you two worked things out?"

When I felt the hand on my back, I peeked up as a tear spilled over and Austin was trying to comfort me. My eyes found Zach.

"No sir," Zach said, looking at us and looking away.

"Well that's too bad." My dad's eyes found mine again, and, as another tear dribbled over the edge, I shot past my dad and into the house.

Our conversation while I was lost had been so normal…so us…so civil. I realized that he didn't want me anymore. I stood in my room, shaking, my eyes roaming over our history in pictures. The Redwoods, Homecoming, San Francisco, Shasta, the day of court, spring break. I plucked them from my wall, one by one, throwing the tacks in a pile and stacking the pictures on my desk. My life was over as I knew it. Zach Owens was graduating from Ashland High and getting the hell out of here and leaving me behind. I collapsed on my bed.

FIFTY

I woke up around 5:30 and the sky was still dark. I wasn't sure but wondered if I was dreaming. My computer monitor was lit and my room was frigidly cold. A shudder waved through my body as I crawled from the warm bed toward the bright screen. My fingers anxiously tapped the name of Zach's website. When his picture flashed up, he looked different than before. His face was dark and sad. I'd never seen him smile without showing his teeth. The other boys looked the same to me. I clicked on his picture. I wouldn't say I was surprised because that word wouldn't have been strong enough…definitely stunned…definitely wounded….possibly damaged. My name—typed beneath Estelle's with the letters BJ next to them. And already updated, Jaycee's name was next in line with an S. I stared for the longest time making sure there could be no other interpretation. E M M A. The letters were all there. I jabbed at the button on the PC to cut the power immediately and the screen went black.

The next time I opened my eyes, the sun exploded into my room and accented the wall that I'd dismantled last night where the pictures had hung. It was bare now. Our time together erased. My room was warm from the sun's rays, and I threw off the covers and instantly moved to the computer. My fingers frantically went to favorites and found his site. He didn't look different. My throat tightened as I stared at his breathtaking picture. He was beautiful. I was a fool to ever think that this would last. I shoved the thoughts from my mind and moved the mouse over his picture. Click.

My mind reeled as an error came up reading that the page was no longer available. I quickly clicked the refresh button and went back to his picture. Clicked again. Nothing. Crap. I went back, this time clicking on Travon's picture. All the names were still there. Will—still there. Jackson—still there. Zach—gone. It was all just dream. I didn't understand...why wasn't it there?

Monday couldn't come fast enough. I'd decided I was going to confront Zach about Jaycee. I couldn't go on not knowing. He was reasonable; I knew he'd listen. He'd have to. I was on the verge of smiling for the first time in days as I passed Ryan in the hallway. His wink gave me the confidence boost I was looking for. Zach was at his locker with his back my way. He was like a finish line I was trying to get to when Claire grabbed my arm. All three queen bees blocked my way and stared down at me. Jaycee smirked. All three perfect as usual. Perfect mean girls!

"Runt," Jaycee said smugly. "Since Zach and I are together now, I'd appreciate it if you'd leave him alone." Her eyelashes beat together several times. Together?

"Em," Estelle said touching my back like she cared. I flinched away from her touch. "You are so cute and so little." She was patronizing me and even talked with a small voice. "But Zach needs a woman. Believe me sweetie," she tapped the end of my nose. "I know."

I hated her. Her words stabbed me like a dull knife. I knew better than anyone that she knew what Zach liked or wanted. She had experienced a part of him I hadn't. My pulse was pounding wildly inside my head. I glanced sideways down the hall and Zach was talking to Brett at his locker. Please look this way.

Jaycee was suddenly in my face. "Stop looking at him. You didn't honestly think that the two of you would stay together...did you?" The three girls giggled as if that was the most absurd thought they'd ever heard.

My mouth came open but nothing came out. I closed it and tried to step away. "Oh my God. You did! That is so cute." Her tone was sticky sweet and condescending.

I back stepped from their unified semi-circle and battled the tears that stung my eyes. Before I got far enough away, Jaycee grabbed a handful of my shirt and yanked me toward her.

"Leave him alone. Got it?" She gritted through clenched teeth.

With every ounce of power I could find, I dropped my Algebra book on the floor and shoved her body as forcefully as I could, sending her sprawling across the floor. She screamed as she fell and slid backward hitting her head on the tile. A single tear escaped from my lid. I glanced up to see Zach and Brett staring at Jaycee lying on the floor and her friends rush toward her. I wanted to pounce on her and punch her but I stood frozen, my eyes locked on Zach as he bent down to her.

"What happened?" he asked with Brett at her other side. I wanted to vomit.

Jaycee held her head and glowered at me. "That bitch!" she yelled pointing with the other hand. At that instant, every single set of eyes in that hallway focused on me. My body trembled from adrenaline still shooting through my veins. I'd never been in a fight in my life and I believed I could take on the world. Suddenly, Jaycee managed to stand and started barreling toward me. Crap! Where was Ryan when I needed him? I was going to be so grounded. I braced myself half expecting her to knock me unconscious, when Zach yanked her back by the hood on her shirt, somewhat choking her. I chuckled and loosened my clenched fists allowing blood to flow into them. Jaycee was fighting Zach now, her arms flailing and legs kicking as I watched his arm wrap around her waist and restrain her. Must be upset she got her ass kicked by a freshman. Brett was jogging to me.

"Runt? You OK?" he asked and picked up my Algebra book.

"I will be. Thanks, Brett." He handed me the book and I looked at Zach. He restrained Jaycee's arms at her side and was talking to her. He'd made his choice. I had to get out of there. I spun around and rammed into Mr. Bowman and Mr. Ming.

Having my father pick me up from school was the worst thing of all. Suspended for three days. What a load of crap. Jaycee got nothing since she didn't act 'aggressively.' Of course my unwillingness to tell officials what she'd said to me didn't help. I was too embarrassed to tell. So now, three more days without seeing Zach. What difference did it make? It was over. They were a couple…I may as well skip the remaining two weeks of school all together. By the time I got back from my suspension, there would be five days left. This year, I couldn't wait to go to Cannon.

During my hiatus from school, I used my better-than-average calligraphy skills to address Ryan's graduation thank you notes. I'd already done his announcements and figured it was the least I could do since I was grounded and couldn't do anything else. I was trying to mentally prepare myself for Monday. Seeing Jaycee and Zach together would be worse than torturous. I think I'd rather have my head slammed in a car door. I wondered if he'd drive her to school…though she already drove. The more I thought about it, the more I realized how wrong she was for him. He deserved someone better than her. I wasn't throwing my name into the bowl because, I knew deep down, he deserved someone better than me.

Monday was interesting to say the least. Ryan and Grant worked together to walk me to my classes. My own personal security squad. First hour was Ryan's and I didn't realize second hour was Grant's until he was standing in the hall when the bell rang. I wasn't sure what their plan was for Thursday and Friday since seniors didn't have to come those days. They both met me after second hour and walked me to algebra—my only class with Estelle. Thank God, I had no classes with Jaycee—but then she had nothing advanced.
Ryan grabbed my arm before I walked in. "Don't let her get to you."
I nodded.
"I got her back," Grant comforted Ryan, and we walked in.
Zach was already sitting in his seat. I thought my heart was going to pop from my chest it beat so forcefully. As much as I wanted to, I didn't have the courage to look at him. I twisted my hair while waiting for Mr. Bowman.
Luckily, I managed to make it through the hour without opening my mouth. I watched the second hand rotate on the clock and held my breath till the bell rang. I glanced at Grant and we met at the door.
"Em. Can I talk to you?"

I hadn't heard his voice in a while and it was music to my ears. I didn't want to look at him. I couldn't. It hurt too much. "I can't, Zach." My feet somehow stepped into the hallway where Ryan waited.

Zach grabbed my arm. "Em, please."

"Please, let me go," I begged. "I can't do this."

Suddenly, Ryan was there and gently put his hand on Zach's chest. "Dude. Let her go." I was impressed; he said it nicely and with no act of aggression.

Zach wore my favorite peach T-shirt. His beautiful brown eyes flickered from Ryan to me then to Grant. I think I could smell him. Resigned, Zach lowered his head and strolled down the hallway.

Ryan's eyes were sad. "You OK?"

My throat was too dry to talk, so I simply nodded as we headed to gym.

My sixteenth birthday arrived without incident, which with my track record was a plus. I was happy for Ryan that his high school graduation day was a perfect day. It was forecasted to be 83 degrees and sunny. It didn't get any better. My sixteenth birthday—a day I'd waited for anxiously to arrive and Graduation Day—a day I'd dreaded all year. Both held broken promises.

But...I was sixteen. I could drive. I was going to be nearly a junior after my summer school credits. I should be on top of the world. Sweet sixteen, isn't that what it was called? Or at least what it was supposed to be. Nothing about this birthday was sweet. My heart was broken, my world turned upside down. I knew no matter what present came my way today...I couldn't have the one thing I wanted.

I had made Zach a picture collage of the two of us over the past year and framed it. I didn't know when or if I'd get it to him and figured he wasn't much interested. I wrapped it and slid it into a sack with his class rings. I didn't want to give them back. But it wasn't fair that I kept them. They belonged to him and I didn't anymore.

After trying on six dresses, I decided on my floral sundress. The straps were dainty and it was short and made my legs look longer than they were. I straightened my hair and wore it down. As I took the stairs slowly, my borderline depression showing in my lethargic steps, I heard Mom and Ryan arguing.

"You are not wearing flip-flips with your khakis."

"Mom. Please. Everyone will be wearing them." He was begging and I laughed to myself.

"Everyone but you," she said, unwilling to give in.

I rounded the corner and caught his eye roll and something he muttered under his breath. He was handsome in his khakis and green polo shirt. After about five hundred pictures and poses and a change of shoes, we headed to the school.

The parking lot was just beginning to fill and I immediately spotted Zach's Jeep parked in the front. The stadium seats were splattered with different groups of people securing their seats, and we parted with Ryan to go get ours. With my sunglasses on, I watched the seniors who were gathering in the corner of the field. Ryan stood with his buddies and Zach was with them. I'm not sure why I found comfort in that, but I did.

Ali and her folks spotted us and she joined me. I couldn't bring myself to say I was happy that she and Ryan were still together, but I wasn't upset about it either. I knew Ryan too well to know the chances of her fairy tale coming true weren't good. As we talked, my eyes roamed the crowd for Mr. and Mrs. Owens. I wondered if Jaycee would be with them, sitting next to Zach's mom. The thought made me cringe with jealousy.

The programs became hand-held fans as the sun beat down into the stadium. The teachers and administration took the stage, and our ROTC flag team carried the flags to the podium as we all stood. When the Pomp and Circumstance march began, my heart's rhythm seemed out of whack. This was not how it was supposed to be; I felt tears build in my eyes. Then I saw Mr. and Mrs. Owens and found relief that Jaycee was not with them. I would have been. I knew we would have come together.

As the march played, the upcoming seniors filed in lining the walkway for the graduates. The queen bees, Estelle, Claire and Jaycee stood together. From where I sat, I could see Jaycee staring at me as I glanced sideways from behind my sunglasses. I was thankful for the darker tint. I contemplated offering her a smile or being a bitch but figured her hateful glare sent a clear enough message. She had won…she had him…not me. I looked away.

When the graduates came down the hill and made their entrance, Ali and I hurried down the aisle to snap some pictures. It wasn't like I only had one person to get on film…I had six brothers graduating today. And Zach. They came one by one…my boys…graduating from high school. Connor Eisenbarth…RYAN HENDRICKS!!!…I gave a fierce shout when they called his name, he rolled his eyes at me then winked at Ali who had a conniption over the gesture. Brett Hess…Joshua Long…Grant Meiers. Now there were the flip-flops, and, of course no pants stuck out the bottom of his gown, so I was hoping at best for shorts. He pointed at me when he walked past and I snapped the picture. Then finally, ZACHARY OWENS! My heart melted as our eyes met for just a brief second before he looked away. I stood numb and braced myself for the beautiful smile that he would flash toward Jaycee—the smile that should be directed toward me. I'm not sure why my tears fell as I watched Jaycee's eyes follow him. But his gaze looked straight ahead never addressing her, then suddenly flickered back to me. His gaze was friendly. I wiped my tears and smiled then quickly lifted my camera into position. He smiled as he rounded the corner to go down the center aisle and that was all it took for me to fall undeniably back in love. What did that smile mean? Had he seen my tears and felt sorry for me? I glanced back toward Jaycee whose face was frozen and fists clenched. My eyes fell to the ground, confident that she was pissed. Ali and I headed back up to our folks.

The ceremony was faster than I expected. As Salutatorian, Zach had to speak to the crowd. I hit the aisle again, this time by myself and met Mrs. Owens. She offered a friendly smile then draped her arm over my shoulders. The overwhelming joy her gesture gave me was incredible. Though I knew there was a possibility of getting beat up later, I didn't dare pull away. It would be worth it.

Good evening. As my fellow classmates know, I am not from Ashland but from San Francisco. When I came here a year ago, I didn't care to meet the people or to fit in or to even be liked. But I quickly found out that this town and the people were just as special as where I came from. Ashland

High has so many good people that I am happy to call friends. This great journey that I have traveled over the past year has been a true lesson to me. I have learned that just because there is change in your life, doesn't mean it's not for the better. The world is round and about the time you think it's ending...it may actually be beginning. And at a time, when I thought my world was crashing down around me...I saw the light. I, along with the help of someone very special, found who I was, who I wanted to be and what I wanted to stand for. I walk away today proud to be an Ashland High School graduate. Thank you.

I stood frozen, silent tears streaking my cheeks and my camera still at my side. I hadn't gotten a picture of one of the most important times in his life, and I watched him return to his seat. Mrs. Owens gently tugged on my arm and led me in the direction I was supposed to go. As I slid in next to my mother, she patted my leg.

"You know he was talking about you, don't you?"

I shrugged, unwilling to feel even the simplest pleasure from the thought. But she was right...it had to be me. He'd spent nearly the entire year with me. Jaycee had only been over the past thirty days. Estelle, I know, meant nothing to him. So...I felt at peace. He didn't hate me. I was 'very special' hopefully in a non-limited way and I'd helped him through this year. I owed him a thank you. Who was I kidding...I owed him so much more than that.

At the end of the ceremony, a flurry of hats flew into the air and roars of happiness, relief and regrets shot across the graduates. It was more difficult than I imagined watching this chapter of my life come to an end. I made a mental promise not to cry.

Suddenly, a pair of hands covered my eyes. "Guess who?"

My heart raced. Could it be? "Give me a hint."

"The hottest guy you know?"

I recognized the voice. "Austin! What are you doing here?"

His face contorted into a shocked expression. "Emma. Are you kidding? My folks wouldn't have missed this. Though you skipped mine last year." I was glad I had graduated to Emma with him rather than Runt.

"I was sick." I defended. "One hundred and three degree temperature."

He massaged my shoulders. "I know. How's it going with Zach?"

"It's not going. I think…it's officially over." I grimaced as the words came out.

His arms pulled me in. "Em. There's going to be so many Zach's for you. You're just getting started."

I knew he was being nice and consoling so I didn't want to tell him how wrong he was. Zach was the only man for me…ever. Knowing I would live without him made it hurt even more.

Austin and I walked onto the football field where the graduates were celebrating and mingling with family and friends.

"Happy Birthday!!"

I flipped around and Grant whacked me on top of my head with his cap, the tassel tickling my nose. "Thanks!" I grinned.

"Sweet sixteen," he said smiling big. "Little Runt is sixteen. I get to spank you later."

I beamed uncontrollably as he jogged off to see his folks and Austin shook his head.

"EMMA!" my dad shouted. "Come on." He waved me toward the group and I hugged Austin.

"I'll see *you* in a few weeks," I said.

Austin stared at me. "You know, this year I look forward to it. In fact, I did you a favor. Now you must do me one this summer."

"I can do that," I agreed with curiosity.

"One date." He waited to speak further, watching my reaction. I was certain he didn't notice my heart skip a beat. "In fact, let's not call it a date. We'll call it a day. That way there are no expectations. A day of fun. We can do Seaside, Astoria, dune buggy in Florence. You name it."

I tried to act cool while my insides were doing jumping jacks, though I knew he was just feeling sorry for me. "You got it. It's a day."

"Happy birthday." He kissed my cheek then met up with his parents. I sighed as he walked away.

Ali and her family were talking with my folks and she and Ryan were standing together. Her dream was still coming true. I was living a nightmare. I had to force myself to look the other way.

"OK. So we'll meet you all in the park?" My dad asked Ryan and Ali.

"Yeah. We'll head there now. Come on." Ryan motioned to us and we walked toward the truck. I turned around and casually scanned the dispersing crowd but didn't see Zach anywhere. The sun was falling and the evening was getting cool.

"Why the park?" I asked heading toward downtown.

"Mom and Dad ordered barbeque and set up some tables. Ali's folks are meeting us there. Grant, Brett, Con. After, we'll head to some parties."

"Oh." I wasn't sure how I'd missed that plan. But of course we'd do barbeque today...it was after all, the graduate's favorite and not the birthday girl's. Whatever. I tried to fight the resentful feeling whirling inside me.

Ryan stopped in front of the bridge where balloons floated at the entrance of the park. White lights hung on the bridge railings. Wow.

"Ali. Why don't you and Em get out...I'll park and be right up."

"OK."

She nudged me and I opened the door. I smiled the moment I heard the fast running creek trickling over the river rock. Outside of the ocean, it was one of my most favorite sounds and the spring rains only made it better.

Ali and I crossed the bridge and as we got closer, I heard music playing.

"So. You'll have to tell me if Zach is at the parties."

"You know I will...but."

"But what? You don't have to protect me. If he's with her, that's OK. I just want to know." The feeling made my stomach knot.

"I don't think he'll be with her."

I stopped walking and stared at her. She knew something. "Why?"

"Cause he'll be with you." Her finger pointed to the left of me and my eyes followed the direction she pointed. Zach sat alone on the park bench staring at me.

FIFTY-ONE

Zach

Oh my God, my heart flipped over inside my chest when her eyes found mine. Planning this moment was difficult enough knowing there was a possibility she had moved on without me. The jury was deliberating that one. I still wasn't sure, but her smile during the graduation processional raised my hopes.

The stubbornness I had come to know and love over the past twelve months left me unsure if she would stay or run. As predatorily as it may sound, I had to find a way to lure her. Ali left the moment Emma looked at me and maybe she had the same sense and got out while she could.

Emma was nothing if not predictable but her desire to want to sleep with 17 guys to catch me was ludicrous. And even more absurd to think I wanted that too. She thought more like a guy than a girl but given her upbringing with Ryan, it wasn't all that surprising. Uh-oh, she took a step backward.

Don't go...

Ready to be in hot pursuit if needed, I stood too. I couldn't go another second not knowing if she was still mine. We'd made this date six months ago on my birthday. A date for her sixteenth birthday and my graduation. A date for us to be together…physically for the first time. I was pretty confident sex was off the table and that was survivable, losing her wasn't.

Her eyes held confusion and I fought every urge to go to her. This had to be on her time. I couldn't push.

"Happy Birthday," I finally said.

FIFTY-TWO

Emma

It suddenly hit me that this wasn't a family event at all. I felt my face twist into a confused mess. What was he doing? I turned back to Ali, who was gone. I lowered my head for a moment before rotating back to Zach half afraid that he would be gone too. He must have noticed my confusion because his eyes narrowed as I took a step backward. His brown eyes were soft and held questions that I didn't know the answers to. He stood, and his khakis were still freshly ironed except near his upper thighs where he'd sat during the ceremony and his burgundy shirt unbuttoned at the top with a white T-shirt around his tan neck. I wasn't sure if he'd ever looked better, and, after all this time, he still stole my breath.

He took a step toward me then hesitated, his eyes measuring mine for some reaction. What was he looking for? My approval? How could he possibly not know how much I loved him? I wanted to go to him but I couldn't. I was afraid. He hadn't wrapped his arms around me in…well…it seemed like forever. I'd prepared myself that it wouldn't happen again, and I couldn't face the thought of feeling it only to lose it again.

"Happy birthday," he said sincerely, keeping the distance.

"Thank you." I didn't smile. I couldn't smile. I was too unsure of what was happening. "Happy graduation."

His teeth shone beautifully even in the dark. I'd missed his smile and I don't know if it's physiologically possible but I think my heart smiled as well.

"Are you hungry?"

I nodded and for the first time looked at the heavy quilt spread across the grass. Plates, utensils, glasses and napkins. My eyes moved back to him and he was closer now. I could smell him. "What is this?" I asked. My voice didn't seem to work as the words barely came out.

He reached down with caution taking my hand in his. When they touched, I closed my eyes feeling the warmth and secretly enjoying the moment. I opened my eyes. He drew me toward the quilt.

"My eighteenth birthday was by far…the best…birthday I've ever had. Having you with me in our own little San Francisco was the ultimate gift. I tried to think of everything you love. The outdoors, the water rushing in the distance, your park. I wanted to take you to the ocean but what with graduation and all…"

"No. This is perfect."

"I wanted your birthday to be as special as mine." He smiled.

It was clear now. He was fulfilling a guilty obligation to pay me back, which was completely unnecessary. "Oh. You didn't have to…I mean…I did that because…" I stopped and it was too late, the hurt, the ache was already back.

His eyes studied mine again. "Do you want to eat?"

The appetite I had a minute ago diminished. "Yes. Let's eat. Then you can get to your parties. I know there are parties," I laughed.

He chuckled and dropped my hand as he reached into a sack shaking his head. "I'm not going to any parties." He pulled containers from the sack. "I have Crab Alfredo and Spicy Crab Linguini."

My two favorites. "Either is fine. They both sound great."

I watched as he dished them out neatly and couldn't help but notice the two wrapped gifts on the backside of the quilt. Obligatory gift? I wondered if Jaycee knew he was here and how mad she would be.

Surprisingly, the pasta was hot and delicious and I wanted seconds but declined the offer. I'm sure he needed to go.

"Well, thank you," I said when we finished eating. "Is Ryan picking me up?"

His eyes hung on my words. "No. I can take you some place if you need to go."

"Whatever. I mean…I can call him or if it's on your way."

"On my way where?"

I rose to my feet and slid my sweater on. I was getting cold. "Zach. What you've done is more than enough to pay me back for your birthday. Most of the stuff was homemade and the food and stuff I ordered I had saved for. It's really totally cool. You're off the hook."

He moved in faster than I expected grabbing my waist. His eyes seemed full of hurt. "Emma. You think I did this because of some silly obligation?"

Then I answered him with a blank expression. "Yes."

"That's ridiculous. We had a date tonight for the past eight months to celebrate your birthday and my graduation. I'm not letting anything get in the way of that."

"But it's OK. I don't want to upset anyone else by us being together."

He winced and his expression seemed pained. "Do you love him?"

"Who?" Didn't he know who I loved?

"Austin."

"Austin, who?"

He puckered his lips and lowered his brow giving me a look like I was clueless.

"I don't know his last name. Your buddy from Cannon?"

"OH!" It hit me. AUSTIN. "Austin? Do I love him?" Why was he asking me that?

"I'm too late. You love him." His words were soft and he wasn't asking, he was telling me. But I didn't love Austin. I just stared at Zach.

"I don't understand what you're getting at. I'm sorry. I'm not dumb but I'm not following you."

He inhaled and exhaled before he spoke. "Emma. I know you're not dumb and I wasn't insinuating that. Are you and Austin a couple?"

"No. Why?"

He sighed. "You said you didn't want to upset anyone by us being together and I assumed he would be upset that you were here with me. I saw you two together tonight."

"I was talking about Jaycee." Her name burned my tongue.

His back stiffened. "Jaycee. Why?"

I wasn't sure I could say it. I thought of different ways to put it so that the tears wouldn't come and nothing worked. "She's your...girlfriend." I bit my lip trying to distract myself and could taste a hint of blood in my mouth.

His look was one of repulsion. "Jaycee is not my girlfriend."

"Well. I mean...whatever she is. I didn't know the word. I'm sorry."

He chuckled out loud. "She's nothing, Em. She's nothing to me."

"But you two..." I shook off the thought. "She was number eighteen. OH." It hit me. It was just sex. "I got it. You two just..." I picked up the bottle of water and tried to wash down the food inching its way back up.

He grabbed my shoulders. "Emma!" He shouted, and it startled me. "I wasn't with Jaycee."

"Yes you were. The night of Grant's party," I reminded him.

He touched my face and I pulled away. "Baby. I wasn't with her. I took her home as soon as we left...she was pissed... but I took her home."

"But you said..."

"I know what I said. I'm sorry." His eyes were sincere.

This didn't make sense. They were a couple. He left with her. "You weren't with her?"

"Never. Not even a kiss."

I shook my head. I didn't believe him. He *was* with her. She said. I couldn't look at him. "But *she* said."

The skin puckered between his brows. "She said what?"

I wasn't sure I could tell him. Was it possible to be in shock without a tragic event? I swallowed. "She said you two were together. That I'd better stay away from you. They said that you needed a woman to meet your needs and that…" I couldn't find the words to finish.

He reached for my hands and I flinched away. He grimaced. "Is that what happened in the hallway?"

I stared off and nodded. "You were talking to Brett at your locker. After I shoved her, you went to *her* and helped *her*." My words were robotic as I recounted what happened but the pain was as real as if it had just happened. "I got suspended. I don't understand. Why? Why would you hurt me by saying she was going to be number eighteen and what happened to the website? Did you change your address to something else?" I finally looked at him as all my questions flooded out.

He ran his fingers through his hair. "Wow. Where do I start? First of all, I'm sorry. I'm so sorry for everything. I had no idea what had happened between you and Jaycee." He said her name with the same distaste as what I felt. "I helped her because I saw a girl lying on the floor in front of me. I didn't know you were even involved until she pointed at you. Then Mr. Ming was there and I don't know. I didn't think you wanted to talk to me." I didn't understand his expression. Worry lines crossed his forehead and he hung his head. "I said number eighteen because I wanted to hurt you." His voice was soft. "I'm so ashamed to admit that…but I did. I was jealous. Grant had just told me about your plan to sleep with him and then you…"

My eyes found his as he struggled to speak. "What?"

"You slept with Austin." Zach's jaw was tight and his eyes were closed. "But it doesn't matter to me. I don't care who've you've been with. I mean, I did at first because the thought…" He shook his head. "But I just want to be with you."

"No I didn't."

"You didn't what?"

"I wasn't with Austin."

His eyes popped wide then narrowed. He seemed as confused as I was. "What do you mean?"

His reaction wasn't what I'd expected. "I mean…Austin and I didn't…scrog." I felt the blood rush to my face and wondered if he knew Austin turned me down.

Zach didn't speak for the longest minute. Maybe he wanted me back because he thought I'd gained some sexual experience which I hadn't. He was still my only experience. His slight hesitation worried me. "You're still…you haven't been with anyone?" He questioned.

My chest swelled in anger and hurt. I knew it. The torrent of pain was present again though I wasn't sure it had truly ever passed. I jerked my hand from his and turned to go. Where? I didn't have a ride. I didn't even have my cell phone.

"Emma? What did I say?" He caught me and his arms wrapped tightly around my waist.

Third time in one day the tears came. Damn promises. My back was pulled snuggly into his chest. "Let me go," I cried and resisted the hold that felt so good.

"No," he whispered through my hair. "Tell me what I said that upset you."

I waited, unable to speak, then finally answered. "I know it…disappoints you that I wasn't with him or at least that I still have nothing to offer you." I felt his lips on top of my head.

"Emma Nicole." His tone was disapproving and he gripped my shoulders spinning me to face him. "I again have to apologize. Somewhere along the line, you misunderstood that I wanted you with other guys." He winced. "That couldn't be further from the truth, baby. I'm thrilled to death that you weren't with him."

"Then…you want to get back together because I'm still…" God I hated the word. "Because I'm still a virgin?" At least I could offer him that.

He released an exasperated breath. "No! Of course not," he laughed. "That has nothing to do with it. In fact, we don't have too scrog…ever. OK…maybe not ever but not now." He smiled caressing my cheek.

"Why did you come back then?"

I watched as his fists clenched. "Em? What am I going to do with you? I never went anywhere. You're the one who wanted out. I've just been waiting. Hoping this would pass. Remember *you* were the one upset with me?"

I tried but couldn't remember that far back. The only memory I could recall was how good it felt to have his arms around me. How could he possibly believe I didn't want him? "You want to be with me?" I asked.

"Wow. You actually heard me? But do you believe me?" He smiled. His hands reached out for me and wrapped around my shoulders then suddenly pulled me into his chest. The warmth of his body felt nice to my cheek. Still a perfect fit. When the tightness of his embrace restricted my breathing, I involuntarily whimpered and he loosened for only a second. I knew there was no turning back. Life as I knew it had changed. And as he ran his fingers through my hair and the warm air from his mouth blew across my cheek, I knew I loved him more than life itself.

"I have something for you." He leaned back and tugged on my hand. He was crazy if he thought for a second I was letting go.

He led me back to the corner of the quilt with the two gifts. "Sit."

I twisted my legs beneath me and sat. He handed me the red foil box first. Very light. I shook it and smiled.

He shrugged. "Shake away. You'll never guess."

"Is it something I wanted?"

"I hope so."

I tried to act cool and not tear in to it like I wanted to. I slowly opened the box and a legal sized envelope was taped to the bottom of the cardboard. I pulled a piece of paper from the envelope.

"What is this?" I asked.

"Read it."

I opened what appeared to be a letter. University of Oregon letterhead.

DEAR MR. OWENS, WE ARE PLEASED TO INFORM YOU THAT THOUGH GIVEN THE TARDINESS OF YOUR APPLICATION, YOU HAVE BEEN ACCEPTED TO THE

University of Oregon. We are honored that given the options available to you, we are a consideration. You have qualified for an academic scholarship in our Pre-Law department and we hope you chose U of O for your educational future. Thank you.

"You're going to Eugene?" I was afraid to get excited, but my heart started racing.

"I have three schools on standby. Three scholarships open, waiting for my decision."

"So when are you deciding?"

He smiled. "Tonight. Which brings in gift number two." He reached behind him retrieving the smaller of the two boxes and handing it to me.

I was a little less careful this time tearing the paper more urgently. A small gold box was inside the larger one. Excitedly, I raised the lid and a small dainty silver band was inside. My eyes instantly rose to find his.

"It's a ring," he said.

"I know."

"It's a promise ring. I bought it for you so you know that wherever I am, I promise to be true to you. If you chose to wear it, you will be true to me."

I stared at him blankly. He wanted to be with me. He was going to go to the University of Oregon. I had to be dreaming.

He reached for the box with a frown. "You don't have to wear it. It was just a thought. Something I wanted to do. You've always had these silly thoughts stirring in your head that you weren't right for me. And I wanted you to know that you are. But...we can do this without the ring...that's fine."

He tugged on the tiny box, which my hand held in a firm death grip. "I want it, please."

A broad smile swept across his face accompanied by a sigh of relief. He placed his hand over his own chest like he was experiencing some sort of chest pain. My heart fluttered.

"You had me worried." He lifted the silver circle from the box and took my hand. I promised myself earlier no more tears. I hoped I could keep that promise. "I'm not sure which hand this is supposed to go on. My mom said the right." He slid it on my right hand ring finger.

"It fits perfectly," he whispered.

"Your mom knows?" My shock was obvious.

He nodded and chuckled under his breath. "I needed to do something. I was in big trouble with her."

"Why?" His mom was so sweet; I couldn't imagine anyone being in big trouble with her.

His hands held mine. "The night of Grant's party, after I'd been a jackass...you came by the house and talked with my mom."

I remembered that night too clearly and I tried to block it from my mind.

"She said I was an idiot for hurting you. Not that I didn't already know that. I told her what I wanted to do for you. But, we were both afraid that maybe I'd already lost you. She worries..." His brow puckered and the look made me anxious.

I raised my hand toward his face almost scared to touch it then cupped his jaw in my palm. His eyes closed and his chin rotated into my touch. "Worries about what?" I asked.

He studied my face, my expression...and my anxiety grew with his silence. "She thinks you are perfect for me."

I knew there was a but coming.

"But she worries you're too young for what I'm asking. A ring...a commitment. She doesn't think it's fair to you."

"I'll be the judge of that," I said softly, assuming my parents would feel the same.

This time, his hand touched my face. "I don't ever want to keep you from doing something you want to do. If someone comes along...that you want to date. I'd understand...I'd try and understand." He corrected with a roll of his eyes. "Maybe it's not fair. Maybe she's right."

For the first time, I lifted *his* chin. "Zach. I love you. I would love to wear this ring. With or without it, I promise to be true to you. I don't want anyone else. So whether I'm young or not...I'm not sure I see this happening any other way."

I'm not sure if I jumped into his arms or if he helped me there but I was there regardless. I bit my lip as he analyzed every inch of my face. His face was closer than it had been all night.

His skin was beautiful and soft.

With my index finger, I traced over his bottom lip right before he pushed my hand down and his mouth met mine. No time was necessary to familiarize myself to him. We picked up exactly where we left off. My heart's rhythm was all over the place as his hands moved from my face to my neck then to my back. His kiss was hungry and I was more than willing to feed it. After a minute, he stopped and we both breathed. He brushed away the hair the wind blew across my face.

"Happy Birthday, Em," he whispered.

I smiled up at him. "Thank you. Thank you for the best birthday ever." I barely got the words out before his lips were back on mine.

FIFTY-THREE

When dad finished loading the two cars with our bags and shut the trunk, I felt my lip move to a full pout. Zach tried to push it back in.

"Don't." He warned.

"I don't want to go." I actually stomped my foot, which was a little disappointing. But the thought of being away from him for a month and a half with no talking was agonizing. He pulled me in for one last hug. I took an extra long breath to commit to memory his scent.

"You're taking half my wardrobe and pictures. What more do you want?" He spoke softly, and, I'm guessing with my dad within ear range, it was intentional.

"I want *you* to come."

"I'm going to visit sometime you know that. I've never seen that part of Oregon and I've heard it's beautiful. My girlfriend told me."

I felt my forehead crease which caused the V between my eyes and he hated that. "Who are you going to hang out with this summer?" He knew what I was getting at. "What if they try to talk to you?" The queen bees were around for another year.

"Well, I'm going to need someone to talk to with you gone," he said seriously. I jabbed him hard in the stomach. Not funny.

He bent forward laughing. "Ow... I bought something very small for you to take."

"What?" I loved presents.

"You'll be in big trouble if your dad finds out," he cautioned and glanced over his shoulder.

I bit my lip. "What?"

He slid something into my back pocket and whispered into my ear. "I'm not going almost two months without talking to you. It's a new cell phone. The number is one number different than mine. Don't get caught. I'm beggin you." He kissed my ear and pulled back.

I smiled. SWEET! "You're breaking the rules." I winked. He didn't like breaking my parent's rules.

"Just one." He grimaced as the words came out.

"Let's saddle up," Dad yelled as Grant and Ryan bolted from the house.

Zach's eyes found Grant for a moment then flickered back to me. He rubbed the delicate silver ring on my hand. "Keep this on," he said raising his brow. "Maybe he'll get the message. I love you," he mouthed.

"And I love you."

He kissed me softly then pulled away. I watched him say good-bye to my folks and the boys then head to his Jeep and drive away.

My dad grabbed my hand. "Good thing you're ridin' with your mom. Cause eventually we will discuss that circle on your finger."

I jerked my hand away but couldn't hide the grin that crept across my face.

"Hey Em. You want to ride with us?" Grant asked.

I shook my head. "Nope."

"Leave her alone. She's got a ring, you know," Ryan teased.

Grant stared at me and then smiled. "Ring, schming… you're all mine this summer."

I rolled my eyes and got into mom's convertible.

BOOK 2   FINALLY...One Summer

Chapter 1

Our first two days in Cannon Beach, the thick clouds hung low offering rain but never delivered. It seems Mother Nature had absorbed my mood. Depressed and pathetic. Two days ago, as my family drove north out of Ashland, Oregon, and six hours up the beautiful Oregon coast, I'd left the man of my dreams...*Zach*. God, I missed him. My heart ached just thinking his name. *Zachary Owens*. I glanced down at the dainty silver ring circling the fourth finger on my right hand. My lungs hadn't taken a full deep breath since he'd left me standing in our driveway in Ashland.

Though my mood hadn't broken, the clouds seemed more forgiving and a flicker of sunlight exploded through on our third day. Our quaint two-story beach house was much like most homes lining Cannon Beach. They'd been here for years. Mom and Dad loved the lower level screened in porch where they spent most evenings but I preferred the upstairs open deck off my bedroom. At some point, on most days of the year, a light mist would fall from the sky and nothing beat lying in a lawn chair, head back with the weightless water providing a natural facial.

I was on the upper deck, now, watching my older brother, Ryan and his best friend, Grant Meiers, tossing the football on the beach. Tide moved out a couple of hours ago and anytime the water abandoned the sand, the pigskin came out. It was as predictable as the tides. They were having fun...laughing and talking as they hurled the ball back and forth. Grant's adorable long blond curls bounced, like chicks in a shampoo commercial, as he ran for the catch. And speaking of chicks, July was the hottest month in Cannon, averaging sixty-eight and definitely the tourist's month, so we'd see the girls start arriving within a couple of weeks. Prime hunting season. I crinkled my nose at the thought and snuggled deeper into my borrowed USC sweatshirt. Three day's into the trip and it still smelled like Zach. My heart fluttered.

Unwilling to surrender to the fun of vacation, I continued my pouting and sulking in hopes of making everyone miserable. I wasn't a mean person inherently, but leaving Zach was so unfair. We'd come to Cannon for the past nine years on an extended summer vacation to stay in a home my mom inherited from her folks. But I was sixteen now and was tired of leaving everything behind to come spend time with a family that I'd spent three hundred and sixty-five days a year with all ready. My *new* phone buzzed in my pocket and I jerked it out quickly. I peeked into the bedroom…nobody.

Hey u.

I smiled. *How are you?* send

This sucks!

I know. Im sorry. send

I miss u.

Me too! Got to go. send

I snuck the phone into the front pocket of the sweatshirt.

"Hey, Honey." My mom was in my room. "Your father and I are going to grab some lunch. Want to come?"

I shook my head not really looking at her.

"Emma." She fingered my hair.

I knew where this was going.

"Come with us. Get out and about. We've been here three days and you've sat in this chair and in that sweatshirt. He loves you sweetheart. He'll be there when we get home."

It was hard for me to grasp but she was right…he loved me. Zach loved me. I struggled with that for a year, not understanding why. He was the epitome of perfect. I closed my eyes and he was there behind my lids…his tan skin and dark hair, face lit by the brilliant smile that seemed brighter when directed at me. And for some crazy reason…Zach chose me. I've never been one of those girls with a lack of self esteem. I could look in the mirror and see that I was cute…but I was short and skinny. Too skinny. And I was a sophomore while he was starting college. I smiled knowing I'd almost earned enough extra credits to be a junior this upcoming school year. That still put me two years away from him.

My folks never allowed texting on vacation and Zach broke the rule by buying me a separate cell phone. He hated breaking their rule but didn't want to go the month and a half without contact. College was his next step and his departure date in August wouldn't be far from our arrival date back in Ashland. The days that I spent in Cannon were days I should be spending with him. But, NO! I left him unsupervised in Ashland with Estelle, Claire and Jaycee. Estelle, he'd already done the nasty with last summer before we were a couple and Jaycee was begging to be with him during our spring hiatus. I never thought of myself as jealous but the distance between us certainly wasn't helping. Especially with those two slutty vultures...waiting to swoop down and attack.

"Hey, Runt?"

"What?" I looked down at my brother.

"Fix us some lunch," Ryan yelled.

Grant brushed the shiny hair out of his eyes and looked at my sour expression. "Let's go help her, man," he said. "Em. You want some help."

I grinned. Grant was going to do whatever was necessary to get this ring off my finger and get into my britches. I chuckled at the thought because had he been interested a year ago, I'd have obliged with no hesitation. My childhood and pre-Zach crush didn't understand why I no longer was obsessed with him. I didn't understand it myself. From the time I was ten till fifteen, I knew I would be Mrs. Emma Meiers until Zach Owens rang the bell of my house looking for my brother.

Leaving last year was nothing compared to this year. Last year, I was bummed...this year was excruciating.

"EMMA!" Ryan yelled.

"What?" I asked.

"Lunch?"

After lunch, I dialed the phone the moment I was alone. It rang only once.

"Hey baby!"

I loved when he called me baby. "I miss you so much!

"I miss you too. What've you been doing?" He asked.

It was embarrassing to say. "Nothing. Pouting. It's been pretty ugly," I laughed.

"Baby. Just have fun. I was thinking about driving up in a couple of weeks."

Weeks? How about days! "Cool. I'll be home in a month and a half and then you'll leave." Disappointment was evident in my voice.

He chuckled. "Em. It's like my probation. It is what it is and we had to deal with that until it was over. But it did pass. This is going to pass. You know what they say, absence makes the heart grow fonder."

"My heart is fond enough. Thank God for this phone. Thanks again by the way."

"It was more for my benefit than yours but you're welcome."

"It's Friday. What are you doing tonight?" Hopefully nothing. Please say nothing.

He hesitated and I didn't like that. "There are a bunch of us driving over to Crescent to the beach around two."

I took a long breath in before answering. "Who all's going?"

"I'm not sure. Brett, Josh and I are riding together."

"Hmm." I stared down at the water hypothesizing different scenarios. He was quiet. Didn't he understand that him going to the beach wasn't OK? I tried to keep my thoughts rational. It was just a couple of hours with friends. He loved me.

"Emma?"

"Yes?" I think I was in trouble according to his tone.

"Do me a favor."

"OK."

"Hold the phone with your left hand," he instructed.

I switched hands. "OK."

"Now hold out your right hand and look at the silver band on your finger."

I smiled catching his drift.

"Do you see it? Tell me you have it on. Lie to me if you don't," he laughed.

I giggled. "I have it on. I've never taken it off."

"So then, you know what that means. It means it doesn't matter who's there. I'll be thinking of you...period. My heart is with you," he whispered near the end.

"I trust you, Zach. But I don't trust them. Don't you see?"

"I do. But don't let that come between us."

"Hey. Mom and Dad just pulled up. I gotta go. Love you."

"And I love you."

"Be good! Bye." I didn't want to hang up but thanked God for the chance to talk to him.

Resigning myself, I headed down to the beach. Typically, I didn't get involved in Grant and Ryan's affairs but thought it might

366

make the summer go faster. As I moved toward them, I plotted in my mind…trying hard not to smile as I walked. Two girls…already? Earlier than usual. One was blonde and the color actually looked real. Her hair was long and she, like most, hadn't dressed for this particular beach. She was thinking sunny and hot like most normal beaches. She'd be heading inside within minutes. I smiled. The brunette at least wore long sleeves. Neither one was all that pretty, though that was never criteria for Grant and Ryan.

"Hey guys." I put my arms around their waists and stood between them. Ryan glanced sideways at me. A smile touched Grant's lips.

Both girls looked at me, my short little scrawny body standing between two giants. "Were you telling the girls about our sleepover last night?" I raised my brows and I wasn't lying. We did crash in the living room, watching a movie.

The brunette looked mortified, her mouth fell open. The blonde was still processing my words. Maybe her hair color wasn't real after all.

"Come on, Jessica." the brunette snarled grabbing the blonde's arm and they plugged away in the sand.

Grant slid his arm around my waist. "It was so nice of you to come play with us, Em. Thanks." His tone was sarcastic.

Ryan shoved me and I landed on my butt. "You're a bitch," he barked.

Grant offered me a hand. "I was thinking about Ali. What were *you* thinking? Do you remember my best friend that you're dating, Ry?"

He rolled his eyes and shuffled his feet in the sand.

"I know why you did that," Grant said.

"Oh? Why is that?" I asked brushing the sand from my pants.

"You were jealous. It's hard for you to imagine me with someone else."

I slapped his arm. "Dream on. I was bored. That's all."

He grinned and ruffled my hair. "Keep tellin yourself that sweetheart. I know the truth and so will you in time."

I flashed my hand in front of his face waving my ring.

Within a quick second my hand was pinned to my side and he was close. The warmth of his breath on my face. "The only ring that would stop me would be a wedding ring. And you're sixteen so we know that won't be the case for a long time. I have the next month and a half to break the two of you up. I predict it won't take that long." He grinned and let go of my arm walking away.

My body shook with anger and I picked up a handful of sand tossing it at him. But the wind caught the gritty particles and blew it back in my face. Why did he do that to me? Why did I *let* him get to me? So much for quality beach time.

I glanced at my watch every ten minutes between six and nine driving myself insane. Straight south, in Crescent City, California, the man I loved was at the beach with other girls. Though we stood with our toes touching the same ocean, the four hundred mile difference was too much to bear. Knots in my stomach tightened as irrational thoughts consumed me. I wanted to call. I went out on the deck…my refuge. The sky was dark and absent of stars. A fire flickered near the edge of the water. I was certain it was the boys.

The screen of my phone indicated no new messages. I decided to dial. It rang four times then went to voice mail. Crap. I looked back at the fire as my heart plummeted into my stomach. I had to do something….so I slid on my shoes and headed toward the flames.

Grant and Ryan were lying back in their beach chairs.
"Hey guys."
"Oh. She came out to play again," Grant teased.
I shot him a squinty eyed look.
"Yeah. Well, if you can't play nice then go back inside," Ryan said still bitter.
"Whatever. You're the one who wasn't playing nice."
He held his palm up dismissing me. Grant grinned and I sat at the bottom of his chair. The fire felt good. The waves wrestled in the distance and I closed my eyes and listened.
"Mind if I join you?" the voice was deep.
We all looked in the same direction. A bulky short guy in an Oklahoma Sooners sweatshirt was across from Ryan.
"Sure." Ryan said. "Where you from?"
"Oklahoma. My family's here for a wedding tomorrow."
"The Sooners. Do you play football?"

It was a stupid question for Ryan to ask. I pictured him as more of a…tennis player.

"Not really."

"How long you staying?" Grant asked.

"Two nights. I'm Dexter."

The poor guy was not attractive.

"Well, Dexter. I'm Ryan, this is Grant and that's Emma. If you're around tomorrow, come down and throw the ball around with us. We can always use an extra pair of hands."

"Thanks. Sounds good." He looked at me and winked giving me the heebeejeebies.

Grant leaned up and kissed my cheek. "She's mine, Dex."

I slapped his shoulder. "He's lying Dexter. I am not his." I started to get up when his arms wrapped around my shoulders and pulled me into his chest.

"Oh Sugar Baby. Do we have to play this sex game again tonight? I get so tired of it."

Ryan laughed and so did Dexter. I rammed my elbow into Grant's ribs.

Dexter waved. "I need to go. Maybe I'll see you guys tomorrow."

I shoved away from Grant's hold. "I'll walk you up Dexter," I added.

He glanced at Grant who shot me an evil look. I smiled.

"Uh, OK." Dexter stuttered as I moved to his side.

"Which way you headed?" I asked.

He pointed north.

"Me, too." I wasn't going north but out of the corner of my eye, Grant was shaking his head.

"Emma," Grant gritted and I ignored him.

"Come on, Dexter."

Dexter's eyes roamed over Ryan then finding Grant who was scowling.

We headed northward.

"Hey, Dex," Grant sang. "If she's not back here within five minutes, we will hunt you down," Grant threatened.

Dexter threw his arms in the air. "Look, man. I don't want her coming with me. She can stay here. I'm not here to cause a problem."

"It's OK," I said. "Just ignore him."

"No. I can't go to this wedding tomorrow with a black eye. Just leave me alone." He held his hands up like I was the enemy and he was surrendering.

I jetted around and kicked sand at Grant. "You're a jackass."

He grinned.

Ryan was smiling. "Revenge sucks, Runt."

I clenched my fists and stormed toward our house. I hated Grant and poor Dexter was running north.

When I reached the house, shaking from anger…or maybe the cold, I phoned Zach from my deck. It rang twice.

"Hey, baby," he said excitedly.

I smiled though I heard music in the background. "How's it goin?" I asked my hands still trembling.

"Fine. You sound upset." It was more of a question as the music faded.

My head was hurting. "You still at the beach?" I rubbed my forehead.

"We are. I think Josh, Brett and I are going to get a room. Crash here then drive back tomorrow."

"Great. Have fun," I said sourly.

I heard his breath on the other end. "Em. I'll drive home tonight. It was just a thought and if it upsets you then it isn't worth it."

I squeezed my eyes tightly shut disappointed I was being a bitch for no good reason. I didn't deserve his patience. "Zach. I'm sorry. I'm pissed at Grant. Are the girls there?"

"By the girls…I'm guessing you're referring to Estelle, Clair and Jaycee?" He seemed annoyed.

"Forget it." I was sorry I asked.

"You don't know how bad I wish I was there to hold you right now. Make you understand there is nothing to worry about." He sighed. "What did Grant pull this time?"

I wished he was here too and I couldn't very well admit to trying to walk some dwarfy dweeb home. No one would ever understand my relationship with Grant. The incident on the ski slope this year gave Zach a peek into the competition between us. That got me in enough trouble so I certainly wouldn't offer up this story. "Oh. Just Grant being Grant."

"Be careful, Em. Don't let him pull you in," Zach's tone was soft and caring. I needed him…wanted him. I stared out at Grant and Ryan by their fire.

"I'm not. I better go. Have fun tonight," I said not wanting to hang up.

"Do you want me to text you when we get in?"

"Sure. If I don't text back then I'm asleep. Love you."

"And I love you. Sleep tight."

I disconnected the call, looked out at the fire, went inside and fell on my bed. I hated summer.

Made in the USA
San Bernardino, CA
29 August 2019